Dear Readers,

Welcome to a brand new world, where evolution split and created more than just humans at the top of the food chain. Kate Reilly's world is much the same as the one we enjoy: she lives at the base of the stunning Rocky Mountains in Denver, Colorado. But there are dark and scary things in that world that most people deny or try to forget exist. Vampires are real, but not the evil undead of our legends. Kate lives in fear of a different sort of vampire—a sentient parasitic species that co-evolved with humans.

The Thrall are a hive, like bees, with a queen who sends out soldiers to bring her food. In this case, *food* is the blood of humans. The Thrall live only *because* of humans, for two reasons. Like a tapeworm or a tick, the vampires attach to us through a bite by another parasite into the blood stream, swim through our veins and bond with our spinal cord, creating a Host. By using their mind control through the hive connection, they force people to bite other people to feed and grow.

But there are two problems with this scenario: Humans can't live on blood alone, and as the parasite grows, there is less and less room in the skull to hold both it and the person's brain. So, instead of long-lived vampires, the ones in this world die quickly. Of course, from the queen's perspective, workers come and workers go. It doesn't affect the hive, and when the queen dies, another takes over. Life continues, except for the human herd, and who cares about them anyway? Well, a few people do—ones who psychically are powerful enough to avoid the parasites' mind control, and physically strong enough to eliminate the infected humans. Kate Reilly is one such person.

We started with the idea of people who seem to be able to cross boundaries in comfort. Some people are equally at home in the biker poolroom as in the boardroom or courtroom. What makes these people special? If they had a deadly foe, who would it likely be? Kate Reilly, along with lycanthrope Tom Bishop, possess that same, innate . . . *something*. They fight for the underdog, have friends at all levels, and experience the hate and prejudice that go along with both. And their foes are terrible indeed. No warm and fuzzy vampires in their world!

We hope you'll enjoy visiting our new world as much as we enjoyed creating it.

TOUCH
OF EVIL

C. T. ADAMS &
CATHY CLAMP

tor romance
A TOM DOHERTY ASSOCIATES BOOK
NEW YORK

TOUCH OF EVIL

Edited by Anna Genoese

A Tor Book
Published by Tom Doherty Associates, LLC
175 Fifth Avenue
New York, NY 10010

www.tor.com

Tor® is a registered trademark of Tom Doherty Associates, LLC.

ISBN 0-765-35400-4
EAN 978-0-765-35400-6

First edition: March 2006

Printed in the United States of America

0 9 8 7 6 5 4 3 2 1

DEDICATION AND
ACKNOWLEDGMENTS

As with everything we do, we dedicate this book first to Don Clamp and James Adams, along with our family and friends, who have offered patience and unswerving moral support through the years.

We would also like to thank those people who helped make this world the best it could be: To Eli Wald, Assistant Professor of Law at the University of Denver Sturm College of Law for his time and expertise in Hebrew translations. We hope we got it right, but if there are errors, blame us, not him.

To Steve Favreau, Kim Wyatt and Sion Crain, for making the initial comments that led to the idea for the world, and to Monica Mika and Voneen Macklin, for help in creating the perfect villain. Special thanks go to our agent, Merrilee Heifetz, and the wonderful Ginger Clark, and our terrific editor Anna Genoese at Tor. We'd also like to thank Linda Nelson for her assistance, because we keep forgetting to do so, even though her help and support have been invaluable.

Without all of you, this wouldn't have been possible. We know that words aren't enough, but they're what we do best.

1

"Katie?" The sound of a familiar voice calling my name made me turn and grin. Peg always has that effect on me.

She was a sight for sore eyes; we didn't get to see each other much, usually staying in touch via email and cell phone. As always, she looked crisp and professional in her dove grey flight attendant's uniform. Her short blonde hair was perfectly coiffed, her make-up flawless. You'd never tell from looking at her that it was four in the freaking morning. With me, you could tell. Oh my, yes!

I had just stepped off my third red-eye in a week, the last in a long string of flights delivering valuables around the globe. I'm a bonded air courier, which sounds glamorous—and sometimes it even is.

This was so *not* one of those times.

Her wide blue eyes narrowed as she looked me over from head to toe. "Here." She handed me the cup of coffee she'd been carrying. "You need this worse than I do. You're limping again. Is that old vampire bite bothering you?"

Had I been limping? As soon as she said it, the whispering in my head started. I slammed down my mental shields and the voices faded, but the cold chill down my spine remained for a moment. "Gee, thanks, Peg. Now you've got me thinking about my least favorite person in Denver."

She grimaced and blushed. "Oops. Sorry. How's the coffee?"

I took a gulp of scalding coffee and let out a small, happy sigh. "Nirvana! If coffee isn't the nectar of the gods I don't know what is. You saved my life." The drink was strong enough to peel the fuzz from my teeth. No cream, no sugar— just the way I like it. Without caffeine I wasn't sure I'd make it to the truck, and none of the airport restaurants or coffee shops would be open for a while yet.

I gestured to her bag with my pinkie. "Where are you off to?"

"Paris, then Rome." She grinned at me, showing white teeth and deep dimples. "Who knows, maybe I'll actually get to be there long enough to see the sights this time." It was a running joke between us. We refer to ourselves as the great young globetrotters. We travel the world—but we're too damned busy to visit the sights or play tourist. Most of the time our schedules don't permit it, and when they do, we're too exhausted to take advantage.

I could, however, write a book about the best sheets and pillows in Europe.

Peg shook her head as I took another long pull on the coffee. I knew that look. "What?"

"Are you *ever* going to retire that blue blazer?"

I glanced down at the jacket. It was looking a little bedraggled, but it had been a long flight. "What's wrong with it? I've only had it a few years."

"Try *five* years, Kate. I was with you when you bought your work wardrobe—remember? Jackets, pants, and skirts in navy blue, black, and green, along with an armful of white cotton shirts. Even the *airline* changes their uniforms more often than you!"

I didn't dignify that with a reply. I just raised an eyebrow and then stuck out my tongue while she laughed. It was too soon for the caffeine to be taking effect, but I would've sworn I felt more alert.

"Um . . . how's Joe?" Peg tried to keep her voice casual as she inquired after my older brother. It wasn't easy. She'd fallen for him hard not so long ago, and he'd behaved like a world-class jerk. I love my brothers, but now was not the time for me to talk about Joe. I was absolutely furious with him, and not over Peg.

I sipped the coffee, trying to think of a response that wouldn't turn into a rant. There wasn't one.

"Same as always." I winced. I hadn't intended my voice to sound quite that bitter.

"Oh God, what has he done now?" Peg steered me toward the nearest bank of chrome and vinyl chairs so that we could both take a seat.

"He bought himself a brand new H2."

"A *Hummer*? But he lives in the city. Where's he going to *park*? How's he going to afford it?"

My voice was cold and hard. I couldn't help it. If Joe wanted a new vehicle—fine. But Peg was right. He should've bought one he could afford. "Oh, he can make the *payments*."

Peg groaned a bit but nodded. Joe's a doctor. He makes good money, especially now that all his student loans have been repaid. But he doesn't think things through too well when he wants something bad enough.

I gritted my teeth, and used my fingers to make the little quote things in the air from around the coffee cup. "But he '*didn't count on*' the increase in his car insurance. So now he *can't afford* to pay his part of the bills for Bryan's care." A harsh laugh escaped my lips. "He doesn't think that's a problem. Do you know that he actually told me I should raise the rents in my building to make up the difference! I just barely got my first tenant and now I'm supposed to raise the rents?"

Peg stared at me, blue eyes wide, her mouth slightly ajar. It was a long moment before she was capable of speech. "I don't believe it." But I could tell from her voice that she did.

I took a long drink of coffee, trying to force myself to calm down and come up with a different subject of conversation. I needn't have bothered. Peg caught a glimpse of my watch, paled and swore.

"I've got to go! I'm late!" She rose in a fluid movement.

She bent to give me a quick hug, promised we'd talk more soon, and took off at a half-run, dragging her wheeled carry-on bag behind her. The rapid tattoo of her heels against the floor echoed through the nearly empty concourse.

I shook my head and rose. I looked around for a waste can for the empty coffee cup. I was still tired, but running into Peg had cheered me up immeasurably. And hey, the combination of caffeine and fury at Joe had gotten my blood pumping nicely.

I was halfway to the shuttle train to the main terminal when I felt the first stirrings of unease.

I was being followed.

The rhythm of my footsteps on the patterned marble floors had been joined by a second set. I would've liked to think it was coincidence, just another weary traveler headed back to the terminal. But the person stepped only when I stepped. Normal people don't do that. They're in too much of a hurry. While I wasn't exactly dawdling, I hadn't been rushing either.

I don't like being tailed. But it happens fairly frequently—and I imagine that it's happening even more often. I'm paranoid by both profession and nature. I've got a huge insurance policy to cover any thefts of clients' valuables, but many of the items I deliver are irreplaceable—and I have a good reputation in the business because I don't take unnecessary risks.

I was busy working out how to lose the person behind me, so I almost missed the announcement overhead. "Adam Dexter. Sam Franks. Mary Kathleen Reilly. Please pick up the white courtesy phone."

I didn't even have to guess who was on the phone. There are only four people still alive who use my full name. Only Joe knew my flight time. He was pissed about something. Otherwise the page would've been for Kate, or Katie. Yeah, right. Like *he* gets to be miffed at *me!* Dream on.

Enough of this shadow business. I turned around abruptly in the darkened hallway, but there was no one there.

That wasn't good. If the person wasn't content with approaching me in an empty, dimly lit spot, it meant they were waiting for somewhere even more secluded. Whatever crisis my brother had in store could wait.

At least I'd come back empty handed. It's a nuisance trying to fight and keep track of valuables. This way my hands were free. It also meant that whoever it was, they weren't after cargo I was carrying. I slipped my hand into my pocket and started walking at a brisk pace past the phone bank. Using the reflection from the shop windows to watch behind me I kept a close eye out. No luck. Whoever it was, they were good. They stayed just far enough back so that I couldn't even catch a glimpse.

Since I couldn't see anything with my eyes, I debated looking with my mind. I don't *like* doing it. It makes me feel so damned vulnerable. The parasites are a constant buzz in the back of my mind at the best of times. Letting down my guard enables me to use my abilities, but it leaves me nearly defenseless if they try to attack. They haven't yet—but that doesn't mean they won't. So I usually rely on the physical instead of the psychic. It's just safer.

I decided it was worth the risk. I lowered my shields and felt outward in a circle with my mind. Nothing. Utter silence. Not even the angry buzz of the hive queens. I felt a shiver of unease run down my spine. That I couldn't hear them meant they were shielding me out—hiding something. That was *so* not good.

One problem at a time. I slowed and did an odd two-step, as though I'd tripped.

There was a solid footstep that wasn't mine during that little dance. Nope, it wasn't my imagination. I ducked into the nearest women's bathroom. I stopped just inside the doorway and flipped open the antique pocket watch I'd pulled from my purse. It doesn't keep time. I have my wristwatch for that. Not being able to carry an actual mirror since 9/11 really sucks, so I've been forced to improvise. I've polished the case to a reflective, albeit slightly fuzzy, finish. I use it for things like applying lipstick and watching my back.

Most tails will either stay nearby or deliberately walk past and then wait further up the hall. I had a couple of options. I could set a trap to confront the bastard, but if it was a Thrall host they could easily have used mind games to get a weapon past airport security. Hell, even a truly determined *human* can manage to smuggle things in.

I sighed. The fact was that I just wasn't really up to a physical battle right now. The combination of coffee and adrenaline had sharpened my nerves enough to recognize the danger, but it wouldn't last. I needed to avoid this fight if I possibly could.

I closed the watch and slid it back in my pocket. I stood utterly still, eyes and ears open, waiting long enough that anyone who'd *not* been deliberately following me would have gone past. No one passed. Shit.

I was still standing there, debating what to do when I heard voices I recognized from the plane. A weary young couple was bickering in hushed tones. I peeked out of the doorway. The woman was juggling her purse, diaper bag, and a carry-on. Her husband struggled with the dead weight of their sleeping toddler. Perfect. I popped out of my doorway just in time to join them.

My stalker kept a distance behind us. More people appeared as I reached the underground train from my concourse back to the baggage claim area. I kept trying to find my tail, but he eluded me. Evidently he wanted to get me alone—probably on my way to the parking lot. Still, I could be wrong. Just in case, I made sure the less-than-happy family was standing close at my back so that no one could sneak up on me as we waited for the train. When it arrived, I bullied my way to the front and sat on the bench facing the crowd.

About half the people stared blankly forward. The other half talked with companions or watched the pinwheels. But today I ignored the pretty, twirly spinners that I usually watch. Instead, I kept my eyes on each of the passengers in the car in turn. All by itself that annoyed me, because I'd rather be oohing and aahing out the window with the little tow-headed girl and her brother sitting next to me. Nobody made me nervous, although I couldn't say the same for them. I got more than a few odd looks.

I couldn't exactly blame them. I stand six foot one in my stocking feet, and have long red hair that I usually wear in a tight braid, plus the kind of attitude that makes most people think twice about messing with me. Joe calls it my "tough act." It's not an act. There's a reason they called me the Terminator when I played pro volleyball—a reason why the Thrall consider me a threat. Joe just doesn't like to admit it.

I made sure I was the last to exit the car when we reached the terminal, jumping out just as the doors were starting to whoosh closed. Everyone scattered to their various destinations. Nobody lurked. Nobody even glanced at me.

I stopped in the middle of the floor and opened my mind again. There was nothing but a solid white wall of static. Despite the heavy blazer, I felt chilled. The Thrall usually aren't active during the day, but the sun wouldn't be up for a while yet, and their human Herds are always a threat.

People on the street call the Thrall vampires. Yes and no. They're not the evil undead of legend. "Thrall" is their own term for the mind control they have over their human Hosts and the Herds. The scientific name for the parasite is complicated and Latin, so people call them either vampires or the Thrall. It's easier.

They have a hive mentality, ruled by a group of queens who control individual Hosts and the human Herds. They despise most humans, referring to them as "Prey." Only a very few humans, perhaps two dozen in the world are "Not Prey." We've earned our place, earned the respect of the queens— usually by dint of killing one of their kind. They have "rules" for dealing with us. Of course, that means there are rules for us to deal with them, as well. Not Prey don't run, don't hide, don't use guns or other distance weapons. If they do, they lose their status. And the status is useful. As Not Prey the Hosts and Herds can't lie to you, and the queens have to treat you as an equal.

There is, of course, wiggle room in the rules—usually in favor of the Thrall, who take every advantage of it.

I earned my title the hard way. I killed the former queen of Denver, but in the process I got bit. Since then, the Thrall have been a constant presence in the back of my head. I hate it, but I've learned to cope. Most of the time even the strongest of them can't cloud my mind—at least, not for long. Still, it helps to have something to listen to. It keeps them from seeing my thoughts. For me, that's usually heavy metal music. But good old distracting conversation will do nicely. So, when I caught a glimpse of my buddy Leroy, I greeted him with more than my usual enthusiasm.

"Hi, Leroy!" The big, ebony-skinned guard turned at the sound of his name. He saw my waving hand and smiled.

"Jeez, Reilly," he replied in greeting. "Do you *live* here? Didn't I just see you a couple of days ago?"

"Actually, it's been a week." I chuckled. Leroy Williams has worked at the airport almost since it opened. You'd think he'd have enough seniority to have his pick of shifts, but I've seen him here at all hours of the day and night, always wearing a freshly pressed uniform and a friendly smile. We'd become fast friends one night when we'd both been trapped at DIA because of a blizzard. We'd played what must have been fifty games of cards while we waited for the storm to clear. I'd learned all about his family life while he'd happily taken a fair chunk of my spending money. The guy's an incredible cardplayer.

Leroy was wearing a jacket over his uniform. He was either just coming on shift or just getting off. I was hoping for the latter and told him so.

His chin tipped and his face grew concerned. "You got trouble, girl?"

"Maybe." I shook my head to clear it. "Hell, probably."

Leroy glanced around the nearly deserted food court. No one looked suspicious.

But then my tail made a mistake. He'd gotten too close and I felt him. *Thrall.* Our eyes locked across the huge room. The moment he knew he'd been spotted the shield of static vanished. The Thrall presence slammed into my consciousness. My head buzzed with the sound of a thousand voices and I clearly heard my name. I shook my head to clear it and slammed my best mental shields into place. I could still sense them, but distantly. Fortunately, with the shielding, they wouldn't be able to read *my* thoughts.

Leroy saw my sudden panic. He moved close to me, projecting menace from every pore. His massive bulk of muscle was comforting. When he removed his nightstick and started to twirl it, the host gave one last glare and left. Good.

If the Thrall wanted something, they'd be back—I knew it. My goal was to make sure I was ready for a fight when they returned.

"Adam Dexter. Leonard Hamilton. Mary Kathleen Reilly. Please pick up the white courtesy phone."

Ah, hell! I'd forgotten all about the call from Joe.

"Watch my back," I hissed as I headed to the phone bank. Leroy took the command literally. He turned his back to mine when I reached the nearest phone and glared at the crowd as though they were all terrorists.

I went and picked it up, stating my name. I looked past Leroy's broad back as I waited on seemingly perpetual hold. An abstract sculpture built into the east wall caught my gaze. Stark metal twisted and soared torturously upward to the white tent roof. It had cost the city a fortune, and was supposed to have some deep symbolic meaning to the residents of Denver. Speaking as one of them, it didn't. But staring at it passed the time as I waited.

I inhaled slowly, basking in the scent of Leroy's lemon grass cologne and shaving soap. It was a comforting scent that reminded me of my grandfather for some reason. Finally the line connected.

"Kate here."

"You're back."

It *was* Joe. He was probably just coming off of his shift in the ER at St. Elizabeth's Hospital. He sounded as tired as I felt so I bit back a smart-ass remark about stating the obvious.

"What's up?"

"I popped by to water your plants."

Oh, *please*! If he thought a ten minute errand was going to get him off the hook about his half of the bills he was wrong.

"Okay. Thanks." My voice was flat and annoyed. I think he was expecting a little more appreciation, but the plants are on automatic misters, which he knows full well.

There was a long pause. I considered pushing the conversation along. After all, Leroy wasn't just here for giggles. Instead, I fought down my frustration and forced myself to wait him out.

"You got a call while I was there." He was pissed. That much was obvious from his voice. "From *Dylan*."

"Shit." The word popped out of my mouth. Dylan Shea was my former fiancé. I'd nearly gotten killed saving his life almost six years ago. In a rush of gratitude he'd run off with my best friend and my cat.

I still miss the cat.

"What did he want?"

"I don't know. He didn't leave a number on the recorder. He just said he'd call back."

Yeah, if I didn't answer, he knew Joe would be watching the place and would try to wring the reason from him, so he wouldn't give any info. Joe just can't help bullying Dylan. He'd said it over and over again while we were engaged: Dylan's weak.

The fact that he's right galls me. Dylan isn't a Host. No, he's a step below that: Herd. Read: *food*. Why he chose that fate is something I will never comprehend.

"Why call me?" It was a rhetorical question, but not a bad one. Dylan had *chosen* Amanda and the Thrall. I couldn't think of a single reason he'd want to contact me. After all, we hadn't exactly parted on the best of terms. My stomach tightened into a painful knot. What an interesting coincidence— Dylan looking for me *right* when I'm being followed by a Thrall Host.

"Katie?" Joe's rich baritone tried to drag me out of the bad memories. It didn't work. It just reminded me of another morning with him, when I was deciding whether to hunt down the queen in the daylight, or wait for Dylan to be slaughtered when nightfall arrived.

That morning Joe had tried to scare me out of rescuing Dylan. He'd dragged me to Dr. MacDougal, the parasitic specialist at St. Elizabeth's. I got a long lecture on the Thrall.

"The queen vampire lays her eggs in the arm vein of a Host human." Dr. MacDougal had said. "When the first egg hatches, it releases a toxin that temporarily paralyzes the Host so that the hatchling can move freely through the bloodstream up to the base of the brain. Once there, it settles in to live. It sends its primary ganglia to wrap around the Host's spinal cord and the two secondary ganglia through the nasal passages and roof of the mouth where they break through the skin beside the eye teeth. Hard and sharp, these hollow tubes are used by the creature to suck human blood, and, in the case of the queen, to lay her eggs."

Dr. MacDougal made sure that I got to view the autopsy of a dead Host. It was supposed to scare the hell out of me. It did. Because of that lecture I'd taken the precautions that saved my life. As a thank you, I'd bought him a bottle of his favorite, very expensive, single malt scotch.

"What are you thinking, Katie?" Joe's voice brought me back to the present.

I didn't answer. Telling Joe the truth wasn't an option. But, funny thing, just thinking of the Thrall had dropped me back into the habit of not *quite* lying.

The silence stretched between us. I could hear his harsh breathing in the background. It was an interesting counterpoint to Leroy's quiet measured exhales behind me.

Joe broke the silence first.

"You're going to do it, aren't you? You're going to talk to him. He nearly got you killed—but that doesn't matter to you."

I shuddered with a chill that had nothing to do with the air conditioning blasting above my head. Oh, it mattered. I'd come very close to being turned that night. The scars on my ankle and the buzz of the hive in my head are a constant reminder of just how close a call I had. I had been saved by preparation and no small bit of luck. I'm Irish. Luck's in my genes, thank heavens.

"Kate, are you still there?"

I realized the silence had dragged on a little too long. "I haven't made up my mind, Joe. I'll have to think about it."

"*Why?* Why think about it at all? It's not your problem. *He's* not your problem. Why would you care if he's called five times? Just let it go."

"Joe, I'm tired. I need to get some sleep before I deal with this. We can talk about this lat—" His words finally sunk home. Too much had been going on or I would have noticed earlier.

My voice dropped a few notes and dripped with suspicion. "Joe, you said you were there when *a* call came in. That's *one*—not five. How would you kno—Joseph Thomas Reilly! You've been listening to my answering machine!"

I'd thrown him off balance and he started to fumble his words. "I . . . he . . . it's . . . it's that blasted BEEP, Katie! Why can't you have voice mail, like a normal person? I tried to just shut it off . . . then I punched the wrong button and . . . and then Dylan called. And . . ." His voice softened. "You're right, I shouldn't have messed with the machine."

Oh, no. He was not getting out of this with a simple apology. My teeth ground audibly and the tips of my fingers were white from gripping the receiver until the plastic groaned. The fuzzy reflection of my face in the metal phone was twisted with fury. "I cannot *believe* you, Joseph! Did you go through my mail? Did you write down the license plates of the cars in the garage and run a check on them, too? We've been over this . . . *how* many times now? I'm a big girl. My business is none of yours."

I heard him take a deep breath, loud enough that it came over the wire. "You're right, Katie. I shouldn't have messed with the machine. But Dylan did call five times. I didn't erase them, I promise. They're all still there . . . well, at least I *think* they are."

"You *think*!" Och! Why couldn't the Reilly heirlooms have included a whomping big sword to smack him over his thick skull instead of Irish lace and china! *Maybe* then I'd get through to him!

It took effort, but I forced my voice back into normal range. People were starting to stare and I could actually see Leroy's back shaking with laughter.

"Before you forget—who called?"

"Um, whats-her-name in 1B called twice about some plumbing things, the diamond guy from Israel called once and said he'd call back. Some guy called about the second apartment—*Chuck,* I think? Mike asked you to stop by this week, and then Dylan's five." I could hearing him counting off the calls on his fingers. "Yep, that's all of them. But I *should* have deleted Dylan's." He was getting his fire back.

"Look, I have to go, but we haven't finished this discussion. Not by a long shot."

He slammed the phone down without saying goodbye.

I hung up my end just as hard. I really did want to throttle my brother, not that it did any good to get angry. Our folks are gone, so he thinks he's the head of the family. He's great in a crisis; it's what makes him a top ER doctor. He's not nearly as good at the day-to-day grind. We spend a lot of our time butting heads—particularly when he tries to run my life for me.

Joe has a redheaded temper. My hair is what most people refer to as strawberry blonde. It hovers on that border between blonde and red—which side of the line it falls on depends mostly on how much time I spend in the sun. But while I may sometimes *look* blonde, my temper is every bit as nasty as Joe's and I don't take well to being bullied. I'm more than up to any knockdown, drag-out if things ever got physical. Not that they ever actually *have*. No, we limit ourselves to verbal sparring matches. I forced myself to count to twenty slowly and calm down. There was no point in *borrowing trouble* as mum used to tell me.

"Calm, Katie. Calm." Calm is not my best thing. My brother Bryan had always been the even-tempered one in the family.

"Man trouble, huh?" I'd almost forgotten about Leroy. He nodded knowingly.

I shrugged. "Not really. One stupid brother, and one ghost from the past." I punched his arm lightly and winked. "If you ignore them, they'll go away."

"Some spooks aren't that easy to shake, Kate." His voice was soft. It held an edge of regret. When I looked up, his eyes were hard. I thought about asking but I believe that personal demons should remain personal. I wouldn't want to tell Leroy about Bryan, so I shouldn't ask *his* story.

I sighed and started walking toward the baggage claim

area with Leroy at my side. Thinking about my baby brother was not going to improve my mood. Sometime this week I'd stop by Our Lady's parish and visit Mike—*Father Michael*—and Bryan. Some days it's hard to put the title in front of Mike's name. We'd grown up together. Mike hardly *ever* called. Hmm, that wasn't good. I should go there today. It might be something important. Maybe Bryan had gotten hurt, or . . .

Stop it, Kate! I shook off the brief moment of panic. If it was urgent, Mike would have said so. There was no hurry. Bryan wouldn't know the difference. I hated that fact, but I knew it was true.

I moved quickly through the slowly awakening airport to pick up my luggage. Leroy remained at my side. Most trips I just bring a carry-on and the package. Since I knew I'd be gone a week in several different climates, I'd indulged myself and brought a suitcase. It had been almost more trouble than it was worth—almost. I have to admit that having my swimsuit for the pool at the Paris hotel had been nice.

I edged my way between an overweight businessman in a rumpled suit, his tie at half-mast, and a stroller with a screaming infant. The metallic whirring of the motor took my attention from chatting with Leroy. The carousel began circling with that odd squeaking/grinding noise that is distinctively multi-national. I watched with one eye for my luggage to come out the chute, while keeping my other eye peeled for bad people.

My luggage is ugly. I make a good living, and could buy pretty stuff if I wanted. But I'd discovered that most "nice" luggage looks pretty much alike. Rather than risk getting somebody else's bag by mistake, I'd bought myself a used, hard-sided, Samsonite bag in olive green, then proceeded to plaster it with bumper stickers. It's unmistakably eye-catching. In all my travels since buying it, the airlines haven't lost it once. Except that it didn't come out this time. The final "rattle-flap-shump" gave way to muffled whirring and then the machine stopped without relinquishing my bag.

I checked the board overhead. This wasn't my flight! No wonder I didn't remember the squalling baby. I walked back to the flight display. Yes, this was the right carousel. I settled down for the wait. Leroy agreed to stay to keep an eye on me. It was nice of him and I was grateful for the company.

It was nearly an hour later when I grabbed my bag from the carousel and stepped out of the way. Jeez Louise! Strip searches in Amsterdam moved quicker than this! Thank God for Leroy's ever present deck of cards. He trounced me, twelve games to two.

I slid a quarter in the machine, tossed my luggage in a liberated cart and went to find Edna in the very expensive covered lot near the terminal. Edna is a fully restored fire engine red 1955 pick-up truck. I bought her as a used piece of junk when I was sixteen years old, and have spent many a weekend with my head buried under the hood. Now that she's restored I've been offered quite a lot of money for her—but things will have to get a lot more desperate than they are now before I'd be willing to sell.

I tossed my bag onto the floor of the front seat and climbed in. She fired up as soon as I turned the key. That was a surprise. Usually I have to coax and flatter the old broad. I cracked the driver's window enough to shout my thanks to Leroy.

He turned and raised a hand. "See you next time, Reilly!"

I watched his broad back disappear into the building before driving out of the parking garage and heading for home and my waiting bed.

It's miles and miles from the airport to the city, and there's nothing like a wide expanse of empty prairie to get your mind working on all the wrong things. I drove through the dark of pre-dawn trying to make sense of everything that was going on. Would the queen of the Thrall have someone tail me? Yeah, if it suited her purposes. There's very little Monica *isn't* capable of. But the big question was . . . *why*? And was it connected to Dylan's calls? I couldn't imagine why my lying, cheating excuse for an ex-fiancé would track me down after all these years.

Traffic was flowing smoothly toward the distant skyline as my mind drifted. Then I saw the first bright red set of brake lights. I nosed over in my lane to see that a lighted directional arrow had been placed on the roadway, just where the airport access joined the interstate. I had to fight a wave of annoyance. Seems like every time I leave town, another construction zone springs up.

Vehicles were supposed to merge into my lane so I stayed put. Still, as always, drivers insisted on zooming past the building line of cars to try to butt in ahead. Vehicle after vehicle sped past at highway speed, only to be shut down when their lane ended. Soon there were cars stacked up in both lanes as we moved closer to the barricades, still at a good clip.

As soon as I realized the barricades were concrete I started swearing under my breath. The type of barricade is an indicator of the length of the proposed construction. Orange cones signify a day or two of frustration. Those orange and white barrels filled with sand mean weeks. Concrete walls mean you're in for months; maybe even *years* of inconvenience. There's one highway in Denver that's been under construction for over two years and isn't even close to finished. I noted with annoyance that there were similar barricades on the opposite side of the highway. I started mentally calculating the extra time I would need for my next trip to the airport. No! Think about something nice!

Okay, how about the renovations to the building entrance? Ahhh, yeah, that's it. I still get the little-girl giggles whenever I think about finding the exquisite mosaic tile floor under the dirty linoleum I'd torn up in front of the elevator in my building last month. The tiny jewel-toned tile bits formed the face and upper torso of a lovely dark-haired woman. Considering the building was constructed during the silver boom of the late 1800s, she could have been anyone from a society matron to a red-light madam. Heck, from the books I've read on the subject, she might have been *both*. It was now covered with canvas until I'm completely done with painting and trim.

A blasting of car horns behind me brought me back to reality with a panicked jerk. We'd reached a section of highway lit bright as day by poles holding banks of artificial lights. The glare was awful. I checked my rearview mirror, but I couldn't see the source of the noise. The horns continued, beeps of all different tones and lengths. The angry squeal of tires against pavement made me twist against my lap belt to look through the back window, but a large panel truck behind me blocked my view. I was two car lengths from the beginning of the construction zone. A Toyota Camry on my left stepped on the gas to try to nose in ahead of me. I'd probably let him when the time came but right now I wanted to know what was going on behind me. I rolled down my window so I could hear better. The sound of screaming metal now joined the horns. As tight as traffic was packed, there was a good chance I was going to be rear-ended by that panel truck, but there was no helping it.

As I reached the barrier, the Camry pulled in front of me from the left lane. I tried to put a little distance between me and the panel truck when a one-ton truck with dual rear tires, towing an oversized trailer, moved up fast and hard along the quickly narrowing emergency lane. The wheels of the trailer were off the pavement on one side. The trailer was clipping off the plastic delineator posts at ground level. I realized in a panic that the stake-bed trailer was headed straight for me!

The next few seconds were a rush of sound and motion. The panel truck behind me honked and swerved. He collided with the car to his left, driving it into the concrete barrier with a screech of protesting metal.

What in the hell is he doing? I couldn't believe it. Was the driver of the dually *insane?* He seemed intent on entering traffic exactly where my truck was. He swerved toward me and then away, sending the trailer careening in my direction. Twice, then three times in rapid succession. I swerved to give him room and touched my brakes to let him enter but it wasn't enough. He slowed and swerved again. The trailer just missed my bumper. I had nowhere left to go. Even stopping wasn't an option. The panel truck behind me wasn't giving way. It was right on my bumper, close enough that I couldn't even see its headlights.

I said a quick prayer, slammed on my brakes and at the same time cranked the steering wheel as hard right as I could. I swerved onto the shoulder of the road behind the trailer.

Edna skittered wildly on the sand and I fought to control her. The panel truck careened by me without the driver giving me a glance. As the road joined the highway, the driver of the one-ton swerved across the double white lines into the far left lane and the whole works ended up sliding down the sloped median. It teetered, tipped sideways at high speed and nearly flipped. The trailer was all that held it upright.

My knuckles were white where they gripped the steering wheel. My heart was pounding a mile a minute and my left eye started to twitch. I had almost regained control when a motorcycle cop sped past me on the shoulder. I instinctively turned the wheel away from him. It was too much for the poor old truck.

The landscape raced by me in a blur as Edna executed a 360-degree spin on the shoulder. The passenger wheels caught the edge of the pavement, and as the driver's side of the truck raised into the air enough that I could look down the steep embankment, every second seemed an eternity.

Edna doesn't have shoulder belts. This could be really, really bad.

2

I threw every ounce of my weight against the driver's door and prayed. My heart stilled as the truck balanced on two wheels. Finally, gravity won and the chassis returned to the pavement with a teeth-jarring thump. I sat there, frozen, remembering how to breathe as wailing sirens filled the air. I patted the steering wheel of my faithful truck like I would a puppy and congratulated her. "Attagirl, Edna!"

My legs were rubbery as I exited the truck and checked for damage. A state trooper came running over and I spent the next twenty minutes trying to convince him, and the off-duty EMTs that just happened to be at the airport, that I wasn't hurt. They seemed convinced that I must have suffered a concussion.

Fortunately, there were enough people who *did* need an ambulance that they let me leave after taking my statement. The Denver cop on the motorcycle made me promise that I would check in at Denver General for testing. While it seemed silly to me, he threatened to write me up for careless driving if I didn't.

As I eased back into traffic, I glanced again at the truck in the ditch. Christian charity aside, I got no small amount of satisfaction from seeing that dually end up there.

I didn't go to DG. Instead, I drove to St. Elizabeth's. It's just one of many sprawling brick buildings on hospital row. Joe was off shift, but I was sure to know someone on duty in the ER.

I crossed the parking lot and came in through the ER entrance. An ambulance was just arriving. I had to leap sideways through the door to avoid the speeding gurney and attendants. I had to wait a few minutes to check in. A pretty blonde nurse who I didn't recognize took the insurance card I pulled from my wallet and made a quick photocopy. As I slid the card back in my wallet she gestured toward the reception area.

"Have a seat. It'll be a few minutes." I turned and looked around. It'd be *more* than a few judging from the crowd. People occupied nearly every chair lining the walls of the waiting room. Most of them looked worried, and were probably waiting for word on a friend or relative. One woman rocked a sobbing young boy of about eight in her arms. His head was a mass of blood from a nasty cut. As I watched, another red splatter landed on the mother's arm. Despite the blood, that they hadn't already taken him to a room was a good sign— head wounds bleed like crazy even if they aren't serious.

I sat down in one of the two remaining seats. Fortunately, it was right at the edge of a busy aisle. If I spotted someone I knew, I could nab him or her and jump ahead of the line. I didn't feel guilty. I'd only take two or three minutes and be out of the others' way.

As I watched the passersby for a friendly face, jet lag decided to settle in. My limbs suddenly felt like lead and my stomach was growling enough to warrant a glance from the man next to me. A quick scan around the room cheered me. While I'm not terribly fond of either vending machine food or coffee, anything is better than nothing. I fished around in my pockets and was rewarded with a pair of quarters. I walked over to the machine debating internally—more caffeine or food? Caffeine won by a hair. I'd pay for it later, of course. I'd probably have a stomachache by noon for having a second cup.

As I stepped up to the machine I noticed something odd. A brand new Gucci purse sat unattended on the chair next to the machine. I shook my head as I plunked the quarters into the coin slot. I didn't remember it being there a moment before. Why would someone leave an expensive purse lying around in a room of strangers? I glanced around. Nobody else seemed to notice the tooled leather bag, but it seemed really familiar to me.

I turned my attention back to the machine as the hissing ceased and coffee began to pour into the cardboard cup. I saw movement in the shiny black surface. I started to turn, but it was too late. A fierce blow hit the back of my skull solidly enough to drop me to my knees. I didn't pass out, but only barely. I rolled out of the way of a second attack by the nurse from the check-in desk, running into the legs of the mother with the boy. She didn't notice. I looked up into her glazed eyes. I realized that none of the people were seeing what was happening to me. With a sudden chill, I remembered the last time I'd seen that expensive handbag—swinging from Monica Micah's slender arm as she backhanded me across a restaurant while all of the patrons stood blindly hypnotized. The queen of the Thrall was paying me a personal visit. Shit.

The nurse came for me again. I shook my head frantically, forcing the remaining cotton candy from my brain. I let her believe that I didn't notice her until she was close enough for me to slam my boot into her kneecap. She dropped to one knee with a grunt but got up so fast that you'd think she'd been kicked by an errant child.

"Enough!" came a voice that crawled along my skin like rows of biting ants. My attacker froze in place, arm raised. A brick fell from her instantly limp fingers.

Monica stood in the doorway a dozen feet away, and she hadn't changed at all. She was still the same vibrant raven-haired beauty with milk-white skin and violet eyes. She looked both elegant and sexy in clothes that had been cut to make the most of every curve. Luring prey has always been easy with her sultry voice, cover model looks and wanton sexual appetite. She could look cherubic, professional or even demure. But underneath the good looks were a mind and a body capable of unimaginable evil. Her enemies tend to scream a lot and then die very, very slowly. So far, I've been the lone exception.

Hello, Kathleen. She spoke directly into my mind, her voice deceptively pleasant. I hate that she can slide so casually into my thoughts. I raised myself stiffly to a sitting position while trying to increase my mental shields. It was a struggle. Her force of will pushed at my body enough to make my muscles ache. My God! I hadn't seen her for a couple of years, but I didn't remember her being this powerful. The scent of her expensive perfume made me sneeze, sending a shooting pain through my skull. Oddly, it helped. By concentrating on the pain I was able to push her mind aside just enough to throw up a stronger shield and not be overwhelmed. She hissed. It was a very inhuman sound that seemed even more evil coming from those perfectly painted lips.

"What do you want, Monica?" I forced the words through a throat that didn't want to work.

Her smile was dazzling. Her laugh was bright but cold, and words again appeared like magic in my head. *Want? Why, what I've always wanted, darling. I want you dead. But not quite yet. We have other plans for you first.*

The last syllable was followed by a surge of pure power that seared my brain. I gasped and brought my hands up against my temples, but white spots and flowers threatened to eat away reality.

When I could force my eyes open past a slit, I saw the nurse taking the cap off a syringe. Monica's eyes glinted with wicked pleasure. *We'll go somewhere less . . . crowded, and we'll chat. Won't that be fun?*

No, it wouldn't. And we wouldn't. Not so long as I had an ounce of fight left in my body. I tensed body and mind to fight. I cast my eyes around the waiting room, looking for something, anything I could use as a weapon. Nothing. But I did see a familiar face walking in the hallway beyond Monica. So, Monica didn't have enough power to do the whole hospital. It was only the people in this room who were enthralled. As liquid leapt from the needle in a broad arc to clear the air, I called in the loudest voice I could manage.

"DR. MACDOUGAL!"

The man turned to my voice and he saw Monica. He knew her. He sees a lot of people who she's *chatted* with. But only for a few seconds before the face is covered and the body is taken downstairs. He ran and grabbed the arms of two burly attendants. Monica bared her fangs and hissed at me.

The blonde was still moving steadily toward me, needle extended and thumb on the plunger.

I couldn't stand. I knew that. Monica's power was too strong. But I knew that if she enthralled the doctor and the attendants, she'd lose her hold over the room, or me. In any case, she was undone.

Or so I thought.

The first attendant grabbed the nurse. He had to struggle to hold onto a woman that couldn't have weighed more than ninety-eight pounds. He was winning, but only barely.

The other attendant reached for Monica. Big mistake. One slender arm shot out and the man was suddenly in the air, held effortlessly by her superhuman strength. A flash of movement later, he was on the ground, his throat ripped into shreds by her perfectly manicured nails. Blood spurted from his torn arteries. I grimaced as she licked the blood from her fingers while he lay thrashing.

This isn't over, Katie.

Both women disappeared. That's the best I can describe it. I lay still on the floor for a second, stunned and grateful. I'd been lucky. She could've killed me in those seconds when she'd clouded our minds to leave. Why hadn't she? What in the *hell* was going on?

With Monica's departure, the waiting room came alive again. The mother looked down at her blood-covered arm with a start. The boy had been bleeding steadily the whole time, and she hadn't noticed.

"Kate!"

I turned to see Dr. MacDougal, a slender middle-aged man

with thinning black hair and a bushy moustache. He was still dressed in a lab coat. He was on one knee next to his fallen employee. I watched as he snapped on a pair of latex gloves taken from his pocket. I could tell the man was badly wounded, but he'd probably live. He was lucky. Monica seldom leaves survivors. A gurney arrived with a contingent of doctors and nurses and the unconscious man disappeared down the hallway in a rush of voices and motion.

I would've expected him to follow along, but he stayed, giving me a long, intense stare that carried the weight of his displeasure.

"Hi, Dr. MacDougal," I replied wearily. I was truly sorry about the guard—and confused as hell.

"What happened here, Kathleen?" He removed the gloves and dropped them into the biowaste container hanging on the wall.

His guess was as good as mine. I couldn't fathom why Monica would suddenly appear. She'd left me alone for years. I reviewed her words in my mind. *"We have other plans for you first." We* had to be the hive. But what other plans? I didn't have a clue. My pulse began racing with fear. One of the benefits of being Not Prey was that they were *supposed* to challenge me one on one, not hunt me like an animal. Somehow the rules had changed. My body started to shake, and it wasn't just a physical reaction.

"I had a near miss on I-70 and promised the police that I'd get checked out by a doctor. I checked in. Monica was waiting for me. I don't know how or why." My stomach tightened into a tense knot. There were too many questions, not the least of which was why my free pass had abruptly expired. I needed to find out, just as soon as I could get my feet back under me and enough rest for my brain to start working again. But I was just too tired, too hungry, and my head hurt too badly to do anything but deal with the immediate crisis.

The anger faded from MacDougal's eyes and his face fell into professional lines. He opened his mouth to begin asking the usual series of questions for accident patients.

I warded off the words by holding up my hands. "I just spun out when someone forced me off the road. I'm fine. The truck's fine. But the cop on the scene wouldn't believe I didn't hit my head." I snorted and shook my head, which brought on a brief wave of nausea. "Doesn't matter much now, since the check-in nurse cracked me with a brick." I used gentle fingers to probe the growing lump. It hurt. A lot. But I wasn't dizzy, or nauseous—both good signs. "I'm probably fine. Really."

MacDougal scowled at me. He crossed his arms over his chest and raised his brows. "*I'll* let you know if you're fine." He grasped my chin in one strong hand, gazing carefully at my pupils. He let out a little snort of air that could've meant anything or nothing.

I heaved a sigh. I wanted out of here, and now. But I knew that tone of voice. I wouldn't be going anywhere until the doctor got a good look at me. If I tried, he'd call reinforcements—possibly in the form of my older brother.

He released my chin. "Come with me. We can take care of this in my office." He gestured for me to follow and I fell into step beside him. I knew where the lab was.

I'm always amazed by Dr. MacDougal's office. Researchers seem to run to two extremes. Some are so involved with their projects that everything else suffers. Unless they are fortunate enough to employ a competent assistant, their office, lab and life are in constant chaos. Dr. MacDougal is the other flip of the coin. His office is meticulously clean— dirt is the enemy. His lab is a model of order and efficiency.

He left the light off, but sufficient sunlight found its way through the blinds.

As I performed a heel-to-toe, straight line walk that reminded me of a roadside DUI test, I asked, "Have you ever finished off that bottle of The Macallan?"

He shook his head. "Nope. I keep it in my desk for special occasions. It was eighteen years old when you gave it to me, and will probably make it another eighteen before I finish it. Every sip is bottled joy, so I refuse to waste it." He motioned for me to stop walking and stepped forward with a small penlight.

He flicked the light into my eyes as I stared straight ahead. "So, have you learned anything new about the Thrall that you can share?" I wasn't surprised at the subject of conversation. Research into the effects of the Thrall parasite is both his job and his passion. I know he likes me as a person, but even that is overshadowed by his endless curiosity about my "link" to the creatures he spends his life studying.

"Nope. I've tried to avoid them."

He stopped in mid-flick and stared at me very seriously. "That's stupid, Kate. You should always know your enemy."

Part of me knew MacDougal was right. I should have spent these years learning as much as I could about them. But the other part had wanted to pretend that if I ignored them, they'd go away. *Denial is more than de river in Egypt.*

I took a deep breath and thought about the call from Dylan and the look on Monica's face. I shook my head. It hurt. A lot. Damn it.

"Okay, okay. So enlighten me with your wealth of knowledge." The words sounded cranky, but MacDougal ignored the tone. He moved behind me and began to lecture as he checked the range of motion of my head.

"Well, as you know, the Thrall have existed since the dawn of time. They've evolved over the millennia from the equivalent of a tapeworm to become a highly intelligent parasitic species with a unique culture and language. Does this hurt?" he asked, pressing firmly on my abdomen where the seat belt had crossed me. I shook my head no so he continued. He knows Edna doesn't have shoulder belts so he didn't bother to check there.

"We've learned since last time we talked that they are extremely sensitive to damage to the Host. This is apparently because the primary ganglia actually *fuses* to the Host's spinal cord."

Hey, that *was* new. "So a gunshot or knife wound to the Host's back will hurt the Thrall?"

Dr. MacDougal nodded. "And damage to the Thrall, such as an injury to a feeding tube in the mouth or a blow to the nesting site at the base of the skull will stun the Host into a comatose-like state.

I pursed my lips. "Is that why all the attempts to operate and remove the parasite have killed the Host?"

"Precisely. It's the same with drugs. Anything sufficient to kill the Thrall will kill the Host. It's only recently that we've learned that the Thrall's body actually merges with and *replaces* human brain tissue. When the parasite grows too big, the hypothalamus is destroyed and the Host dies. The usual life span seems to be about three to four years. Your friend Monica is a notable exception."

He reached up and ran cool fingers over my forehead, searching for lumps or swelling. His probing at the back of my head produced a quick flash of pain. He saw my reaction and then carefully moved to my jaw. I reached up and felt the sore spot. It wasn't much of a lump, but it was certainly tender. There was a clicking sound as he moved the jaw back and forth.

"Make an appointment with your dentist," he commented. "You're a little out of alignment. Could give you headaches and change your bite pattern."

"Anything else new on the research front?" I changed the subject away from a possible dental visit. Not my favorite place.

He ignored the question, stepped away and dug in his pocket for a moment. He withdrew a ring of keys and selected one. "I've got something here that will take care of the swelling and concussion."

The key opened a cabinet on the wall and he removed a large white plastic bottle. "Take two now and one tonight *with food,* and again for the next two days. I'll write up a prescription that you can fill at your normal pharmacy."

I glanced at the pair of red and white capsules he dropped in my hand, and raised a leery brow. "They have drugs to get rid of a concussion now?"

He smiled and handed me a plastic bottle of water from the little refrigerator on the countertop and I popped the pills. "That's the nice thing about the best minds in the world researching the effects of the Thrall. We've learned a lot about head injuries since you played ball." My stomach took that moment to comment on the word "food." He glanced down at the sharp rumble.

"And I *mean* with food, Kate. You don't eat nearly as often as you should. Go to see your old chiropractor if he's still practicing, too. This looks about the same as the knock you took in your last game, so your back's probably out of place. I'll file a report with the police. But I want you to take the usual precautions."

He handed me a printed leaflet from the counter that discussed head injuries. While I read what I already knew, he scribbled on a pad. "If you experience any dizziness, increased thirst or if you still have a headache in twenty-four hours, give Joe a call."

I sniffed in amusement. "Calling my brother *gives* me a headache."

"And you him." MacDougal chuckled for a moment, handed me the square of paper with an unreadable scrawl that I presumed would mean something to the pharmacist, and then changed the subject back to his personal obsession.

"You asked about my research. I think I've found out something very valuable that would be of interest to you. Someday it could help Bryan."

That caught my attention. I moved to sit down on the couch.

"Just by accident, I've discovered that EKG patterns of drug zombies like Bryan are identical to those of Hosts."

I gave him what must have been a quizzical look. "What does that mean? That the Thrall are somehow responsible for the zombies?"

"Not at all. But it *may* mean that improperly prepared Eden, which causes the zombie-like state in its junkies, is similar in composition to the yolk of the Thrall egg which enslaves the Hosts. It's just a theory, but I'm putting together a grant application to study it."

Interesting as the conversation was, my stomach took the opportunity to remind me, again, how hungry I was. The rumble was loud enough that MacDougal let out a low growl. I shrugged but blushed.

"Sorry. I haven't eaten since lunch yesterday."

He nodded and crossed his arms over his chest. "Like I said earlier, take the pills *with food*. Go—eat."

I grinned. "Yep. Food and then bed. That's second on the short list."

He shook his head and gave me a stern look. "Not with that head injury. You need to call someone to sit with you—or at least set the alarm and wake up every hour until the medication kicks in." I stepped out into the hallway through the door he held open for me. I immediately felt the familiar tickle and buzzing in my head. It was almost dawn. Normally the hive activity would be winding down. The fact that they weren't meant something was going on. It was a forcible reminder that MacDougal had been right about more than the head injury.

Apparently, ignoring the Thrall was no longer an option.

3

The sun was past the horizon by the time I reached LoDo. The orange brilliance that chased away the night struck the mirror and caught me right in the eyes. I had to flip the rearview to night mode, which meant I couldn't see cars behind me very well, and the lancing pain I got every time I turned my head made me want to scream.

Gee, it wasn't even eight o'clock, and the day already sucked.

Traffic downtown was moving at a crawl. I can remember a time when there was almost no traffic in the early hours of the morning. That time is long gone. The Denver area is growing faster than the city facilities can support it.

The long, slow drive gave me far too much time to think about things I'd rather not have contemplated. Dylan Shea was at the top of that list. But I didn't have enough information to make a decision about Dylan. Better to think of something else.

Probably because of the conversation with MacDougal, my thoughts were of my brother Bryan. I originally became a courier because I wanted to travel. Be careful what you wish for. I now spend the bulk of my life in foreign countries. But

I'm good at the job, and it pays well. I need to make good money to pay my share of the costs for Bryan's care.

I fought down the wave of hurt and anger that threatened to overwhelm me. My nose and eyes burned for a moment until I slapped myself sharply on the cheek. Don't knock it—it works. I can't afford to cry while driving.

Bryan had been the best and brightest of our family. Captain of the football team; class valedictorian. Why in the hell he'd gotten involved in drugs, especially something so horrible as Eden, is beyond me. It breaks my heart to look into those vacant green eyes and realize that he doesn't recognize me, Joe, or anyone else. No glimmer of intelligence is left. He does what he's told if the commands are simple enough. Eden zombies have even less will than the Herd. He eats because Mike tells him to. He sweeps up the church and helps with the lifting in exchange for food, shelter and protection. Between them, Michael and his small staff keep Bryan and the others from wandering off and either starving to death or getting run over in traffic.

I took the highway exit that goes past Coors Field. Downtown was deep in shadows, still and cool. The open window let in a chill breeze that was filled with city smells. I love city smells. Cold steel, exhaust and brewing coffee, with a hint of morning dew. I slowly calmed down. Drivers racing to work cut me off more than once but I was just too exhausted to cuss them out. Now that the adrenaline and caffeine were both gone my entire body felt leaden. I turned the corner, stopped and entered my code on the keypad. A metal grate rose and I drove down the ramp to the parking area beneath my building. It was good to be home.

I own a converted factory, a four-story red brick building, with huge multi-paned windows. I bought it with my inheritance and the last of the volleyball money, back when the neighborhood was bad. The price was reasonable enough for an injured pro beach volleyball player to afford, and that's saying something.

When they moved in Coors Field, Six Flags, and the Pepsi Can—oops, I mean the Pepsi *Center,* the neighborhood became upscale and expensive. Now the place is worth a fortune. Renovating it helped me get through the pain and anger of Dylan leaving me for Amanda.

Joe is probably right that I should either sell the units as condos or raise the rents. But I love the place and want to get in tenants who will stay forever and love it too.

One of the biggest selling points for this particular building was that it had parking. The previous owner had been foresighted enough to convert part of the basement. It only has six spaces. There will be one for each of the other tenants, plus one for a guest. As the owner, I take two. One for Edna, and one for my motorcycle.

I watched in the rearview mirror to make sure no one tried to sneak under the gate as it came down. It was just that sort of a day.

The grate clanked as it hit the ground, and I pulled the truck forward into its usual slot. I didn't feel like unpacking right now, so I left the bags in the cab and locked up. I felt the wave of exhaustion flood my muscles and make them ache. All I wanted was to get up to my apartment, grab some food and rest.

When I want exercise, I take the stairs. They're narrow and steep, guaranteed to give me a great workout. Not this morning. I wasn't taking one extra step I didn't have to. Mornings like this were why I kept both elevators during the renovations.

The freight lift that opens into the garage is a massive, fully functional relic of the industrial age. It's noisy and it's ugly, but it works. I got used to it while hauling things upstairs during the remodel of my apartment. The freight elevator is now walled off on every floor but mine.

The elevator in the lobby is small and elegantly decorative with ornate brass that matches the kick plates on the door. I'm sure the tenants will love it. But, perversely, I like this one better.

My body felt leaden. It was almost too much effort just to climb out of the truck. But I was alive, and I was *home*. I closed the door of the truck and started across the parking area. My footfalls on the concrete echoed off of the brick walls. I could hear the street sounds through the grate behind me. There was a long honk and a screech of tires. I held my breath for a moment and waited for an impact. Nothing. Another accident narrowly avoided.

I made it to the elevator without meeting another person. As soon as I got upstairs I planned to lock the door, turn off the elevator and collapse in bed after some food. I don't usually turn off the elevator, but I was feeling more than a little paranoid. My mind kept repeating the same thing over and over—*I'm Not Prey. That means they're supposed to leave me alone or issue a one-on-one challenge*—as if by repetition I could undo the events of this morning. I couldn't, and I knew it. But I was afraid enough that I was only a half-step away from panic. My home was supposed to be off limits, but what if *all* the rules changed? I reminded myself that Monica shouldn't know where I live. I'm unlisted and keep a low profile—but I couldn't be sure. Dylan shouldn't have had my telephone number. We haven't spoken since I left my old apartment. The fact that he had tracked it down, or gotten it from someone I knew was unnerving. If he could get the number, there was a good possibility he, and they, had the address. *Shit.*

The elevator took me smoothly but noisily up to my apartment. I pulled open the reinforced gate and stepped into the foyer of my apartment. I had thirty seconds to shut down the alarm system, so I hurried across the kitchen to where the controls are discreetly mounted on the wall next to the fridge and entered the code.

Then, before I could forget, I grabbed the spare key to the elevator out of my junk drawer. I'd given Joe my copy of the elevator key and the pass code for the system ages ago so he could take care of the plants when I'm away on business. I was beginning to think that had been a mistake, but in the meantime I'd use the spare. I glanced at the answering machine next to the phone on my way back to the lift. There were four new messages, but judging from the small amount of tape still showing through the window, Joe hadn't managed to erase the calls he had heard.

But first I needed to unwind. I turned the key and heard the elevator lock "snick" into place. The tension in my shoulders relaxed a bit.

It was good to be home. My apartment takes up what was once the entire third and fourth floors of the building. I left the red brick walls mostly unadorned; the only exception is a six foot framed coat of arms with the Reilly family history that has a place of honor on the north wall.

The only interior wall is on the lower floor where a set of wide steps curve up to the bedroom loft. The wall's painted a pale peach. The walk-in coat closet and downstairs bathroom are behind it. The north and south walls have no windows, but the east and west walls more than make up for it. The thick rippled glass of the old factory windows seems to capture rainbows and then spray them across the room. I love to lie on the floor and watch the colors dance across my skin as the sun sets behind the mountains. They're not energy efficient, but I like them. So do the plants—the living room is part jungle.

I walked directly into a large living room with a ceiling that is open to both floors. Industrial size ceiling fans circulate the air, making the custom vertical blinds rattle sharply if the setting is on high. Joe had left the blinds open when he watered the plants, and the sunlight streaming into the living area was almost blinding. I crossed over to the wall by the entertainment center and hit the switch for the motor that would close them slightly. I hit the button to rewind the tape on the machine, and then straightened one of the picture frames on my way back to the kitchen.

I keep all of my important pictures on the wall above my stereo system. They're all different shapes and sizes, with a variety of frames. It gives it an eclectic look that contrasts the smooth clean lines of the curving staircase that leads to the open loft I use for my bedroom.

I opened the fridge. It was achingly empty. Only a half-empty carton of eggs, a partial stick of butter and a six-pack of bottled water. My trip had been planned, so I hadn't bothered to go grocery shopping before I left. There was more in the freezer, but I didn't have the patience to wait for something to thaw.

Beep! "Kate, hey . . . um, well, I've got some good news and some bad news." I recognized Chuck's voice. He's my brand new tenant in 2B, right underneath my apartment. He's a cop on the Denver force. I pulled the egg carton from the fridge and unhooked one of the copper-bottomed fry pans from the rack on the wall. I flicked the switch to open the gas jets and put the skillet on to heat. I didn't really need to hear any more bad news, but with Chuck it probably just meant he'd lost the lease I gave him to sign. Not critical, but a pain.

Excitement filled his voice. "The third time was a charm! You were right. I passed my Detective test yesterday. I really appreciate you taking the time to go over the materials with me. It really helped." Now his voice was nervous, filled with worried sighs. "Which is why it's so hard to tell you—"

I closed my eyes so I didn't have to watch the boot drop on my head. "Actually, it's good news, but I know you've been strapped for cash. I got offered a slot on the Fort Collins squad, as a full detective. The guy who's leaving got a promotion and is going to Boston. He, um, said I could sublet his apartment until the lease expires. I hate to, Kate—I really do, but it's a hell of a drive from here to Fort Collins every day. I won't be able to take the apartment, and I feel just rotten about it. I know I promised."

I rubbed my temples with tired fingers and angrily grabbed a plastic spatula to turn the eggs. He was right, it was good news. And he was also right that the drive would be hell. It's over an hour on a good day. I was happy for him . . . sort of.

"So, I guess that's it. I'll check around the squad room to see if anyone is looking for a place. I really liked what you've done with the building, but I just can't sign the lease. Hope you're not mad or anything. Anyway, well, I have to get to work. You can keep my deposit if will help you right now. You can get it back to me when you can."

No. I'll give him back his security deposit. It's in a different account, and that's just . . . well, just no. I'm not that desperate. *Of course, I haven't checked the mail yet, either.*

I slid the fried egg onto a plate and punched down the bread in the toaster. While I was waiting for it, I clicked off the machine. First things first.

I grabbed the portable phone and the White Pages, and still managed to catch the toast just as it was popping up. Considering the size of the Denver phone book, that's no small feat. A quick slather of butter later, and breakfast was served. The scent of the frying egg made me hungry enough that the entire meal took about five minutes to finish. I flopped to the business listings, found the number for the *Denver Post* classifieds and dialed. Might as well get it over with.

The bright perky voice almost made me more grumpy. "Thanks for calling the *Denver Post* Classifieds. This is Tina."

I sounded even more tired than I felt, if that was possible. "Hi, Tina. My name is Kate Reilly. I placed an ad for an apartment for rent a few months ago, and I've got another vacancy. Do you, by any chance, still have that ad on file?"

"Is the ad under your name personally, or billed to a business?"

"Nope. Just me. I think it was about two months ago. Do you keep them that long?"

"We do on business listings. Okay, let's see—" I heard clicking in the background as perky Tina tip-typed the search for my file. I held the phone to my ear with my shoulder and rinsed off my plate.

"Ah. Kate Reilly, here we go. Sure, we can . . . oh, wait." Tina's friendly voice dropped a few notes and became more businesslike. "I'm sorry, Ms. Reilly, but we seem to have an outstanding invoice for the last time you ran this ad. We'll have to get payment for that bill before we can place this new one. Would you like me to connect you to accounting?"

I felt heat in my cheeks. "Are you sure? I could have sworn I paid that bill last month."

"Well, I don't have your payment files down here. I just have a flag on the account so that I can't place it again. I can transfer you to one of the bookkeepers, though."

I sighed and shook my head. "No, not right now. Let me

check my bank statements first. I'll give you a call back later today."

Bright and animated was back in a flash. "Okay, then. Thank you for calling the *Denver Post* Classifieds."

A perfect ending to a perfect morning.

I stumbled up the staircase to my bedroom. I was on the verge of collapse, but I was a good girl. I followed Dr. Mac-Dougal's orders and set the alarm.

I barely managed to pull off my shoes before falling on top of the bed fully clothed.

I couldn't have been asleep long when the dreams started. Dreams starring the two people who were the focal points of my frantic life today.

I was suddenly entering my apartment again and the phone was ringing.

I looked down. I realized I was wearing a sweater that I'd thrown away because of all the blood, and black jeans which had followed the sweater into the trash because one leg had ripped puncture holes with more blood. My brain recognized this memory. I started to panic. I did *not* want to dream about this! I felt myself thrashing on the bed, my heart pounding. It was no use. The dream rolled relentlessly forward. I watched helplessly as my dream self walked over to the phone.

I tried to pinch myself to wake up, but couldn't figure out in the dream why I was pinching. No, no, no, I don't want to answer that phone!

I'd just returned to town from a trip to Israel, and had tried to reach Dylan, my fiancé, at work to tell him I was home. But his secretary hadn't seen him for two days and was getting worried. I called his apartment and was very surprised— read *shocked*—to have the phone picked up by my best friend, Amanda.

"Oh, hello, Kate." Her voice was oddly smug. It raised again those nagging fears in the back of my head that I'd been trying to avoid. My real brain, the one in my body on the bed, knew that I should have listened to the nagging.

"I'm looking for Dylan, Amanda. Where is he?" My voice

was harsh, but I felt oddly disconnected from my emotions. It's how I deal with stress.

"You don't have to worry about him, Kate. He's in good hands."

"I don't consider your hands all that terribly *good*," I snarled.

Her laugh was a joyful tinkle of sound over the wire. "Oh, but *Dylan* does. I've tried to convince him to tell you about us for a couple of months now. But he didn't want to *hurt* you. He can be such a wuss sometimes."

I could feel my heart still in my chest, in both places. A *couple* of months? We'd only been engaged for a couple of months. That *bastard!* Salty wetness burned at my eyes and a buzzing filled my ears. I tried to hide the hurt from my voice. It still sounded strangled and harsh, but from anger, not pain. "That doesn't explain where he is, Amanda. He hasn't checked in at work for two days."

"He's interviewing for a new job. One that pays *very* well."

"He could have taken a couple of vacation days, or even a sick day. Who is this *job* with?"

Her voice was becoming huffy, tight. "Not that it's any of your business—but his new friend, Larry, offered him a position. It pays *very* well. I told him to take it while he could."

Panic flowed through my veins. "Dylan wouldn't work for Larry, Amanda. He knows what Larry *is*." Larry is the Thrall queen. The Thrall don't care if the Host is male or female. They just have to be strong, healthy and psychically gifted. It helps if they are good looking. They lure the victims in with sex. Back then, I'd heard the rumors that the Thrall had started *recruiting* and were actually paying people a regular salary to join the Herd. I hadn't believed them. Evidently I'd been wrong.

Once again her laugh filled my ear. "You just don't get it, do you, Kate? Dylan does what *I* tell him to do. You're ancient history. Dylan is going to be part of the Herd for the new queen. Larry's already picked his successor, and Monica picked Dylan as one of her first. They'll pay him two thousand bucks a month just to stay healthy and help feed the queen. It's the same amount he makes now, for a lot less work. You don't make that kind of change donating a pint at Bonfils!"

I stared at the wall of my apartment in horror, listening to Amanda casually compare donating blood to save someone's life at the Belle Bonfils Blood Center to being sucked dry by a stinking parasite! I had to believe—*had* to believe that Dylan was under some sort of mind control to even consider such a thing!

I'd hung up on Amanda without another word. I didn't even know if I could believe her. I didn't *want* to believe her. It was easier for me to think that she'd somehow turned him over to the Thrall. My mind imagined Dylan fighting for his life as they dragged him screaming to the lair. It was easier to consider than thinking of him walking into the hive and baring his neck.

I called Joe. I managed to not cry when I told him about Dylan and Amanda, and he managed not to say "I told you so." When I told him I was going to save Dylan he insisted that I at least come down to visit him at the hospital first.

He'd taken me to his office after I'd spent a half-hour in the morgue, staring at the dissected body of a Thrall Host. Joe had expected the display to scare me, and it did. But the devastation to the internal organs only made me that much more determined to save Dylan. God help me. I loved him. Even if our relationship was over I *couldn't* just leave him to . . . that.

Joe was furious. He kept saying "no better than he deserves." It didn't matter. Eventually, reluctantly, he gave up on making me come to my senses and dragged me back to the staff lounge at the back of the ER saying he had something to show me.

I'd tried to argue. "I don't have *time,* damn it! They could be bleeding Dylan as we speak—or infesting him." But Joe wouldn't take no for an answer.

I had been wrong. It was worth the delay. Because in a box on top of the fridge in the staff lounge was something he'd been working on with one of his friends from the police department.

In the dream I watched Joe pull the box down onto a

bench. He reached his hands in, drawing out a vaguely torso-shaped chunk of what looked like plastic. Two separate pieces of rock-hard fiberglass had been joined together on one side with a hinge. A small tongue and hasp was visible on the other side.

"What in the *hell* is that supposed to be?" I asked with suspicion.

"It's a prototype of a neck shield, Kate! My friend designed it for patrol cops and paramedics. Not even the toughest Thrall can bite through it. You can't even sink a knife in."

"A neck shield . . ." It was a good idea. Hell, it was a *wonderful* idea. While the vamps *can* munch on any major blood vessel—they almost always go for the neck. Hidden under a turtleneck sweater the thing would be invisible—giving me the element of surprise.

Silence stretched for long moments as I ran my hand over the cool hard surface of the shield.

"Don't do this, Katie. Don't risk your life for that piece of trash." His voice was harsh. When I looked up, I could see the fear behind his eyes. We'd already lost our parents, and then Bryan. He'd be all alone if I didn't come back.

The image jumped abruptly. I was in a dim stairwell, my stomach leaden with dread. My heart was pounding so hard I could barely breathe. The smell of beer and stale cigarette smoke couldn't quite mask the underlying scent of blood. My present self tried again to end the dream, but I couldn't seem to wake up. Instead, I lived it all again. The dry-mouthed terror of entering the Thrall nest *knowing* I might not survive.

It was mid-afternoon, full sunlight. I'd hoped, *prayed* that all of the Hosts would be sleeping off a long night of carousing. The neck shield scratched at my neck and was almost unbearably hot and uncomfortable. From the minute I'd heard the "snick" of the tiny padlock securing it at my throat I'd wanted it *off*. But I'd promised Joe. That promise, and the fact that it *was* daylight were the only things that had kept him from either demanding to come with me, or trying to have one of his friends commit me under a forty-eight-hour "suicide watch."

I heard Larry's pleasant voice right behind me. "G'day, Kate. I wondered when you'd get here."

I turned my whole body to the warm Australian voice. I didn't want him to know about the shield. It was nicely hidden under the green turtleneck sweater and my leather biker jacket—a present from Dylan. It made my shoulders a little broad, about the same as when I was working out every day, but Larry had never met me so he wouldn't notice.

The man standing behind me was handsome, but ordinary. His wavy sandy hair highlighted pale green eyes and full, red lips. He was shorter than me, about 5'8", but the arms and shoulders looked muscular. I hoped I could take him.

"I've come for Dylan."

"Then you've come to the right place. Sorry." His smile was open and inviting and his accent made him sound like everyone's buddy. But there was something . . . *odd* about him. As I looked at him I would catch glimpses of a different Larry. The flashes lasted less than a second—but showed me the image of a much thinner man with straw-like hair and lips that had sunken in as his teeth had rotted. This other Larry was very obviously ill.

It was disconcerting as hell, but I forced myself to stay on point. "Sorry? What do you mean, sorry? Where is he?"

"He's here—but he's not mine to give. I'd tell you to ask Monica, but she's a little *under the weather.*" His eyes narrowed as he watched me, but he pointed to the corner.

I turned so I could see where he pointed without letting him out of my sight. In the corner, chained by her wrists, a gorgeous brunette was thrashing around. She emitted a high-pitched scream and then sighed and stretched like a contented cat.

I started toward her when he spoke. "You'd best not bother her. She can be a real tiger. As soon as the hatchling takes over, she'll be fine. She's *one of* my choices for my replacement."

Something in his phrasing stopped me in my tracks, sending a chill up my spine. His eyes burned into mine with frightening intensity. His slow, satisfied smile made me dry-mouthed with terror. I couldn't tear my eyes away as he casually walked the length of the brick basement and lowered himself into the leather recliner that waited for him next to a pool table.

The whole situation was surreal. I'd been prepared for a fight. Instead I stood here having a perfectly civilized conversation with the local Thrall queen while his successor alternately screamed in pain and moaned with what appeared to be a world-class orgasm.

"Yes! Oh, *yes!*" She screamed and writhed. Foam flecked the edge of her mouth. She screamed again, her body arching, wrists struggling against their chains.

I turned to look at Larry again. My expression must have been priceless because he responded. "Yeah, she seems to be enjoying it, doesn't she? I was a lot less *vocal.* Of course, it affects everyone differently—and *she's* not fighting it." He smiled easily, his eyes twinkling. Again, that flash of vision.

I shook my head. Very weird. I rolled my eyes and shrugged. "I really don't care what gets her off. I just want to walk out of here with my fiancé. I can't imagine why you would care about one guy. You've got the whole city to choose from."

He stood and started to walk toward me. "You're absolutely right. I *don't* care about that one guy. I gave him a quick bite—just so's he wouldn't be able to change his mind about joining the Herd. My people are watching him in the other room. Again, just in case. But I wanted *you.* He was the quickest way to bring you right to me." Larry rose from his chair.

Huh? My back stiffened, my throat constricting so that I was barely able to speak. "What does this have to do with *me?*" The fear was audible in my voice. I started to back away from his casual approach. I was already reaching with my fingers for my knife, hidden in a wrist sheath under my coat.

"Your boyfriend says you're psychic."

I continued to back up, turning the corner smoothly. I wasn't sure what I was going to do when I reached the pool table directly in my reverse path. I tried to downplay my abilities, but I didn't quite know why. "I've had better than average luck with woman's intuition, I guess."

He gave a hearty bray of laughter. But an instant later the humor slid from his face as though it had never been, leaving his green eyes cold and hard. "Don't lie to me, darls. I've seen the way you look at me. You can see right through my illusion—and you're not even trying. And those 'feelings' of yours? They're not intuition and you know it. I checked around after Dylan bragged you up. You found your brother Bryan when he'd been dumped on the streets of a strange city—went right to him. You're always in the right spot at the right time. Just like you showed up today. You *knew just where to look for us*. You *knew* that I would kill Dylan if you didn't come. Admit it."

I had known, but to hear him say it scared me. How many people had he talked with? Who'd told him about Bryan and the rest? I've always had some very unusual gifts, but it's not generally something that I discuss. My butt suddenly bumped the pool table, stopping my progress. Larry stopped as well, waiting.

"Okay, fine." The tiniest edge of fear was settling into my voice. I cleared my throat and continued with a little more strength. "I'll admit that I plan for people to live down to my worst expectations. They usually don't disappoint me. So sue me."

He chuckled and started forward again. He was only a few steps away. I tensed my muscles, preparing to fight. "I don't plan to sue you, Kate. That very rare talent is just what the hive needs in a new *queen*."

I forgot to breathe. It was quite easy to do the moment my heart stopped. He'd been hinting at it before, but hearing it spoken so . . . casually . . . . Me? A Thrall *queen?* No. Oh, no. No. . . . The moment slowed. Every detail had a crystalline sharpness—Larry's pleasant smile, the sound of chains rattling and Monica's screams. I pointed to the corner without taking my eyes from Larry. The movement distracted him enough to pull the knife from my sleeve and hide it behind my arm.

"You've *got* your queen!" I wanted to shout the words, but what emerged from my throat was a strangled croak. "Monica's the new queen."

As I said the words, Monica went silent.

He shrugged and pulled back his lips to bare long, narrow fangs. "Oh, Monica will do in a pinch. She's got big plans for the Denver hive. But you'd be better, and a part of you knows it. As for me, I've always believed it's a good idea to have a couple of candidates in case one doesn't work out. I figured I'd lay eggs in both of you and let you fight it out. I'll keep her chained until your hatchling has you under control. I've got a couple of weeks left. So I'll live to see the outcome. I always did like catfights."

I was shaking my head, over and over. "No. I won't let you do that to me."

With a movement fast as lightning, he was next to me with hands on my arms, holding them tight to my side. "You act as though you'll have a choice, luv."

He bent me back over the pool table. I couldn't move the knife. His voice was a whisper, a hiss of warmth in my face that smelled of wintergreen breath mints. "I'm betting you'll win. She's vicious, but you're strong. We'll all have a lot of fun in bed before I turn over the Herd to either of you."

Oh, that was *so* not happening! I let out a roar of frustration and rage. I brought my knee up sharply and caught him in the thigh. It shifted his position and gave me back a measure of control. I broke away from him by pulling down and away. I took off at a run, heading for the stairs. There had to be a better location for fighting, one where I would have the advantage. It was no good. He reached me before I could go two steps and brought me to my knees. I pulled away again and threw myself into a flying dive under the pool table. I came out near where Monica lay.

"Feisty little thing, aren't you?" Larry laughed. "Right, then." He was on top of me in a flash. I could feel his body tense and could imagine his mouth opening wide. Instead of the sharp pain that I was expecting in my neck, I heard a sharp thud and a gasp. I didn't wait to find out if he hit Joe's special collar. I plunged the knife up and back into the bulk of his body. There was no response. His body was just suddenly so much dead weight. I scrambled from beneath him and turned on my knees.

In death Larry's face was that of an old, weary man: pale and bloodless, eyes vacant. The knife had caught him right in the heart and one of his fangs had broken off.

The screaming started. Shrieks and moans and thuds sounded in the building above me. I glanced up. It was the wrong thing to do. Monica's eyes shot open and her teeth—sporting brand new needle-sharp fangs—bared. There was panic in her eyes.

"They're dying! No! It's not time yet." Her expression changed from fear to rage in the blink of an eye. "You've *killed* them!"

I recognized the danger too late. Monica shot forward as far as the chains would allow. She caught my leg in a grip of steel. I kicked at her, but she steadily dragged my body toward her. I grabbed at the table, but she just pulled it along with me.

Her words were a hiss that turned her model features into a monster mask. "You'll pay for this, bitch!"

Her fangs sunk through my jeans and sock and into my calf. I screamed, long and loud. A mind not my own invaded my head. "You'll be the first of my Herd, Kathleen." Monica's mouth was still filled with my leg, but I could hear her voice as clearly as if she was speaking. "You'll pay. Every day of my life you will *pay!* Feel my pain. Feel what you have done!"

A veil ripped open and my mind shuddered under the impact of the death throes of the nest. Blinding pain, aching, wrenching sorrow as one by one the dozen voices in my head, in her head, were silenced. There was only emptiness without the hive. There was hollow loneliness, paralyzing fear. I realized that my body was still fighting her without the use of my head. I was kicking, scratching and beating that lovely face. And screaming, I was doing a lot of screaming as she ground her teeth further into my vein, pulled my blood from me as her first meal. I pulled open her jaws with my fingers, but she bit down again, ripping the holes in my leg into bloody gashes. More and more screams echoed in my brain.

I knew—just suddenly *knew*—that Larry's death had killed dozens of his Hosts. They hadn't tied to Monica yet. They had died with their master and she was *alone*.

I woke screaming, the afghan I keep at the foot of the bed tangled around my feet from my kicking. My breath was coming in gasps, my heart pounding fit to burst my chest. I wasn't sleeping, but memory took over where the dream had left off. My head insisted on replaying that day's events even as I sat completely awake on my bed.

I managed to get her mouth off of my leg, but she had a grip on my thigh that would end up leaving bruises for weeks, so I continued to beat at her. Monica was fending off my blows with the shackles around her limbs. My mind rang with her awareness, her terror. So *alone!* I fought back, fought for control of my own mind. I had to be free of the voices, of the screams.

A sudden buzzing: a soothing, melodic chorus of voices joined Monica's. The words came from multiple minds, thousands upon thousands of individuals. *You are not alone, young queen. We are here. We are many.*

I felt the unique presences of each of the other nests, responding to the crisis to Monica. Here, then, was the true hive, and I was nothing to them. I was food. I was *prey*.

"I am not prey!" I shouted my defiance at the collective. "I am not *food!*" I wrenched my body free. I grabbed a pool cue, brandishing it like a bat as I spit words of defiance at Monica. "And Dylan is not *food*! I will kill you here and now if you don't release him!"

Monica's face contorted in fury. *"No!* He's mine. He is my only, my only *living . . ."*

I slammed my fists to my head as the united Thrall hive suddenly spoke directly into my mind. The hiss grew until it seared through me. The sound was bell-like—sharp and loud and repeated over and over. The words frightened me more than Larry and Monica both. *You are part of us now. You are ours.*

My eyeballs felt like they were going to split open, but I managed to beat down the mental attack, not even knowing quite how. I screamed my refusal in two words—*Fuck you!*

The shrill sound of a telephone ringing brought me to my senses. I sat up in a panic, trying to focus on the room and then collapsed back into my pillow when the machine picked it up. I shuddered anew at how very close a call I'd had that night. I wasn't theirs. Thank God. But I wasn't free of them either. The hive was a near-constant presence, always in the background, but always *there*.

I glanced at the small, wind-up alarm clock on my bedside while I waited for my heartbeat to return to normal. God help me, but I'd only been out for three hours. My body hovered right on that border of nausea from too little sleep, and gratitude for *any* rest at all.

I tried not to dwell on the dream. I knew how it ended without having to relive it. With Monica chained to the wall and the rest of the hive dead, the other queens and I had finally come to an understanding. I would be *Not Prey*. I could take Dylan—if he would come. I would not kill Monica or any of Larry's Herd who had survived. They would not reveal to the police who had killed Larry, although I had a damned good case for self-defense if it came to that. They would not hunt me down. They would not allow Monica to hunt me down.

Monica had fought them. She screamed and cursed until she was breathless. But the chains held and the bargain was made. The other queens would control her until a new hive was established and would establish the equivalent of a restraining order so that Monica could never come near me without turning into a drooling zombie. Most of the surviving Herd would become Hosts—except Dylan. Otherwise Monica would go insane. *Denver will fall if that happens,* I was tersely informed. I wasn't sure I believed that, but I hadn't argued. I was too grateful to be walking . . . limping out of the nest in possession of my own body and soul.

I'd found Dylan easily enough. He'd been unconscious and drained nearly bloodless, with bite marks from a dozen different Hosts. Their corpses littered the floor, creating a macabre obstacle course as I dragged him up the stairs to daylight and sanity.

I had reached the street before I heard one last comment in my head from Monica. *Go ahead. Take him. He wasn't a very good lay anyway.* Her bitter laugh was part tinkling chimes and part hissing snake.

I looked down at Dylan's pale face and *knew*. She wasn't lying. Dylan had cheated on me with Amanda, and on Amanda with Monica. It made me seriously consider just dropping him on the pavement to let the paramedics find him. But as much as I hated it, I still loved him. So I'd kept dragging, crying the whole way, until I reached the hospital.

The phone rang again downstairs, but stopped in the middle of the third ring. Whoever was on the line was letting it ring until just before the machine picked up, then hanging up and starting again.

"Asshole." I grumbled under my breath as I forced myself upright on the edge of the bed. My clothing was covered in sweat. The crusty salt on my temples said that I had cried in my sleep, just as I had at the time. I was worn out, exhausted and weary from the memories. I ignored the ringing. I knew who it was. Pretty soon Joe would lose patience and actually leave a message for me. Or not. I didn't really care which. I just knew that right now I was in no shape to talk to him.

I heard the machine beep, then Joe's voice on the line. "Mary Kathleen, it's your brother. I know you're there. Pick up!" There was a long pause. I didn't move toward the phone. This wasn't the time for him to push me. "Come on, Katie. *Please* pick up. I'm really getting worried." Another pause.

I really couldn't deal with Joe right now. I'd probably start bawling and then he'd come over and I didn't want any company right now. I stood and walked into the bathroom. I turned on the cold spigot and splashed my face. I might as well face the day. I wouldn't be able to go back to sleep. More precisely—I didn't *want* to go back to sleep. I was too likely to dream. Besides, the sun was high in the sky, the buzz of the hive had diminished to next to nothing. Anything I planned on doing outside of the apartment I'd be doing in broad daylight until further notice.

Joe's voice was barely audible over the sound of running water. "Okay, then. Maybe you're out. Call me as soon as you get home."

Maybe. We'd see how the morning went. If Monica came after me again, I'd probably end up visiting him in a professional capacity.

I decided that just a splash of water on my cheeks wasn't going to be enough, so I took off my travel clothes and stood under the shower. I set the temperature to lukewarm, guaranteeing I would be shivering when I got out. It's amazing how much that wakes me. By the time I brushed my teeth and dressed, I was as ready for the world as I was going to get.

The lump on my skull hurt a bit when I combed my hair, but otherwise I didn't seem to have any serious ill effects from this mornings misadventure. *Thank God for a thick skull.*

I *should* probably take it easy. But I did need to shop, and running always clears my head. So I grabbed my black leather backpack, slipped the straps over my shoulders and secured the lower strap around my waist. A glance in the mirror showed my freshly scrubbed face, hair tied in a ponytail, with a still-muscular body poured into loose fitting shorts and a yellow cotton T-shirt. Fortunately, the scars that remind me of my battle with Monica stay nicely hidden under crew cut socks. Some days I can wash my leg without getting angry. Today wasn't one of those days.

I discreetly clipped a knife to the inside waistband of the shorts. It might chafe a bit, but I was willing to risk it rather than going out unarmed. That I took the precaution, in full daylight, with the hive asleep said something about just how paranoid I was getting. But it's not paranoia if they really are out to get you, and Monica definitely was.

I took the stairs two at a time and was out the garage door without seeing anyone I knew. When I reached the street I did a couple of stretches. It was awkward with the backpack, but I didn't want to cramp up.

I started at a slow jog. The nearest decent supermarket is on Speer at about 13th Street. That's a good long haul from LoDo, and it had been a rough day. Better to take it easy for now.

I used to be a night person before my run-in with the Thrall. Now, me and daylight are buddies. I picked up speed, using the run to release the tension that I couldn't seem to shake from the dream. I turned onto Wazee, then picked up Speer near the Auraria campus, where several local colleges were already starting fall classes. I caught a glimpse of the big Ferris wheel at the Six Flags amusement park to my right as I bounded down the stairs to the bike path.

Speer is one of the main arteries through Denver. Day or night, there's always traffic. I was really grateful that they built the bike path low, along the river, putting distance between the pedestrians and fast-moving traffic. Casting a quick glance behind me when I reached the bottom of the second flight, I took my place behind a speeding bicyclist. I didn't want to get rundown by a careless rider. There are a lot of blind curves on the path, but most of the cyclists don't seem to care. They take the path at racing speeds. I've learned that when I hear a quiet command of "Left" behind me, a cycle will be speeding by in the next second, nearly clipping my left elbow. Those are the polite ones. A lot of them won't even mention their presence until they race past.

"Morning!" called a pair of power walkers as they passed by going the other direction. I smiled and nodded.

The path was still steeped in shadows. Traffic was a steady hum in the background, but the quiet murmur of the flowing water and quacking of bobbing ducks almost made me forget about Dylan, Larry, and Monica—almost.

My senses were alert and my brain was utterly my own. The vague smell of car exhaust blended with the flowers and trees growing along the path. It felt good to move. My legs formed an easy rhythm with my pumping arms. I had a light bead of sweat on my brow by the time I reached my exit on Broadway. I could go further on the bike path, but the grocery isn't near an exit, so I'd have to overshoot it and come back to reach it. I went up the stairs two at a time, but just missed the crossing light.

"Can you spare some change, ma'am? Maybe for a donut and some coffee?" asked a tired-looking man of about forty who was standing on the corner of Broadway. He held a sign that read, "War Veteran. Anything will help." His blond hair was oily and uncombed and his blue eyes were bloodshot and fuzzy. Probably from last night's bender, if the smell of whiskey that hovered over him like a cloud was any indication.

That's the only problem taking Speer. A lot of the street people live under the bridges and panhandle on the corners until the cops run them off. Still, I removed my wallet from my pocket and handed him a ten.

"Go get a hot meal at Denny's," I said, with a warm smile that wasn't faked. His return grin said that business hadn't been too good. A lot of those guys would die without a handout. As much as I hate that there are people who are willing to beg for a living, it's reality, and charity is a big part of my religion.

As I started toward the crosswalk, a droning, sing-song voice chilled my blood. "We wish to speak to you, Not Prey."

My head immediately started to throb as the combined force of the queen collective entered my skull like an icepick. I turned and saw the pale eyes of the bum take on an inner light. When he opened his mouth, a chorus of voices froze me in place.

I hated that my voice sounded strangled, because the words were not only entering my ears, but beating behind my eyes directly into my mind. "What do you want? You've already broken your word to me. Why should I talk to any of you?" Being a hive mind, I didn't need to explain the situation. They already knew.

The queen collective possessing the man made his back straighten. His face grew confident; assured. He was suddenly a warrior in the prime of his life. Aw, man. I really didn't need a fight right now. "We only learned of Monica's deceit when you did, Not Prey. Her insanity risks the collective, and we feel it necessary to eliminate her. We ask your indulgence while we find another to take her place."

Indulgence? Like they cared what I thought. I snorted and crossed my arms over my chest so they wouldn't see that I was shaking just a little bit. I hated that we two had disappeared to the minds of everyone around us. Businessmen stepped around us quickly, looking down as though we were a doggie doo-doo pile in their path.

"*My* indulgence? She tried to kill me! Why shouldn't I just track her down and eliminate her myself?"

The cold sureness in the voice sounded almost condescending. "This is not just a matter between you and Monica, Not Prey—as you well know. There are many other lives to consider. Hosts and Herd with families; jobs. Would you risk all of them for such a small favor? You saw the result when you eliminated Queen Larry without regard for the others."

I did, and I've been paying for it ever since in the confessional. I cocked my head suspiciously. "*How* small? When can you replace Monica with another queen?"

"Two weeks, and—"

I picked my jaw up off the ground. "*Two weeks!* She'll have me dead and buried about thirteen days before that!"

The man began to pick up his backpack and sign. "We can contain Monica for that long. You have no reason to fear, Not Prey. We thank you for your indulgence and—" the man's eyes cleared like magic and the deep, grateful baritone finished the sentence, "thanks for the money, lady. You really made my day! I haven't had a square in almost a week."

He dashed across the street, leaving me rubbing my arms to get some warmth into my blood again. Could I trust the queens to "contain" Monica? They *had* managed it for almost six years, but what caused them to lose control earlier? They were right about the others—including Dylan. I wouldn't willingly send them to their death.

A flash of sad anger rushed through me. Had he taken the extra step yet? Was he now a Host? Is that why he was calling? Lord, I hoped not. I took a deep breath and stepped from the shadow of the bridge into the bright sunlight. I tried to shake off the feeling of dread. I had to, or I'd go insane.

It was only a few minutes more before I reached the tastefully low-key grocery store on the ground floor of an apartment high-rise. I kept the backpack strapped to me as I entered, and grabbed one of the hand baskets. Technically, you're supposed to check empty bags at the store, but if it ever came to it, the cameras would show that the pack never left my body and I never reached into it. No hints of shoplifting. I'd already had one pack disappear after I'd checked it with the nice service people, who naturally swore that the person who accepted it had gone home for the day. So I keep the pack with me.

After a quick visit to the pharmacy, where I asked for one monthly refill and left the illegible prescription from Mac-Dougal, I started through the throng of people. My pace slowed to a walk as I moved down the aisles. I started in the meat department, where a pair of T-bones begged me to take them home. I followed up the steaks with a nearly frozen chicken. It was about time to restock my ready-made meals.

Every few months, I do a mass shop and a factory-style cooking session. I make homemade pasties—meat turnovers like pot pies, but with potatoes. Mom used to make them with turnips *and* potatoes, but I can't stand turnips. I'd always spit the little cubes into my fist by faking a cough and then sneak them under the table to the dog. He had a strange addiction to turnips that made him the gassiest basset hound on the block.

I backtracked to the meat section and added a couple of pounds of burger to the basket. I suddenly had a craving for burritos with lots of salsa, or maybe some thick meaty lasagna. Heck, I'd probably make them all. I freeze everything in individual portions anyway. That way I can have a good meal even when I'm on the run. It makes sense with my crazy schedule.

Going through the store I remembered I was out of freezer bags, so I moved over a few aisles and grabbed a couple of boxes and tossed them into the heavily loaded basket. There was no way this was all going to fit into the backpack. Screw it. I'd walk home and carry a couple of bags. If any of the Herd tried to stop me, I'd beat them senseless with a frozen chicken.

I shouldn't have gone down the frozen food aisle. I normally don't. There's nothing behind those glass doors that isn't pure carbs, but I convinced myself it was the quickest way to the check-out. My eyes cheated. They were supposed to stare straight ahead, moving only to avoid shoppers, but they flicked sideways at one of the frozen offerings. I couldn't believe it! My hand reached for the silver handle before I could slap it back, and one more item was added to my pile. Well, there went my *walk* home. I'd have to run to keep it from melting all over my backpack.

Fortunately, the check-out line was short. Mornings are the best time to shop, if a person can manage it. I waited as the groceries were scanned and wrote out a check for the balance. The clerk glanced at it and looked at me for the first time since I'd emptied the basket.

"You wrote the wrong date on here, Ma'am. Today's the 17th, not the 16th."

I furrowed my brow and looked at the check-out display, but didn't believe what I saw. "No, today's the 16th. I just flew in at the airport this morning."

The customer behind me in line interrupted. "No, it's the 17th all right." He pulled from his basket a newspaper and handed it to me. Oh, man! It *was* the 17th! No *wonder* Joe's been calling over and over. He was afraid of exactly what happened! I'd slept for over twenty-four hours! Eek!

I owed my brother a major apology.

4

I was huffing and puffing by the time I reached the building. It wouldn't have been so bad had I not taken the last two blocks at a dead run. But the shriek of the burglar alarm, combined with the sight of flashing police lights at the entrance to my building gave me an incentive to hurry.

It had to be my apartment. None of the others have an alarm. I looked up and saw a cop standing on the fire escape outside my apartment. A second one joined him on the fire escape landing, and spoke into his radio before heading down the iron steps.

I hurried to where Connie stood just inside the front door, talking animatedly to a third uniformed officer.

"Kate—you're back! I thought your brother said you'd be out of town until tomorrow. But I should have known when I saw your truck in the garage."

I blinked in surprise. Joe hadn't said anything about actually visiting with one of the tenants.

"What's going on?" I dropped my backpack and grocery sacks onto the floor and turned my attention to the cop. He was probably in his late twenties or early thirties, with short blond hair and wide blue eyes. He had a fresh-scrubbed look and the kind of soft skin that made me think he'd have a hard time growing a beard.

"We got a call from the alarm company about a possible break in. When we arrived, Ms. Beltaine here met us at the front door and said the owner of the building was out of the country. . . ."

"My name's Kate Reilly, I'm the owner of the building."

He nodded and wrote that fact in his notebook. "Ms. Beltaine here says she saw a teenage female running away from the scene right after the alarm went off, but by the time we got here she was long gone. The ladder to the fire escape was pulled down, so my partner and Officer Phillips went up to investigate further while I took Ms. Beltaine's statement."

He nodded in the direction of the two uniformed officers who had come down to join us. Both were large men of middle age with close-cropped hair. The redhead on the left had a small brass name plate that said Scott. By process of elimination, the brunet carrying a crow bar must be Phillips.

His face looked familiar, but it took a long moment before I recognized where I'd seen him before. Joe had introduced us—after Phillips' neck brace had saved my life. A weird coincidence after the dream I'd had earlier. I promised myself I'd check with him and make sure Joe really had built him a second brace, and see whether he'd found anyone willing to manufacture and sell them—as soon as we finished dealing with this mess.

"Ms. Reilly." He shifted the handkerchief and pry bar to his left hand long enough to extend his latex covered right for me to shake. "Good to see you again. Sorry about the circumstances."

"Me too."

Officer Scott had a soft tenor voice that seemed odd coming from such a bulky body. "We took a look around. It looks like she got scared off before she got inside, but you'll need to come up and take a look around and let us know for sure."

I gathered up my grocery sacks and started over to the elevator, the cops and Connie at my heels. I wasn't sure why she chose to come along, but it seemed a little ungracious to ask her not to—particularly since she was the only witness.

We rode the elevator in silence. The hallway we exited into wasn't large. Since I had taken all of the third and fourth floors for my apartment, I'd claimed virtually all of the usable space, only leaving enough for visitors and pizza delivery types to make their way either to my front door at one end of the short hall, or the door to the stairs at the other.

The wailing of the alarm was making all of us wince. I hurried the few steps to my front door.

Connie looked around as if she was confused. "Wow, the hall's much bigger on my floor. And the ceiling's lower." She was almost shouting to be heard over the siren.

I suddenly realized she hadn't ever been up to my apartment. It was kind of a surprise, although maybe it shouldn't have been. She's always called me on the phone instead of stopping by to discuss repair issues. Fortunately, Connie's never needed much. I'd worked hard to make sure the building was in good shape before I rented the space—and I work hard to *keep* it that way. That reminded me of my conversation with Joe. He'd mentioned she had a plumbing question. As soon as the cops were finished I'd need to talk to her about that. I hoped it wasn't serious. But whether it was or wasn't, I'd have to deal with it. In my experience, ignoring a plumbing problem almost always leads to serious water damage.

I juggled my bags to retrieve the keys from my back pocket and opened the door to let us all in. The front door of my apartment is original from the factory days. It's heavy fire-resistant steel. Adding the locks had been a royal pain. Still, nobody's going to be breaking in through it. Not in this lifetime. Any burglar with an ounce of sense would do exactly what this morning's teenager had—go for the fire escape and windows. I immediately went for the burglar alarm keypad and entered my code. The infernal wailing finally shut off, and the next words echoed in the silence.

"Some door." Scott commented a little too loudly. "No one's coming through this without dynamite."

I grinned in acknowledgment of the compliment and

stepped aside to let everyone in while I gathered up my groceries. Connie's eyes widened as she stepped over the threshold, and her mouth formed a little "o" of appreciation.

"Wow! This is . . . *beautiful*. And the elevator opens right into it like a penthouse. That is *so cool*." She'd stopped right in the way—staring at the elaborate painted tin ceiling with the pattern of flowers and geometrics. The cops and I had to edge around her. It wasn't easy with my hands full of the backpack and groceries, but I managed.

"Thanks." I set the bags onto the kitchen island. The cops were here on business, so I didn't want to dawdle, but I did take a second to stuff the frozen item into the freezer, bag and all, before beginning an inspection of the place with Officer Scott.

Nothing was missing. Other than the window next to the fire escape being jimmied, nothing much seemed to have been disturbed.

"The alarm must've scared her off."

It was possible. It was even probable. But the thought of someone having invaded my home made me angrier than I'd been in a long time. Home was my *haven,* damn it! I was grateful for the police response, glad that the burglar alarm had worked, but *pissed* that it had been necessary. I was even more furious when I saw the damage to the window. I'd be spending a chunk of my afternoon replacing the lock and the trim, and sometime soon I'd have to repaint the whole works to cover the gouges in the paint. *Damn it!* I ground my teeth in frustration and fury. One more thing to do. One more expense. *Just what I need.*

The cops didn't stay long once I reassured them nothing was missing. They filled out their reports, assured me they'd check the crowbar for fingerprints and left. I didn't get to talk to Phillips about the neck guard as I'd hoped, because Connie pounced on me about her plumbing problem before I could even escort them out the door.

"I had a plumber come in to do some work yesterday."

I sighed. Another bill to pay, or at least she would deduct it from her rent. "What's wrong with the pipes?"

"Well—" she began, and fidgeted nervously. "It wasn't the pipes *at first.*"

My eyes narrowed a bit and I growled, "At *first?*"

As usual with her, she spilled everything in a rush. "It was just the faucet. It was dripping a little. I left you a message on your machine, but you didn't call back—"

"I was ou—"

She didn't even give me a chance to finish the word. "So, anyway, this guy I'm seeing, Clyde, he's really nice, and he said that he could fix the faucet with a little kit from the hardware store, so he went out and bought one, it's this cute little set of rubber pieces with an itty-bitty screw—"

Okay, at this point I was just amazed at her ability to make all that one sentence without drawing a breath. I continued to stare, open-mouthed.

"And he turned off the water, or at least I *thought* he turned off the water—"

I winced and closed my eyes, waiting for the next admission.

"So off comes the faucet and there's this *geyser* of water coming from the sink."

"Did you get the water turned off?" I asked. Well, at least she had a ground floor apartment. None of the ceilings would cave in. And no, I wasn't paying the bill now that I knew the story.

"He couldn't get the valve to turn. He said it was stuck. So he got a wrench and started hammering on it. I didn't watch it because he kept the door closed, but I could hear him in there, swearing a blue streak and banging away."

Oh, man! My poor plumbing! "Connie, it shouldn't take a wrench to turn those valves. They're brand new!"

"Yeah, if he had turned the *right one* it would have been easy!"

"Wha—" I started, and then understanding settled in. Connie was the first person to sign a lease, so she got some control over what her place looked like. She had gushed over the old claw foot tub in the bath, which was a pretty unusual item to have in a factory, I had to admit. Maybe it was for the owner. Anyway, I had told her she could keep it. I'd had to run a separate water line and drain to hook it into the new plumbing. But she'd liked the look of the old water intakes that came down from the ceiling, so we'd left them in, as *decoration*. A chuckle escaped me. "No doubt those old lines were a little hard to crank!"

"No shit! The *idiot!* I didn't even know until he finally unlocked the door and the place was flooded. It took hours to mop up all that water before it ruined the hardwood!"

"But you got it turned off?"

"Oh, sure! I walked in and turned it right off. But he had bent one of the pipes going into the tub, so I had to bring in a plumber. Don't worry, though. I'll pay for it. You're welcome to come in and look at it to make sure that we don't have to bring in someone to redo the floor."

I opened my mouth to reply but she interrupted, "I told Clyde I'd take it from his hide!"

If she didn't, I might.

"This really is an incredible place." Connie shook her head in awe. "I don't suppose—" She looked longingly at the loft. I could tell she wanted a tour. But I wasn't giving her one. There's not much to see in the place that can't be viewed from the front door. The loft is my bedroom and not really up to a tour right now. It was a pit.

"I've really got to give my brother a call before he goes on shift. Since I was out of town, he probably got the call from the alarm company." It was a logical lie and I tried to sound apologetic. "I really appreciate you chasing off the intruder. That was really brave!"

She blushed to the roots of her dyed hair. "Aw heck, it was nothing, Kate. She was a skinny little thing—probably just looking for loose change for a fix. I deal with a lot worse types than *her* every day. Yep, you should give Joe a call, 'cause he's probably a wreck. He seems to really care what happens to you. I'll let myself out."

I realized she was right. Connie is a bail bondswoman and a good one. She's been in the business long enough that she's probably seen everything. A teenaged junkie was just a minnow in the sea of bad guys *she* knows. And she was right about Joe, too. I realized how much restraint it must be taking for him not to be here right now checking up on me.

I waited until she left and slid the deadbolt home. I took a deep breath and dialed Joe's cell number. He always has it with him unless he's in the ER—no electronics allowed because of the equipment. After the fourth ring, his voice mail answered. I left a short message that I was fine, was sorry that I didn't call him, and had picked up the prescription that Dr. MacDougal had given me.

It was time to get back to life. Cooking would take awhile, and would be messy, so I decided to throw on my paint-splattered coveralls in lieu of an apron. They're comfy to slop around in and virtually indestructible in case anything spilled. But first, I figured I should get the mail. I was getting increasingly nervous that if I had forgotten to pay the classified advertising bill, what else was past due? I left the apartment, making sure to lock the deadbolt behind me and went down the grate metal stairs two at a time. The building inspector had assured me that they would last until my great-grandchilden died of old age, and it would please the insurance company if I didn't replace them, because they don't burn.

The postal boxes are ugly—brushed steel and aluminum that are an embarrassment to the rest of the room. They don't match the Art Deco lobby at all and I just hate it. But the post office has *standards*. If there had been existing boxes in place, I could've used them. There weren't. So I had to put up boxes that are really too small to hold much of anything *and* clash with the decor.

The biggest reason they clash is that I had succumbed to reality. I'm gone often enough on trips that my mail backs up. Before I put in the large drawer, I'd have to go visit the post office to claim things every other day.

The key turned smoothly in the lock, but the drawer wouldn't open. A peek inside told me why—it was overflowing, and several of the envelopes had annoying yellow and red stripes on them that indicated past due notices. Ick!

No, I just couldn't deal with it now. I pushed and squished the contents until the drawer reluctantly shut and turned to go back to my cooking. But my eyes lighted on a package on the floor next to the elevator. They'd delivered the moldings while I was gone! I opened the long reinforced cardboard boxes and eased out one of the thin strips of custom cut hardwood. I placed it next to the one I'd just finished stripping and nearly jumped up and down with joy. It matched, down to the smallest leaf!

My original goal for this room was to replace about a dozen missing hammered tin ceiling tiles, fix the broken light fixture, put in new linoleum and take down the damaged moldings. But once I actually got up to the ceiling, I realized how delicate and detailed they were under the dozen layers of (probably lead-based) paint. I decided to see if I could salvage them and used the last of my savings to get three more strips made so that they would all match.

Well, no time like the present to get started! Maybe actual physical work would help shake off the vague dread.

I hauled out the big ladder from under the table and balanced the long strip in my hand as I climbed. It bounced and flopped over the ladder's top while I fumbled for my hammer, but then remembered that I'd forgotten to set up my helpers and had to climb back down.

I'd figured out a way to install the ten foot lengths of trim by myself early on, while I was pulling down the others to strip them of paint. Two lengths of two-by-fours on a crossed stand rose up like a Christmas tree. Each held a wide notched piece of scrap plywood. Once standing, it nearly touched the ceiling, so that all I had to do was position one in each corner, lift the trim onto them and start hammering.

I was completely engrossed in making sure that the brads countersunk into the trim without leaving big ugly hammer marks on the wood, so I didn't notice someone appear outside the front door glass.

What happened next could take the prize on *Funniest Home Videos*. A visitor opened the door, which knocked over one helper. It hit the floor with a bang. The suddenly loose trim strip smacked the man on the side of the head and the whipping motion ripped out the three brads I'd been able to hammer in. The other end smacked *me* in the head before clattering to the floor. I nearly lost my balance, and *did* drop the hammer, which knocked over the almost empty can of paint on the table and splattered paint onto the ladder, my arm and the side of my face.

I stood there on the ladder, stunned, rubbing the sore spot on my head.

"Wow!" said the visitor, likewise rubbing his scalp. "I can't think of any way that I could have made a worse first impression. I think I'll just quietly slip out now. I was looking for the owner. Really sorry to bother you."

He turned to leave so quickly that I had to shout. "Hey, wait a minute!"

I climbed down off the ladder. He stopped and turned his head, so that I finally got to see his face. He was my height exactly, with dark curls the shade of brown that is almost, but not quite black. Intelligent, chocolate brown eyes looked out from behind long curled lashes. The standard business uniform of grey suit, white shirt and patterned red tie couldn't hide the amazing build. This was obviously an athlete. He was without a doubt the most handsome man I'd ever seen, and I suddenly couldn't speak. All I could think of was that I probably looked the worst I had in my life. I was dusty and sweaty, wearing paint covered overalls and, of course, had a wide swatch of cream-colored paint next to my ear.

I offered my hand, but then hurriedly pulled it back and cleaned it on my pant leg before holding it out a second time. He smiled, revealing deep dimples and perfect white teeth. This guy's girlfriend is one lucky lady! Yeah, I looked for a ring. There wasn't one, but a guy like this wouldn't be without female companionship—probably blonde with a *Penthouse* figure. "I'm Kate Reilly. I *am* the owner. What can I do for you?"

He shook my hand. The laugh that came out was both sad and annoyed. "Naturally you're the owner. I'd heard rumors that there was an apartment for rent in this building, but after wrecking your project, I can't imagine you'd offer it to me."

I chuckled. "You hardly *wrecked* it. Trust me, I've spilled a lot more paint than this during the renovation!"

He bit his lower lip, which made him look like a naughty

six-year-old. "Actually, I sort of did." He pointed down to the trim strip that had hit him in the head. I could see now that one whole corner of it had snapped off. "I have a pretty hard head. Sorry."

"Oh, man!" I knelt down on one knee next to it. They *just* got here! I picked up the index card size piece and held it up against the main strip. Well, then again—with some wood glue and clamps . . . hmm, *maybe.*

"Like I said," he interrupted. "That probably cost a pretty penny. It looks like vintage stuff. I'd offer to pay for it right now, and I know I should, but I really need to find an apartment in a hurry and I barely have enough for a deposit. In a few weeks I might be able—"

I looked up at those frustrated eyes and dimples and melted. Boy, if I could look at that every morning, even if just when getting the mail! "Then it would be in my best interest to keep you around, huh?" I watched him and saw the surprise on his face.

"But first, how about a name?" I held up a hand to shake his again, but he misunderstood and pulled backward, helping me to my feet. He had a nice, firm grip and wonderfully soft hands.

He grinned with astonishment and hopeful anticipation and held onto my hand longer than required. "Tom Bishop. Would you really be willing to show me the place? I don't care if you're done with it or anything. Heck, it could be a broom closet off the pool!"

I laughed. "No pool, I'm afraid, but there is covered parking."

He laughed in return. "No car."

I could feel my eyebrows raise. No car, no home, and he's wandering the bad part of town. Okay, cute or not, he was beginning to set off my little alarm meter. He could tell, and waved his hands quickly. "No, no, it's nothing like that. I have a good job and can pay the rent. It's just that—" He looked undecided suddenly.

"Yes?"

He took a deep breath and rubbed the bridge of his nose.

He wouldn't meet my eyes. "Okay, fine. I've probably already blown my chances anyway. I'm a lycanthrope, Ms. Reilly. I'm also a fireman. My landlord found out about the werewolf part when Channel 4 did a news story about me. Now I'm getting kicked out. Of course, we *werewolves* aren't allowed to drive, so I have to find a home close to the station." He clenched his fists and his jaw set angrily. He raised flashing eyes to lock with mine. "So, go ahead, say it."

I probably looked somewhat dim-witted, because I couldn't for the life of me figure out how he was expecting me to respond. "Uhm, say what?"

"You know, *'oops, I almost forgot. I already promised the apartment to someone.'* Don't worry, I'm used to hearing it." His words were biting and sarcastic.

I shook my head and sighed. I sat down on the edge of a chair in the corner, filled with cans and tools. I offered him the matching one nearby, but he noticed the paint splatters, wood shavings and dust and then looked down at his spotless, perfectly creased pants. He bit his lower lip, glanced at me to see if I'd be offended—which I wasn't, and squatted down instead. It put him at just about the same height, and showed off totally ripped thighs underneath the charcoal pinstripe. He stared squarely into my eyes, giving me his full attention.

I tucked my heels onto the top leg brace, rested my palms on my knees and returned the favor. His eyes were like chocolate melting in the sun, shiny and luscious and drowning deep. I probably stared too long. He winked suddenly and flashed a smile, which made *me* melt, too.

I cleared my throat and dragged my mind back to business. "Look . . . Tom. First, I don't play that game. I don't care if you're black, white, yellow, green or furry. If I think I can trust you and you can pay on time, you can rent from me. I have one apartment available. The guy who I'd promised it to just left me a message today saying he couldn't take it after all, and it's ready to move in. The appliances, wiring and plumbing are all new, and the boiler works . . . so far, anyway. You'll have to put up with me finishing the renovations, though. It'll be noisy, dusty and . . . well, *slow*. I'm gone on business a lot, so I can't give you a for-sure date of when I'll be done but I do work on it whenever I can."

I'd watched his face go from angry to amused to hopeful, but finally ended with absolutely ecstatic. He stood up and started grinning broadly. "Wow! Plumbing *and* lights. A definite step up from my last place!"

I couldn't help but laugh at his enthusiasm. "So, do you want to see it? You might change your mind. It's pretty simple—not like some of the high-dollar lofts over on Wazee or in Cherry Creek."

His face grew serious. "I wasn't kidding, Ms. Reilly. Consistent electricity and water really *are* a step up from the dive I was in. Noise, dust, dirt? No big deal. I don't even care what the rest of the apartment *looks* like. I'll manage. If it's not too high, I'll take it, sight unseen."

I shook my head. "First, I'm *Kate*. Ms. Reilly is for my customers, not the people who live downstairs from me. Next, I can't do 'sight unseen.' Not only is it illegal, but it's not fair to either of us. I'll give you the tour, and you can decide if it's worth it. I'm only charging what I have to get to pay the bills for the place. I'm not trying to get rich off the tenants. I want people who will live here for years and be happy, so I don't have to keep interviewing new people." I smiled, but it was with a healthy dose of chagrin. "I'm not very good with people."

His reared back in surprise and his face showed honest confusion. "Really? I think you're terrific with people. Heck, you're even nice to someone like *me*."

I just shook my head and stood up. "In this building, Tom, there is no 'like me'. I know that Connie works with some people with lycanthropy, and the people I know don't have jerky attitudes. It's not like it's your fault. It's like being born with blue eyes or with Down Syndrome. You just *are* a werewolf. I mean, you're not dangerous or anything, are you?"

He was staring at me very intently with flared nostrils. I guess I passed whatever test he was throwing out, because he grinned. "Well, my shift commander says I'm a pretty dangerous pool player and I'm dangerously competitive in sports and running, but that's about it."

I smiled and then turned, twitching my finger for him to follow and threw open the stairwell door wide enough for him to catch it after me. "So, unless you somehow manage to kick my ass at pool—which is highly unlikely, beat me at volleyball, or don't pay the rent, you're probably safe here. Okay?"

I could feel him walking behind me up the staircase, just far enough back not to step on my heels, but just close enough that I could sense his presence. It made me shiver, in a nice way. Yeah, I could do this every day. "Sounds good to me," he said lightly. "I probably won't beat you at volleyball. I can't play to save my soul. But I may take you up on a game of pool or running, if it won't get me kicked out. I run every morning in the summer."

He reached out past me when we reached the landing and opened the fire door. Walking past him, I couldn't help but notice the amazing musky cologne he wore and he stood so that I had no choice but to brush against him as I went through. I don't think either of us minded.

The apartments are pretty much standard issue. None of the terrific features in my place are in them, with the exception of one wall of brick and glass that looks out over the roadway. I just couldn't bear to cover it up. If you stand just right, you can see the mountains between the buildings across the street. I waited in the living room while he wandered around, opening cabinets and closets and flipping switches. When he returned, he was shaking his head and muttering to himself. I couldn't hide my disappointment. I just had a feeling he would be a terrific tenant, and hoped he'd take it.

"You don't want it? Something not work for you?" I tried to keep my voice neutral and professional.

He held up his hands in panic. "No, no! I *love* this place. It's absolutely perfect. I was just feeling a bit in awe. I am totally amazed that you did these renovations *yourself!*"

I felt my back go up just a bit. "Why? Because I'm a woman?"

He snorted and rolled his eyes and lightly squeezed my bicep. "Hardly. Your arms and shoulders are a pretty good indication that you could pull it off. But it's a *very* professional job," he said seriously. "There are no paint splatters or crooked wall outlet covers or dinged cabinets that usually happen with one-person jobs. It's tough to do stuff like this single-handed."

Well, I couldn't argue, but I blushed anyway. It had taken a lot of time to get it right. I shrugged and tried to be modest. "I've really been enjoying it—learning how to do wiring and drywall and painting properly, finding a way to manage it alone, and then getting each thing just right." I looked up and around the room. The satiny warm ivory paint was a bit sterile, but not nearly as bad as flat white, and the multi-colored Berber carpet would go with anything. With one big bedroom, a full bath, separate dining room/eating nook, kitchen and office—at least that's what I called the smaller second room—it was just the perfect size for a single person. It really *is* a nice apartment.

He took a deep breath, held it and winced a bit. "So, how bad is it? What's the monthly rent?"

I laughed, because it was the same reaction that both Connie and Chuck had given me. Apartments in converted lofts are *exclusive* and 99.9% of them in LoDo are therefore *expensive*. The only reason mine aren't is that I just can't justify charging it. It's all that Catholic guilt in my system, I guess.

I named my price, and smiled as his jaw dropped and the pent-up air exhaled in a rush. I'm well aware it's about half what the other lofts are getting. "I pay the utilities, unless they get out of hand. It's cheaper for me to have a single meter into the building for water, gas and electricity. You get a parking space in the garage with the apartment, but since you said you don't need it, I might park my motorcycle there. The security deposit is one month's rent, and you get it back when you leave. I keep it in a separate account and don't use it for anything, even damages. We'll handle that separately if it happens. If you find anything that needs fixing, please tell me before you call someone, if there's time. I'd rather try to do the work myself to save money. If I have to pay too much for outside help, I can't afford to keep the rents where they are. Of course, if I'm out of town, do what you need to so it doesn't get worse."

"For *this* place? The place I checked a block over was half this size and wanted more than twice that! Jeez Louise, get me a lease before you come to your senses and change your mind!"

I laughed, because he was the first person I'd ever met who used that antiquated expression. 'Jeez Louise' is something Mom used to say almost daily. I picked up on it when I was a toddler. It drove my dad insane listening to me walk around the house, screaming it over and over at the top of my lungs.

"So it's in your budget? I don't want you to have to choose between your bed and food every month. I've done that. It sucks."

"Hell yes! That's right square in the middle of my budget. I can probably even pick up the stuff I had to hock to get the deposit for the other place!" He raised his eyebrows and gave me a wicked grin. "There's even enough left in my pocket to treat my new landlady to an early dinner, if she's willing."

I felt my mouth go dry and my heart rate speed up. I hadn't been out with a man other than my brother since Dylan and I ended. "Uhm—I don't know, Tom." I couldn't think of a way to refuse gracefully without him thinking it was because he was a lycanthrope. Plus, I really did like him and I *was* starved. "Where could we go with you looking all gorgeous and me looking like—" I held out my hands and looked down at my painted arm and clothing. I could see some wisps of red hair from the corner of my eye that were a lovely shade of warm ivory. "—well, *this*?"

He laughed, so apparently I hadn't offended him. "Hardly *gorgeous*. But for saving me almost five hundred bucks each and every month, and letting me get my beloved microwave out of pawn, I could probably wait a few minutes for you to shower and change. I'll just bet that you'll end up stunning. You're already damned gorgeous, even with paint all over you." He stared at me with a look that seemed to burn right through my clothes. It gave me goosebumps on my goose-bumps.

Eek! What does a girl say to that? "Okay, then. Well—uhm," I managed to stammer, "Do you want to do it here or come up to my place?" He fought not to smile, and I blushed furiously and put my hands over my face. "Oh God! That came out *so* wrong!" I peeked through my fingers. Fortunately, he was keeping a straight face. "Do you want to *wait* down here?"

His dark eyes twinkled merrily. "Sure. I can figure out where to put the furniture, if I can borrow the measuring tape on the table downstairs."

The blush was growing the longer I looked at him. *Please God, let this not be the way dinner would go, too.* "No problem. My place is upstairs. I'll shower and change and be back down in a few minutes."

His smile was warm and inviting. "I'd say 'take your time', but I really hope you hurry. I'm really enjoying talking to you."

I didn't bolt up the stairs, but damned close. Before I forgot in all the excitement of actually putting food in my rumbling stomach—with Tom—I dug for a moment in my desk and tucked a copy of the lease form into my purse.

I tried to figure out what to wear before I went in the shower, and finally decided to keep it semi-professional. He was going to be my tenant, after all. I managed to find a scoop-necked silk shell in soft yellow that was ironed. The white and green embroidered roses went well with the dark green slacks. I opted for my black flats because it was sort of nice to be able to look a guy in the eyes for a change. The hair and arm took some work to remove the latex paint. I finally had to resort to a green kitchen scrubber, leaving the side of my face a little pink. By the time I'd finished that, there was only time to blow-dry my hair, spritz myself with some cologne, and throw on enough makeup that I didn't look dead. It wasn't perfect, but it would do. After grabbing my purse, checking the elevator once more and then locking my front door, I nearly skipped down the stairs to the second floor.

I had to admit, the result was more than I could have hoped for. Tom was crouched down, busily measuring walls and writing figures on the back of an envelope when I walked into the empty apartment. He heard me arrive, and turned his head back and up so he could look at me. His eyes got wide and his jaw dropped and then he actually fell over. Yeah, I know he was off balance to begin with, so it shouldn't make me so freaking happy. But it did and I smiled.

"Wow!" he exclaimed as he quickly got to his feet and dusted off his pants. "You look *amazing!*"

I shrugged. "Thanks. It's nothing special, but it's clean. I just got back from a long trip and haven't had time to run the laundry."

He walked past me and held open the door. "Boy, I can't wait to see your 'first-string' clothes then." As I turned to leave, he put his head close to my neck and sniffed. It made my stomach lurch pleasantly. "Mmm. I like your perfume and shampoo, too. Most people don't consider picking complementary scents."

When he saw my surprised expression, he smiled lightly and shrugged. "Hey, when you have as good a nose as we wolves do, it's a big deal."

"Ah," I replied in a nicely noncommittal way. I followed him down the stairs and made sure that the entry door was locked before we exited into the garage. Our footfalls echoed against the low ceiling. "So, where would you like to go? It's still pretty early." It was only 3:38 according to my honking big diver's watch. It's not particularly ladylike, but it has a nice big lighted dial that I can actually *see* while flying at night and changes automatically to whatever time zone I'm in. Very cool feature.

He waggled his head and thought for a moment. "Well, if we walked slow, we'd get to the Old Spaghetti Factory just about opening time."

"Wow! What a terrific idea. I haven't eaten there for ages!"

His eyes were twinkling and he started to open his mouth to say something, but then stopped and shook his head with a chuckle.

"*What?*" I asked suspiciously. "What were you going to say?"

"Promise you won't hit me?" He was grinning fully now and holding up his hands as if to ward off a blow.

I crossed my arms over my chest. "Yeah, well—we'll see when you tell me."

He chortled, low and inviting. "I was going to ask if we were going to have dinner in bed. That could be a lot of fun."

I managed to close my dropped jaw before a big bug flew into it. *Bed? Huh?* My mind searched for whatever the double entendre might have been. He was obviously teasing by the rolling laughter that was almost bending him double. I liked the sound of his laugh. It was deep, genuine and, well, happy. I hadn't heard happy in a really long time.

I missed it.

Wait—bed! Yay, I finally got the joke! The Old Spaghetti Factory is famous both for being the former trolley station and for having really unique seating arrangements. You can sit in an actual trolley to eat, or a bathtub, and there's even a four poster brass *bed* to sit on. You have to be quick to get that one, though. It's a favorite of families with little kids. The staff lets you bounce.

I couldn't help but smile and shake my head because he was leaning against the wall, wiping away tears and heaving for breath. "You should have seen your face, Kate! It was *priceless!* You just about swallowed that beetle!"

I swatted at him and he ducked. "Keep it up, laughing boy. You'll be eating your spaghetti through a straw tonight."

5

We were third in line at the restaurant and only had to wait about fifteen minutes for it to open. A few people lined up behind us as we chatted about living the walking life in Denver. A person actually doesn't have to drive here. The buses run on time and unless you need to go to the 'burbs, you can pretty much live your whole life in a two square mile area and never realize you hadn't left.

"Shhh! He'll hear you. Do you really think that's him?" The words caught my attention, because they were followed by so much girlish giggling that I had to look to see the ages of the speakers. They were a little older than I'd thought, in their early twenties. They noticed that *I* noticed and stepped a little farther from the entrance. But I have good hearing, and while Tom was looking at the menu pasted behind plexiglass on the wall, I listened in.

"It is, Julie! He's the guy in the fireman calendar. That's Mr. August." I glanced back at Tom and tried not to gawk. Well, he *could* be a calendar model. He's certainly gorgeous enough.

"Omygawd! I think you're right, Megan. Man, he is soooo hot! My sister had to wipe her drool off that page when she bought it."

The doors of the restaurant swung outward just then as the manager unlocked the upper and lower locks of the second towering door. Tom reached back his hand expectantly and pulled me toward him. He put his hand firmly against the small of my back and then fixed the giggle girls with his full attention. He winked and flashed a smile at them that could have melted solid steel before following me inside. I heard their delighted squeal just before the door shut behind us.

"You're a calendar model?" I asked quietly with awed amazement while we waited for the greeter to return from seating the people in front of us.

He shrugged and managed to look both modest and pleased. "Yeah, sort of. The department did their annual charity calendar last year, and I was Mr. August. No big deal. The police do one, too."

I chuckled. "It was a big deal to *them*. You probably made their whole week by smiling at them."

I noticed that his hand was still warm against my back and his eyes were locked with mine. Boy, did I notice. His words were more serious than I think he planned. "I'm a lot more concerned with whether I've made *your* whole week."

I was thankfully saved from responding when the greeter returned. The lights were dim enough that hopefully he couldn't see the blush that reached all the way to the roots of my hair.

There's nothing like low lighting and the smell of pasta sauce to stimulate conversation. I don't know why. We were sitting in the back of the trolley car since there were only two of us, and they were saving the bed and bathtub for larger groups. It wasn't long after we started sipping our wine that we were both spilling our life stories to each other.

"Yeah, I think I've met your brother," Tom said, nodding. "Doesn't he work over at St. E's? When Denver General gets full, we take victims over there."

I nodded with a mouth full of hot crusty bread, slathered with butter. I figured I'd earned it by sleeping the whole previous day, so I wasn't too worried about the calories.

When I finally swallowed, I replied. "Yep. He's worked in

the ER since med school. He really seems to love it. It takes a special breed to do that day after day. I sure couldn't deal with the stress."

He was devouring his salad with gusto. Mine was long since gone. Hungry? No, not me. I started to reach for another slice of the wonderful bread but stopped. The man was going to think I'm a pig. I reached past the basket and grabbed my water glass instead.

He let out an exasperated breath, put down his fork and reached for the bread basket. He removed a slice, buttered it and put it down on my plate, while I watched with raised brows.

"Eat the bread, Kate. I can hear your stomach rumbling from here. Starving yourself for your figure won't impress me much."

I had to laugh, which surprised him. God! Did he think I was *that* vain? "This has nothing to do with my figure, Tom. But, for the record, I *love* your attitude! No, I just discovered earlier today that I'd slept the entire previous twenty-eight hours because I got cracked on the head with a brick and didn't hear the alarm clock when I was supposed to. I'm trying not to gorge myself as much as my body wants me to."

Worry replaced the surprise and he sat back into his chair to stare at me carefully. I bit into the slice of bread and shrugged. There wasn't much else to say.

His face grew serious and slightly angry. "So, you were standing at the top of an eight-foot ladder looking at the ceiling, *after* a concussion and without food for over a day? Are you *nuts?*"

It was my turn to be surprised. No questions about how I *got* the concussion, which is what I expected. Of course, I hadn't planned to tell him about Monica. Werewolves and the Thrall are mortal enemies—another good reason to have him live in the building, I suppose. But I didn't want him in danger *because* of me, either.

When he saw my surprise, followed by my annoyance whenever I think about Monica, he got the wrong impression. He swore under his breath and waved his hands in front of him. "Hey, sorry, that's the EMT in me kicking in. I know it's none of my business, but you really could have been seriously hurt if you'd gotten dizzy and fallen from that height. I'll shut my mouth now." He lowered his gaze to his meal and picked up his fork silently.

I actually hadn't considered falling off the ladder and I should have, because he was right. I reached across the table, and put my hand on top of his to stop his self-conscious stabbing at a garbanzo bean. I sighed and nodded. "No—you're right. I shouldn't have been up there, which means that I took a harder crack than I'd realized for even thinking I *could.*"

He smiled just a bit and released the fork. He flipped his hand and gave mine a quick squeeze before picked up his fork again. The food arrived, so conversation was replaced with contented eating sounds. Neither of us seemed inclined to talk until most of the spaghetti was safely nestled in our tummies.

After I was sitting back happily, letting my food settle before finishing the plate, I asked, "So, what made you become a fireman? There seems to usually be a reason why people go into fields like fire fighting or police work."

He nodded calmly. "There is. And it's the one you'd expect. Some people I cared about were killed in a fire."

I always hate hearing things like that. "Oh, I'm so sorry, Tom. What happened?"

He let out a slow breath and then wiped a bit of sauce from the corner of his mouth with his napkin. "I was about fourteen, I guess. It happened at night—an electrical fire." He let out a sad chuckle. "They always seem to happen at night, don't they? Anyway, I woke up coughing and tried to wake everyone. I managed to wake Dad. He insisted that I take out my younger sister first, and he would get Mom out. That whole part of the house was already engulfed, but I managed to find Liz and lift her over my shoulder. I tried to get back to where I'd left Dad so we could all go out together, but I couldn't see through the smoke. A fireman found us near the front door, both unconscious from smoke inhalation. I found out later that I was the only one they could save. Liz died at the hospital before I woke up."

I hadn't realized that the waitress had stopped at the table, but she was busy listening, too.

"Oh God! That's terrible, Tom! You lost your whole family?" My voice showed my sorrow and horror. The thought of it made me a nauseous. I'd lost my own parents to a car accident about the same age, but at least I still had Joe and Bryan. What would it be like to be completely *alone?*

The waitress interrupted, and her voice was a little shaky. "I'll just get these empty plates out of your way, folks. You go on talking and ignore me."

Tom smiled sadly but then his eyes cleared and he was suddenly fine. "No, it's okay. There's not much more to say. It was a long time ago. Do you want some dessert, Kate? I hear their chocolate cake is to die for here."

The waitress saw a chance to lighten the mood, and took it. She chuckled and raised her brows. "You *hear* it's to die for? You've had a slice for three nights in a row now!"

I looked the question at Tom and he laughed, only a little bit embarrassed. "Yeah, so sue me. I like the food here, and my *electricity* was out in the apartment."

He held up two fingers to the waitress and winked. She smiled, nodded and removed the plates on her way back down the narrow aisle. She had to move sideways, and say "excuse me" more than once. I was suddenly glad that we'd arrived when we had. We'd been so involved in talking that I hadn't realized the place was now packed with people. I glanced at my watch and saw that more than an hour had slipped away. For some reason that reminded me of the lease. Segues are weird things.

"Oh!" I exclaimed, and reached down underneath the table for my purse. I had to worm it out carefully from where it had secured itself between the bench seat and the wall of the trolley, nearly resting my chin on the table to reach it. "That reminds me. You don't have to look at it now, but I wanted to give you the lease to look at. No hurry. I'm not trying to push. I was afraid I'd forget if I didn't bring it along."

His smile broadened and he lifted his glass of wine in a salute. "To the woman who is going to save me from a life of darkness and cold canned food!"

I removed the tri-folded paper from my purse and handed it to him with one hand, raising my glass in the other. "And to the man who will help *pay* the electricity to stave *off* darkness in my own house!"

The walk back to the building after dessert was pleasant and quiet once we hit the side streets where few cars travel after working hours. The sun hadn't quite set behind the mountains, but the shadows were already deep between the skyscrapers. Wailing sirens in the distance made both of us perk up our ears until they faded into the distance.

I'd already told him all about the courier business over cake and coffee, and surprisingly, started to talk about Dylan. He wasn't nearly far enough from my mind today, and I just hated it.

"When I learned he'd cheated on me with Amanda, I just couldn't accept it. I guess the thing that made me most mad is that nobody who knew us was surprised." I let out an exasperated breath.

Tom nodded, and put an arm around my lightly shivering shoulders. The breeze was kicking up, or so I told myself. I hadn't realized I was rubbing them until I felt his hand settle onto my shoulder.

But his warm hand felt good deeper inside than just on my arms.

"Yeah, I know all about betrayal," he said quietly. "You always seem to think that you're on top of things when you're in a relationship. That somehow you'd *know* if the other person was cheating. But you never do. It always comes as a surprise."

I nodded, not quite sure what to say. We'd only known each other for a few hours, but it felt like years. That made him a bit nervous. It just seemed—I don't know—too *comfortable* being with Tom.

When we arrived at the building, he seemed a little nervous. "So, I guess I'll see you in a few days then. I need to find one of the guys at work with a truck to get my stuff over here. I'm on vacation this week so I could find a place, but none of the other guys are. So it might be the weekend before I can get started. Will that be okay?"

The words came out before I even realized it. "Heck, I've got a truck if you need one. Edna's old, but she can carry tons of stuff."

He turned to me, and apparently I had completely stunned him. He opened his mouth a few times to speak, but nothing came out. He even raised his hands as though he was talking. Finally he shook his head. "Wow. I mean, nobody's ever *offered* to do something like that for me. I wasn't fishing, I swear. But I couldn't, really. You're already giving me the place for a song, and—"

I put a finger to his mouth, which seemed too personal, but just right, too. "Tom, stop. It's not as generous as you're making it out. You're going to do the packing, and the hauling. I'm just providing the truck and driving it. I'm betting that you can handle the moving part, right?"

He laughed lightly. "Yeah, the werewolf stuff isn't worth much in the real world, but I *can* do grunt work. I'll just rent a dolly for the balance issues and you won't even have to get out of the cab of the truck."

My questioning look brought an answer. "A couch isn't too heavy for me, but it's clumsy. One good gust of wind can knock me off balance."

I opened my purse and pulled out a pen and a deposit slip from my checkbook. I scratched out the account number, and wrote down my home phone number before handing it to him. "The printed number is my cell phone, but call me at the home number when you've got everything packed. I'll try to let you know if I get called out of town on a job."

He folded the paper and then wasn't quite sure what to do. So I decided for him. "Talk to you soon, then, okay?" I turned and unlocked the glass door and went inside the darkened entry. I saw from the corner of my eye as he started down the street, whistling.

Two things happened almost at once: I heard the glass door shut behind me, and the toe of my boot caught in the canvas underfoot. I started to fall at an awkward angle and could see the brass scroll work quickly approaching my head. My next recollection was being in Tom's arms, even though he had been outside and the whole fall had only taken seconds to occur.

I looked up into those pretty brown eyes and thought I saw something more than just gallantry deep inside. His voice was husky. "Wouldn't want you to crack your head and forget that you offered me the apartment." His smile was warm as he pulled me closer, but I flinched and he stopped.

Too much pain, still too close to the surface. It wasn't his fault, but the last thing I needed in my world at that moment was a man. Without a word, he stood me back onto my feet and let me go, which was nice.

"Uhm—well, try to be a little more careful, huh?"

I nodded and smiled shakily, because part of me really wished that he hadn't stopped. I found myself watching him walk out the door and down the street as I locked the deadbolt behind him. Only when he was finally swallowed by shadows did I turn to go upstairs.

Sigh. It really had been a long time since I'd been *happy,* even for one night.

6

Well, certainly the *quickest* way to get rid of a happy moment is to deal with reality. I took a deep breath and turned the key in the mail drawer. I pulled stacks of past due bills, envelopes with return addresses and no name, but a first class stamp, plus sales flyers out in handfuls. I finally found what had been lying at the bottom of the box that had caused it to be so full. A small cardboard box was holding the rest of the mail aloft. I tried to remember what I had ordered, and turned it over to see the return address.

My spirits lightened a bit! I'd waited for this package for *weeks*. It was just what I needed to help forget the rest of the mail—or at least keep up my humor.

My steps were a little bouncier as I headed back to my apartment. I dropped the mail onto the little space left on the counter and went upstairs to change. Every few seconds I heard the characteristic *beep* of my thoughtful machine, reminding me I had more messages. A quick glance when I came back down told me that Joe had been busy! The lighted display read 14 since I left for my run. God, was that only this morning? Man, what a day it had been!

I shook my head as I walked back toward the kitchen. The messages and the repairs to the fire escape would just have to wait until after the bills and cooking—mainly because I'd forgotten that the raw beef wasn't in the bag I'd put in the freezer when the cops showed up. Damn.

Twenty minutes later, three pots were cooking on the stove, and the oven was heating. I laughed abruptly at the scene on the television while I was boiling pasta. I flicked my thumb on the pause button on the remote and tracked back to the previous scene.

The wonderful antics of John Cleese and company sailed across my screen. They were presently trying to hide a rat—which the Spanish waiter swore was an endangered hamster—from a visiting hotel inspector in one of my favorite episodes of *Fawlty Towers*. It's a British sitcom that was made shortly after the demise of *Monty Python's Flying Circus*. Cleese was brilliant as Basil Fawlty, but the show was apparently even too eclectic for the Brits, because there were only eleven episodes made. I'd just bought them all on DVD. There were even interviews with the cast and some wonderful outtakes on the three-disk set. I watched an amazingly realistic pratfall as Basil the person tried to capture Basil the rat, while crammed up against the counter with my head at an angle so I could see the television in the sunken living room.

I almost didn't hear the elevator start to move when the audience howled. I hit the pause button again. There was no mistaking it—the freight elevator had started to move down. But it was supposed to be locked off. I distinctly remembered locking it. What the hell?

I stepped across the kitchen, removing a large carving knife from the block on the counter. I held the knife at my waist for an upward swing to the body, searching with my mind to see who the intruder could be. By the time the elevator dinged and the doors opened, the knife was back in its slot. Some days I hate having a brother.

"So! You *are* home! I have been worried *sick* about you!" Joe snarled at me as he stalked into the room and sat down on the couch, arms folded angrily. I shook my head and kept stirring the noodles.

I snarled right back at him. "Jesus, Joe! Did it ever occur to you to use the *door*, or maybe even knock? And I left you a message. Sorry if you didn't get it."

He snorted. He crossed his arms over his chest and raised his feet to rest on the coffee table. "You have that damn television so loud you couldn't have heard a missile strike! You wouldn't have heard me if I had knocked, and yes, I got your message. Was it supposed to make me feel *better* knowing you could have died?"

I decided to ignore that one. "Y'know, you were almost a shish-kabob, big brother. I was all ready to slice and dice the person walking out of the elevator with the carving knife." I walked down the couple of steps into the pit living room and knocked his feet back onto the floor. "Feet off the furniture. You know better."

He readjusted himself on the couch, but kept his feet on the rug. "Oh, puh-lease, Kate! Like with those woo-woo psychic powers of yours you didn't know full well who was coming upstairs. Besides, I shouldn't have to announce myself like some guy off the street. We're *family*."

I spun the wooden spoon around in the water just long enough to confirm what I'd smelled. A couple minutes of inattention and now the bottom of the pot was coated with burned lasagna noodles. Guess I was going to use the 9x12 pan instead of the big one. "Even family *calls* before they drop by."

"You checked your messages lately?" His voice was sarcastic, but held an edge of fear. "There's probably a half dozen from me! First you wreck your truck, then get attacked by the *Queen Thrall* and get a concussion! But do I get a call from *you*? No. I get a *message*. So, did you get the 'scrip filled? Have you taken the second dose of the medicine?"

I turned back to the noodles before he could see my blush. I'd completely forgotten about the second pill. "I've been fine, Joe. I told you—I'm a big girl. I went grocery shopping. I got the prescription. I had some dinner. Now I'm cooking and trying to relax a little. I took the pill *with food*, like I was instructed." Okay, so it was a lie. But I would take it before I went to bed.

He grunted agreement, which worked well. I didn't tell him about the police visit or about Tom. There are some things he's better off not knowing. I changed the subject by hitting the play button on the remote. Basil the rat scurried out from underneath the tablecloth of an unsuspecting diner. I chuckled and pulled the pot from the stove, spilling a bit of the water/olive oil mix onto the burner before pouring the works into a colander in the sink.

Joe grabbed the second remote from the coffee table and turned off the DVD player. "Hey!" I shouted, but couldn't reach the remote in time.

I winced when the VCR came on. I didn't want him to see what I'd been watching before I left for Tel Aviv last week. I tried to turn it off with my own remote, but the batteries decided to take that precise moment to fail. I sprinted from the kitchen, but didn't make it to him before delighted laughter filled the speaker.

The camera was obviously held by an amateur. The screen remained black until a woman's voice said, "Um, Timothy, it would be easier to see if you removed the lens cap."

Joe hit the pause button and then looked up at me with wonder. "Kate, is this—"

I nodded. "Yeah, it's Bryan's tenth birthday party. I found it the other day when I was cleaning."

His face softened and he patted the seat next to him. I took a deep, shaking breath. I'd cried my eyes out when I'd watched this the other day. I hoped I'd do better today, because I was out of tissues. Forgot to put them on the grocery list.

It was an ordinary home movie of an ordinary event—a child's birthday party. Two parents, three kids. But the parents were both dead now, and the birthday boy might as well be.

"C'mon, Bryan! Make a wish!" Joe's younger self was mugging for the camera, making funny faces to make his little brother laugh.

"Is it chocolate, Mama?" asked the laughing boy under the pointed paper hat while the candles were lit. "With lots of cherries?"

A slender redhead who looked a lot like the woman I see in the mirror every morning knelt down to get into the video. "It sure is, sweetie! Black forest cake. Just like you asked for. And tonight we're having all the pasties you can eat!"

I heard Joe whisper the next words, even as my younger doppelganger said them. "You made mine without turnips, didn't you, Mom? I don't like turnips."

Joe turned on the couch and smiled. "I don't know why you asked every time. She *always* made some for you without."

I started tearing up, and I hated it. "Yeah, I know she did." I stood up and walked back into the kitchen and started to pull noodles out of the colander while I listened to the laughter and screams as each present was opened. I glanced at Joe and he was enraptured, laughing along with the happy family. I'd done the same right up until the end, and then I was without them again.

I was concentrating so hard on not getting wrapped up in reliving the past that I didn't notice that Joe had turned it off and was now standing across the center island from me.

His eyes were a little redder than when he'd arrived. I had to go back to the sink or I was going to start to bawl. His words stopped me.

"I stopped by the church today, Kate. Why didn't you tell me?"

I turned to him, confused. "Tell you *what?*"

"Why didn't you tell me that you've been paying for most of Bryan's care?" He let out an exasperated breath. "I agreed a long time ago to cover half, but you never told me that the bill had gone up over the years."

"That's not fair. I tried. But every time I'd start to talk to you about it you'd change the subject or 'have to go, there's an emergency.' What was I supposed to do?"

He shook his head and stared at the ceiling. His eyes were a little shiny in the light. "No *wonder* you went ballistic when I leased the new car. Six thousand dollars a month—God, Kate! I'm amazed you haven't already lost this place trying to cover that. I've been sending you, what, like eight hundred?"

I shrugged, because I didn't know what else to do. "I've been managing."

He snorted and stepped back to lean against the counter. "Yeah, right. You've been *managing*. I saw the notices on your desk, Kate. You're in trouble, and you've been working like a dog trying to get by."

I felt my back go up a bit. "I make good money, Joe. I can take care of myself."

He stepped forward abruptly and grabbed me by the shoulders. I looked up into his eyes. "Then *take* care of yourself. Quit trying to save the rest of us." He released me and turned away. "I canceled the lease on the Hummer. It was still in the rescission period. And I paid Mike for the next three months of Bryan's care."

He turned around, probably to see the shock on my face. You could have *driven* a Hummer into my wide-open mouth. He sighed. "I try not to be a jerk, Kate. Try to get back on your feet in the next three months, though, because I have to tell you—that payment *hurt*. Unlike you, I can't work myself into the ground forever. I'll be out of town for a few days at a conference, so just promise me that you'll take care of *you* for that time. Not me, not Bryan—and *not* Dylan."

All those warm fuzzy feelings crashed down around my feet. Damn it! I *knew* there was more to this than him being decent! I should have seen it coming. "Joe—" My tone was a warning.

I saw then the anger that was boiling just beneath the surface. "I'm concerned about you, Kate. Doesn't that mean anything?"

"Your concern means a great deal to me, Joe. But I won't satisfy your need for instant answers. You can't force me to make the decision you want me to. Thank you for picking up the bill with Mike. It was nice of you. But leave now, while there's still hope of my being rational about Dylan."

His back had straightened more and more with each of my words until he was ramrod military perfection. His voice took on a rolling Irish brogue and flames beat around each word. "You've always been stubborn, Mary Kathleen Reilly!"

"Don't start with me, Joe. Really truly don't."

I turned the television and DVD player back on and went back to stirring the boiling potatoes while the noodles cooled enough to handle. I turned my back on Joe and tried to concentrate on the sound of laughter that had nothing to do with my family. I glanced at the crusted pot bottom, turned on the hot water and added a splash of dish soap. At least I hadn't burned anything important. They always give scads too many noodles for the way I make lasagna. One layer on bottom, one on top, with the middle all steak chunks and ground sirloin in a thick tomato sauce. Five kinds of cheese mixed in and on top make it almost too rich to eat. Almost.

I watched from the corner of my eye as Joe walked toward the door. "The keys, Joe. Leave them on the counter."

He stopped, frozen in his tracks. He knew what I was talking about and had hoped I'd forgotten. "Who'll water your plants when you have to go out of town?" He was smart enough to guess that the return of the key was permanent.

"The timed misters don't question my judgment." I pointed to the bottom drawer in the cabinet, next to the dishwasher. "There's a replacement lock set and deadbolt in that drawer. I'll change the locks if I have to."

Joe let out a heaving sigh and crossed the room to the breakfast island. He set the key carefully down on the countertop and walked to the door.

"Joe?" I heard him pause with his hand on the knob. "Thanks. I really didn't have the money to pay Mike this month."

"I know." I heard the door click shut behind him.

7

I alternately cooked and froze meals, and watched my DVD while dipping into the pint of rum raisin ice cream with a tablespoon. It really hadn't been too horrible of a day overall. I had expected worse. The more time passed from when Monica attacked me, the easier it was to believe that the queens could control her until she died.

I knew I would have to deal with everything eventually. Spending an evening like this was irresponsible at best, and quite possibly stupid. But for just one evening I intended to ignore reality and pretend to have a normal life. Tomorrow the world might come crashing down on my head. But for tonight, Bryan's care was paid for, I had survived a nasty concussion, and I had actually had a dinner date with a cute guy . . . who was going to move into the building . . . and thought I looked *amazing*. Wow!

When the last of my cooking was safely stored in the freezer, I loaded the dishwasher and climbed the stairs. There was one last self-indulgent thing I wanted do to before bed.

I love bubble baths. It's one of the few really "girly" things I do. Showers get me clean. Baths relax me. They're a luxury my schedule can't often accommodate. Considering everything I'd been through in the last forty-eight hours I deserved a good, long, soak. I set the taps running and set out my fluffiest towels before going over to the sink to make my selection.

The cabinet under my bathroom sink is filled with some of the best products from around the world. There are concoctions in every conceivable scent and color, each claiming to be the best in the world at something in whatever native language. Tonight I picked an aromatherapy mix that promised to relax me. I poured the mixture into the water filling the tub with a sigh. The herbal scent was heavenly. Just *exactly* what I needed.

It was still early when I finished the bath, but I was tired and completely relaxed for the first time in ages, so I pulled on an oversized T-shirt and shorts and put myself to bed. I dreamed of chasing rats and haughty guests, and a cute guy named Tom, *not* Larry and Monica.

I woke early the next morning, but actually felt rested enough to face up to my responsibilities. I went downstairs and started the coffeemaker brewing before settling in at the breakfast island with the stack of mail I'd brought up the day before. Bills and junk mail, just as I'd suspected. Unfortunately, the letter telling me I could "stuff envelopes in my spare time for big money" started to look good after I'd calculated how much I'd better have to pay my monthly expenses, even without Bryan's care. The situation was grim. With the added expense of fixing the window and fire escape from the attempted break-in yesterday, I'd better make the meals in the freezer last as long as possible. It wasn't *impossible* to manage. I'd just have to do some juggling. I silently thanked Joe again for paying Mike.

I dropped the junk mail into the waste can. The bills I carried across the room to my desk. I'd sit down with the checkbook and pay the worst of them later.

The insistent beeping of the answering machine finally got to me. I had to know. I grabbed a pen and paper, went to the kitchen for a huge mug of steaming coffee and then settled in next to the telephone.

His was the first message. A bare few words, "Kate, it's me."

He paused, "Dylan." He said it as though maybe I wouldn't recognize the voice. Not unlikely after five or six years, I suppose, but no such luck.

"I . . . I left a message with Joe, but I'm not sure he'll give it to you." Not a bad guess, since my jerky brother never said *anything* about actually talking to Dylan, *or* taking a message.

"I have to talk to you. It's life or death. I wouldn't call you otherwise. Meet me at Bernardo's Thursday at one. Please?" All the muscles I'd worked so hard to relax last night tightened into knots at the sound of his voice. Shooting pain in my jaw told me I was clenching it. I rubbed my temples with my index fingers as I tried to decipher the nuances of the message. Of course, today was Thursday. Naturally.

Bernardo's is a 24-hour pool hall. It's within walking distance of the loft. It's considered neutral territory by the monsters. Dylan is part of the Herd, but he's still a yuppie. Bernardo's is not a place he would normally choose. That he had was . . . odd, and that set off little alarm bells in the back of my mind. At one o'clock in the afternoon most of the vampires would be off of the streets. While they *can* do sunlight, they don't like it. Joe has a theory that it's a vitamin deficiency caused by the parasite. I personally don't care. I just know that I like staying in sunlight.

"Why Bernardo's?" I muttered to myself as I wandered across the room to grab a bottle of water from the fridge. I twisted off the cap, pulled a vitamin tablet from a bottle in the cabinet and swallowed it with a long pull as I waited for the next message. It was nearly a full minute before the machine beeped again and I realized that there had been a long silence before Dylan had hung up.

The next message was from the diamond exchange. "Ms. Reilly, this is Mr. Goldstein. We have a shipment that has to be picked up in Tel Aviv no later than next Wednesday. Are you available? Please contact me as soon as you return from Paris. The cutter, ahem, *specifically* requested that we send you."

A chuckle escaped me. The cutter in Tel Aviv is Gerry Friedman. For a seventy-year-old man, he's quite the flirt.

I hit the rewind button. Goldstein works out of several different offices, I wanted to make sure I called the right one when I took the job. I couldn't afford to refuse it.

Something about Dylan's call was still bothering me. I rewound the whole tape and listened to Dylan's message three more times. I still couldn't quite put my finger on the problem, so I moved on. Mike called to let me know that the nursing company had raised their rates for the day nurse, again, and that we'd need to talk. *That* was seriously unwelcome news, but no surprise. And it was handled for the moment.

The rest of the calls were from Joe and Connie. Fifteen calls for three useful messages. What a waste.

I checked the clock. Morris Goldstein's office wouldn't be open for a while yet. I had plenty of time for breakfast and a run. I went downstairs to check the weather to see what I wanted to wear. Yeah, I could look out the window, but being on the third floor in Denver is like its own little world. Once I dressed for cold and snow flurries to find that a Chinook wind stole the snow away before it reached the ground. I was boiling hot all day. Weird, yeah—but it's how it is.

I was standing at the front door in an oversized T-shirt and shorts when I heard a sultry baritone behind me.

"Hey Kate!"

I turned at the greeting and found Tom standing there. He looked good enough that my mouth went dry and my heart skipped a beat. This morning he was dressed in running shorts and a flame red T-shirt with black lettering that read "Firefighters like it hot." It stretched taut across his muscular chest and the shorts showed off the buff legs I had imagined were under those pinstripes last night. Unlike a lot of people with lycanthropy, his body is perfectly proportioned, not gangly at all, and his face. . . .

I was staring. Damn it. I just can't seem to help it. He *did* notice. Tom smiled at me, flashing deep dimples, his eyes lingering over the length of leg showing between my shorts and cuffed socks. Yeah, I blushed. His grin widened, and his brown eyes began sparkling merrily.

"Want to join me for a run?"

I crossed my arms over my chest and threw a teasing look his way. "You ran all the way over here to ask me to *run?* Boy, if *that* isn't contrived."

He laughed, just a few short chuckles. "Nah. I ran over here to pick up the key to the apartment. I was sort of . . . well, *distracted* yesterday." He pulled a thick, folded letter envelope from the back pocket of the shorts and held it out to me. "I signed the lease, and the money's in the envelope, too, so I hope it's okay." He smiled, but there was tightness around the corners of his eyes. "I'm afraid there's been a change of plans, and I need to get some boxes into the place today, if that's okay."

"Yeah? What sort of a *change of plans?* What's up?"

He shook his head, tiny little annoyed movements. "It's not your problem, Kate. I'm just really glad I have a place to move into. That guy is a royal pain in the ass." White knuckles showed how hard he was clenching his fists.

I understood the feeling. "It's about the landlord of your other place, huh? What did he do?"

Tom was getting more and more agitated as I watched. He was staring at the sidewalk and was lost in internal thoughts that made his jaw muscle bulge. I put a hand on his bicep to bring him back to this world. He jumped and then stared at me, startled. He took a deep, slow breath with his eyes closed and seemed to center himself.

When his eyes opened again, he was back to normal—or at least as normal as he was yesterday. "Sorry. I shouldn't let him get to me like that. But he barely told me two days ago that I had to move by the end of the month, and this morning there's a knock on the door and two guys say he's paid them to move my stuff onto the street!"

I opened my mouth in shock. "*What?!*" My hands went to my hips and I barely suppressed a scream. "They can't do that, Tom. It's against the law!"

He shrugged and threw up his hands. "Not much I can do about it. A couple of guys I know are watching the boxes to make sure that nobody rips them off. But I really need to get the key and get back there. Do you mind? I know it's not the first of the month or anything—"

My brain immediately started working. This was wrong on so many levels that I couldn't even count them all! "Oh, we'll get your boxes all right. Just let me slip on a pair of jeans and grab my keys. I don't have the spare back from the other tenant yet, but mine will work just fine. It's a master."

I spun around but he grabbed my arm. His look told me that he was afraid I was going to do something that get him into trouble. "Really, Kate. You don't have to get involved. I can bring the key right back."

I smiled tightly and removed his hand. "No, it's okay. We'll get you moved, and I'll be nice. But then your landlord is going to hear from the Housing Authority, the D.A. and anyone else I can think of very soon. I'll make sure of it! Guys who pick on people with no room to make waves really yank my chain."

He looked uncomfortable, but waited downstairs as I took the elevator up, turned off the coffee pot, grabbed my cell phone, keys, and wallet, and changed clothes.

The trip over to his building only took a few minutes. The building was one of the pre-renovation models, with crumbling brickwork and peeling paint on swollen doorways. It looked just like one of the crack houses on *Cops*—*after* the police raid.

A couple of clean-cut burly guys were leaning against a growing stack of boxes, angrily watching the other two burly guys who were carrying boxes out of the building.

We pulled up to the curb and Tom hopped out. I waited for a break in traffic and then quickly opened the door and shut it before the next big delivery truck could clip me. A large green and white sign caught my eye as I started to walk toward Tom and his friends. I immediately recognized the logo and lettering, but *no way!* I heard the swear words that I muttered under my breath while opening the passenger door of the truck to grab my cell phone.

Tom walked up to me with his friends, just as I started to dial.

"What's up, Kate? You suddenly look pissed off on a whole new level." He stared at me curiously, and I noted that his nostrils were flared wide again. I wondered what a werewolf could smell that a human couldn't. I'd have to ask someday.

I held up a finger to stop him as the woman at other end of the line greeted me. "Hi, is Keith there? This is Kate Reilly."

Tom cocked his head and narrowed his lids a bit, but then looked at his friends and shrugged. He opened the soda that his buddy handed him and took a sip.

"Hey, Kate! Good to hear from you. Did you change your mind about the property?"

I put on my best professional tone. "Hi, Keith. No, actually I'm calling about something different today." I put a bit of concern, and a hint of confusion in my voice intentionally. "Do you have the property over on—" I looked up at the building. "1840 Baker?"

"Hmm, that sounds familiar. Let's see." I heard clicking from his rapid fingers on the keyboard. "Yep, that's one of ours. It's not for sale, though. We just have the management contract."

I let out an annoyed breath that would be obvious over the phone. "Boy, I was really hoping you *weren't* going to say that, Keith."

Caution edged into his voice. "Yeah? Why not?"

"I just took on a tenant who lived there, and I'm standing in front of the building as we speak. There seem to be a pair of movers that were hired by the owner of the building and they're putting his stuff out on the street."

Keith could hear the other boot starting to drop, but he didn't quite know what to say. "Uh-huh. And . . ."

I learned a lot about the process of renting and evictions when I bought my building. Interviews with property management companies taught me more. One thing I learned from *Keith* was that managers tend to get stuck in the situation of being a buffer between the owner and the tenant. They always hate to hear that the owner is going around directly dealing with the tenants without involving them.

"No three-day demand, Keith. No FED complaint, no

court appearance, no Order of Restitution. Nada. Please tell me that you've got a renegade owner on your hands and that you didn't authorize this *incredibly* illegal situation. I'd hate to think that about you guys while I'm still considering hiring your company."

One corner of my mouth curled up as I heard him put down the phone and mutter violent swear words in the background. I winked at Tom and his buddies, who were trying to hide their laughter and failing miserably. Tom was staring open-mouthed at my side of the conversation.

Keith's voice was very serious when he finally picked up the phone again. "Kate, I swear to you that we had no knowledge of this action. I just checked the file on that building and we are supposed to be *fully* involved in evictions. We don't have anyone in violation of their lease. Everyone is paid up to date. I'll call our client, and if there's a legitimate reason for this, Kate, I *promise* you that it'll be handled in the proper way." He let out a frustrated sigh. "Can you grab one of the movers and let me talk to him, please?"

I walked up to what appeared to be the head mover and held out the cell phone. "Excuse me, but the gentleman on my phone is the property manager of this building." I pointed to the posted sign on the building wall. "He' d like to talk to you."

I stepped over to Tom and accepted a Coke from his grinning blond friend. "You go, girl!" the blond whispered. I wiggled my eyebrows briefly while popping the can and taking a sip. Tom couldn't quite figure out what to say. He just looked confused and was watching it play out.

The middle-aged Latino mover stepped away from us, toward the management sign. I could hear bits and pieces of the conversation—the name of the man who hired him and what they were to be paid. No, they didn't have the tenant's name; just a description and the apartment number. Finally, it was over and he returned and handed me back the phone.

When the other mover—a slender pale guy in his twenties, came out with stack of boxes, the first one said, "Hey, Dale, grab your stuff. We just got pulled off this job."

The man named Dale pulled a red paisley handkerchief

from his pocket and wiped his face. "That sucks. We gonna get paid for the whole day?"

The older man nodded. "Yeah. I told him it was a flat rate. I got the address to pick up the check."

"Oh. Okay, cool." Dale ripped open the hook and eye fastener on the front of his black nylon back belt, leaving it dangling from the shoulder suspenders. They walked away without another word and got into an old, beat-up pick-up truck.

There was a moment of silence while we all stared after the departing truck, trying not to choke on the thick blue smoke that belched out of the tailpipe.

Finally, the tall Latino friend with the Sprite waved his hand to clear some of the fumes away and spoke up. "Jeez. Any chance you could call my landlord, too? I could use a new fridge."

We all burst out laughing.

Tom couldn't seem to get a grin off his face. He leaned back against one stack of boxes and shook his head. "I can't believe you just did that! In fact, I'm not quite sure *what* you did!

I shrugged and swilled down the last of the Coke. "Nothing much. I know the guy at the property management company. I was going to hire them to run *my* building. Basically, the *owner* doesn't get to tell you to get out. He hired a company to represent him, and is under contract to let them deal with the tenants. There's a whole legal process to remove a tenant. It takes days and days to go through. Since the owner doesn't have a leg to stand on for kicking you out, you don't *technically* even have to move into my building. You can stay here if you want."

"Oh, hell no!" said the blond. "My wife would shoot me dead if she ever found out I let Tom stay in this hellhole!" He held out his hand to me. "By the way, since Tom is being rude and didn't bother to introduce us, I'm Marty, and this is Paul."

I shook his massive hand and gave as good as I got, which earned me a startled look and then an appreciative nod. I was too far away from Paul, so I nodded a greeting, which was returned.

Tom looked embarrassed and stepped forward. "Oh, hey guys! I'm sorry. I should have introduced you right off. Kate Reilly, this is Marty Bell and Paul Tolwake. They work out of the Northglenn station. Guys, this is my new landlord."

"Damn, Tom!" exclaimed Paul with jealous admiration in his voice. "You do manage to fall into the sweetest deals! Now *that's* a landlord! If only I didn't live a mile from the firehouse already—"

Tom and I laughed, while Marty guffawed and punched Paul lightly on the arm. "Pfft! And if *only* you didn't have a jealous wife and four kids, too!" He shook his head and turned to Tom. "C'mon, let's get this stuff back upstairs."

I held up my hand to stop them. "Hey, I've got the truck right here. Why don't we go ahead and load the boxes? It's just a few blocks to my building, and then you've got some of your stuff already there."

Tom looked at me hopefully. "Really? You wouldn't mind?"

Paul nodded thoughtfully and glanced at his watch. "I don't have much more time today, guys. I promised to pick up my sister's kids from the doctor and take them back to school. It's the only way she'd let me borrow her truck tomorrow to move the furniture. I can probably stay a few more minutes, though."

With four of us working, it only took about half an hour to load the boxes into Edna. Tom's every other sentence on the way back to the building was spent thanking me for the apartment, thanking me for calling Keith, thanking me for helping with the boxes. I was just starting to enjoy the wanton gratitude when we arrived. Damn!

I was really glad he'd purchased file storage boxes from the office supply store. Having boxes that stacked neatly, with removable lids and *handles,* was a nice treat. I'd have to remember that the next time I need to move things around. After discussing the best method, we decided to put all the boxes on the freight elevator and take them up to my apartment. Then I could block open the door and turn it off so we could unload it easily. As a bonus, carrying the boxes down one flight of stairs would be a lot easier than carrying them *up*.

With careful arranging, all the boxes fit in the elevator, with just enough room for us. I wiggled backward into the space, so I was squished between the steel grate and the boxes, and Tom entered face first so we could talk. But when he kicked out the block in front of the door with his foot, it slid shut with a dull clang and latched, but nothing else happened. I realized the motor was still turned off. I fished in my pocket and removed the key, handing it to Tom.

"Turn on the elevator, would you? It's the keyhole under the fire alarm."

He turned his head and spotted it. He took the key and tried to reach around. But he was stuck tight between the boxes and couldn't move. He bent, he twisted, but it was just out of reach. He looked at me and bit his lower lip. "Uhm, Houston, I think we've got a problem."

I dropped my head into my hands. "Yeah, I can see that. Why do I get the feeling you planned this?"

He chuckled. "While I can think of *worse* places to be stuck with you, I'd like to think I have a bit more tact. Any ideas?"

I sighed. "Actually yes." I could put in the key, but it was going to be slightly uncomfortable and more than a little embarrassing. "All I ask is that you hold still and not make any sudden moves. I promise I'm not getting fresh."

That raised his eyebrows. "Well, now you've got me curious. Please *do* proceed."

I took a deep breath and wiggled forward until we were touching along the full length of our bodies. His eyes bored into mine from inches away, and he chuckled low and deep. Then he noticed my discomfort and tried to make light of it. But the tone was too honest. It wound up sexy enough to make my face red. "Well, so far I'm liking your idea."

It took more than one try to talk, which made me even redder. "Just don't move. Please?" I slid my arms between the grating and his muscled hips, holding onto the key carefully so it didn't drop. I wouldn't get another try at this. I realized that his wonderfully broad shoulders and chest were in the way, and I couldn't quite see where I needed to be. "Well, okay, I was wrong. You do need to move. Can you pull up your arm up so I can see the panel?"

"I think I can manage that." He slowly wormed his arm upward until it touched the ceiling of the elevator, and then lowered it down over my shoulders, lightly stroking my hair on the way. Flames beat at my face from the inside and I couldn't meet his eyes.

"Is that better?" Tom's voice was getting husky and the silk shorts didn't leave anything to the imagination.

I glanced down under his arm and could see the keyhole, along with other things that made my stomach clench unmercifully. "Much," I whispered, and then coughed when the word caught in my throat. "I mean, yes, that's better. Thanks. It should just be a second now."

He twisted and moved his head slightly, which made it easier to see. But his nose also nestled in my hair and his reply was warm and moist against my neck. "No hurry. Take your time." The shiver went all the way to my toes.

Eek! I held my breath and reached forward quickly, trying desperately to concentrate on the key, instead of his amazing cologne tickling my nose, the feeling of muscled legs against mine, and the little moan that huffed into my ear when I made the final, desperate attempt. The key went into the lock and I turned it on in one triumphant movement.

But I'd forgotten about the initial bounce at start-up when the car was fully loaded. The jolt knocked me backwards. Tom caught me before I hit my head. We wound up squished against the back of the elevator. He was pressed against me in ways that my body was very happy about.

I noticed that he didn't try to untangle us for the short trip, and I was embarrassed to admit that I didn't try either. I think he very deliberately nibbled my ear as we scuffled around trying to catch our balance. I could be wrong, but I was sort of hoping I wasn't.

When the door finally, thankfully, opened on the third floor, part of me was sorry. But the more staid, rational part of my brain was screaming to get out of the car, and he could tell.

I nearly kissed the carpet when I exited the car, but instead turned into a flurry of energy. That happens when I get stressed. I found the big chunk of iron that I used as a doorstop during construction, blocked open the elevator, unlocked the apartment door, nearly ran down the stairs to open the other apartment, and ran up the stairs again. My heart was beating nicely by the time I'd returned, and I knew that part of it wasn't from the stairs.

Tom was wandering through the apartment, which I don't normally let people do. But it was better than a warm and fuzzy moment after being wrapped around each other. I didn't think I could handle *that*.

"Okay, let's get moving," I declared with a loud clap of my hands. I grabbed two of the boxes and spun around to take them downstairs.

"Kate—"

"No time now, Tom." I said the words behind me as I tore out of the apartment again at a fast walk. I saw him shake his head from the corner of my eye and grab a pair of boxes.

I worked like a madwoman but even still, it took nearly an hour to unload the boxes and take them to his new apartment. I did try to follow the directions he'd written in pen on the boxes, placing some in the kitchen and some in the bath and others in what would be the bedroom.

"These are the last two," he commented on the way past me down the stairs and the thought made me nervous. Could I really stand to have a guy that was giving me this bad a case of the whim-whams right downstairs? What *was* I thinking! And what was I going to do when he stepped back through the door? I felt really guilty that my first thought was to slam the door shut and lock it. But that would be rude and, in reality, I really didn't want to.

As Mum always said: *When in doubt—cook!* I retreated to the kitchen where I felt safe. Some food really *would* hit the spot. Dinner had been a long time ago. I thought about diving into the freezer stock, but eggs sounded good. I like food that's heavy on protein—with the exception of my pasties and the occasional rum raisin ice cream. Stick to the ribs, but simple. Dylan had complained endlessly—and insisted on eating out most of the time. French food, with fancy sauces. Things I could never possibly have replicated in the kitchen.

Just thinking about Dylan brought my mind back to the message, and I glanced at the clock. It was already after ten. *To go, or not to go. What a really sucky question!*

I heard Tom bounding up the stairs, which he must do a lot of. He has the best-looking butt I've ever seen. My mood improved measurably with each step he took, and that scared the crap out of me.

He tapped on the open door lightly before poking his head inside.

"Come on in."

He poked his head into the kitchen and smirked. "I guess you're hungry?"

I shrugged one shoulder and cracked an egg into a bowl. "I haven't eaten since dinner. I was feeling a little lightheaded."

His voice was completely neutral and I didn't turn to see his face. "Ah. Is *that* why you were moving at a dead run?"

I didn't answer. I just grabbed a whisk and started to scramble the eggs. "I can make some for both of us, if you want. Are you hungry?"

I felt him behind me before I realized he'd moved. I felt my heart skip a beat when he stroked one finger down my arm. "Kate? Could you look at me, please?"

The scent of his cologne was driving me insane. I put my hands down on the counter and took a slow breath. He backed up and gave me some room to think.

I turned and looked into those warm, drowning deep eyes. I had to be honest with him. "I just can't do this, Tom. I'm not ready to get close to another man."

He stepped forward, closing the small gap of space that made me feel safe. My heart started pounding again like a triphammer. "You can't lie to a werewolf, Kate, even if you can lie to yourself."

He leaned forward just a bit. I could feel his chest brush against my shirt with each inhale and my body responded almost without registering in my brain. I was suddenly flushed, my breathing fast and shallow. Then his nostrils flared and my stomach did a flip-flop when he abruptly pressed his lips against mine. It wasn't what I'd expected and I didn't know how to react. His hands reached for my waist and pulled me tight against him. I stopped breathing. My mind was numb, but my body knew *exactly* what it wanted. I melted into his embrace and kissed him back, meeting his probing tongue with my own.

Strong hands circled my waist and one slid up my back. His finger caught briefly in my braid and pulled a few hairs out of the loose band.

I allowed my hands to explore the muscles of his chest as I leaned in closer. I could feel a hint of his incredible strength as he tightened his grip around me. Time stopped as his mouth worked over mine. His lips and tongue were warm and soft and his increasingly urgent breath in my ear made tingles thrill across my skin. Yesterday's intruder could have come in and looted the place. I wouldn't have known—or cared.

Tom let loose first, taking half a step back. His hands remained on my waist and his eyes were slightly glazed.

I had to force myself not to whimper. I wanted this man. Oh how I wanted this man. It took a second before I was able to speak. Even then my voice was a little breathy. "Apparently I'm not very good at lying to myself, either."

His grin was a triumphant flash of white teeth and deep dimples. My mind was on leading him upstairs to the loft, but my stomach would have none of that. It growled—audibly.

Tom laughed out loud and shoved me gently in the direction of the stove. "Eat. *Then* we'll exercise." Somehow I didn't think he was referring to a run anymore. I really hoped we were talking about something much more entertaining.

"Why don't you put on some music while I cook?" I suggested. My voice was still a little shaky and it made him grin.

He wandered into the living room. The sound system is in a huge oak cabinet that sits next to the stairway. I would never have bought a stereo that elaborate but a friend on the volleyball circuit was in dire financial straits after her husband left her. She sold it to me for about half of what it was worth, but more than I could afford at the time. The sound quality is phenomenal and the acoustics of the apartment make the most of it.

"What do you want to hear?" he asked. I didn't bother turning around. I just started cracking more eggs into a bowl and grabbing anything that might work in an omelet from the fridge. I found peppers, onions and some ham to go with the cheese. I grabbed a spatula from the old crockery cookie jar on the counter where I store them.

"Whatever."

I expected the music to come on right away. When it didn't, I turned my attention from omelet preparation to see what Tom was up to. I found him staring at the picture wall— at one particular photo. Dylan's. All of the humor had left his face. He looked more serious than I'd ever seen him. He didn't bother to look at me. He seemed to know that I was staring. "Is this him? Your old fiancé?"

Honestly, I had forgotten it was there. "I should've taken that down." Hell, I shouldn't have hung it up in the first place. I still wasn't quite sure why I had.

"But you didn't."

"It'd leave a hole in the wall." I tried to make it a joke. Of course it fell flat. I turned the heat off under the eggs and walked over to where he stood.

He made an inclusive hand gesture that took in my one-woman demolition and make-over of the building.

"A woman who could do all this, afraid of a little spackle? I don't think so." He tried for humor, but there was definitely tension underneath.

I stopped when I was standing barely an inch away from him and stared into his chocolate brown eyes.

"Maybe I'm just waiting for someone to give me something better to put up in its place." Like him, I put a hint of playfulness in my voice, but I was serious. Dylan had been gone from my life for years. Phone messages be damned, I knew he wasn't coming back. I didn't even want him to. I wanted Tom. Not just for a roll in the hay—for real. Funny, sweet, intelligent and honest. All the things I like in a man. Needless to say, I haven't found a lot of men with all of those qualities, and none of the relationships have been casual. I'm not the casual type.

"I see." Tom's voice was soft, thoughtful. He gave me a

long assessing look. It took a minute, but finally there was a hint of sparkle as his natural good humor started to reassert itself. "So, you're saying that if *someone* gave you another picture the right size you'd get rid of this one?"

"Absolutely."

"Stay here. I'll be right back." He dashed out of the apartment, leaving the door wide open. I could hear his footsteps thundering down the stairs.

I went back to the kitchen. If I was lucky the omelet wasn't ruined. If I wasn't lucky, too bad. I don't waste food. I was going to eat. *Then* I was going to make damned sure Tom understood that Dylan was no longer a part of my life.

The eggs were finished by the time I heard his footsteps coming back up. I cut the omelet in half and scooped an equal amount onto the plates and set them onto the counter before walking back over to the picture wall. I pulled down the frame holding Dylan's picture.

Tom came in without knocking, shoving the door closed behind him. When he stopped in front of me his eyes were merry with mischief and dark with challenge.

"Here you go."

I took the glossy paper from his hand and glanced at it. I wasn't sure *what* to say. I knew I was blushing. My face was hot with it. Good God! They had sold *these* at 7-11?

He was nearly naked but stared at the camera saucily from under his yellow helmet, an erotic smile curling one side of his mouth. Only a well-placed fire hose covered his hips. It was the ultimate dare. Would I actually hang his original calendar photo right in the center of my living room wall?

"Good choice." I was still blushing, but I met his eyes. I removed the backing from the frame in my hand, handed Tom the old photo, and watched without comment as he dropped it into the nearby waste can on top of my discarded junk mail. *He* watched as I slid his picture into the frame. It was a perfect fit—just like the fire hose. I turned and hung the frame on the wall without another word. While my back was turned, Tom stepped closer. He slid one arm around me, pulling me against him. He used his other hand to push aside my braid so that he could nibble at my neck. I could feel his groin swelling and pressing against me through the thin silk of his shorts. A small, needful sound that was almost a whimper escaped from my throat as I turned to face him. The smile he gave me was knowing and predatory. The kiss that followed was filled with wanton lust. It made my knees weak and my breathing ragged.

He pulled back a fraction of an inch. "Lunch first."

I could barely catch my breath, but I blurted. "You've *got* to be kidding."

"I want you at full strength." His grin was wicked as he pushed me gently away. "You'll need it."

"I certainly hope so."

8

I have never bolted a meal that fast in my life. I shouldn't have bothered. Tom deliberately took his leisurely time eating his omelet while I cooled my heels, but not my libido, on the couch.

"Wouldn't want to cramp up later," he explained. I could tell that he was actually *enjoying* the omelet, but something close to indecision clouded his face. He closed his eyes about every other bite and his mood was darkening, his face shutting down; losing warmth. I could almost feel a chill drift toward me.

I wished I knew what the issue was. I wanted him, he obviously want me, or *did* want me ten minutes ago. Maybe some light bantering would help. "I can't imagine why you like my cooking. It's just eggs and cheese, some veggies, and a few spices."

He swallowed and gave me an incredulous look. "Are you *kidding?* You're a great cook. I mean, even the fact that you *can* cook is rare today."

My brows shot up. "Everyone can cook, Tom. You throw ingredients into a pan and take them out when they're done."

He shook his head. "Hmm-mmm," he mumbled before he swallowed again. "I can honestly say that I will probably never use the stove or oven you provided in my apartment. If it isn't fresh, or microwaveable . . . ."

Inside I was smiling, because the chill was fading away, but I really did have a hard time believing him. In my opinion, most microwaveable *food* is barely deserving of the term. Then again, I'd been spoiled. When I was little every meal my mom prepared was amazing. Sunday dinner was perfectly seasoned roast beef or chicken and Christmas was formal rack of lamb with all the trimmings. Even breakfast was from scratch—pancakes or oatmeal with plenty of fruit and milk.

I shook my head. "Honestly, I only do really simple stuff. I've never been able to live up to my mom's cooking."

"Trust me on this, Kate," he said as he licked off the back of the fork. "You cook like a master chef as far as I'm concerned. I can burn water, and the guys at the station aren't any better. It's hotdogs, hamburgers or chili when I'm on shift. The reason I eat so much fruit and veggies is that you don't have to cook them. When it's my turn to cook, they get vegetable trays with store-bought dressing. If I'm feeling daring, I might slice up some sausage and cheese with crackers."

I just shook my head. I couldn't quite grasp that concept. When he finally finished his meal, he stood, turned toward me and stretched. My little heart went pitty-pat as I watched all those perfectly toned muscles twist and flex, and compared them to the photo on the wall. I vowed never to get him hooked on pasties. Fruits and vegetables did well by him.

I knew that he was watching me gawk at him but I couldn't seem to stop. Hell, I couldn't seem to blink. Every one of his dozen graceful steps to the couch mesmerized me. The half-shut blinds provided a slow motion strobe effect as the light and dark played across his bare arms and legs. His shirt disappeared in a movement so quick and fluid that I only saw it out of the corner of my eye. When he stopped directly in front of me, I blushed as my gaze caught a glimpse of his painfully tight shorts. His scent was stronger with his shirt off. I didn't know whether it was soap or shampoo or just him. But it smelled terrific.

He dropped to his knees and we were suddenly face to face. "You know what I like about you?" he asked with a warm smile.

I honestly couldn't imagine what *anyone* would like about me. I tried to say that, but I actually couldn't talk past the lump in my throat. It had been a really long time since I'd been this close to sex. I shook my head almost numbly.

"Your honesty." He must have seen my brow furrow in confusion, because he continued. "You don't try to hide anything. If you're angry, it's right out there in the open for the world to see. And when you're excited . . ." He reached forward and slid his fingers slowly along my jaw, brushed my ear and tickled my neck. "It captures every part of you."

He pulled me to him as he leaned in closer. The kiss was everything that I could have hoped for. His tongue teased and explored my mouth, then turned needy and demanding, causing shudders to pass through me in waves. I had thought that he would roll over me onto the couch but instead, he pulled me on top of him onto the floor. Well, okay, the bed would be softer, but who was I to complain?

His mouth moved to my neck and his hands to my braid. The fragrance was strongest along his jaw; clean and sharp, with hints of musk and citrus. I closed my eyes and just breathed, feeling his lips caress my neck. I slid my fingers though his hair and he returned the favor. Practiced fingers removed the little blue pony-tail holder and began to unplait my braid. He could do whatever he wanted as long as he didn't stop nibbling my ear.

He ran his hands through my hair over and over, easing the tangles, until it flowed like curly satin through his fingers. I'd never gotten such an erotic feeling from a man playing with my hair before. He pushed me up until I was sitting on his chest over him. His eyes were locked on mine as he slowly began to unbutton my blouse. My skin was covered with goose bumps by the time he slipped it from my shoulders and my breathing was deep and ragged.

He rolled me over so suddenly it took my breath completely. His hands smoothed across my stomach as he planted tiny kisses along the edge of my bra and then placed his whole mouth over my breast through the cloth and teased the nipple.

I gasped at the sensation and felt my hands clutch at his back. I began exploring the warm tanned expanse of his back and his silken hair as he pressed his hips against me firmly and wiggled until my legs moved apart.

The sound was so sudden that we both jumped—BANG, BANG, BANG. The whole front door vibrated with the force.

Tom turned his head and raised his nose to the air, his nostrils twitching slightly. "It's a man. I recognize the scent, but I can't place him."

But I recognized the pounding. I'd heard it enough times on the bathroom door when I was a kid.

"Oh, I know who it is. *Not now,* Joe." I yelled. Tom recognized the name and rolled over, too quickly. By the time I had the second word out, he was pulling on his clothing. I reached out my hand, intending to stop him. "Go *away!*"

"Mary Kathleen Reilly, open the goddamned door." Joe's roar was followed by more pounding.

"You told me your brother's as stubborn as you are, Kate. He's not going to take no for an answer." Tom whispered the words in my ear, kissed me gently, and handed me my top. But I could tell from his movements he was relieved at the interruption. I just wished I knew why.

The pounding resumed.

The metallic echoes were beginning to annoy me. "Just a *minute,* damn it!"

Tom was already dressed, so he rose and walked over to the door. He glanced over his shoulder to make sure I was fully clothed before unlatching the door. I was—sort of. My blouse was on, but it was buttoned crooked.

Joe stormed into the room with a glare for me. He turned to Tom with a full head of steam on. Whatever he'd intended to say died in his throat. His eyes widened and his jaw dropped open from shock. *"Who are you?"*

"None of your business, Joe! Who the hell were you expecting?" I knew it was a mistake the minute I said it.

"Dylan."

Tom's expression changed with the flick of a switch. His face flushed, his eyes narrowed and darkened to near black. The look he gave me could've frozen lava.

"*Joseph Reilly!* I haven't seen Dylan Shea in years and you know it!"

"But you kept his picture . . . and he called . . ."

"He called?" Tom's voice was suddenly cold with an edge like a razor.

"His wants me to meet with him for something." I willed Tom to understand. He didn't.

"Are you're going to do it?"

"I don't know." I admitted. "I honestly haven't decided."

Tom stared wordlessly at me for a long moment. Jealousy, anger and hurt were all rolled into the look. I didn't back down but I felt my face flush. Joe, mercifully, had fallen silent. He's tactless but not stupid.

"Maybe you were right. Maybe you *aren't* ready yet." Tom's voice was harsh with emotion, but I didn't know which one. He walked out without another word. The door slammed closed behind him, vibrating on its tracks from the force.

I let out a roar of rage and frustration.

Joe cringed. "Kate . . . I . . . I'll go catch him; talk to him. Uhm, whoever he is."

"The hell you will!" I snarled. "You've done enough damage for one day, thank you very much." I clenched my hands into fists and then kicked the wall hard enough for the pot hanging on the other side to fall and hit the floor. "*Damn it, Joe!* Tom Bishop was actually *interested* in me! Do you have any idea how long it's been since someone has looked past the leather and the weapons and wanted to spend time with *me?*" It sounded even bitchier than I'd intended it to.

Joe flinched as if I'd hit him. I didn't, but a part of me wanted to.

"I'm sorry, Kate. *Really* sorry." He looked sheepish and forlorn, despite the outfit he'd chosen. When he's not on duty at the hospital, Joe normally wears faded blue jeans and a plain white shirt. His hair is darker than mine, almost exactly the color of carrots. He keeps it very short so that he doesn't have to bother too much with it. Today he wore black jeans and a tight black T-shirt that showed every bulging muscle. Heavy black construction boots added a nicely menacing touch. The gel he used to spike his hair made me know that the choice of clothing wasn't accidental. The look was deliberately aggressive. Joe had obviously been planning to intimidate someone. Whether it was Dylan, me, or both was anyone's guess.

I took a deep breath and counted slowly to fifty. It didn't work.

"I'm going to take a shower."

I turned my back on my brother and went upstairs. As I opened the door to the master bath, I heard music start. Don Henley. Joe knows it's one of my favorites and is usually guaranteed to calm me down.

I turned on the water, shaking my head. I grabbed the shower cap from where I'd stuffed it with the bubble bath bottles under the sink. I have a lot of hair. Washing it would give me time to cool down, but it'd take hours to dry and I was not in the mood to deal with it.

As I got ready for the shower I tried to reason with myself. I knew Joe cared about me and was just trying to protect me.

That line of thought lasted until I stood up. The mirror showed the truth. My loose hair flowed around my face in thick waves. My lipstick was smeared across my chin. The mis-buttoned shirt made me feel like I'd been caught behind the bleachers. I *felt* like I'd been caught; interrupted. *DAMN* him! He had no right!

I slammed the cabinet door closed and stalked into the bedroom. A quick glance over the half-wall showed Joe tending my plants. He'd grabbed scissors and was snipping dead leaves. I wanted to bounce something off his head right now. I glanced around the room. My eye lit on the poor innocent wind-up alarm clock on the night stand. If it had known the fate of its predecessors, it would have hid under the bed like a smart clock. One quick swipe and a sudden throw with all of my serving strength made it all worthwhile. No, I didn't aim it at Joe, though God knew a part of me wanted to. The south wall of the bedroom was the target. The sharp sound of exploding plastic against the brick was followed closely by a bright 'bing'. A feeble death knell was last and then the shattered clock lay silent on the floor. I glanced over the wall to see Joe standing stock-still with his back to me. He carefully put down the scissors and darted for the kitchen. Point for me. It was childish, but satisfying.

I stepped into the bathroom, closed the bathroom door and stripped. I set the shower head to heavy massage and climbed in, sliding the glass door closed behind me. I stayed under the spray for a long time. I was hoping to relax my knotted shoulder muscles. There's nothing like interrupted sex to make a girl tense. The hot water heater gave out before the tension did. Not a big surprise. My anger with Joe was useless. He is what he is.

I was fairly confident I could convince Tom he had no competition from Dylan Shea. We *should* be able to get things back on track. If not, it was going to be a long and miserable lease.

I had been going to blow off Dylan's meeting, but now I might as well go. I was certainly in the mood for it. I replayed the message in my mind. No matter how hard I tried I could not pinpoint exactly what was wrong. But the message, coming at the same time as the incidents at the airport and the hospital set off alarm bells in my head. And speaking of alarm bells . . . .

I tossed the shower cap back into the cabinet and patted myself dry before wrapping my body in a towel. I grabbed the broom and dustpan from the linen closet and went out to the bedroom and swept up the remains of the clock and tossed it in the trash. Then I walked to the closet and reached up on the shelf for another clock. Hmm. Last one. I'd have to remember to pick up more.

I flipped through the clothes in my closet. What do you wear to meet with the man who you almost married who dumped you for your best friend? Of course I didn't have to meet with him. I could say no. Hell, I probably *should* say no. I tried to tell myself that just meeting with Dylan wouldn't do any harm. I didn't believe me. And I couldn't help remembering Dr. MacDougal's advice. When it came to the Thrall, ignorance was probably not going to be bliss.

I took a deep breath and began getting ready, deliberately taking my time. I needed to calm down before I went downstairs. It was hard. I was so very angry—at Joe, Dylan, and most of all, with myself. I was the one in control of my life, and I'd chosen to bury my head in my work rather than deal with my problems. And my problems might well kill me.

"Courage is doing what you're afraid to do. There can be no courage unless you're scared." I muttered Sister Elizabeth's favorite quote under my breath. I couldn't remember who originally said the quote. That would bother me all day until I remembered.

I kept worrying at it while I pulled on my clothes. Black underwear, black jeans, a black silk blouse. I even braided black and silver ribbons in my hair. The dark color made me look wan, so I washed my face and started over, choosing darker, more dramatic blush and lipstick. I looked grim—but grim was not a bad thing. Grim might get my brother to back off. We were certainly going to look like twin goths today. But it would keep Dylan from thinking this was anything but a business meeting. Not that I thought he would try anything. Last I had heard he and Amanda were happily co-habitating in the suburbs.

"Eddie Rickenbacker!" That's who said the quote.

I hadn't realized I'd said it out loud until Joe shouted "What?"

"Never mind." I came down the steps to find Joe staring at the newest photo on the wall.

"Where's Dylan's? It was here this morning."

"And now it's not. It's none of your business."

He motioned toward Tom's photo. "*That's* where I've seen him! Mr. August, right? Firehouse Eight?"

"Drop it, Joe."

"Kate . . ." Joe gave me an awkward, uncomfortable look. "I don't know if you know, but he's a *werewolf*."

"Yeah. So? You told me that it's not contagious."

"But . . ."

I gave him a long stare. He changed subjects. Smart man.

"You're going to the meeting." It wasn't a question. "Won't that piss off the new boyfriend?" That last was hopeful. He might not want me to pair off with Tom, but he wasn't above using the possibility to manipulate me into doing what he wanted.

"It isn't Tom's decision to make," I observed coldly. "It's not yours either."

Joe straightened to his full height in umbrage at my tone. He pulled his shoulders back and his eyes darkened. "You're not going alone." He glared at me. I didn't wither. I never do. You'd think he'd stop trying to intimidate me but he just can't seem to help himself. Joe was always bigger than everybody else through school. He's still big, but a lot of the rest of the kids we knew caught up with him. Me included.

He growled low in his throat, turned on his heel and stomped past me. He flung himself into his usual recliner with a viciousness that made the chair creak in protest. "I shouldn't have told you."

"You *didn't*, which I am incredibly ticked off about, by the way. Dylan called and left another message."

Joe used an oath he usually saves for special occasions. I wasn't shocked. I've heard it before. I use it more than he does.

"I can't believe you didn't just tell that bastard to go to hell."

"I did. Years ago."

"You know what I mean!" Joe's face flushed with anger so that the freckles all blended together.

"You don't have to come."

"Right." One word, but it was heavy with scorn.

My own eyes darkened. "If you're going to cause trouble . . ."

"I will *not* cause trouble."

"Your *word?*" That meant something in our family.

He hesitated, then his green eyes narrowed dangerously. "I give you my word."

"Good."

He looked me up and down. His features were heavy with disapproval. When he spoke, his voice was almost an octave lower than usual. "I can't *believe* you dressed up."

I didn't bother to explain. If he wanted to think I was trying to impress Dylan, fine. It was none of his damned business. I love Joe, but he can be an overbearing pain in the ass. More importantly, he doesn't know the "rules" for dealing with the bad guys. Having him around the Thrall would be a recipe for disaster. Of course we would be out in full daylight. And I didn't *know* the Thrall was involved. All I had were a series of unconnected incidents and that little trill of intuition. But until just these last couple of days both my past and the monsters had been leaving me pretty much alone. Having both resurface at once seemed a little too much of a coincidence. And I believe in being prepared. Especially since I could feel the hum of voices in the back of my head. Daylight or no, some of the hive were awake and aware. *That* was unusual enough to make me worry.

I opened the coat closet tucked under the stairs. It was going to be a warm day. I'd roast in my black leather biker jacket but decided to wear it anyway. Bernardo's is air conditioned. Better safe than sorry. Most clothing is just too thin to provide any protection against bites. Biker leathers are thicker and have lots of metal zippers and studs that catch at razor sharp fingernails and teeth. But there were more than just practical reasons for the outfit. I looked intimidating and I looked good. I might not want Dylan back, but a part of me wanted him to regret leaving me. Maybe not even such a small part.

"It's too hot for leather." Joe observed.

"I wish you were wearing some."

He rocked forward in the chair, giving me a long intent look. "Why?" That one word held a world of suspicion.

I shook my head. If I couldn't pinpoint my misgivings to myself how in the hell could I explain them to him? I turned my back to him so that he couldn't read my expression. "We'd better go."

"Kate?"

I didn't answer and he let it go. I was glad. He pulled himself up from the recliner, stretching in a way that made it clear he was as tense as I was. "Want to take my car?"

"Nah. We'll walk. Wouldn't be able to find parking any closer anyway."

He grunted in acknowledgment. When I pulled on the jacket, he didn't say a word.

It's a five-minute walk to Bernardo's. I play pool there at least once a week. Most of the neighborhood regulars know me by sight. They'll usually call friendly greetings. Not today. Joe and I got more than a few long stares and nervous glances. I suppose we looked dangerous. The closer we got to the pool hall, the more angry Joe became until the rage roiled in the air around him in an almost visible cloud. He'd given his word. He wouldn't *cause* trouble. That didn't keep him from hoping there'd be some.

We didn't say anything on the way there. I *was* doing this. He disapproved. There was no point in arguing. We turned the corner, crossed against the light, and there it was.

Bernardo's is housed in a section of LoDo that hasn't become trendy and upscale yet. It's a long, low red brick building and takes up most of the block. The only windows are high up on the walls and too small to be of any use; particularly since they haven't been washed since God was a baby. The grime is so thick it's almost impossible to make out the neon beer advertisements shining behind the glass. Zombies huddled in the shadows, their vacant eyes staring at nothing. The harsh sunlight made the neighborhood look even worse than it really is.

Bernardo's is neutral territory. You're liable to run into anything or anyone here—but the monsters will leave you alone so long as you're on the property. Once you're one inch outside however, you're on your own. It's not a place Joe would normally go, but it didn't frighten him the way it does most people. It's a dangerous place, and probably why I like it. There were no Hosts outside the building. I hadn't exactly expected any—but Dylan is Herd. What he knows, they know. Unless he was strong enough to deliberately block them from his thoughts. I didn't believe he was.

I checked my watch—12:30.

Joe's voice made me jump just a bit. "You're nervous," he said, his voice tense.

I thought about it a minute as I reached for the door handle. Was I nervous? Yeah. Part of it was my instincts acting up. Paranoia may or may not be part of my psychic abilities. In any event, I understand but don't always trust my instinct very well.

The Thrall are incredibly dangerous. They would not only know I was coming but what my next move was, unless I concentrated to prevent it. Another part was less pragmatic. It had been a long time since I'd seen Dylan. I want Tom. I think I'm over Dylan. But the fact is there *hasn't* been anyone in my life since him. It hurt so *damned* bad when he left me for *her*.

Amanda is everything I'm not: petite, dark and delicate. She looks exactly the way I wanted to when I was growing up. In school I caught a lot of crap for being over six foot with the shoulders of a linebacker. I used to slump and slouch, trying to minimize my height and shoulders. I outgrew that habit when I started watching the videotapes of my volleyball games. I *was* pretty damn good and everyone else was as tall as me.

Now I sort of like my build. Probably a good thing since there isn't much I can do about it. Regular work-outs, running and martial arts keep everything taut and toned. I'd started on a strict regimen back when I played. I've kept it up because I'm vain enough to appreciate how well my body has held up compared to the rest of my peers at our class reunion.

Joe gave a cough of annoyance, which brought my mind back to the present. Old, best-forgotten memories were making me spacey. I couldn't afford that. I needed my wits to be sharp and they just weren't. I opened the door and we stepped inside.

I blinked, letting my eyes adjust to the relative darkness. Even over the throbbing bass of the latest rap music I could hear the crack of billiard balls breaking and the murmur of voices. When I could see again, I looked around. There were plenty of patrons, but not a real crowd. I gave a friendly wave to Leo. I was glad Leo was the bouncer-slash-manager on duty. He's about 5'10", but built as solid as a brick wall. The prison-blue sleeve tattoos and eyebrow piercings give him character. His eyebrows and goatee are a medium brown. His head is shaved to a perfect, shining smoothness. He looks like the bad-ass he is. Not a bad thing in a bouncer. A lot of jerks think twice before causing trouble with Leo around. He probably qualifes as Prey to the Thrall, but nobody's ever bothered him.

His hands were full of empties as he walked toward us, giving an approving glance and nod to my clothes. Predators like other predators.

"How you doin', gorgeous? Been a few days." He leaned in and gave me a quick kiss on the cheek, keeping the half-full glasses safely away from me. It brought a look of disgust to Joe's face. He covered it before Leo saw. That's probably best. Joe probably never even noticed that Leo had sized him up, memorized him, and determined that he could kick his ass before a word was spoken.

"Just back from a run. This is my brother Joe."

Leo nodded briefly in his direction. "I sort of figured from the hair."

I motioned to the glasses in his hands. "Your bar-back not show up again?" Normally managers don't do the dishes here unless someone calls in sick.

He let out a frustrated sigh. "Him *and* the morning manager. Damned *kids*. The two little shits got in a money game last night and won. Them and their stakes spent the whole night celebrating. I was supposed to be off-shift an hour ago."

I winced. That's a long damn night. But I knew the morning manager. It's when I normally come in. "Bobby's a pretty good 9-ball player, though, Leo. He could make it to Vegas."

"Probably. That's what the boss says, too. But it doesn't wash my dishes or get me any shut-eye." I shrugged my condolences. He shook his head before moving off again.

I checked out the room and then steered a course to a bar box in the farthest corner of the building. It was the closest thing we were going to get to privacy and I like walls at my back. Joe followed without a word. The waitress appeared like magic as I was sliding quarters into the pool table. Joe ordered a beer for himself and a Coke for me. Diet was probably better for my health, but I was hoping that the combination of sugar and caffeine would give me back my edge.

I racked the balls. For the next half-hour or so Joe and I killed time playing 8-ball. He won.

At precisely 1:15 the front door swung open. Two men stood blinking in the doorway as their eyes adjusted. One of them was Dylan.

He still looked good. There was a little bit of gray in the wild black curls, and a few crinkles at the corners of sapphire blue eyes. It didn't detract a bit. He was wearing the brown leather bomber jacket I'd bought him a lifetime ago and worn blue jeans that were tight enough that I could tell he still went to the gym regularly. That startled me a little. He'd been a member of the Herd for a long time now. After one or two years most Herd members look like junkies and suffer from malnutrition. Maybe living in the farthest suburbs kept his master from calling him too often. Perhaps my negotiations with the queens had really saved him. Or maybe Monica was keeping him to use against me. There was no way of knowing.

I expected to feel a tug on the old heartstrings. I didn't. It was a welcome relief. I found myself wearing a genuine smile as the two of them got their bearings and headed back to our table.

"Thanks for coming." Dylan extended his hand and I shook it. "Sorry we're late." He grimaced, "I forgot how bad parking is down here. Good to see you, Joe." He gave his best dimpled smile to my brother who uttered a noncommittal grunt. Joe did at least thaw enough to shake the hand extended to him.

"No problem." I forced myself to hold on to the smile. It wasn't easy. Something about the man standing in Dylan's shadow bothered me. He was good looking in an ordinary way. Middle aged and well dressed in a navy suit that cost more than Edna and my motorcycle combined. His hair was thinning, but beautifully coiffed in an attempt to hide the fact.

His ice-blue eyes looked at me with distaste. Whatever he'd been expecting, I'd apparently lived down to it.

Joe glanced at the man and raised his eyebrows just a bit. I didn't know why, but it seemed significant, because he looked . . . well, *impressed.* I let the smile slide from my face, leaving my eyes hard and cold. I didn't really care who he was, but I didn't like the feel and smell of him. Expensive cologne couldn't quite cover . . . something. He made the hairs on the back of my neck stand on end. I didn't ignore the psychic scream of warning. I'm alive because of my instincts and my power. Oh, and brains. The brains help.

A nervous tic had started above Dylan's left eye. It was obvious he was tense but his voice was controlled as he made the necessary introductions. "This is my brother-in-law Matt Quinn. He's Amanda's brother. Matt, this is the woman I told you about."

My eyes widened and I felt Joe stiffen beside me. I felt light pressure as Joe lightly gripped my arm. But he didn't need to stop me, or even console me. While I hadn't realized Dylan and Amanda had married, it was logical. And it's not like I would have received an invitation. Still, I was surprised at my own lack of reaction. I had expected . . . well, *something.* But I felt no hate, no sadness or anger. I would be more upset if Gerry Friedman got married than I was at hearing Dylan had.

Matt extended a leather gloved hand and I took it. "Nice to meet you, Mr. Quinn."

"*Councilman* Quinn, Ms. Reilly. Your duly elected representative, I believe. I surmised from Dylan that you live nearby and this is my district." Ah, so that's why Joe had raised an eyebrow. He reads the papers more than me. I shook his hand and managed not to snort derisively. So he was a city councilman—big whoop. I'm not much interested in politics. But I *was* interested in why he was wearing gloves on a warm July afternoon. It was odd, and I felt another prickle on the back of my neck.

Dylan was babbling on, oblivious. "His daughter is missing."

That would make the girl Amanda's niece. It took a moment, but I thought I remembered her. I could vaguely recall a young blonde girl coming to visit Amanda, back when we used to be friends. The girl couldn't be more than fifteen or sixteen now.

"I want you to find her." Matt's voice was heavy with the authority money and power give in the "real" world. Money and power don't impress me much. Matt could sense it. It didn't make him happy.

"*I* want her safe." Dylan said softly.

I gave Dylan a wry smile. Found and safe can be two *very* different things.

"How long has she been gone?"

"Three days." Matt answered.

"The police haven't had any luck?"

Dylan shrugged. It was a gesture that said nothing, and everything. She might be fine. Some runaways are. Most aren't.

"How old?" I asked, even though I thought I already knew. Dylan answered. "Sixteen."

Yep, it was the one I remembered. "Picture?"

Matt reached into the pocket of his jacket and withdrew an elegant leather wallet. He pulled a photo out of a thin plastic sleeve. It was old enough that the blue background was getting that greenish tinge, and the surface was cracking. The kid in the picture looked to be about ten years old. An angelic looking blonde with wide blue eyes stared out from one of the generic school photographs kids hate. I absolutely remembered her now, but the picture was useless six years later.

"You don't have anything more recent?"

He glared at me. I was supposed to wither. I didn't. Instead, I handed the picture back.

"She's gone goth." Dylan announced.

I tried to convert the white lace schoolgirl in the photograph to a teenager with oddly dyed hair and body piercings. It wasn't easy. She could look like anything. But it explained why Matt didn't have pictures. Goth would not be a style that made him happy. It was, no doubt, why the kid had done it.

"Name?"

"Her name is Becky." The brother-in-law's voice was heavy with disapproval. Which probably meant that the kid went by something else. Becky is too vanilla for a goth.

"What's her street name?" I asked Dylan. He might not know, but sometimes a semi-cool uncle gets confidences a stuffed-shirt stepfather doesn't.

"Dusty." Matt spit the word out like an obscenity.

I looked over at Dylan. He appeared to be counting to ten, or maybe fifty. I didn't blame him. His brother-in-law was an ass. Still, if Dylan thought the girl wasn't ready to be on the street she probably wasn't. Probably. I would at least check. Make sure she was still alive.

"I want her safe." Dylan repeated.

Matt glared at him and turned the cold steel gaze to me. "*I* want her *back*."

My eyes locked with Dylan's. "I can only do so much." It was a warning. The girl could be gone or dead. More people die in this town than make the news. Street people and runaways can and do disappear without a trace.

"Try?" Dylan was begging. It made me frown. First, it wasn't like him. Too, it reminded me of feelings I'd rather forget.

"No promises."

He agreed. "No promises."

"All right. But I'm going to need a few things."

"Like what?" He grinned at me then, sapphire eyes sparkling. For just a moment there was a glimmer of the old magic.

"How much?" Matt's voice cut between Dylan and me like a knife: cold, startling and a little bit painful.

"Excuse me?"

Matt had his wallet out. He was thumbing through a sheaf of bills thick enough to get him rolled. Even though it was mid-day and neutral territory, it wouldn't keep the human predators at bay. A junkie with a gun can kill you just as dead as a Host or werewolf. At Bernardo's, it's even a hell of a lot more likely.

"Matt!" Dylan was shocked—not only by the offer, but the

tone. He shot me an apologetic look. I shrugged to show him I wasn't insulted, although I did have the right to be.

"What?" That one word from Quinn was both defiant and aggressive.

I interrupted the glaring contest between them, and started reciting a list of what I would need to find the girl. "I'll need a copy of Dusty's most recent yearbook, and the names and addresses of her friends, if you know them. If she hadn't gone goth when school pictures were taken, a *recent* picture would help. I'll also need a phone number where I can contact you to let you know what I find out." I spoke to Dylan, ignoring the asshole brother-in-law. From the corner of my eye I saw Matt's face flush. Apparently he wasn't used to being ignored. He was insulted. Aw, darn.

Dylan pulled a business card and a pen from his pocket. He scrawled his home and cell phone numbers on the back. "I want her safe." He handed me the business card.

It was the third time he'd said that. His voice was almost panicked and his eyes a little too wide. I reached out and touched his hand. The minute my skin contacted his, he flinched. He jerked back and tried to pull away. I held on tight and tried to concentrate.

The minute they felt me, they fell silent. The Thrall was involved somehow. And they knew I knew.

What in the hell was I getting into?

"Katie, what's wrong?" Joe's hand fell onto my shoulder. "You've gone white as a sheet."

"Dylan," I spoke very carefully. "I am Not Prey. You *cannot* lie to me."

His hand twisted and squirmed in mine like a captured snake. "I haven't lied, Katie. I swear." He was just suddenly sweating, beads of water appearing like magic on his forehead.

"Kate?" Joe's voice had deepened by almost half an octave till it was a rumbling bass.

Matt stood up from the table, his expression sour. "I need to get back to work. *You*," he glared at Dylan, "need to get back to your *wife*." He took one menacing step forward. Joe stepped in front of him, blocking his way. I felt, rather than saw, Leo coming toward us. My focus was Dylan. Either Joe or Leo would take care of Matt.

"Is there a connection between your brother-in-law and the Thrall?" The tension that sang through his arm told the tale.

"I won't stand here and be insulted." Matt snarled.

"Then go." Joe suggested. "Nobody here's stopping you." Matt gave my brother a long, assessing look. He apparently decided that Joe was too tough to take on because he gave a growl of frustration before turning on his heel and stomping off to the door and out of the bar.

"Katie, I . . ." Dylan's voice was a hoarse whisper as he tried to speak.

I felt a flash of intense pain through the connection I'd created with Dylan. A crushing headache was coming on as Monica fought to assert dominance over Dylan's mind. Tears streamed from his sapphire blue eyes and his knees buckled. I had to catch him to keep him from falling to the floor. I steered him clumsily to the nearest chair. He collapsed into it, leaning forward so that an elbow was on each knee and his head was between his legs.

Physical contact makes the psychic bond stronger, so I squatted in front of his seat and took one of his hands in both of mine.

"Dylan, why do they want me?"

He opened his mouth. He fought to speak, his face contorting with the effort. The pain was blinding. As clearly as if she were in the room, I could hear Queen Monica's voice. "Tell her *nothing!*"

Answer enough. I released his hand.

"I'm sorry, Katie." Dylan whispered. He looked up, his eyes locking with mine. "I'm so sorry."

"I know. So am I."

He reached forward and grasped my hand once more. "I'm so glad you're safe." He struggled against their control to whisper to me. "They tried to wreck you yesterday, but I knew you'd get away . . ."

His body slumped forward as he gave up a fight he

couldn't win. I thought back to the one-ton truck with the trailer. Had that been intentional? I would have asked Dylan, but he had gone still and motionless as the Thrall called to him, weakened him until there was nothing left of his own personality. I leaned forward and kissed his forehead. It was a maternal gesture, and a pitying one. I stood. He didn't look up.

"Leo." Leo moved around Joe to stand next to me. He looked down at Dylan, rubbing his hands along his tattooed arms as if suddenly cold.

"He gonna be all right?"

"Probably not." My voice was tired and sad. Dylan had made his bed, but I wasn't happy seeing him lie in it. I reached into my back pocket and withdrew my wallet. I pulled out a twenty and handed it to Leo. "Give him a couple of shots of whiskey. I'm going to call his wife."

Joe stared at me wide-eyed, and Dylan started shaking his head no.

I squatted down next to Dylan and looked into his panicked eyes. "You're in no condition to drive."

Nobody disputed it. Dylan might have, if he could have talked. But he couldn't. So I pulled the cell phone out of my jacket pocket and dialed the home number listed on his card.

Amanda answered on the third ring. I didn't waste time on pleasantries and neither did she. I explained the situation and told her the list of items I needed that I'd given Dylan in case he didn't remember when he came to.

"I want to talk to him."

I wasn't sure Dylan could talk but I passed the phone to him anyway. Leo was back with the shots and my change. I tipped him, and he hurried off. It was almost as though we'd spooked him. Surely not.

"Are *you* going to be all right? You look like hell." Joe spoke softly so that Dylan wouldn't hear.

"I'll let you know when I find out." I gave him a wry grin that earned me a scowl.

"Don't joke. Not about this."

"Why not? We don't *know* what's going on."

"Maybe not, but *something's* happening. Otherwise why would their Queen have attacked you in the hospital yesterday?"

"If I knew what was going on I'd tell you. I'm being careful, Joe." I gestured toward the leather jacket I was wearing for emphasis. "I'll check around; try to see if anyone has any information, but I'm not going to panic." I gave a long sigh. "But I sure as hell don't look forward to running into Amanda. That's something I'd avoid if I could."

"Then go." Joe suggested. "I'll babysit Dylan. We can meet back up at your place."

"No. Thanks, but no." Call it a hunch, but something told me that I needed to stay. Amanda wasn't a Host or even Herd so far as it went but if it had to do with the Thrall, she was in it up to her pretty arched eyebrows.

Joe's eyes narrowed, but he didn't argue. He also didn't leave. Apparently he considered himself my bodyguard. Kind of silly, but he is my big brother.

It was forty minutes later when I saw Amanda walk through the door. It wasn't a fun forty minutes. It's hard to concentrate on a pool game when there's a drooling man half-comatose on the floor. There isn't much else to do in a pool hall, so we sat and drank and talked, after first propping Dylan up against the wall. We'd tried to help him keep his dignity by sitting him in a chair. But he kept falling over and bonking his head. I told myself it would be funny a year from now over drinks.

The air almost crackled around Amanda when she stalked through the bar. She'd always been strong-willed, but there was an aura of power that hadn't been there when I last saw her. She looked good. She'd held onto the whole tiny stacked cheerleader thing she had going in high school. I'd expected to feel . . . something. Again, my lack of reaction surprised me.

"What the *hell* do you think you're doing with my husband?" she snarled, repeating the same question she'd asked on the phone. The answer hadn't changed. That she was *jealous* of *me* was just weird. Wow.

I saw Joe's back go up and I reached over to squeeze his leg to silence him. He wouldn't buy it. He has even less restraint than I do.

"I think a better question would be why is your husband begging to see Kate?" Green fire flashed in my brother's eyes and I sighed.

Amanda's head spun in my brother's direction, "Dylan would never beg to see Kate!"

"Oh, no?" Joe shot back. "Five messages in two days. Yeah, I'd say he was begging." I gave Joe a hard look. Needling Amanda was not going to improve this situation.

Amanda took a menacing step forward. I stood. She shoved past me, dropping to her knees next to Dylan. A second later, she noticed the condition of the carpeting, sticky with spills and ground-in dirt, so she changed to a squatting pose with a look of disgust.

"Dylan! Wake up and tell me what the hell is going on!" I winced as she slapped him hard across the face. I knew it was the best way to pull him out of the trance but I didn't have to like that she seemed to enjoy it. She was about ready to deliver a second blow when I grabbed her arm.

"Dylan called me to help Matt find Dusty." I said quietly. I was hoping to avoid a big confrontation. I'd hate to get bounced out on my ear by Leo. Bernardo's is one of my favorite haunts.

Her brow furrowed and I had to admit it did my heart good to see the wrinkles she was trying to hide with her brunette bangs. "Who?"

"Your niece, Becky. She goes by Dusty now. But I think his contacting me has something to do with Dylan's *masters,* too."

I forced myself not to grit my teeth. It's none of my business, but seeing him so helpless . . . I can't imagine how Amanda can actually believe that it's not only okay for Dylan to be a Herd member, but actually believes it's *beneficial.* Like death from parasite-related anemia is a good thing.

She yanked her arm out of my grasp. "Queen Monica would never send Dylan to you."

She used Monica's name the way a Brit would say "Queen Elizabeth."

"You're absolutely right." My agreement surprised her. "Who do you think made Dylan into a drooling zombie, Amanda? He contacted me without her say-so."

The implication was clear. To hide an action from a group mind took a huge effort. That Dylan had been willing to risk Monica's fury meant that whatever he was up to was very important to him.

Amanda's eyes narrowed into slits. She sprang up from her crouch directly at me fast enough to take me by surprise. I didn't even have time to back up before her hands were around my neck.

"You lying *BITCH!*" she screamed. Her nails dug into my flesh and I gasped. Joe leapt to his feet and immediately grabbed her around the waist and tried to pull her away. It was obvious she worked out, and hard. Ropes of rock-hard muscle appeared under the thin skin of her arms. She kicked backward and caught him in the stomach, pushing him onto the floor beside Dylan.

Amanda pressed me against the table. Her fingers tightened, cutting off my air. I was off-balance enough that I would fall if I used my hands to fight her. Hmmm. I tensed all the muscles in my neck and shoulders so she would have to work to choke me. Then I raised my arms and let her momentum carry us backwards. The table tipped, hovered and then fell out from under us as I rolled sideways, carrying Amanda with me.

Her hands loosened but she didn't let go entirely. She'd been training. Fortunately, those few seconds were all I needed. In mid-air I raised one foot, braced it against her stomach, slid my hands up her arms and grasped her wrists. I tore them away from my neck at the same time that I pushed against her stomach with my foot. She catapulted over the top of me. A crash, followed closely by a scream, sounded behind me and a nine ball slammed into my shoulder. That's the problem with fighting in a pool hall. Someone's bound to end up on a table.

I rolled to my stomach and coughed until I retched. I really hate being choked. I used a nearby bar stick to raise me to my feet. I held it crossways to protect myself while I tried to find Amanda's position. Problem two with fighting in a pool hall—an overabundance of weapons.

I didn't have to worry. Amanda lay prone on the bar table across the aisle from our table. Balls lay scattered on the green felt around her and probably under her. Even if she didn't crack a rib, she'd be sore for a week. She was breathing raspily and moaned slightly, but I still didn't get close enough to check on her. Instead, I stood over her with the pool cue at the ready.

I felt a presence behind me and spun around, stick raised to strike. Leo had finally entered the fray. He grabbed the cue quicker than I could move and yanked it out of my grasp.

"Knock it off, Reilly." His voice was the stern growl of a professional bouncer.

I opened my mouth to explain . . . and broke into giggles. Leo's brow furrowed. I guess he wasn't used to fighters laughing after he'd broken up a brawl.

"Sorry," I gasped when I could breathe. "But the first words out of my mouth were going to be, 'well, *she* started it.'"

A wry smile turned up one corner of his mouth. "Then I guess my line is, 'and I'm finishing it.'" He pushed me an arms-length back and helped Amanda to her feet.

"Take your man and *go*," he commanded after he was sure she could stand. "And if the slate on this table is cracked, you're getting a bill."

Amanda's eyes went wide and her mouth opened. Then storm raged again across her face. "If that table is broken you can send the bill to *Kate,* thank you very much! I'm the injured party here!"

Leo crossed massive arms over his chest. "No. You were the aggressor. Kate took care of your man until you got here and then you attacked her. I'm not stupid. I've been watching the whole scene since you walked in." He turned and pointed toward the door. His voice raised until it was a bellow. Grown men have quaked in their boots at that voice. "Now, if you don't get your ass *out* of here and take that drooling zombie of yours with you, I'll call the cops so fast your head will spin!"

9

I helped Leo clean up the place after Amanda left. Joe wanted to be a big brother and follow me around all day but I had no intention of letting him. So I lied. I told him that I was going to go back to my loft, and I would . . . eventually.

Whether he actually believed me or not, he gave in. I think the way I dealt with Amanda had opened his eyes a bit to what I was capable of. Or he had his own agenda. I'd like to think the former, but the latter was far more likely. Still, you know what they say about gift horses. I'd get more done, quicker, without my brother dogging my heels and I needed information, fast.

With that in mind, I headed toward the center of downtown. The 16th Street mall runs from Civic Center Station by Colfax a couple of miles down to Wynkoop. It's the beating heart of the downtown area. They've closed it to all but pedestrian traffic and the shuttle buses that run north and south along a central boulevard with street vendors, seating, and the occasional fountain. The shuttle is free, with stops on every corner. It's always crowded with an eclectic mix of business and street people; going to work or going nowhere.

I seldom take the shuttle; it's too crowded and despite the

bus company's best efforts—including video surveillance—I know of more than a few people who've had their pockets picked. Walking is good exercise, and it gives me a chance to see people.

I've made friends with most of the regular street vendors. Pete's my favorite, for a very particular reason. He's a small man, probably only 5'2", if that. Today he was wearing his standard uniform: jeans, a Rockies baseball cap, sunglasses, baggy Hawaiian print shirt over a sparkling white undershirt and faded jeans. He sells overpriced sunglasses from a wheeled wooden cart that sits in the center island between Stout and Curtis streets. I have a bad habit of losing sunglasses, so I visit him often. Today, I was hoping to pick up both a pair of shades and information.

"Hey, Pete."

"Uh, Kate. You're back." He didn't sound happy to see me, which was unusual enough that I commented on it.

"It's just . . ." Pete looked around nervously, licking his lips. "Monica . . ."

I nodded. "Yeah, I know. Monica wants me dead. But the queens are taking care of it."

Pete's lifted his sunglasses so that I could see the earnestness in his beady brown eyes. "You're joking, right? No, Kate, you're confused. Monica wants you *alive*. And I sure as fuck wish I could say that the queens were controlling her. It's getting a bit dicey for me to even be seen with you."

He stared at me intently, *willing* me to understand. My mind went back to Monica's words in the hospital: "*I want you dead. But not quite yet. I have other plans for you first.*"

Pete dropped his shades and turned away. He didn't look at me, but began wiping fingerprints from a pair of glasses as he spoke in a near whisper. "She had somebody else picked out, but the girl up and disappeared. The replacement the queens sent is dead; and *they don't know how she did it.*"

I heard "girl" and "disappeared." My warped brain immediately tied it to the pretty blue-eyed blonde in the photo. I didn't have any proof but it made sense. Amanda might think the Thrall was a godsend. I was pretty sure Dylan didn't. As

Herd he'd know if Monica had plans for Dusty. He'd also know their plans for me. Was he setting me up? I tried to think clearly, but terror had tied my stomach in knots. The queens couldn't contain Monica? What had she *become?* I felt my head moving from side to side and I felt cold in the warm July sun.

"Not only no, but hell no. Not only *hell* no. *Fuck* no. No way. I am *not* playing Host to one of those *things*. I'd *rather* be dead."

"You're thinking too small, girl. No mere Host for you. Uh-uh."

His words made it crystal clear. She wanted me to be queen. It was finally her time and now it was my turn. Mine or Dusty's. Monica would *know* that adamant refusal would be my reaction, which is why it would be the perfect revenge, but also why she had a back-up. She'd been smart enough to try to drug me first—suicide was *not* supposed to be an option.

"You should leave town."

I took a slow, deep breath. I wouldn't panic. I *would not* panic. "Leaving town would be running, Pete. Prey run. I am Not Prey." I heard my voice as if from a distance. It sounded strangled and almost a full octave higher than usual.

"Prey, Not prey, who gives a fuck?"

I took another deep breath. When I spoke again I managed to sound calm. Nothing could make me feel it. I was terrified. My pulse thundered, pumping adrenaline and blood through my veins.

"If I run I am Prey. They can hunt me down and kill me like an animal. If I am *Not* Prey they have to treat me as an equal." I said it as much to reassure myself as to educate him. Because right now I needed reassurance.

"Better you than me." He shook his head. "Shame you couldn't have been out of town a couple more days. Then the whole thing would've gone down without you winding up in the middle of it."

"I should be so lucky." I grabbed a pair of sunglasses from the cart at random, and pulled out my wallet. I let him keep the change from the twenty. The warning he'd just given me was worth at least ten times that much. But oddly, an offer to pay more would probably have insulted him.

"Thanks Pete."

He gave me a look that held pity and worry in equal doses. "Watch your back, Katie—watch it like a son-of-a-bitch."

"I will. Believe me!"

I pulled on the glasses and turned back the way I came. Despite the sunshine and the heavy black leather, I was cold. I felt . . . exposed and, damn it all, terrified. What I most wanted was to get home and get my neck guard on. The zippered leather jacket would protect my arms long enough for me to fight. The inner thigh . . . they'd have to have me pinned or unconscious to get me there. But my neck was vulnerable right now and that was terrifying. Because one little nip is all it takes for them to be able to use their mind control on you. Strength of will was all that had saved me when Monica chomped onto my leg last time—and she'd just been a baby.

A sudden hand on my arm made me reach to where my knives should be, but of course they weren't there. What in the hell had I been thinking? The answer to that, of course, was that I hadn't. Been thinking, that is. I'd been too distracted by Tom and pissed at my brother. I mentally kicked myself for being an idiot and prayed that I'd actually *live* to regret the mistake since dead or infested I wouldn't *regret* anything.

I spun on my heel to face . . . Morris Goldstein. He jumped back a half-step, as if startled by my hostile reaction. He coughed slightly, covering his mouth with a pudgy hand. "Ah! Ms. Reilly! I'm so pleased you're back from Paris. You were on your way to see me?"

Morris is one of the least threatening men I've ever met. Short and balding beneath his skullcap, with hazel eyes made wider by thick square glasses. His suits are perpetually rumpled, and his English, while good, is very heavily accented.

"Actually," I started to argue, but Morris had already tucked my arm into his and was pulling me down the mall in the direction of his office. I'm almost a full foot taller than him, but the pace he set was fast enough that I was actually struggling to keep up.

He was talking a mile a minute, the words a blur of Hebrew-accented English.

"Marta has been trying to reach you all morning! We need you to go to Tel Aviv at once. Such luck I have to run into you! I've acquired the most amazing stone! It's a 2.37 carat D-flawless, just arrived from a small town in Arkansas. Found by an elderly tourist—never in my life—purchased it for a song. I'm certain it will be very soft on the wheel to become a stunning pear cut. Yes, yes, God is on my side! One package to deliver and another to bring back."

He was still babbling about his latest find as we reached the Diamond Exchange Building where he has his office blocks down the street. Whew! I was breathless, and I wasn't even the one doing the talking.

Always the gentleman, he had me precede him into the elevator. He chattered all the way up to the eighth floor, mostly scolding me about my absence of jewelry. He punched the series of numbers that unlocked the outer office door, then held it open for me. Marta was not at her desk. He called out, but there was no answer. He frowned, stepping behind the desk to look at her computer. He furrowed his brow and then looked at the printer. His eyes widened and he smiled. "Ah! The ink has finished. She must have gone to the supply room in the back."

He bounded around the desk once more and moved me toward one of the plush cushioned chairs. "Sit. Sit, and I will call the cutter to tell them you arrive Wednesday. Marta will return shortly. You will wait, yes?"

I glanced at my sports watch, and frowned. "I really don't have much time."

"Of course, of course! You're a busy woman. I know this. Please, just spare an old man a few moments." His expression was exaggeratedly woeful, but the effect was spoiled completely by the bright sparkling eyes behind his glasses.

"I suppose." I didn't want to. I wanted to go home. But I really couldn't afford to alienate one of my best clients. I thought about the stack of bills on the desk, and then about

Monica. I'd give him ten minutes. No more. "But *just* a few minutes. I really do have another appointment." An appointment with my closet and my weapons.

Morris nodded assent before scurrying in to the inner office.

I took off my sunglasses to look around and tucked them into the pocket of my jacket. The front office of G&S Jewelry Design hadn't changed much since my last visit. Very "office neutral." The actual "work" is done in a workroom discreetly sealed off behind Morris's personal office and guarded by a formidable security system. This was the public face of the business. The walls were pale dove gray, the carpet a deep turquoise. There was one difference. A brightly colored Monet print had been replaced with an expensively framed article from a jewelry industry magazine. I stood and walked over to get a better look.

I could hear Goldstein's voice booming from his office. He was speaking Hebrew.

When I started getting regular runs to Israel I had decided to learn Hebrew. With my looks, it's not something most people would expect—but it's come in *very* handy. Without even meaning to, I found myself translating the conversation I was overhearing.

"Ken, ani amtin." (Hello. Yes, I'll hold.)

I forced my attention back to the article. It was a personal profile of Morris Goldstein, and spoke very highly of his ability to see a rough stone and determine what the final cut and size will be before it gets to the scaife. Unique talent, that.

"Ken, ken. He kan. Lo, lo Raiti. He loveshet meil" (Yes, yes. She's here. No, I didn't see any. She is wearing a jacket.)"

That perked up my ears. The cutters know and like me but they would not give a jolly goddamn about my wardrobe—except possibly my jewelry. I glanced at my watch again. It was almost eleven o'clock at night in Tel Aviv. My stomach lurched and my mouth went dry. Who in the *hell* was Morris talking to?

"Ani yachol Le-aker ota Le-reva shaaa, avl Atta tzarich le-maher Ani Hoshev sh-Araba-atenu hochel Le-hishtalet alia." (I can probably stall her for another fifteen minutes, but you must hurry. I would think that between the four of us we can control her.)

Yep. There was that nasty tingling again. I was being set up. Steeling myself against the upcoming onslaught, I opened my senses completely as I heard Goldstein leave his office. There was an angry buzzing in my head and then the murmur of a hundred voices. Damned if he wasn't a Host! I'd never noticed! Then again, I hadn't seen him in person for nearly four months.

I debated simply being gone when he arrived in the lobby. But no, that would be running.

Goldstein was beaming his usual smile when he reappeared. "Good news! The shipment from Sierra Leone has arrived and the stones should be cut by Wednesday."

I kept my body loose but ready. I didn't know what he would do next so I needed to be prepared for anything. My smile probably had a sinister edge.

I chose my words carefully. *"Atta Tovmeoz meod. Lo Hay-iti Choshedet. Aval Atta Yachol Le-Msor La-Malka Shelcha sh-ani lo chelck me-ha-eder sk-he osseffet."* (You're very good. I never would have suspected. But you may tell your *queen* that I am not part of the Herd to be *collected*.)

Goldstein froze. He began to sweat profusely as his Thrall and through him the queen realized that I not only spoke Hebrew but knew their plan.

My voice was cold and harsh as I continued in English. "Monica, I will deal with you on my terms in my own time. Make no mistake that any of your children who try to control me will pay dearly for it."

I slammed down my mental shields. I started listening to heavy metal songs in my head, reciting the periodic table, anything that took concentration so the Thrall wouldn't be able to read my mind. I half-expected Morris to try to stop me when I turned on my heel to leave, but he seemed frozen in place. That happens sometimes when the Host tries to fight off the Thrall parasite's commands. It's different than what happened to Dylan, but has a similar outward appearance. Once upon a time Morris had been my friend and I appreciated his effort. I'd have hated to have to kill him.

I'd no more than stepped in the hall when the elevator bell dinged. Taking no chances, I ducked into the stairwell. A full eight flights to reach the ground. Ick. I took the stairs two at a time. I considered finding another floor and taking the elevator down but frankly, they would probably think of that. An access door opened above me, and I heard feet thundering down the stairs toward me.

I gripped the handrails and tried a tactic that was both quicker and quieter, sliding down the flights using the handrails the way Bryan and I had when were kids. It takes a long reach and good upper body strength. By the time I'd done four flights my left shoulder was giving me hell. Thank God there were only two more floors between me and the ground. The footsteps stopped. They were listening for me. Their hearing is almost as good as a lycanthrope's. I felt a prickle at the back of my mind as they searched with their minds for mine. I gripped the handrail tighter, stopping my descent. I hovered in mid-air two flights below my pursuers, deliberately concentrating on composing a thank-you note to my old coach for insisting on parallel bar training to strengthen my triceps.

Two more steps and they stopped again. After more agonizing moments, the steps retraced upward and an access door opened and closed. I hovered for another full minute, ignoring the knifing pain that let me know the shoulder wouldn't stand for much more. Were they both gone? I just didn't know.

I carefully lowered myself down and stood silently, listening for any movement; any breath. I didn't dare open my senses. If there was still someone above me, it would be like sounding an air horn in the echoing stairwell. On my tiptoes, I eased one boot down onto the next step, using the far corner of the tread, where the rubber was still new and silent. Twice more and I reached the landing. I silently leaned over and rubbed my hands on the floor. There was just enough dust from previous shoes to lightly coat my hands. I carefully removed my watch, tucked it into my front jeans pocket and pushed up the sleeves of my jacket, so the zippers wouldn't contact the metal handrail. They wouldn't cooperate, and kept falling down to my knuckles.

Ah, the hell with it! If anyone heard, I'd deal with it then. Grasping the handrails, I slid down quickly and nearly silently. Nobody followed.

I didn't stop at the lobby, but went down the extra floor to the parking level. I'd fight if I had to, but without weapons, and with my shoulder giving me hell it was a risk I'd rather not take.

I carefully opened the door to the garage. It was cool and silent. Here I could safely open my senses. Unless someone were in the structure with me, the thick concrete would block my telepathy. No buzzing, no headache. I was alone. My bootsteps echoed off the parked cars, but I didn't care. I just wanted bright sunshine and people around me. I bent almost double to get under the crossing barrier, and the guard gave me a strange look, but I was out! I walked quickly down the shadowed street. Now, back to the house for my neck guard and every knife in the drawer.

"Psst. Kate!" The hiss of a familiar voice caught my attention. I glanced into the souvenir store to my left and saw Dylan frantically motioning me inside. He pulled my arm and took me to the back of the store. We knelt down behind the racks of overpriced, cheesy T-shirts with pictures of baby wildlife and pithy sayings, sporting "Always Buy Colorado" labels.

I had to gasp when I finally got a look at him. He was transformed—no longer a sweating, shaking mess. He seemed confident and intense.

"My God! Dylan, what's happened to you?"

He shushed me with a look as his eyes raked the area. "We have to do this fast. They'll know I'm missing soon. Here!"

He shoved two photographs into my hands. The first was of a group of kids admiring a tricked out Mini Cooper. The second was a pair of dour looking teens trying to act cool and goth. Both photos had been taken from a distance. You could just make out features. He pointed to the painfully thin girl in a long black skirt, sporting Jell-O green hair and white lipstick. "That's Dusty last year. I think she's gone to pink or red hair this year. The girl next to her in the tie-dye cropped shirt is her best friend, Voneen. I remember Dusty mentioning that she thought it was cool that Voneen had her own place. It was somewhere over on East Colfax near Clarkson Street by that triple X theatre. If Dusty went anywhere, it was probably to Voneen's."

Wow! That was the last section of town where I would have looked for them. I knew the place he referred to, but couldn't remember the name. It was something like Nancy's Pleasure Castle. . . . It's a twenty-four-hour triple X arcade and book store, with attached lounge and theater. It covers about a full city block. I'd heard there were some sleeping rooms above the lounge, but never had the nerve to go look. I was afraid I would catch something really icky.

I saw movement and felt a touch on my hair. In my somewhat paranoid state, I immediately lashed out to strike. But Dylan was quicker. He grabbed my wrist in a blur. My heart lurched in my chest as I realized how he'd managed his "miraculous" change.

I looked into those sapphire eyes and croaked, "*Why?* For God's sake, Dylan—how *could* you? I can't believe you'd let one of those *things* . . ." I couldn't believe he'd actually taken that last step and become a Thrall Host.

He smiled sadly. "It's not what you think, Katie. Vickie isn't like Monica. But I couldn't fight Monica's influence without help."

"But you'll *die*." I felt tears well up and hated it: hated that he could still move me to tears.

He reached out and touched my hair, stroking a gentle finger down my face to push away an errant strand. "I'd forgotten how beautiful your hair is."

I frowned and pulled at my arm, but he wouldn't release it. "Don't change the subject, Dylan."

An amused hint of a smile curled one side of his mouth. "I'm *not* changing the subject, Katydid."

The familiar endearment cut through me like a knife, but I couldn't seem to get any words out of my mouth.

"I don't want Monica to have Dusty, and I don't want her to have *you*. I want you alive, and happy and with me for the rest of my life. I've been checking around. Vickie treats her people right. One of her Hosts is still healthy after twelve years."

His words were a buzz in my head. Even with him touching me, I couldn't feel the Thrall Host inside him. "With you?" I finally blurted. "That's insane. What are you talking about?"

He gently traced a warm line down my jaw and I felt my body react. His face grew serious. "Just what I said. I was a fool, Katie. I've regretted what I did every waking moment for the past two years. I've never loved Amanda like I loved you. I hurt you, and I can't tell you how sorry I am. But I want to make it up to you." He suddenly looked lost. "I . . . I mean . . . oh, *hell!*"

He moved forward like liquid and pressed his mouth to mine. His hand reached behind my head and pulled me tight against him. His tongue slid in between my lips before I could breathe. Then I was lost in the feel of his jaw moving against mine, lost in the sweet, familiar taste of the man I used to love. The careful shell that I'd constructed around my heart was cracking. He held my wrist tight in his and I could feel a fine trembling running through strong new muscles. My other hand was trapped against his rock-hard chest.

But I was terrified that if I searched with my tongue, I'd find fangs behind his teeth. I tried to pull away, but the fingers sliding through my hair held me like steel. The kiss was hungry, needy, and part of me was reminded of nights long ago filled with cries and moans on cool sheets. The beginnings of a beard scratched my chin as his kiss deepened. When he moaned, my breathing grew ragged and he tore feelings from me that I'd thought were gone. But just when I was about to give in to my own need and free my arm to clutch at him, I remembered the truth. He wasn't mine anymore. He could never be mine. And I wanted someone else now.

I pushed and pulled at the same time, separating us. "Stop it, Dylan." He let me go and I moved back even further, clutching the photographs like a lifeline to the present. "Don't make me think that there's a chance for us again. I can't believe you. I don't trust you. I'll find Dusty, but please—go back to your wife and stay there."

He met my eyes and stared long enough with darkness in his gaze that I shivered. "No, Katie. I'll go, but not back to my wife. I have to leave until Monica is gone." He pushed himself to his knees and then got to his feet as though raised on strings. It was unnerving. He turned started to walk out of the shop, but then turned his head and looked down at me, still huddled on the floor. "But I'll be back, Katydid. I won't let you get away a second time."

I couldn't think what to say to that. My jaw just kept working silently long after he walked out the door. It took a few more moments for me to collect myself enough to get to my feet. I stood in the shop for a minute longer. If he was going into hiding, it was better that we not be seen together. But the fact that I still *cared* enough to wait scared the be-jeebers out of me. It wasn't fair to Tom, or to me. I looked again at the pictures. Of course, none of this was fair to Dusty. Not at all. I put the pictures in the back pocket of my jeans.

Why was Dylan hiding and whose side was he on? From what he said *Vickie* must be a different queen—but from where, and what was she doing here? I had too many questions, and not nearly enough answers.

I kept worrying at the problem, trying to make sense of the conflicting information I'd uncovered. One thing was certain, if Monica's Host was reaching the end of its life she'd be desperate—and even more dangerous than usual. I shuddered at the thought. I'd be safer if I went to ground, but then I'd be abandoning Dusty. I barely knew the kid, but I couldn't do that. Not when I knew what Monica had in store for her. I'd have to be very, very careful if I wanted to survive the next couple of days. The good news was, if I did, I'd never have to worry about Monica again.

I was alert to the point of paranoia as I exited the store and started walking down the mall again. It was mid-morning, and the street was a hive of activity. I lowered my shields and tried to concentrate on finding Morris and the other Hosts. I couldn't find them, but I knew they were there. More important, I could sense an argument was in progress.

I will have my revenge!

No. She is too strong. She is Not Prey.

"Got a cigarette?" The voice from the alley startled me so much I jumped a good foot. My concentration broke, and the Thrall had thrown up shields of their own. I could no longer hear the argument, but it was interesting to know that the rest of the hive wasn't behind Monica.

"Don't smoke." I answered.

There were three of them, a boy and two girls. None of them looked older than sixteen but they had a the hard look of kids that have been on the street for a while. One of the girls had spoken. She was tall, only an inch or so shorter than me, and still pudgy with what my aunt had always referred to as "baby fat." The spiked purple hair added a couple of inches and made her skin look even paler under the goth make-up. There were dark circles under her red-rimmed grey eyes. She'd been crying. I felt a twinge of unwanted sympathy. It usually takes one hell of a lot to break through the tough shells street kids develop. Whatever it was, it had to have been bad.

The boy was about 6'2", rangy, with long arms and legs and oversized hands and feet. His eyes were dark brown, his body language cautious and unfriendly. His hair was shaggy but clean, straight and shiny—a brown so dark it was not quite black. His forearms were covered by thick hair of the same color.

The second girl had hair bleached almost white, with wide black stripes like a zebra. She had striking ice-blue eyes that were set off by wide black eyeliner. Her black nylon halter top barely covered breasts that overpowered her small frame and seemed almost too large to be real. A good wind would probably overbalance her. Her jeans were hip-huggers that were barely decent, even by street standards. A tattoo peeked out from the top of the jeans. It looked like the tip of a wing but not enough showed for me to be sure. Neither of the girls had the facial structure to be Becky, a.k.a. Dusty.

I forced myself to smile. It wasn't easy. I didn't want to talk to these kids. I wanted to get the hell back to my apartment and get some protection. But I'd told Dylan I'd try to find Dusty and these were just the type of kids who might know something. If I didn't talk to them now, I'd probably never get another chance.

"Bummer." The purple-haired girl gave an exaggerated sigh. "Don't suppose you have a couple of bucks?"

"Hungry?"

She shrugged, admitting reality. She *was* stressed. "A little."

"If you're willing to answer a couple of questions, I'll buy you some burgers." I gestured to include the three of them. I didn't want any misunderstanding. I only wanted information, not sex. One on one might be construed as a come-on.

The boy pulled himself away from the building he'd been leaning on in a smooth, liquid movement. I'd expected him to be awkward. He wasn't. It caught my attention, roused a memory. Suddenly I knew. He was a wolf. If he was a member of the local pack he probably knew Tom. I didn't know where Tom fit in the structure but from what I understood from the grapevine, the group wasn't that big. Most of them didn't advertise what they were.

I locked glances with him for a long moment. He tilted his head back in a practiced gesture that looked like flipping his hair from his eyes. Nostrils flared as he took the long sniff that was a dead giveaway. I wondered if he smelled Tom on my hair. I'd showered, but I hadn't shampooed. If he did smell Tom, would it be a good thing, or bad? I didn't know. Or did he smell Dylan and the stolen kiss?

The three of them exchanged glances. At an almost imperceptible nod from the boy the blonde spoke. "Sure, why not." She held out her hand, "I'm Ruby. This," she gestured to the other girl, "is Jade. That," she gestured to the boy, "is Jake. He's a *wolf*." Her voice dropped when she said it—as though I should be frightened, or impressed. I just nodded, which earned me a small frown from Ruby and a nod of acknowledgment from Jake.

I gestured for them to precede me. Jade and Ruby moved on ahead but Jake fell in beside me. His eyes were constantly moving. He wasn't nervous; just alert. I knew he was aware of everything going on around us. I didn't think he'd noticed one thing that I had, however. Ruby's walk was a studied sexual strut, but Jade was walking with great care, as though each movement was painful. It wasn't exactly a limp but it was obviously awkward.

They led me a couple of blocks up the mall to a corner where one of the chain burger joints took advantage of both the mall and a major cross street. Jake played the gentleman, holding open the door for the three of us girls.

The chill of the air conditioning hit me like a welcomed slap in the face. I was dressed too warm for the day and was nervous enough to be sweating buckets. I didn't want to take off the coat but unbent enough to open my jacket. When I unzipped it, the cold air hit the wet silk and I gave an involuntary shiver.

There weren't many patrons scattered at the shiny plastic tables. The old bums sipping coffee eyed us warily. A couple of suits in the corner stared openly at Ruby's impressive figure. She ignored them completely and held her hand out to me palm-upward. I pulled another twenty from my wallet. She snatched it from my hand and made a beeline for the counter.

"Order for me, will you?" Jade called to her friend. "I need to go to the john."

"No problem." Ruby answered.

I started to follow Ruby but a firm grip on my left arm stopped me. Jake was holding me back to get in a private word.

"I've heard about you, Reilly. I can't *believe* you'd work for that man!"

I guessed he was talking about Matt Quinn. I knew that word on the street got around quick but this was just plain impressive.

"I'm working for her uncle, not the stepfather. He's worried that the girl's gotten in over her head and he wants me to keep her safe. What can I say?"

Jake uttered a short burst of sound that was close to a bark and then lowered his voice to a hiss. "Oh yeah, right. The guy's trying to sell his nearest and dearest to the *Thrall*. You go looking for her and you'll lead them right to her. That kind of *help* she don't need!"

So, I'd guessed right. Dusty was the girl in line to be queen.

Jake shook his head angrily. "Dusty found out some things she shouldn't about her stepdad. He's a bad man, Reilly. She knew what would happen if he got hold of her, so she bolted. When he couldn't find her, he offered her up to the vamps—and *hired you*. You're being used. And I'm telling you now, you'll have your ass in a wringer if you find her and deliver her up to either the dad or the bloodsuckers!"

"I hadn't intended to give her up, Jake."

"Yeah, right. And that's why your jacket and hair smells like two different Thrall hives. Don't bullshit me, Reilly."

I flinched a little. Guilt will do that. "Sometimes there just *aren't* any right answers to the questions being asked. I'm not working for anyone except Dusty's uncle."

Jake's kept a wary look and a low growl hissed through his lips. "I won't let you find her. She's in danger, so know this—I'll *kill* you or anyone else hunting her before I let them take her."

"Her uncle said he was worried, and wanted her *safe*." I kept my voice calm and soothing, but it had no effect. There was no reason for Jake to believe me. In his place, *I* wouldn't believe me. Great. Now I had new people to watch my back from. *Jesus, Dylan. Did you have any idea what you were throwing me in the middle of?* I shook my head again. Of course he had. Otherwise he wouldn't have risked Monica's wrath to bring me the pictures. But then the questions started again.

No. Dylan believed I could save Dusty *and* myself. He as much said so. Wished I could be so sure.

Jake's arm was still on my sleeve. I shook it off.

"A bit of advice," I hissed. Ruby was near the front of the line, and Jade was limping her way back from the hall that led to the bathrooms. "Dusty's going to need protection from people who won't be bought and *can't* be bit."

"We've taken care of that." Jake spoke with confidence.

"Really? I don't think so." I inclined my head in the direction of Jade. Jake turned, his eyes widening as he saw what I had. There was a small spot of blood spreading through the jeans on her left upper thigh. Right where a vampire would've munched. She wasn't a Host. He'd have been able to smell that. But she'd been bitten and was Herd.

A low, menacing growl, deeper than the one he'd given me, left his lips and he started to swear.

Maybe she heard him. Maybe she sensed our attention but she turned toward the two of us. She looked directly into my eyes and smirked. I had a flash of intuition. There weren't just bathrooms in that hall. There were telephones. The Herd can't talk telepathically—they can only receive their instructions from the queen that way.

Jake saw it too. "Shit! Go." He practically shoved me toward the door behind us. "Hurry."

Jade's smirk turned to panic as I casually moved toward the exit. No running; no tales to tell Monica. From the corner of my eye I saw her half-run towards us but Jake was blocking her path. I heard her cry of protest just before the door closed behind me.

I sensed Hosts in my vicinity. They felt like the ones from Morris's office. Glancing about quickly I saw that there were four of them. The two from the stairwell had been joined by friends. I shut down the brain again and tried to think typical mall-crawler thoughts to confuse them with one part of my brain while I tried to plan with the other.

I suppose it was flattering that they thought it would take four of them to nab one measly human. But I wasn't flattered; I was scared. They were converging on the restaurant from the 16th Street mall. I didn't stop to think. I turned onto the cross street and walked the few feet past the storefront before ducking into the alleyway between the restaurant and an art supply shop.

The alley was narrow and straight as an arrow. I could see a trucker unloading racks of clothing into the back of a building about halfway down the block. Other than that, it was deserted.

I needed to hurry. When the vamps found out Jade had failed to keep me at the restaurant, they'd come looking. I needed to get out of here. Fast.

I hate it in movies when the hero runs up a staircase. There is, after all, only so far up you can go. Then you're trapped. But the fire escape was my first thought. If I was lucky they wouldn't think of it. If I wasn't, then at least I might have a bit of a head start before they found me. Unfortunately the rusted fire escape on the nearest building hung too high on the wall to help me. After all, they want tenants to get down, not potential burglars to get up. Although I could probably reach it, I was not going to waste time trying to jump to grab it when I wasn't sure my shoulder would hold.

I felt rather than saw something coming at me from a recessed doorway to my left. I ducked, so the first blow missed. Training took over. Without even thinking about it, I stepped backwards into the attacker's body, bringing my right elbow back in a sharp blow to the diaphragm that forced the air from his lungs in a whoosh and bent him nearly double. I stepped forward slightly and then put my whole body into a backward blow that rammed the same elbow into his bent-over chest. A third blow smashed into his face in a quick one-two. My fingers started to go numb from the shock of the three blows. I heard the sharp crack of bone breaking as his fangs snapped off from the strength of the impact.

I bounced out of reach but he didn't keep coming. Breaking the two secondary ganglia had thrown the Thrall in his head into shock—leaving the human Host helpless. I owed Dr. MacDougal another bottle of scotch. I'd only have seconds before the others closed in on me. I needed out of here *now*.

I was out of time. I could sense it, *hear* the frustrated fury of the nearby vampires as a hiss in my head. I ran down the alley. Shoving the trucker inside the building, I dived through the doorway. I slammed the heavy steel fire door shut and threw home the bolt.

"HEY!"

I ignored the trucker's protest, looking around for something to brace the door. There wasn't much. I was in the receiving end of a sports clothing store. There were racks of clothes but not much else.

"Shit." I swore under my breath. There was no more time. The lock would either hold or it wouldn't. Angry vampires are not easily stopped or even slowed down. What I'd done to their brother was definitely going to piss them off.

"If I were you, I'd get the hell out of here," I shouted in the general direction of both the trucker and the sales clerk who'd appeared in the doorway.

I didn't wait to see if they listened. Instead, I took off through the front door, dodging the clothes racks. I emerged onto the mall, nearly taking out a camera-carrying tourist. The sound of bodies impacting the steel receiving door spurred me onward. I didn't run, but it was one hell of a fast walk.

The southbound shuttle bus was pulling to a stop in front of the burger joint. I dodged behind it, making for the northbound bus that was ringing its bell prior to taking off.

A last-second leap threw me into the packed throng. I made it just as the doors whooshed closed. I muttered apologies to the other passengers, my eyes glued to the far window. Two pale men emerged from the sports store. A third female rounded the corner, having doubled back around the restaurant. The taller male gave a hand gesture and the three of them split up, each taking a portion of the mall.

The bus lurched forward. I lost my footing and fell into the lap of a dark-haired businessman. He had taken off his suit coat, loosened his tie, and rolled up the sleeves of his white shirt in response to the temperature. It *was* pretty toasty.

"I don't know how you can stand to wear leather in this heat. Why don't you take off your jacket?" He smiled when he said it, and I realized with a shock he was *flirting*. It's not that men don't flirt with me but in the present circumstances it just seemed so . . . bizarre.

"I dress for the situation, not the weather." I hadn't meant it to be harsh but my voice was flat and cold. It gets that way when I'm stressed.

He gave me an odd look at the comment and it seemed to cool his interest. Guess he was probably wondering what situations would require this much leather. Then I caught the smell, and saw the red smudge on his shirt where I'd bumped him. Blood. Apparently our boy in the alley had fed recently. There was still enough blood in the teeth when I'd broken them to make a mess. I tried to turn the jacket on my body to take a look at the damage, and felt the telltale stinging that told me that vamp boy wasn't the only one bleeding. *Shit.* Still, it had to only be a scratch, or I'd have felt it before now. Shock and adrenaline can mask minor injuries. Major ones still let you know they're there. Funny thing was, my attacker had gone down so quick I couldn't for the life of me figure out how I'd gotten injured. I'd have sworn he hadn't landed a blow.

Shirt sleeves made his way rather hurriedly off the bus at the next stop. I watched the incoming boarders carefully. No vamps. Good thing because despite the crowding all of the other passengers had pulled away from me as much as they could.

"You're bleeding." A small girl with long dark braids announced it loudly before her mother could shush her.

"Yeah. I hurt myself a little."

"Oh. Do you need a Band-Aid? We have some at home. They have kitties on them."

I smiled at her earnest concern. "Thanks, but I have some at home, too."

My pleasant conversation with the little girl seemed to soothe the nerves of my fellow passengers. The crowd closed more tightly around me to make room for new boarders as the bell rang and the doors whooshed open. A different female vamp was outside, looking into the bus. I tucked my bright red braid into the back of my jacket and turned up the collar. Then I slouched and ducked my head down so that I disappeared into the crowd. I thought of a little girl with kitty bandages in her bathroom.

The bell rang again, the doors whooshed closed and the bus lurched forward. This time, I used one of the metal poles to brace myself so I didn't bleed on anybody while scanning the crowd. No vamps—but I'd never know if any of the passengers were Herd. They look just like ordinary humans. Hell, they *are* ordinary humans. They eat and love and raise families. At first, they're healthy specimens. Joggers and health-food nuts. All the better to bleed iron-rich food for their masters. But the feeding wears them down. Soon they look like junkies and die an early death. I wondered again why Dylan had been spared.

But speaking of being spared—I'd snuck a look behind the bus to watch and see what direction the vamps were heading. All three were standing as still as statues. Then they started to shake all over and I could just spot froth at the corner of their mouths before they each dropped like stones.

I felt a flash of blinding pain behind my eyes, sensed Monica's rage. What the hell was going on? I couldn't help but stare at the scene through my tear-filled eyes. A couple of people clapped before they realized that it wasn't a display of performance art. Then there were screams. Mounted and bicycle cops converged on the scene.

The warning bell rang and my bus pulled away from the curb. Most of the passengers strained to get a better view of the scene out of the windows. I closed my eyes and prayed. At the end of the mall, I stepped off the bus. I still had to make it about six blocks before I could board the cross-town bus to take me to the other end of lower downtown. Either that, or I'd have to walk the whole way. If I was being hunted, I wanted to be in something large and metal and moving.

I made it to my building unmolested and unseen. Running is a prey behavior, but they hadn't actually witnessed me running and I'd fought the one who confronted me. Besides, even a jaguar will run from a *pack* of dogs. At least that's what I told myself.

Just as I was reaching out to unlock the deadbolt, my cell phone rang.

"Shit!" I jumped a foot and promptly dropped my keys. Me, nervous? Nah. "Kate here." I bent down to pick up the keys, my voice a little bit breathy.

"Kate, it's Mike." I propped the phone between ear and shoulder and began fiddling with the lock. "Joe stopped by. He told me you've been back a couple days. I'm surprised I haven't seen you." There was more than a hint of reproach in his voice. Damn it!

Mike continued before I could explain. "I know you're busy, but we need to talk." His intonation gave the word 'talk' all sorts of ominous overtones.

"Mike . . ."

"It's important." Of course it was. It always is. Frustrated fury welled up in me. Damn it! Joe couldn't get me to do what he wanted, so he called Mike in as reinforcements. I should've *known*. He'd left Bernardo's too willingly. That interfering, manipulative, son of a . . .

"I have a meeting with the archbishop this afternoon, so I'll expect you tomorrow." Mike hung up before I could argue. He had to know I would've. Not even Mike gets away with ordering me around like that. I let him get away with a lot because he's my friend, my priest, and my ex-boyfriend. He gets even more slack because of the way he takes care of Bryan. But there are limits, and if he pushed too hard he'd find out just what they were.

I slid my phone back into the pocket of my jacket and opened the door. Home. I felt a surge of relief. I'd made it. Now I needed to get my knives and find that neck brace. Not for the first time I wished I could pack a gun. But I knew the rules all too well. No distance weapons. I'd have to rely on my own physical, mental and psychic strength and whatever I could use hand to hand.

The message light was blinking. I figured I'd might as well listen to the messages while I armed myself. As I pulled the wooden box that held my wrist sheaths off of the closet shelf in the bedroom a familiar voice wafted up to me.

"Kate, it's Ramon. Celeste told me that you wouldn't be available for any deliveries and will be closing your business, but I need your help. I have a special project for you. It's not your usual thing, but I just don't trust anybody else. Please call me back as soon as you can!"

What in the hell was he talking about? I walked downstairs, carrying the knives with me. Ramon and Celeste Ortega owned Tres Chic, an art gallery just a few blocks away in LoDo. Work for the Ortegas made up about a third of my business. They've always paid well and promptly, two things I absolutely adore in a client. But why would Celeste tell him that I wouldn't be available for any deliveries and would be closing up shop? Hmm, either Celeste had come up with a cheaper courier she wanted to use and was making up stories to buffalo Ramon, or . . .

Since few things were beneath her, I was definitely going to have a little *chat* with Ms. Ortega. If she had information, I'd get it from her. Oh, yes indeed. Celeste is a very stylish, but not terribly disciplined, cream puff. Getting her to answer a few pointed questions should be positively easy, and in my present mood, more than a little enjoyable.

The machine shut off, leaving silence in its wake. Almost immediately I could feel the pressure in my skull, hear the "buzzing" of the angry Thrall hive. No words this time, they were shielding me out too much for that. But I could sense Monica's rage. It beat against my mind. I felt the beginnings of a throbbing headache that would become incapacitating if I didn't do something about it. It wasn't just me she was angry with either. But that wouldn't keep her from taking it out on me.

10

I used the speaker phone to call Ramon. It left my hands free to strap on the wrist sheaths and slide in my knives as we exchanged initial pleasantries. He seemed genuinely delighted to hear from me, which was nice. He'd been very *concerned.* "Something in Celeste's voice when she spoke about you frightened me."

"Really? So why didn't you call her on it? You've never been scared of her before."

"Kate, Kate, Kate. Since *that afternoon* we barely speak except through our attorneys. But the business is in both our names, and there are things that simply must be taken care of."

"That afternoon?" I had to ask. Stupid me. The question just popped out of my mouth before I thought. If I *had* taken time to think I would've known the answer and stayed out of the middle of it. Their personal life was their business, not mine. I didn't need to get in the middle. But, like most people, he took the words at face value. "I still love her, Kate. I swear I do. But she did the unforgivable. We had a new artist. Brilliant, really. He took postmodernism to a whole new

level. We were grooming him, as we always do with a new find. Celeste apparently decided to take a more *personal* role in his development." The words were harsh—wet with long spilled tears. I knew that sound.

"You caught them." It wasn't a question. It didn't need to be.

He sighed and it spoke volumes. "In my own bed. Surrounded by the beautiful art that we collected together over a decade." He paused. "I threw her out. On the spot."

My eyebrows dropped so far that I could see the individual hairs at the edge of my vision. "So what exactly is it that you need me for?"

His voice brightened a bit. "The judge awarded me the house in the divorce. Five days ago, I went to work like normal. Apparently while I was out, she got there with a locksmith and changed all of the locks. I went to court and got an order of eviction. She never showed up at the hearing, so it was easy. The problem is, nobody can get her served."

Ah! Now the problem was becoming clear. "I don't do service of process, Ramon."

"It's just a delivery, Kate. She likes you. You can get close enough to give her the papers."

I intended to get close to Celeste. Close enough to do a little intimidation. I needed to know if she had any information on Monica's plans. I was pretty sure she did. Just one of those *feelings* of mine that Larry had been so enamored of. But it didn't make sense for Ramon to call me. He knows full well what I do, and what I *don't* do. I *don't* do process service. I leave that to the professionals.

"Did you try a private process server? That's what they do."

"I've tried five different companies. Twice. Nobody will go back."

What? Some of those guys would saunter into Five Points during a Bloods/Crips war. What could be so bad that one wouldn't be willing to walk into the situation? "Why the hell not? Is she violent?"

"Not per se. When she sees a car, she goes out on the balcony of the second floor. From what I hear, she's been pelting people with elephants."

It was so utterly ridiculous that a smile caught me unaware. "With *elephants?*"

Ramon's voice was angry now but clearly a little part of him found it funny. "My prized elephant collection. Crystal elephants, stone elephants, elaborately carved wooden elephants. I've collected them since I was a child. From reports that I've been getting, a good half of them have been destroyed. She's got a good arm and can reach precisely to the property line. She was the pitcher for our company softball team."

I couldn't help but get an image of tall, willowy Celeste standing on a balcony, winding up and pitching elephants at a process server. I had to fight not to laugh. I was on the verge of hysteria from the day's tension and this was just *so* ridiculous. But I made sure my voice was steady before I spoke. "I'm sorry, Ramon. I really am. But I'm not in the mood to get an elephant heaved into my skull. It is an FED, though. Just post the notice. It's allowed."

"FED?"

"Forcible entry and detainer. That's what they call an eviction in the court system. Just have someone wait until she's gone and post the notice on the door. Then the sheriff can bring the swat team to get her out."

"She won't leave." Apparently, someone had already told him he could post the notice.

"What do you mean, she won't leave? She has to leave *sometime,* Ramon. She can't stay holed up forever."

"And yet, that's *exactly* what she's doing, Kate. She's having groceries delivered. She's meeting clients at the house. She *never* leaves."

I shrugged my shoulders. Heard it before. "Freeze her out."

"Like how?"

"You have possession. Call the electric company, the gas company, the phone company. Stop into their offices. Turn everything off. She'll leave. Trust me."

I could hear his dark hair rustling in the phone as he shook his head. "I love her, Kate. I couldn't do that to her."

"Then you'll never get your house back. She's won." It was a fact.

"It's a game. I know it is. If I can get her served, she'll know I'm serious and she'll go."

I shook my head. A note of anger found its way into my voice. "You're deluded, Ramon. And I don't care to be involved in that particular delusion. Call someone else."

His reply was almost a sob. "Kate, I can't. I've called everyone I know. You're my only hope. I know you can do this. She won't hold it against you. She won't throw an elephant at *you*. You've been too good a friend for too long."

"Which is precisely *why* I won't do it, Ramon. I like you both. If I serve her, I'll be taking sides. There are always two sides. I've only heard one." Cold, but the truth.

His response was too fast. He'd planned for my refusal. "Then let her tell her side. Let her tell it in court, where it belongs. But she won't know when the hearing is if she doesn't get the papers." God, those last words sounded smug.

Fortunately, my personality won't allow me to get bested in a debate. "You're required to mail the papers to her in addition to serving. Mail it from out of town and don't put a return address. When she gets the envelope, she'll know when the hearing is and if she doesn't show up, it'll tell you that she doesn't *want* to tell her side."

Now he was sounding desperate. "I'll do *anything*, Kate. I'll *pay* anything if you'll just do this!"

I knew it wouldn't be all that hard. I could sneak up on Celeste in my sleep, and I actually wanted to talk to her, to find out what she knew. But I had way too much on my plate right now with other things and she was way low on the list.

I finished buckling the final strap on the left sheath, and started on the right. I needed to finish this and get moving. He'd said he'd pay anything, but I knew Ramon. If I named a figure outrageous enough, he'd back down and find someone else. I just needed to go high enough. "Ten thousand. I'll serve her for ten grand."

There was a cough and silence on the other end. His voice was a mix of shock and outrage. "For a *service?*"

I shrugged and it sounded in my voice. "Take it or leave it, Ramon. I've got a busy schedule today."

"I didn't pay that much to have you deliver the *Picasso,* for God's sake!"

"And the collector didn't heave elephants at the messenger. Like I said, Ramon, take it or leave it."

I nearly dropped the phone when he agreed, and my feet wanted to do a happy dance. Apparently I hadn't chosen a number quite high enough. My checkbook would appreciate the transfusion, if I stuck around long enough to deposit it.

I'm a woman of my word. Like it or not, fifteen minutes later I pulled Edna into the loading zone in front of Tres Chic. It should have only taken ten minutes, but I discovered daring new levels of pain in my shoulder the first time I shifted the old truck into third gear. First gear was no problem, second was fine, too. But that tiny bit of twist up and over to put it in third put little sparkles in my vision and turned my breathing into rapid pants.

I drove in second gear the whole way.

I got nasty looks, too, because second doesn't come anywhere close to the speed limit.

As I pulled up to the curb, a group of about five teenagers surrounded the truck to admire it. Five years ago, Edna was just an old truck. Today, she's a *classic.* I've spared no expense to restore her to her original beauty. She's a '55, which was a great year for Chevy. As I stepped onto the sidewalk, I put a hand on the nearest shoulder. "Admire to your heart's content. But if anyone lays so much as a hand on it, I'll track you all down and decorate her with your intestines." My steady gaze and cold smile did the trick. Well, that and my pulling up the sleeve of my jacket to reveal the knives. He motioned to his buddies and they all stepped back a pace.

"Thanks, guys. Keep an eye on her for me." I reached into my pocket and handed the nearest kid a twenty. It would keep them honest for a space of about—oh—ten minutes.

"Cool, lady! Another one like that and we'll wax it for you!"

I smiled. "No, just make sure it stays in one piece."

Ramon wasn't in the store. Starla, the receptionist, handed me an envelope along with Ramon's sincere apologies that he couldn't be here to see me. He had a very important meeting to attend. Yeah, right. I opened the envelope. Inside was the Summons and Complaint and Order of Restitution. There was also a check for ten grand, payable to me. It almost made it worth the trip. Edna was fine for the fifteen seconds I was inside. I could have saved the twenty. The boys were all whispering and looking at me with the strangest expression as I came out. They backed away slowly as I approached. Weird, but oh well.

Ramon and Celeste live in a trendy foothills neighborhood, where the ticky-tacky houses all have identical rooflines and colors, while trying without success to appear unique and individual.

Luck was with me! Celeste was in the front yard, trimming hedges as I puttered slowly up asphalt so new it was still a smooth sheet of vivid black. I wondered if I would sink into the tarred depth of it when I stepped out of the truck.

While I wouldn't have chosen her outfit in my wildest nightmares, it was classic Celeste. Her flowing, knee-length tunic was in earth tones with geometric patterns and finger-paintings of ancient cave art. It mostly covered a pair of matching capri pants. Silk slippers and a matching cap completed the surreal image. The pants were her grudging acknowledgment to physical labor.

I tucked the papers into my back pocket and sauntered up casually. When her back was to me briefly, I stepped onto the neighbor's property. The hedge was neck-high between us.

"Hi, Celeste!" I said cheerily. She stiffened at the noise and reached a hand into the hedge. Damned if she didn't come out with an elephant. It was heavy lead crystal. Rainbows patterned on her tunic and bare arm. But when she turned and saw me, she dropped it to the grass with a thud.

"Oh, my God! Kate! How *wonderful* to see you, darling!" She gave me a long, searching look. Whatever she'd expected to see wasn't there. Her smile faded, her body stiffened slightly. She cast a panicked glance towards the house, but decided it was just too far a distance to run for it. I watched the whole process take place in a matter of a second. Impressive, but not enough. I knew now that she had information about what was going on with me, and I intended to get it.

I smiled, but kept my eyes squarely on hers. "You know why I'm here, don't you?"

A cunning expression flickered across her face. She made the decision to lie, to pretend that it was only the situation with Ramon. "It's not fair, Kate. I found this house. I *love* this house and he's punishing me forever for one moment of weakness."

I decided to play along for a bit, make her comfortable and see if anything slipped. I could use intimidation with the best of them, but sometimes an indirect approach works better.

"You're rationalizing to the wrong person, Celeste. I'm Catholic, but it's one of the big ten thou-shalt-nots in pretty much every religion." I pushed a little harder, wanting to make her emotional enough to drop her guard. "Was it worth it, Celeste? Was it worth throwing away everything you have? Everything you worked for?"

She looked at me for as long as she could. But then her eyes dropped to the ground and tears glittered brightly. I almost didn't hear her response. It was a whisper that was nearly lost in the growing wind. "No. I've betrayed everything—everyone I care about . . ."

"I'm sorry, Celeste. I really am." I took the papers out of my pocket and set them onto the neatly manicured hedge in front of her. "But you have to make a decision, who do you want to be? What do you want your life to stand for?"

She looked up, her tear-filled eyes meeting mine. She opened her mouth to speak . . . and I felt a surge of the power of the hive. As I watched her knees buckled, her eyes glazing over as she collapsed to the ground, spittle trailing from the corner of her mouth.

I started around the edge of the hedge to help her, but movement at the edge of my vision stopped me. A handsome young man glared at me through the French doors for the up-stairs balcony. He opened his mouth to hiss, giving me a clear glimpse of pointed fangs. With one smooth movement, he leapt from the balcony and landed on the grass in a crouch.

"Shit!"

I didn't run. I did draw one of my knives. With the knife in my right hand, keys in my left, I backed slowly, carefully across the lawn to where my truck was waiting. He followed me, keeping the distance of the width of the perfectly tended lawn between us. When he reached Celeste, he picked her up and hissed at me again.

I tried to appear casual as I opened Edna's driver's door, but my heart was racing a mile a minute. I swore and berated myself for most of the slow, slow drive home. I should've known Celeste wasn't strong enough to go against the hive. Hell, she was weaker than either Dylan *or* Morris. Damn, damn, damn.

Still, the more I thought about it, the more I *thought* I knew what was happening. The problem was that the players had been wrong.

I was dealing with more than one queen, which shouldn't be possible. That was like one foot consciously refusing to move after the first one stepped. But Pete had said the same thing, and I couldn't ignore the blindingly obvious clues anymore.

I started analyzing what I knew as I carefully made my way home, both knives drawn and visible. No one tried to sneak into the parking garage after me. No one was waiting in the shadows, no matter how many times I spun around and scanned them. Part of me was almost disappointed when I made it to the apartment unmolested.

But by the time I got there, I had some of it figured out. Tossing the keys onto the kitchen counter, I strode over the stereo, slid in an AC/DC CD and turned the volume way up. I could only hope keeping them out of my head worked in reverse as well. I couldn't afford for them to know what I was planning.

So far as I could determine, Amanda, Matthew Quinn, the nurse at the hospital, and the bozo in the pickup truck at the airport were working for Monica. That left Dylan, who obviously was fighting her, and the vamps chasing me on the mall who collapsed. What about Morris? Where did he fit? And who held Celeste's chain? Between all of these thoughts and the pounding bass beat from the speakers, I was getting the mother of all headaches. And I really, *really* needed to find my neck brace.

Where in the hell is *it?* I wanted to scream with frustration as I tore afghans and sheets from the closet shelf one-handed. I was saving my bad shoulder for important things—like staying alive. Every second seemed an eternity. But I was not leaving here again without my neck guard and my knives in case I had to fight. Monica *should* have challenged me. Any Thrall should have to attack one at a time. Of course, if you have one hundred of them come at you one at a time, one after another, you're going to go down. My bet was that the purpose of sending four of them was to overpower my mind and will so that I wouldn't fight at all.

My strategy, for what it was worth, was to avoid groups of the Thrall. If cornered, I would challenge Monica to a duel. She'd have to fight me herself or face the wrath of the other queens. Of course, that didn't seem to mean much at this point. But I didn't know how hard they were trying.

I was hoping that she wouldn't be able to withstand their collective power if they were really pushing themselves. Not a great plan, but it was the best I could think of. It had worked last time. But last time I'd been wearing my neck guard.

"ARRGH! Where *is it?*" This time I did shout it out loud to the air. I was losing control. Not good. I took a long deep breath. I stared at the mess I'd made of the contents of my walk-in closet. Calm. Take deep breaths. Try to remember . . .

My concentration was interrupted by the sound of Tom's voice accompanied by knocking on the apartment door.

"Kate, are you home?"

I didn't really want to get into a discussion with him right now. It had been a bad day. But he didn't deserve to get shut out either. I went downstairs and opened the door a crack.

"Tom, nothing personal, but now really isn't a good time to talk. If you need the key, I'll get it off my ring."

He sighed and pushed against the door lightly. Against my better judgment, I let him. I backed up and he walked in past me. "Kate, I know what's going on. Your brother came by while I was bringing over some more boxes. He explained everything. That you're working to protect a girl from the Thrall, and that Dylan is married now. He's worried about you, and now so am I. He says he heard Dylan calling your priest, and—"

Oh, that was just *super!* Joe *explained* things to Tom. There went any hope of a normal relationship! And no wonder Mike Wants to talk to me. Father Mike is firmly of the opinion that Dylan is just "misguided."

My voice raised to get over the sound of Bon Scott's singing. "I know he's worried, Tom. But he doesn't need to be. I'm fine. I just stopped by to get my neck guard and more knives before I get started searching for the girl."

"Wait, you *know?*" Tom finally stopped to actually look at me. What he saw made him wide-eyed. He took slow steps around to the back of me.

"What in the *hell* happened to you?" I supposed I should be a little concerned that his voice held at weird mix of fear and horror.

"Long story." I started back up the stairs. Guest or no, I was running out of time. The plants were moving into deep shadows as the sun started down the west side of the building. The tiger lily blossoms had already begun to slowly fold in on themselves to prepare for the night.

"Kate." His voice cracked with fear. It was dry as dust and was pained enough to make me turn around. "The back of your jacket looks like it was shredded by claws. You're bleeding all over the floor."

I stopped in my tracks, frozen. Then I turned around and looked down. Tiny spots of red were making *CSI*-style splatter patterns on the floor. My gaze swept the room and I realized the bleeding was growing worse, not better. I didn't remember the vamp doing anything that would've shredded my back—which meant he'd used mind control on me. The fact that he'd succeeded scared me shitless. A baby Host had clouded my mind and nearly taken out my back. I'd always believed I earned my Not Prey status. Had Larry simply gone into shock when I broke his tooth? I wasn't that good with a knife. He just hadn't been able to fight. Lord protect me! Without the shield, Monica would have me for lunch!

Tom saw me shiver and strode past me to the kitchen. I saw him sniff the air a bit, and then open a cabinet in the center island. He pulled out a bottle of whiskey he seemed to know was there and grabbed a pair of cut crystal glasses. He walked back and placing a glass in my hand, and then poured a generous portion for each of us. I didn't complain, even though it was my whiskey. I needed something to calm me down enough to think clearly.

He raised his glass and touched it to mine. "*Slainte!* Here's health to your enemy's enemies and the hope and blessings of the three on you!"

The toast made me wonder what his background was, because it's a very old, very Irish toast. But it lit a memory, and I let out a whoop. "The hope chest!" I set the glass down on the counter so fast that liquid spilled from the glass onto the tile surface. I took the stairs at a dead run. Flinging clothing and shoes aside I made my way to the cedar chest at the foot of my bed. With trembling fingers, I undid the latch. When I flung back the lid, there it was, right on top.

I felt some of the tension leave my shoulders as I ran my hands over the slick acrylic. It felt cool, rock solid and comforting. I immediately started pulling off layers of clothing until I was down to my bra, tossing everything on top of the pile spread over my bed.

"Tom?" I called down. "I may need some help up here."

"On my way." There wasn't a hint of teasing in his voice. It was rock solid and business-like.

"Wow." Tom stared at the mess I'd made of my room from the top of the stairs. "I guess you had a hard time finding this thing?"

"Just help me into it. It might be the only thing that saves my life today."

He frowned and picked up the guard. I held my hair out of the way. He touched my back and I flinched and let out a harsh hiss of air. The cuts must be deeper than I had thought.

"I want to clean and bandage those claw marks first. Nothing gets infected like human nail scratches."

I held my hair up again and nearly shrieked when he touched my back.

"Jeez Louise, Kate! What have you been up to?" He bent my right arm backward. The elbow felt a bit swollen, but it was nothing compared to the shoulder. I guess driving hadn't done it any good.

"Are your fingers tingling? I'm not an orthopedist, but that rotator cuff doesn't look too hot."

"It's fine," I replied stubbornly. Actually, it *was* fine, since it was so swollen it was numb. Tomorrow would be ugly, though. I wiggled my fingers for him, surprised at the effort it took to make it look effortless.

"Uh-huh. And I suppose that this doesn't hurt a bit?" He bent my left arm at the elbow with one hand and with the other pressed down on my palm. Shooting pain made me cry out. I yanked my arm away.

I turned furious eyes to him. "What the hell was that for?"

"You try to use a knife with that hand and it may be the last thing you ever do with it. I can't let you go out and risk ruining yourself like this."

I'd heard that before, from the surgeon who repaired me after my final match. The arm's not perfect, mind you, but there's nothing like someone telling me I *can't* do something to ensure that I will.

"Don't lecture me, Tom. And don't get all warm and fuzzy on me. Now is not the time."

I saw his eyes go cold, and realized that he wasn't always a happy-go-lucky nice guy. "Fine. I'll clean you up, and don't worry—you bleeding all over the carpet doesn't really get my engine going." He turned abruptly and stalked into the bathroom. I heard him banging cabinet doors harshly and almost went to help, but I knew that part of what he was doing was releasing some stress. I understand that. He returned in a few moments with a wet washcloth, a tube of antibiotic ointment and a box of bandages.

He was as good as his word. Warm and fuzzy never came

into play. My breath hissed between my teeth from the sting of the washcloth as he roughly scrubbed it against the opened skin.

"Hmph. It's not as bad as I thought from the amount of blood. None of them are deep at all." Tom made the observations as though to a colleague while he smeared ointment onto the wounds.

"Most of the blood was his."

I could sense him smile. "Attagirl." He stood and went back into the bathroom for more bandages. It took quite a few of them to cover it all. When he was finished, I checked my mobility by twisting at the waist and bending over. I could feel them pull with the movement, but not enough that it would inhibit me in a fight. They did sting like an S.O.B., though.

"You'll need something to cover up that neck guard. If they see it, they'll take it. Maybe a turtleneck sweater?"

I shook my head. "Too heavy. I have to wear a coat." I went upstairs and dug through the clothing on the floor. The arm was starting to ache now, but I couldn't afford to let Tom see the struggle just to look natural. I finally found a flimsy cotton dickie to cover the guard, and then found a T-shirt over the top of it. It would only *look* like I was wearing a turtleneck.

Tom retrieved his drink from the counter and took a long pull of the harsh amber liquid that emptied the glass. He rested his hands on the tile, head down. "I want to help."

"Tom, that's a bad idea and you know it."

"You shouldn't be facing them alone." He met my eyes in the glass of the mirror. His face was flushed; his jaw thrust stubbornly forward.

"I'm not that easy to kill. If I was, they'd have gotten me last time." Brave words. But not a lie, and he could tell. He settled the neck guard over my shoulders and snapped the lock with an annoyed shake of his head.

I ignored him and went back upstairs. I put on the dickie and the T-shirt and then began rummaging through the pile of clothes on the bed once more. Down at the bottom was my Colorado Rockies jacket. It's purple, white, and gray, but at least it's leather. With the biker jacket trashed it was the heaviest thing I had. Unfortunately, it's lined, so I was going to be miserably uncomfortable. I'd have to drink water every hour to make sure I didn't wind up with heat prostration. I pulled it on, zipping it closed over the sweater. The elasticized sleeves made it possible to get to the knives at my wrist, but it was slower than I would've liked. The biker jacket had zippers I could open that made drawing the knives much quicker. The rays of sunlight streaming in the west window were already making me sweat. I pulled my hair out of the braid and ran a quick comb through it in the bathroom. The wavy hair falling around my shoulders would give further concealment, and allowed some air movement to my neck. I drew the knives in front of the mirror, one at a time. Then I tried pulling both at the same time.

Tom gave me a long hard stare. His eyes never left me as he watched me draw and redraw the knives. He was staring at me like he'd never seen me before. I walked out of the bath and drew again. The shoulder ached. Slow, too slow—but the best I was going to get.

Tom didn't say anything for a long time. When he finally spoke his voice was harsh and strained. "I hate this. I absolutely hate this. I'll go move furniture. If you get hurt, have the ambulance take you to St. E's and make sure that Joe calls me." There was a long pause before he continued. "But if they get you, or you die, so help me God I will kill Dylan Shea with my bare hands."

I didn't doubt it a bit.

11

We left within minutes, after I gave Tom my building key—and after multiple promises that I would be careful and I would keep him advised. It was sort of nice to have someone worried about me. But it was also scary.

I drove down to Colfax to look for Dusty, Voneen or both. I had to admit that driving was a bit easier with the shoulder all numb. But I didn't look forward to tomorrow; again, if there *was* a tomorrow. Boy, aren't I just a ray of sunshine?

The rules said I couldn't run and couldn't leave town, but it's harder to hit an unpredictable moving target. *That's me all right. Unpredictable and moving.*

I parked Edna at a burger stand and sprinted across Colfax with the light. You have to sprint on Colfax, even when you *have* the light—and suddenly I was standing in front of the place. The building is both unassuming and gaudy. Neon screams at passers-by about the variety of X-rated offerings available inside, but the building itself is low-key, with wood paneling and brick, and tastefully small windows. It's right at the edge of the Capitol Hill residential area, full of old towering houses that are once again becoming trendy. The shop has to stay low-key or it will die.

A pair of bikers were just swinging off their bikes as I walked by. The first guy, a blond, wearing a scarf tied around his head, lowered his sunglasses as I walked by.

"Whoa! Now *there's* something worth stopping here for!" I continued to walk, ignoring the comment and the resounding whistle from his buddy. I'm used to fending off catcalls when I run. "C'mon, baby. How much for a couple of hours?"

"Not for sale," I finally said when I felt movement behind me. The pair kept following. They smelled of gasoline, oil and sweat. I was really not up to dealing with these two. I wanted to get what information I could and get off the street. I shrugged off the jacket. Most guys, when they see the wrist sheaths over my thick forearm muscles, will back off.

A low whistle eased into my ears. The voice that followed was a whisper of excitement so strong that I knew it wasn't faked. *"Hit me, hurt me, beat me, burn me—take me with you, mistress."*

I stopped cold with wide eyes and blushed to my fingertips. *That* was not the reaction I expected. I did what any sane person would do. I retreated. The light just turned, so I bolted over to the next block. The pair didn't follow. They just laughed and elbowed each other in the ribs at my discomfort and entered the lounge.

I put the jacket back on quickly and tried to figure out my next move. I didn't know if I could go inside to ask questions. I could do violence just fine. But sex *and* violence?

"If you keep running from the customers, honey, you won't last long in this business. Mmm-hmm. Take it from someone who knows." I turned to the rolling alto voice. My eyes scanned the corner. They passed over a middle-aged black woman sitting on the bus bench twice before settling on her. She was the only person who could have spoken.

She wasn't dressed provocatively. She wore blue jeans and a v-necked T-shirt. While it did show off her ample chest, it didn't appear intended to entice.

She smiled, showing strong white teeth. "Don't look so surprised, honey. I'll share this corner. You'll be attracting a whole different crowd than me anyway."

"No," I stammered quickly, "You don't understand. I'm . . ."

"Well, sure! It's obvious you're new. I haven't seen you anywhere down here, and I *would* have. You're very distinctive. You'll be popular if you can just get over being embarrassed."

I shook my head. "No. I'm not a hooker. I'm a courier."

That raised her eyebrows. "Well, okay. I should warn you, though—the cops work this area a lot. You carry anything harder than weed, and they'll bust your ass."

Shit! Wrong kind of courier! This conversation was going badly. I took a deep breath and worked for control. The woman watched me. I opened my eyes and held out my hand to her. She eyed it suspiciously.

"Okay, let's just start over. My name is Kate. I work as a *bonded* courier, but I'm here looking for a couple of missing girls. I'm hoping someone has seen them."

Now the woman's face shut down. She didn't take my hand. Her voice was harsh. "We don't want no trouble down here, and we don't tell tales. Maybe the girls *want* to be missing."

Okay, now this was more of the reaction I was expecting. I could deal with this. I pulled back the offered hand.

"You're right. They probably don't want to be found. But bad people are after them. I've been sent to keep them safe. I can't do that if I don't know where they are. They're just kids."

She snorted a short blast of air that was close to a laugh. "Honey, I've been on the street since I was twelve. I've seen my share of bad people and I haven't seen any down here. The neighborhood's gotten better. They're safe enough."

I noticed that the bench where the woman sat was in the shade of a large tree growing from a hole in the middle of the sidewalk. I moved over and sat down next to her. She scooted over to keep the same distance between us. I could smell her perfume now. It was an older fragrance, one that my mom used to wear sometimes. I think it's called Evening in Paris. It felt a little surreal—something in my brain connected it as a comforting smell. I smiled at the woman and shrugged my shoulders.

"Sorry, but I'm *dying* in this outfit."

Her reply was the stern voice of a mother. Why didn't it surprise me that she might be one? "And you're a fool to wear it. You need to get some sense, girl. If you're going to do detecting, you aren't doing so hot at being low-key. You stand out like a sore thumb."

I chuckled. "No shit. I'm going for protection." I stared at the woman's hard, life-weary face with intensity. "The *Thrall* is after one of the girls. I *have* to find them." I was hoping that she'd been on the street long enough that she understood that the vamps aren't just myth.

I got the reaction I was hoping for. She hissed in a deep breath and her face grew worried. Her voice lowered to a whisper. "So you believe they're real, too?"

I laughed then, a startled sound that ended with a deep breath. "Oh, I *know* they're real. I've met the queen. It's why I'm wearing leather in the middle of a hot July afternoon." I pulled the two photos of the girls from my pocket and passed them to her.

She glanced at them and started to cackle. She held the photos aloft. "I *knew it!* I just knew it!"

"You've seen them?" I asked eagerly.

Her face sobered suddenly and she handed back the pictures. "Oh, I've seen 'em, honey. But you won't be finding them. No, ma'am!" She pointed to the girl in tie-dye. "That one's dead—not more than a couple of days ago. The other girl ran off."

I looked down at Voneen's young face, trying so hard to look cool in the photo. "Are you sure? How do you know she's dead?"

"Why, honey, they only lived a few doors down!" She pointed at a decrepit brick building less than a block away. She saw my look and shook her head. "Won't do you no good to go look there, neither. The cops have already cleaned out the place, and the landlord, he's already got a new tenant in the spot. Rooms are hard to come by down here, and someone dying in the room don't matter to folks round here."

"So how do you know *which one* died?"

"I called the ambulance, girl!" She pointed a long finger at

Dusty's face. "This one here—she comes screaming into the street that her friend was dead. I held her in my own arms, honey! I went upstairs with her, and she was right. The other one was stone cold, lying on the floor of the bath. I called the ambulance and told that little bitty thing to get moving, or the cops would have her downtown for questioning in two shakes. That scared her. Yes, it did. You could tell she was running from something." She made small clucking noises and shook her head with pity.

She leaned toward me and lowered her voice to a harsh whisper. "But I saw the marks, honey! I saw the *teeth* marks, right on that dead girl's arm. Mmm-hmm. Yes, I did. I know some boys on the squad—we've met a couple of times. I asked them what she died of. The coroner said it was a drug OD." She tapped her temple. "But I *know,* honey—I've seen the people that have been bled down. The *evil* ones, they got that poor girl."

I stared at the hooker, and returned my gaze to the photo.

She shook her head. "And there was something wrong with that bite, too—something bad wrong. The arm was all swollen up and bruised. And there was foam on her mouth. But she'd been bit. That's for sure. I *know* the marks of the evil ones." She lowered her voice even further, until I could barely hear her. "They're *everywhere,* you know. That queen they've got now, she's got her fingers in *all* the pies. Not like it used to be. Mmm-hmm."

"Do you . . ." I saw movement from the corner of my eye, and waited until a street person, his shopping cart full of his life's belongings, shambled by us. His hair was a dirty mat of brown.

"Morning, Martha," he said with a leering grin at the black woman. Two lower teeth were missing.

She made kissing motions in his direction. "Morning, Billy. You get any money on your corner today, you come see me, hear?"

He chuckled and licked his lips. I smothered my initial reaction. It was her life, her choices. Martha turned her attention back to me once he was past.

"You were saying?"

I cleared my throat. "Do you have any idea where the other girl went?"

Martha nodded. "She called a friend. He came and picked her up in a cab. Real nice looking fella, too. I've seen *him* before. He was in one of those sexy calendars, for the firemen. They sold them down at the 7-11. Mmm-hmm—he's a *fine* one, honey!"

My breath stilled. Maybe it was a coincidence, maybe not. There were eleven other firemen in that calendar. But how many ride in a cab?

"Thanks, Martha." I rose, but then stopped. I should at least ask. "You want anything for your time? I've kept you from a customer."

She raised her hand and flipped it dismissively. "Old Billy? Nah. He never has any money left after his bottle." Her eyes stared at me with intensity. "No, honey, you just go and keep that girl safe. You keep the evil ones away from her. She's a nice girl. She didn't belong on the street—and she don't need to wind up dead."

I nodded and turned toward my truck. I needed to go back to the house. I hoped Tom was there, because I needed to talk to him. A brief glance toward Martha's bench showed that she wasn't alone. A tall black man had just sat down and rested his arm on the bench back. He was smiling at her and tracing a slow line down her arm. She raised her hand and waved at me as I got in the truck. I waved back, feeling a little strange for just leaving her there. *Her life, her choices.*

I drove back to LoDo, trying to think of what to say. "Gee, Tom, been hanging around Colfax lately picking up young girls?" "Have any firemen friends who date sixteen-year-olds?"

I had misgivings about looking for Dusty. Jake could be right. I could be leading the enemy right to her. But Dylan had begged me to help her—and *he* believed that she needed my help. I didn't trust the stepfather, so I believed *Dylan.* Of course, I'd believed Dylan in the past, and look where that got me. And now Dylan was a Thrall Host, so any hope of trusting him was out the window. *Plans within plans—who was bullshitting who in all of this?*

There were no easy answers: no way of knowing what was the right thing to do. If I dropped it, and the girl was killed or worse, I'd never forgive myself. If I *didn't* drop it, and she wound up dead or turned, I'd blame myself. Damn it.

I started to turn the truck into the parking garage, which is a real trick with one arm and no power steering. I stopped short, because a sedan was parked right up to the gate. There was no driver in the car, which ticked me off. It seems to run in streaks that someone will think that any place off the road is a great parking spot, and then I have to get them towed. It's worse during baseball season, because the stadium is only a few blocks over. I try not to be really mean about it. I just have the tow company pull them off into a street spot and then boot the car so that they have to go to the tow company to pay for the tow. Some of the other building owners call the cops. They have the car towed all the way to the impound lot. The owner won't know where it is until they call to put in a police report that it's been stolen. Then they have to pay for an illegal parking ticket *and* the tow.

I parked at the corner in front of the fire hydrant, which would earn me a ticket if I didn't reach the tow company before the cops spotted it. I could probably talk my way out of the ticket, but I'd have to go to court and show them a picture of the car blocking my garage, and my truck next to it. Then I'd have to get the tow company logs and my phone bill showing the times matched. I've done it, but it was a royal pain.

I'd just started to walk around the back of the car to add the license plate number to the make and model I'd written on the back of an envelope, when two things happened simultaneously: The hive roared to life in my head, causing a blinding pain right behind my eyes, and I heard Tom shout a warning.

"Kate, look out!"

Instinct took over. I dropped to the sidewalk and rolled toward the building with every ounce of my strength, ignoring the screaming in my shoulder. It was just in time. A Thrall Host sailed over me with a flying kick that would have hit me squarely in the head. He landed on the car and rolled over the trunk. It's just not fair when vampires can do martial arts. We poor humans should have *some* advantage. I quickly got to my feet and scanned the area.

Not good.

Four Hosts converging from different directions, and they all looked pretty young and athletic. Two were coming from across the street, one was next to my truck on the right and the kicker was sliding behind the car on my left. I saw movement from almost behind me and risked a quick glance before I moved, since I'd heard Tom's voice from that direction. Sure enough, two white boxes were lying on the floor of the parking garage by the elevator. Silverware and kitchen canisters were scattered across the cement. He lifted the garage gate up a few feet with sheer brute strength and rolled underneath it to wind up beside me. There was a deep growl rumbling from his chest as he faced the Hosts closing in on us.

Mortal enemies. I wondered what that meant in the real world. "This isn't your battle, Tom. It's me they want." I said it quietly, as we both moved into better position to fight.

He never took his eyes off the opponents as he spoke. "Yeah? Well, they'll have to come through me to get you."

Truthfully, I was glad to have someone fighting with me. Four of them was a bit much and I was hardly in tip-top shape. Monica wasn't kidding around anymore. My head felt like it should have a wide crack down the center from the level of pain, and my arm was throbbing. Anything I was going to do would have to be quick and dirty. I wouldn't be able to fight for long.

Never one for defense, I burst forward in a run toward the nearest vamp, the one by my truck. He was a male with a runner's build. The attack, combined with a very cleansing primal scream, took him off guard. He was even more surprised when I ran squarely into him, past the punch he tried to throw. I'd planned for the collision, so I was better prepared. We slammed into Edna, and I heard a satisfying thud as his skull hit the solid steel mirror brace.

I grabbed his left arm and got a firm grip on his belt buckle as he fell backward off balance. I lifted him off his feet and all of my upper body strength went into slamming him face first into the building, just like a whomping big alarm clock. It didn't even hurt—adrenaline is an amazing thing. They should really bottle it.

Fortunately for me, supernatural strength does not give you supernatural mass, and a brick wall is an immovable object not to be messed with. He dropped to the ground and stayed there. I could see that both fangs, along with a couple of regular teeth, had snapped off at the gum line.

A second later, the shoulder reminded me of its existence, and it was *not* happy. The pain nearly took my breath away, but I tried not to let it show. The other three Hosts couldn't quite grasp what was happening quickly enough, and Tom was able to step inside his female vampire, throw a straight finger punch to her throat at the same time as he blasted a kick squarely through the side of her knee. She crumpled to the ground with both hands around her neck, which was emitting a strange gurgling sound.

Now we were down to two. But predators aren't stupid, and Hosts have the whole Thrall group mind behind their actions. They took one look at their fallen comrades, saw that we were both standing and moving toward them and did the smart thing—they took off running down the street. They almost ran into a police car making regular rounds. The cops saw bodies on the ground and made the logical assumption. The officer in the passenger side took off after the runners before the car even came to a stop. He didn't catch them.

It was the second time the police had been to my place in two days. I didn't lie to them about what I knew or didn't know, but I did bend the truth into little salted pretzels. After explaining about the attempted break-in and a quick call to the dispatch, they decided they weren't terribly surprised to be returning. I was betting that Connie would be able to identify the female vamp as the "junkie" from yesterday. The police took away the Hosts without issuing *us* any warnings, which was nice.

They did tell me that I'd have to get the car towed myself, because they couldn't say it belonged to one of the muggers, which is how they defined them. That part sucked big slimy river rocks. At least they pasted a parking pass on Edna until the sedan could be removed.

Tom went back inside while I took care of the details. When I was done with the police and the tow company had removed the sedan, I parked Edna and went inside. It felt sort of strange to knock on the door of 2B, because I was so used to coming and going. Now there was this invisible barrier of *propriety* there.

He answered on the first knock and held the door wide so I could come in. As I walked past him into the apartment I could suddenly smell that amazing cologne again. It reminded me of the feeling of his hands on my skin. When he closed the door behind me, I jumped. I was suddenly nervous, and not just about Dusty or about Monica.

He must have found another truck to help him move, because the whole place was set up except for a few stray boxes here and there.

"Wow, you're quick! I like what you've done with the place." Talking helped distract the butterflies inside, but I wasn't lying. I *did* like the furnishings. They were distinctly male. The couch was upholstered in chocolate leather with accents of pecan wood. The tables were in the same pecan, with strong, clean lines and a solid feel. Color was splashed here and there—a bright burgundy pillow, a fringed throw with ducks in green and russet. All in all, it was very similar to my own style; earthy, solid.

"Thanks. It helps to have a nice place to put the stuff first." He'd moved up behind me as I was looking around. My heart quickened. I felt his hand touch my shoulder and I flinched. He pulled back as if burned. I turned to see him, and was embarrassed that he looked annoyed, bordering on angry.

"Tom, I'm sorry. I didn't mean—I guess I'm still a bit flinchy. I really appreciate your help out there."

"Gee, I can't *imagine* why you'd be flinchy." His sarcastic tone masked barely contained fury and it made me search his face for answers. I didn't find any.

"Um, what's up with you? I said I was sorry."

He stared at me open-mouthed and then shook his head

and blinked. "What's wrong with *me*? Good Lord, Kate! What in the hell is wrong with *you*? You got hit with a brick just before I met you, ruined your shoulder doing God knows what, got your back *clawed* to ribbons and just were attacked by vampires!" He threw up his hands and fell backward into an overstuffed chair. "So far, I think I've been pretty nice not to ask any personal questions about *why,* but if you've got some sort of sustained death wish that could get me killed too, I think I ought to know the details."

I blushed, because he was right. He'd been remarkably tolerant and hadn't asked any stupid questions. I had thought it was a nice change from other people I knew.

But then again—the best defense is a good offense. *Why* hadn't he asked any stupid questions? Any other normal person would have grilled me until I spilled at dinner after the brick incident. It's not a terribly common event. I hated to be so suspicious, but I haven't been having much luck with people playing fair lately.

I crossed my arms over my chest and leaned against the nearest wall. "Fine. You want details? How about this—the queen vampire is trying to capture a young girl named Becky, who goes by Dusty. I'm trying to stop her. They don't want me to. End of story."

He shook his head and laughed bitterly. "Oh, that is *such* bullshit. This has nothing to do with the girl."

I raised my eyebrows. "So, you *do* know something, huh? Where is she, Tom?"

I saw his back stiffen. His anger was replaced with frustration. I could tell from his body language there was something else going on. I pulled the two photos from my back pocket and held them out to him.

"Go ahead. Look at the face of the girl who's going to get killed if I don't find her." He stood up without meeting my eyes, and without looking at the photos, and entered the kitchen. It's in the same location as my apartment. All the better to string the plumbing together.

Something occurred to me just then, when he wouldn't look at the photos. Maybe he really didn't need to. Maybe this has nothing to do with me, and I'm just a bit player.

I walked to the kitchen doorway and leaned on my good shoulder. He wouldn't meet my eyes. He pulled an apple from a basket on the counter and bit into it almost violently.

"You know, I was about to say that you have no idea how insistent Monica can be, Tom. But maybe you do. There are a lot more Thrall than lycanthropes right now. How do I know the vampires weren't after *you?*"

He looked at me, but just smiled tightly and shook his head. "You don't have a clue what's going on here, Kate. You're not a detective, and you don't know the players. Don't you realized you're being lied to?" His made his voice sound concerned, but there was a hint of tension to the way he held that gorgeous body.

I acknowledged his comment with a nod. "No, I'm not a detective. And yes, I'm aware I'm being lied to. I'm just trying to figure out *who* is doing the lying." Little things were starting to fall into place in my head, and they weren't pleasant. "How did you just *happen* upon my building the other day, Tom? Have you been getting close to me to keep me occupied, to throw me off track? Or is it the other way around? Are you staying here hoping that the Thrall won't mess with me?"

The scowl that darkened his face said that I'd either hit the mark, or hit the opposite end of the spectrum and insulted him.

"So, what—you think I orchestrated that whole scene at the other building? Jeez Louise, Kate! You're paranoid enough to be two people!"

Perfectly true, and skillfully misdirecting. I walked to the other side of the kitchen island and leaned against it, willing him to listen. "I don't want to play games, Tom. You said I was honest. I'm also direct. The girl could be in a lot of danger. Dylan wants me to find her and protect her."

His barking laugh was cut short. "*Protect her.* Now there's a good one!" He took two steps backward, keeping his eyes on me, and leaned against the far counter so we were facing each other with the island in the middle. He crossed his ankles and bit into the apple again.

"Are you saying you don't think I'm *capable* of protecting her?"

He looked at me very seriously, and used the apple to emphasize his words. "No, that was pretty obvious outside. I'm saying that Dylan's lying to you. He wants her found, all right, but not for the reason you think. If you find her and tell them where she is, she's as good as dead. Back away from this one, Kate. For your own good."

I shook my head and sighed. I really *don't* like to play games. Tom might be my best hope for finding the girl before she wound up like her friend. I couldn't afford to be gentle and worry about his feelings. "I'm not working for her stepdad, Tom. I don't know what he wants with her, but I agree with you. Whatever he's planned isn't good. But I was told to keep her safe, and that's what I'm going to do." I realized as I said it that I'd made my decision. I *would* find Dusty. And I *would* protect her. With my life if I had to.

I guessed that I didn't have to pretend anymore, so I used names he should recognize. "Look, Tom, you were spotted picking Dusty up in a cab after Voneen died. If I know that, so does Monica. If you don't tell me here and now, I'll keep digging. That really *might* get her killed. If that's what you want—so be it."

His eyes closed and his jaw stopped working on the bite of apple. His shoulders fell and he shook his head. He swallowed hard, like it wasn't just apple going down his throat. I wondered if he would get defensive or lie to me about it. I really hoped not. It might cause me to say things I would probably regret.

He sighed. "I knew I should have sent Rob to get her. And I'm figuring out just how stubborn you are. Fine. Yeah, I know Dusty. But you need to drop it, Kate. You're really making waves out there. The wrong people are noticing."

"I know. That's why I have to get to Dusty first."

He shook his head and took another bite of the apple. He spoke with his cheek full before he started to chew. "There are things going on that you don't understand, Kate. We *can't* let Dusty get hurt. We'll protect her until Monica is gone."

I thought I probably knew who *we* was, but I needed to make sure. "I'd like to believe that. I really would. But I need more assurance than your word, because there are things that *you* don't understand."

"I understand that if we keep Dusty under cover long enough, Monica will die or she'll pick someone else for the new queen. That's all we're concerned about."

I laughed tiredly and rested my forehead on my arms. I could hear crunching as Tom continued to snack on the apple. I could also still smell that wonderful cologne, and hear his breathing. I looked up at him, and my voice was both sad and determined.

"Tom, you don't understand. Dusty is already Monica's *second* choice, because she's not going to get the first. Dylan believes I'm strong enough to save her. I'm not so sure, but I *do* know that if it's just you and Jake watching her, Tom, she's dead. You have a job, and the kid won't last ten minutes against a true Thrall attack. Monica will send dozens of Hosts if she finds out where Dusty is hiding."

"And we'll deal with it. We've battled the Thrall before, and we're still here. The only loose cannon is *you,* Kate. Just back off and let us take care of it."

I let out a harsh breath. "I can't do that. So, if that's been your goal while snuggling up to me, it won't work."

Tom's eyes were angry and hurt over the bright red apple. "No, it wasn't my *goal.* I *thought* you might be someone I'd like to get to know."

His next words were flat and cold. They hit my heart like a lead weight. "Apparently, I was wrong." He shook his head and walked out the door to the living room. "Look, I'll find another place to live and get this stuff moved out in a day or two. Obviously, there's no future for either of us with me living here."

I swallowed hard and tried to stay mad, but it was no good. If he was being straight with me, and we really were on the same side—to keep Dusty alive, then I'd insulted the hell out of him. If not, then I couldn't trust him farther than I could see him, and needed to keep him close until I knew where Dusty was.

I really hate trying to figure this stuff out. It's why I'm *not* a detective. I followed him to the living room, where he had already opened the door for me to leave. "You don't need to move out, Tom. Frankly, I can use the money, and you said you need a place. Fine. I'll do my best to believe that we're on the same side. But I can't stop searching for her. I just hope neither of us winds up dead."

His eyes met mine for a moment when I turned around after stepping over the threshold, but there was little warmth in them. "I hope so too, Kate, because I can't stop protecting her. And if that means one of us *does* wind up dead, so be it."

He closed the door—on a lot of things.

12

Well, wasn't this just turning out to be a ducky day! I wanted, *needed* to talk to someone to try to get some perspective. But I remembered that Joe was going out of town for some sort of class, and Peg wouldn't be home yet. Who did that leave? Mike.

Maybe my priest could help me sort things in my head. He's pretty good at that. Plus, I could visit Bryan, and I felt safe at the church. The best of all worlds.

I wouldn't even admit to myself that I might be visiting just to say goodbye. Goodbye would mean I thought I would lose. Surely not.

I hopped in Edna, realizing I *still* hadn't taken my suitcase upstairs. Oh, well. The luggage was the least of my worries. I drove out of the garage, stopping long enough to be sure that the gate was securely down and that nobody was lurking outside the building. That's actually a trick while wearing the neck guard. I have full range of motion, but it cuts into my neck when I twist quickly. I drove around the block once, checking for suspicious people. I didn't see anyone. I would think that Monica would have *someone* at least watching my place after the attack, but hell, who knew? Nothing made any sense to me anymore. I was tired. Physically, mentally and emotionally tired. And much as I hated to admit it, I was terrified.

The sun was setting, so I drove down 17th Street with the sun right in the rearview mirror. The cell phone rang shrilly, and I jumped, letting out a little yipping noise. Damn Monica anyway. Damn her ability to terrify me. Fear gave way to good old fashioned anger—at least temporarily.

"Hello." My voice sounded rough, deeper than usual. Even the one word seemed angry. Good. I pulled the truck to the side of the road to take the call.

"Kate, it's Tom." His voice sounded tight and the tone was very carefully neutral. "Our Acca asked me to tell you that she wants to meet with you. The Shamrock Motel, room 150. Day after tomorrow at 3 p.m."

"Your what?"

"Our leader, the head of the wolves."

His pack leader. I was going to meet with the Acca of the local werewolf pack. Good.

"Tom . . ." I wanted to apologize to him, and I wasn't even sure what for.

His voice came across the wire once more, curt and thick with warning. "Don't say anything you don't want people to hear, Kate."

I shut my mouth. He'd felt free enough to tell me the time and place of a meeting, but I wasn't supposed to talk freely? What was up? "I'll be there."

"Good." He hung up the phone without saying goodbye and without giving me any additional information. Pressing a few buttons gave me a call back number but when I dialed it nobody answered.

I pulled back onto the road, mulling today's events. I had my hands full driving in downtown traffic to reach the church, so deep thoughts weren't terribly bright. Colorado Boulevard was out of my way, but I wanted to grab food first and driving around helps me think. There aren't many places to eat by the church. I pulled into a drive-through burger place and waited in line for an overcooked burger on a soggy bun, and suddenly remembered the last pill resting in the little amber bottle back home. Sigh. *Maybe tomorrow, if I last that long*. I was still snacking on salty fries as the church came into sight.

Most Catholic churches have towers and spires that soar gracefully heavenward and attempt to typify the best of the human spirit. But Our Lady of Perpetual Hope is just a little red brick building with a steeple. Once upon a time this part of the central city had been a lower middle-class Irish neighborhood with enough of a Catholic population to justify a church and private school. Over the years the middle-class abandoned the inner city for the suburbs. The school is boarded up, the underground tunnel linking it to the rectory sealed off by a locked iron gate. Located in what's one of the worst neighborhoods in Denver, all Our Lady's church can typify now is harsh reality. Unshaven old men with shopping carts and forlorn women with vacant-eyed children wander the sidewalk. The masses are empty in summer, crowded with homeless looking for warmth in the winter. The soup kitchen does a booming business year round.

Michael O'Rourke and I grew up in the neighborhood in the "old days." We dated in high school, long before he realized his calling. He's a good man and a great priest, but he gets disillusioned at times. I can't blame him. He gets to see the worst life has to offer on a daily basis. His knowledge of the Thrall comes from the folks that visit the parish shelter. He offers blankets in winter, meals when he can, and solace year round. When a "regular" doesn't show up for a few days he always checks around, even though he knows the news probably won't be good.

I parked my truck on the one-way street across from the arched double doors that serve as the front entrance. The brass railing matched the hammered brass door pulls. All are kept polished to an almost blinding brilliance. I walked up the first two concrete steps; then stopped. I always stop and look up at the stained glass window. It's an absolutely stunning rendition of the Pieta, the famous painting by Michelangelo which depicts Mary cradling Christ's dead body. It's always struck me as an odd choice for the window of a church that is named for hope. What do I know? It's been there since the church was built. That it's remained unbroken all these years in this neighborhood is a true miracle.

Our Lady's is small, but immaculately tended. It's how Michael keeps Bryan and the rest of his zombies busy and off the street. He has the equivalent of a mission, with twelve zombies that he and a few workers care for 24/7. I'm awed by his dedication. I sure as hell couldn't do it. The best I can do is donate time and labor to keep down expenses. The coat of spotless white paint on the doors and trim were contributed in good part by Joe and I one sunny weekend last summer. So were the shutters that closed up the belfry. The metal fire doors on all the other entrances were required upgrades to meet fire code.

Joe hated having to close off the belfry. Back when the neighborhood was better and the church school was open, it had been a family right of passage to break into the belfry and ring the old church bells just before high school graduation. It wasn't easy, either. The bells hadn't been used regularly in decades. A shame really—they have a beautiful tone. The real thing sounds so much better than the canned tape recording they use now. Unfortunately, the real bells are loud. You can hear them for miles around. The neighbors complained. So Mike plays the tape, and the real bells are sealed up in the belfry gathering dust.

I pulled the brass door handle and stepped from the noise and light of the street into the cool dim interior of the church foyer. I stood for a moment. While my eyes adjusted, I took another look up at the window. The afternoon light was streaming through the glass, sending patterns of brilliant color across the smooth gray-veined marble floor. I felt a warmth seep into me as I gazed at the bold russet of Mary Magdalene's robes, the angry gray-green of the storm clouds, and the vivid red of Christ's blood staining his weeping mother's robe. While the Roman soldier in the background reminded me that there is always a price to pay for your convictions, the window calms me. There is peace here. Sanctuary that has nothing to do with the stone and mortar of the building. I glanced over the railing toward the font. An eerie trick of the building's design causes the water in the old marble baptismal to reflect the image of Christ's weeping mother back up at me when I glance at it sideways. I suppressed a shudder at the intensity of the grief and defiance captured in that face by the artist.

The foyer is a reminder of better days. It was a gift from a wealthy patron back when there were such things. The floor and walls are all covered in gleaming white marble veined with gray and black from the quarry in the western slope town of Marble. The ceiling was hand painted by an unknown artist with real talent. At first glance it's a summer sky filled with clouds. But it's like a Doolittle painting. If you look long enough you can see angels and saints in the cloud formations. It needs to be cleaned and restored but the parish doesn't have the money for both that and the soup kitchen. The poor won out. It was a decision I agreed with, so I don't complain.

"Michael?" I called out softly. There was no answer. I poked my head inside the first door and called again.

There are three doors that open off of the foyer. They're painted a glossy black that looks stunning against all that white marble. The two on the east side lead to a unisex bathroom and the choir loft and bell tower. The bathroom's kept unlocked for the street people. The choir loft door isn't. In fact, the same day we'd shuttered it closed Michael had installed a heavy steel deadbolt lock to make absolutely sure no one would go up there and wind up falling through the half-rotted floorboards.

The door on the west side of the lobby was propped open, giving me a glimpse of the smallish room that doubled as Mike's parish office and a changing room. There was no one sitting at the scarred gray metal desk, but the computer sitting on the typewriter shelf was running. The closet doors were closed, hiding the multi-colored priest's robes and the altar boy outfits from view. Someone had been busy with the brass polish here in the office as well. A row of elaborate candlesticks sat on the long counter redirecting golden beams of sunlight from the window across the room. The six-foot brushed steel cross that the altar boys carry to the front of the church at mass has a polished brass Christ hanging from its limbs. Even the fruit bowl had been polished to a mirror finish.

Michael has a sweet tooth. He started gaining a little weight a couple of years ago and stopped keeping candy around. Instead, he keeps fresh fruit in a silver bowl on his desk. I started to snag an apple from the top of the pile, but changed my mind and walked back through the foyer and the open arches into the church proper.

I dipped my right hand into the basin of holy water and crossed myself. The movement hurt, both from the shoulder and the fact that it made the bandages pull just enough to remind me the scratches were there. I paused for a second inside the door to say a silent prayer of thanks that things weren't worse, followed by a plea that they stay that way.

I heard murmuring in the main chapel. The decor in the body of the church doesn't match the foyer at all. It's much more modern, and more plain. A 1960s remodel tore out most of the old church. Only the original stained glass windows and dark-stained pews remain.

I started down the main aisle, my footsteps silenced by the burgundy carpet installed over tile flooring. Otis, the janitor, was in the corner by the prayer candles. I heard him call out "Mike, I need to get us some more votives. Where are they?"

"In the basement, in the closet under the stairs that lead up to my rooms. There should be a whole case of them." I followed the sound of his voice to the front of the church. Father Michael O'Rourke stood near the pulpit in his traditional black priest's "uniform" next to a woman I'd never seen before. She was tall and sturdy looking, with blonde hair put up in a bun. She looked at me with wide, panicked eyes and then quickly turned and walked toward the other two occupants of the room. My brother Bryan and a girl of about fifteen with vacant eyes were rubbing lemon oil into the dark wood of the pews. Bryan didn't look up. Just polishing the pews took his entire concentration.

Mike's face lit up when he saw me, but fell into stern lines a split second later.

"*Kaaate.*" The word ended in a low growl, showing his annoyance. I fought not to turn around and walk back out. As both one of my oldest friends and my priest, he gets to lecture me—up to a point. Mike dropped the cloth he'd been using to oil the pulpit onto a first row pew and walked down the aisle toward me. He ran a hand through his thinning blond hair in the unconscious gesture he always uses when he's worried. Moving the hair back revealed a pair of blue eyes the exact color of a summer sky. Funny, I keep forgetting how attractive he is. His face is handsome, not pretty—with sharp cheekbones and a strong jaw. In fact, his features would be devastatingly perfect if he hadn't broken his nose playing hockey in high school. The nose doesn't ruin his looks. Instead, it makes him more human and approachable. A good half of the females he encounters wind up with a crush on him, but it's a waste of their time. Mike takes his vows very seriously.

He let out an exasperated breath. "Kate, when are you going to stop trying to save everyone from reality? We're all big kids now."

"What do you mean?" I could try to play dumb, but I knew he'd see right through it.

He sat down on the pew nearest to me and patted the seat next to him. I genuflected automatically, crossing myself again before reaching out to touch the smooth surface. I sat down the next row back, forcing him to turn to look at me.

"How many times have I asked you if you were keeping Joe in the loop? How long have you been—well, *lying* to me that he was paying his share and he knew that Bryan's condition was deteriorating?"

I leaned back onto the smooth polished wood and stared at the ceiling. I did not need this right now. "Look, Mike—"

He raised his voice, which he almost never does, and it caused me to jerk my head forward to stare at him open-mouthed. Each word had a knife edge, which I haven't heard in years. "NO, blast it! *You* look, Kate! I just had to endure nearly thirty minutes of tail chewing from your brother, and it was *deserved!* I trusted you, Kate. Joe has the right to know what's happening with Bryan. You have no right to protect him from the truth! And don't even get me *started* on dealing with the whole Thrall mess! I swear, if you don't start letting people help you manage things, you're going to wind up *dead!* Dylan—"

I stared at him coldly. Fine. If he wants reality, he was going to get it right between the eyes. "Dylan is one of them now, Mike. Did he mention that? He's a Host now. Anything he says is suspect. Yeah, I'll have to deal with Monica. I don't get a choice. But it doesn't have to involve anyone else. It's *me* she's after."

There was no flinching in his face when I told him about Dylan. Had he actually told Mike? "There are always choices, Katie."

"There aren't always good ones."

We stared at each other for a long moment, but neither of us was going to give in about this. Ever one to change the subject, I glanced again at the woman and then motioned toward her with my head. I raised my brows at Michael.

He sighed and shook his head. "Fine, then. Change the subject. But fair enough, you haven't met Carol yet." He raised his voice slightly. "Carol, come over here and meet Kate." The woman turned her deer in the headlights gaze to me again. She stooped and picked up the rag that Bryan had dropped. He just knelt there, not even knowing enough to pick up the cloth. Once he had it, though, he again began to polish.

"Kate, this is Carol Rodgers. She's a registered nurse. She just showed up the other day, offering to help me with our charges." Michael always refers to the zombies as charges.

I leaned toward Michael and lowered my voice. Carol was just starting to walk down the aisle to greet us. "Obviously, I'm thrilled, Michael. I guess I'm just surprised you can afford a *registered* nurse. Have donations picked up, or is she the *new expense* you mentioned on my machine, because—"

He actually gave me a bit of a smile. "She's a *volunteer,* Kate. Isn't it great? She believes that helping the charges is her calling, just like it's mine!"

Carol reached us but waited hesitantly for an invitation. I held out my hand to shake hers but she stepped several pews away and nodded her head. "Nice to meet you."

I smiled and stood, continuing to hold out my hand. Panic flowed across her face, causing one eyelid to twitch. She looked around frantically and then deliberately placed her palms down on the slick wood of the pew next to her. When she released it a second later, her hands were covered with oil. "I wouldn't want to get this oil all over you, Ms. Reilly. But it's nice to meet you."

I felt my brow furrow. Maybe I'm just paranoid but it didn't seem normal behavior for a nurse. They're generally a little brusque, but always polite. And how did she know my last name? I tried to open my senses, to read her, but came up against a complete blank.

"Are you new to the area, Carol?" I tried to keep any note of suspicion from my voice.

She shook her head and crossed her arms over her chest. All of that slick oil smeared across the front of her shirt. Curiouser and curiouser. "Not really," she said. "I actually grew up in Georgetown, but graduated from nursing school back east. When my parents died, I decided to move back here and help take care of zom . . . I mean, the charges."

Michael's the only person I've ever met that actually *wants* to take care of zombies. I had no doubt there were others, but this person didn't look the type. Her makeup was too perfect. The nails that peeked from under her crossed arms were long and exquisitely maintained. I didn't know what her angle was, but I was probably going to mention to Michael in private to check her references. Still, he's a big boy. He's been in the business long enough that few people can take advantage of him.

There was a thunk of plastic hitting wood. Carol turned and saw that the vacant-eyed girl had knocked over the bottle of oil. "Oh, Tiffany, whatever will we do with you?" She dashed to the rescue with a mumbled, "Sorry. Nice to meet you."

When I turned back to Michael, he was beaming. "Isn't she wonderful? It's so nice to be able to attend to my other duties, knowing that the charges are cared for." His face again grew serious. "Which reminds me, Kate. You're wearing your collar?" He made it a question.

Oh, suddenly I'm lumped in with Bryan and Tiffany? I tapped on my shoulder. Through the cloth, it sounded like thumping on a cantaloupe. "Never leave home without it. You wearing yours?"

He gave the joke the weak smile it deserved. "Good." He swallowed hard. He looked toward the front of the church, as if checking with the cross for guidance. Taking a deep breath, he spoke.

"Dylan said they're after you, Katie—the Thrall. They say that the local queen's Host is dying and she doesn't have an heir."

"So I've been told."

He nodded grimly at my confirmation. I started to say more, but stopped. Bryan had reached the end of the pew he'd been working on. He now stood vacant eyed, incapable of doing anything further without another direct order. Carol was still helping wipe up the oil Tiffany had spilled and didn't notice.

Michael didn't say anything. He just watched me watching my brother. "How is he?" The words were choked with pain. No tears. I'd cried myself out over Bryan long ago.

Mike shrugged his shoulders. "We've been over this before. He's healthy and strong. Same as always. What do you want me to say, Kate? That he's getting better? He's not, and he won't. He's getting worse, just like they all do. Every day when I wake him I have to remind him who I am. It used to be every other day. He has to be told his own name so he can respond to instructions. He can follow direct orders, but only if they're simple enough. Anything else is just beyond him. Look at him. A year ago, he could have polished all of the pews in here with one instruction. Now he doesn't even know to move to the next pew unless I tell him. I can keep him and the others alive and busy but they'll never be who they were— never recover. There's too much damage from the drugs."

It was brutal, but the truth. The shell lived, but the essence that had been my brother was just . . . gone. God help me, it would almost have been better if he'd died. Then I could mourn him the way we'd mourned my parents and be done with it. "Can I say hello?"

Michael sighed, giving a gentle shake of his head at my never-ending stubbornness. "Bryan, come here."

Bryan raised his head, turned obediently and shambled toward us. His face was an expressionless mask. Attractive enough, but lifeless. Without thought or emotion, there was no animation. Carol watched attentively.

"Bryan," said Michael, "This is your sister, Kate. Say hello."

"Hello, Sister Kate."

I gave a wry chuckle. It made me sound like a nun! Michael laughed. Bryan's face lit up when we laughed, and he joined in even though he didn't understand. When we stopped, so did he; the laughter cut off as if by a switch. He gave Michael a vacant look, waiting for his next order.

Michael stood and took Bryan's arm, walking him down the aisle to the next pew past the girl who was still rubbing oil into the wooden bench with vigorous movements, oblivious to everything but the task she'd been given. She had never stopped her task to even acknowledge my presence. Michael handed him off to Carol, who placed an oiled cloth into Bryan's hand, then steered the hand down to the wooden surface.

"Bryan, rub the cloth on the wood and make it shiny from here—" Carol moved to the other end of the pew. "To here. Then stop."

Bryan set to work at once, his brow furrowed with concentration. When Mike was sure his charge had understood Carol's command, he walked back down the aisle and sat next to me.

He spoke softly, as though we might be overheard. Of course, maybe Michael wasn't as sure about Carol as I thought. "Dylan told me something else, Kate. The eggs and the hatchlings can't stand alcohol. That's why none of the drunks on the street has ever been infested. He . . . he couldn't tell you himself, so he asked me to let you know. Said for you to get good and drunk and stay that way."

When Carol left the room to fetch more oil, I raised my voice a little. "I can't fight when I'm drunk, Michael."

"If you stay drunk you may not *have* to fight."

"You can't trust what he says, Mike. He's not human— he's not *Dylan* anymore."

I didn't like the way Mike was squirming in his seat like a guilty schoolboy. He didn't answer or meet my eyes. Instead, he turned to watch Bryan and the girl. They scrubbed the pews as if their lives depended on it. I winced. The thought was closer to the truth than I cared to think about.

Mike turned his attention back to me. His blue eyes had gone very dark, and his voice was as serious as I'd ever heard it. "You're in terrible danger, Kate. You need to leave town, make it impossible for her to find you."

I shook my head and stared past him toward the front of the church and the bright stained glass. "I can't do that. It's not just about me anymore."

Mike looked crestfallen and weary. "You're right, Kate. It's *not* just about you. Other people are depending on you. Don't leave them without you."

I closed my eyes and clenched my hands into fists. "Don't go there Mike. Really, don't."

"Fine, if you won't leave, then get drunk. It's your only hope if you stay in town."

I let out an exasperated breath. "Why can't you get it through your head? He's *theirs,* Michael. They own him." It was the truth. Dylan might still be alive but I sure as hell hadn't saved him. He was a Host now and I couldn't change that. I hated that I was completely powerless.

Michael shook his head. Once, then twice. "I know you think Dylan betrayed you by doing this, but he wouldn't lie. Not about this. Not to me. They may own his body, Kate. They don't own his soul."

"I'm not sure I'm ready to take that chance. Do you know where he is? I can find out if he's telling the truth."

He gave me a blistering look that I hadn't seen since his hockey days. "I've told you everything I'm allowed to, Kate."

Ah, the sanctity of the confessional. Mike would take Dylan's secrets with him to the grave if need be. "Then there's nothing I can do with the information you've given me. I can only treat it as a lie. I'm sorry, Michael."

"For God's sake, Kate!" Mike threw up his hands in a gesture of exasperation. "Will you at least think about it? Please?"

I nodded my head and stood to go. "Goodbye, Michael." I raised my voice a little bit. "Bye, Bryan." No response, but then I hadn't really expected one.

Michael looked at me with serious eyes. "See you next week, Kate." Not goodbye. Never goodbye. Then he turned and walked back to his charges. He didn't look back as I left the church.

13

It was nearing dark. I kept replaying the conversation with Mike in my head. Dylan's place in the scheme of things was still a question mark. He might truly be trying to save me with the tip about alcohol. On the other hand, getting drunk might be just a trick to get my guard down enough for Monica and the rest to dominate my mind. I've never heard of a queen being able to separate from the Hive, and I wouldn't be able to tell whether Dylan was one of Monica's Hosts or not, even if I found him. I'm not that talented. I supposed that someday I could forgive Dylan for doing what he did, but I couldn't trust him. I had too much to lose.

I was about two blocks from home when the cell rang, startling me from my musings. I knew before I picked up the line that it was Mike, and that something was seriously wrong.

"What's up, Mike?"

"Is Bryan with you?"

I had to clear my throat twice before I could get words out. "Why would Bryan be with me, Michael? I left him with you polishing pews. Maybe he just went downstairs to his room."

"Jesus Christ, Kate! If I hadn't already searched the church, do you think I'd call you?" When Michael falls back into old swearing habits, it says how much stress he's under. I slammed on my blinker and forced my way into the right lane. If I turned around right now, I could be back at the church in fifteen minutes.

"I'm on my way back, Michael. Which way did you send Carol, so we can cover more ground?"

There was a long pause where the only sound was the honking of horns as I swerved around a car pulling out of a parking place. Edna's hard to drive with one hand—no power steering. And it's impossible to shift.

"Michael? Are you still there?"

His voice was careful; hesitant. "I'm here, Kate."

"Then talk to me, damn it! I'm doing almost fifty in a thirty zone to get back there before he can get too far. Which direction do I start from? Where's Carol? Does she have a cell phone with her?"

"Carol's not here, Kate. I don't know where she is." Sadness and worry flowed through the phone line. If I knew Michael, anger would be next.

"Damn it, Michael! Are you telling me that Bryan's been kidnapped?"

I slammed on the brakes just in time not to run a red light directly in front of a cop car. *Pay attention, Reilly!*

I could almost see Michael running fingers through his hair. "I don't know, Kate. I just don't know. I made a call in the office. I was only gone a few minutes but when I came back, Bryan was gone and so was Carol. She only works half-days on Friday, but she said earlier that she was going to stay all day."

I took a deep, steadying breath. If I opened my shields now, I could find him. I knew it. But I'd also might as well be lighting a homing beacon for the Thrall to find me. *Damn, damn damn!* To hell with it. I dropped my shields.

My mind's eye searched the city, feeling for Bryan's presence. I can't really explain how I do it. It's sort of like walking in a familiar dark room and *knowing* where each piece of furniture is. You have to feel around for them, but you know with absolute certainty they're there. I groped in the darkness for my brother, but finding him was like catching a jumping frog. It took a few seconds of spreading my mind over the city, but I found him.

He was in a car. Carol was driving but had stopped. I might have gotten more had I not been distracted by the blaring of car horns. The light had changed and the cars behind me expected me to move. I pulled around the corner, pulling up to the curb in a no-parking zone. I tried to open my senses again, but came up against the smooth white wall of Monica's shielding.

Shit!

"He's with Carol." I didn't bother to explain how I knew, and Mike didn't ask. "They're in a car. Is there any legitimate reason for her to take him somewhere?"

Mike's voice was flat and cold. "No."

"Fine, give me Carol's home address. I'll head there first. Maybe she's taking him there." I didn't think so, but it was a start.

He read me the information from her application, while I once again turned at a yellow light to head in the direction the address pointed me. I hung up the phone so that he could start to call in some of the church regulars to help search.

I reached the building in moments. It was only a few blocks away. Naturally, there was no parking on the street, but I didn't have time for that now, anyway. I pulled into the alley next to the older brick building and turned off the ignition. Few vehicles other than a trash truck can move Edna out of the way. A brown and white dog behind a tattered chain link fence barked furiously at my intrusion. I opened the outer door and bolted up the stairs to Apartment 204. I heard sound behind the door, and pounded on the molded steel. "Carol, it's Kate. I need to talk to you!"

A Hispanic woman holding a baby opened the door. "*¿Que?*"

The apartment behind her was furnished in early Salvation Army. Besides the young boy in the mother's arms, there were two more at a table, eating dinner. The television was blaring the Spanish version of *Sesame Street*.

I wasn't really good in Spanish in school, and I have to struggle to remember even the simplest of lines when I'm in any of the South American countries. I do a little better with understanding. *"Hola. ¿Hables Ingles usted?"*

She glanced down at my hand and shook her head. *"No, Señorita."*

Great! Um . . . well, I can at least tell her I don't speak Spanish very well. Then maybe she won't start into a torrent that I won't be able to follow. *"Yo hablo mal el español."* She raised her head and then nodded in understanding. She waited patiently for me to come up with the next phrase while the baby pulled at her shining hair. I wanted to ask if she knew Carol, but I couldn't think of quite the right words. Maybe— *where* is Carol? *"¿Dónde está Carol Rodgers?"*

She shook her head with furrowed brows. *"¿Quién? ¿Carol Roggers?"* She shook her head a second time, and transferred the infant to her shoulder as he started to howl. *"No. No está."* She pointed to herself. *"Rosa Rodriguez. Aquí tienes mi casa."* She held up five fingers. *"Ser de aquí cinco meses."*

Of course. Rosa and kiddies had lived in the apartment for five months. It was a fake address. *Dear Lord, Michael. What's happening to you?* He must be getting desperate for help not to even check out the woman's application.

I nodded my head and likewise glanced at her hand. A simple gold band gleamed softly on her finger. I turned to go and apologized for bothering her. *"Gracias, Señora Rodriguez. Lo lamento molestarle."*

"No para nada, Señorita." She smiled as she shut the door. Well, at least I didn't butcher the language enough to make her mad.

I took the steps back down three at a time. I didn't even have to wonder about Carol's motives now. She had Bryan and Monica was protecting her. Monica was breaking the rules again. I had no doubt she was planning to use Bryan as a hostage against me if I didn't stop her. The only way I could was to get to Carol before she got back to the nest.

I tried to remember if anyone had ever told me where Monica had her headquarters. I knew she'd abandoned Larry's old haunts, but had anyone told me? I wracked my brain as I doubled back to the church. I just didn't know.

My only hope was that maybe one of the street people had seen something. I stopped when the next light turned red and checked my wallet. I only had about thirty bucks on me. Still, even a few bucks will loosen a lot of tongues down there.

I picked up my cell phone again and clicked the down arrow five times to come to the church phone number without even looking at the display. Knowing in which order I've saved the numbers really helps when I'm driving. I hit the send button. It didn't even ring on my end before it was picked up.

"This is Father Michael!" His voice was two shades above panicked.

"It's Kate, Mike. Have you heard anything?"

He sighed, and I could imagine him running his fingers through his hair once more. "Not a thing. Any luck with Carol?"

I hesitated. I wanted to spare him any additional anguish, but this wasn't the time for it. I plowed on, trying to keep any hint of reprimand from my voice. "I got to the address, but someone else lived there. I'm on my way back to the church now to talk to some of the street people. Maybe we can get a lead if we're both looking."

His voice sounded tight and pained. "Kate, I'm so sorry. I'd never have imagined that she would use a fake address. My God in Heaven! What have I done?"

I tried to think of something to say that would console him, but it was a little difficult under the circumstances.

When I got back the church, Michael had already talked to the people around the church. Nobody saw anything. It was their story and they were sticking to it. Even money couldn't pry information from them, so maybe they really didn't know. Neither of us could find Joe to tell him. He either hadn't taken his cell phone, or was out of range. I either couldn't remember where the seminar was being held, or he hadn't mentioned it. Mike finally insisted that I go home around eleven, because after that many hours, searching in the dark would do no good. We'd pick up the search again in the morning.

I only agreed to go because I knew what I had to do. I

drove in to the parking garage, knowing that nobody would be waiting for me. Monica had the only thing she needed to bring me to her. I noticed lights on in Tom's apartment as I drove in, and nearly took the stairs to knock on his door to just have someone to talk to. But I didn't.

I called Joe on his cell phone. He answered on the first ring, and sounded panicked. Apparently, Mike had finally reached him.

"Kate! Thank God! Have you found Bryan?"

I closed my eyes and tried not to cry again. "Not yet. It got too dark. We couldn't see anything in the alleys or side streets. We're going to start again at dawn. But I need to ask you something."

"Anything. I'm just packing up my things. I'm catching the first flight out that I can find. But the airport here in San Francisco is socked in, so I don't know if it'll be until morning. But I'm going to the airport anyway."

Oh. I didn't realize he was in California. I'd presumed the conference was local. A little bit of the overwhelming worry slipped into my voice. "Please don't rush so much you get hurt, Joe."

His voice was tense, but determined. "I won't. I promise. What's your question?"

"Tell me about werewolves."

As an ER physician, Joe is required to treat anybody and anything that comes through those doors hurt. That includes the "furballs," as the hospital staff less than affectionately refer to the lycanthropes. He might or might not have information, but it wouldn't hurt to ask.

The outrage in his voice took me by surprise. "Werewolves! The vampires have Bryan and you're worried about your love life?"

"Joe! This *is* about Bryan! It's important!"

It was probably my tone that silenced him. I heard a shuffling sound and faint squeak that told me he'd sat down on the bed.

"All right." He launched into a monologue that was probably going to make him miss at least one flight. He didn't even ask any questions until he'd finished.

"Lycanthropy is a hereditary condition. It is not contagious in any form. Female lycanthropes are sterile. They protect the males. The pack system is matriarchal. Each pack recruits a human female to be the surrogate and give birth to the puppies for the pack."

"A surrogate—" I thought about Jake's words in the restaurant, and Tom's in his apartment. "*We've* taken care of it" and "We *can't* let her get hurt." Was Dusty going to be a mommy? More importantly, who was the daddy?

Joe continued as if he hadn't heard the interruption. Maybe he hadn't. "The change is linked to adrenaline. Most of them have very little control over it. They get in a crisis situation and boom, dog time. It's why the state won't issue driver's licenses to known lycanthropes."

"That's got to be a pain in the ass."

"No doubt. Now tell me the truth. This isn't about Tom, is it?"

"Nope. I've got a meeting with the local Acca tomorrow. It's about Dusty. And they might know what's going on with Bryan. They seem to have their ear to the ground in anything involving the Thrall. Thanks. That's enough information for me to meet with the Acca."

"Yeah, right. Talk to me, Kate."

"Look, I don't know much more than I did a couple of minutes ago. But, if it makes you feel any better, I'll call you when I do."

"Promise?"

"Promise." I hung up the phone before he could press for more and went upstairs to try to get some sleep.

The bedroom was a mess from my frantic search for the brace earlier, so I spent a few minutes hanging and folding clothes, but that woke me up again. So I unpacked my suitcase and put a bag of laundry down in the truck to take to the dry cleaners. Nope. Still too wired to sleep. Well, maybe some food and warm milk.

I grabbed a pasty from the freezer and popped it in the microwave. The tantalizing smell told me that I was hungrier than I'd thought. I ate the first one while walking around the living room watering the plants and trimming the leaves that

Joe had missed yesterday. I was too wired to sleep, and dreading what I knew I had to do.

The first tasted good enough that I treated myself to a second one. I took another pill and had to admit I was impressed with the little capsule that made the goose egg, and a possible concussion, completely go away

I sat down to start the real searching, the kind I couldn't do with Mike around. He doesn't like to believe that the stuff in my head is real. He knows it is, but he works hard to delude himself, so I try not to beat him over the head with the truth too hard.

I sat down in the recliner and took a deep breath. I closed my eyes and opened my mind. I let it flow outward slowly; carefully. Perhaps the hive wouldn't notice me if I moved slowly. But no such luck. I gasped when I suddenly heard my name in my own head. The buzzing grew louder and louder. The hive was angry; livid, but Monica was smug.

You know I have him, Kathleen. Surrender to me or I will bleed him out before you can find him. Come to us, Kathleen . . . come . . . COME!

I realized I was crying, because I knew she'd do it. I knew I wasn't thinking rationally, because I started to wonder where I'd put my car keys and tried to remember where her lair was located.

I shook my head hard and tried to back out of the connection. It wouldn't break. So I turned on the stereo and plugged in a loud rock CD. For the first time, it didn't drown out her voice. My head started to pound and my wounds ached in response to the quickening of my heart.

Come to us, Kate. Be our queen . . . take care of us. Please don't let us die.

I turned up the music, but the desperate chorus of voices grew louder in response. A hive of bees was nesting in my skull and I couldn't make them stop! I shut my eyes and threw up shields. I sang old Celtic drinking songs, and played the CD louder and louder even after I felt vibration underfoot as Tom banged on his ceiling.

. . . we need you, Queen Kate. Help us.

I caught myself twice with the doorknob in my hand and

tears in my eyes. Finally, I did the only thing I could think to do. I took a sleeping pill, even though I'd never used them before when the Thrall was actually *trying* to control me. It could work—but it might backfire and make me susceptible to the hypnotic, sing-song droning. I didn't know how it would interact with the other medicine, and I doubted that Joe and Dr. MacDougal would approve. But I wasn't sure I was going to win this battle in my current state. I had to get some sleep.

Warmth spread through my stomach in a few minutes and my arms started to feel heavy. I lay down on the bed and didn't fight the fuzzy numbness as the drugs quieted the voices and the room faded away.

I felt the cool sheets caress my skin sensuously as Dylan whispered to me in my sleep.

I'm so proud of you, Katie. You're strong and powerful and I've always loved that about you. We'll be together again soon forever.

It made me happier than I could remember. I wanted so desperately for him to approve of me; to want me back. But wait—didn't he used to *hate* that I was stronger than him? Didn't he? I couldn't remember. But I wanted so much to believe.

We'll be together soon, Katydid. I want to touch you again; taste you. I want to be with you and hear you scream my name as I take you again and again. I need to touch you, taste you so bad . . . so very bad. Yes, Katie, let me taste you—

His low, frantic whispers prickled the hair on the back of my neck. I could feel his hunger and lust and need flow through me. A flutter of excitement quickened my heart as his teeth sunk in. The pain in my stomach washed away in a sweet, metallic rush. She wasn't me, but it *would* be me so very soon. Part of me wanted to swim with him in that sensation, feel the climax overtake my body, but still I fought to get away.

This was wrong. This wasn't Dylan. No, no, this can't be the Dylan I knew. I struggled against the whispers, screamed again and again, but I couldn't wake up.

We're sending someone and Monica will be gone, and you'll be mine again. Soon now. We're sending someone—

My eyes flew open and I *was* that someone, stalking Monica in her own lair. She was asleep, surrounded by a bevy of Hosts, when I slid into the room. But I didn't move like I would in real life. The attack on Monica was sudden and violent. Mind and body struck out in unison, but she was ready. I saw her face thin to almost skeletal. Her hiss was unearthly and inhuman. An answering blast of psychic energy hit the dream-me in the chest and knocked me back against a wrought-iron spiral staircase. The metal groaned and bent before the bolts sheared off and the whole works collapsed.

So they've sent you to replace me, have they? The words whispered and hissed through my brain even though her lips never moved. I tried to move, but was trapped in the crushed metal. *You fool! Didn't they learn when I killed the last one? My children will live and they will be more powerful than you can ever imagine. I will not live to see it, but neither will* you!

A blinding flash of white light and dark magic and pain that was like a stiletto to the heart: sudden and deadly. My eyes flew open on the bed and I realized through my pounding heart that it wasn't me that Monica had been fighting. There was abrupt panic in my mind—a fear so strong that it took my breath away. They had been right . . . and so very wrong. The other queens had tried to control Monica by sending one of their strongest to eliminate her. But they had underestimated her. She was more powerful than they had imagined, and now they feared her. Even at the bare ends of her life, she was stronger than the strongest of them.

What in the hell was I going to do?

14

Dawn arrived steeped in dreary mist. I yawned wide and long, but it didn't help to clear my fear that still pounded in my heart and flowed through my veins. Sleeping pills always make me feel wooden and fuzzy the next day, but I supposed it was better than terrified. A shower helped a little bit, but it took two cups of coffee before I could think well enough to put up my mental shields.

I was just picking up my keys when I heard a knock on the door. I risked a quick psychic search, but all I found was a blank wall of sizzling energy. It wasn't Thrall, but what *was* on the other side of the door?

I grabbed both knives in one hand and walked to the door. "Who is it?"

"A name from your past and perhaps an ally to ensure your future." The voice was soft, female, and alto. She did sound familiar, but I couldn't place her.

Opening the door always puts me at a disadvantage, especially now that my shoulder hurt. I unlocked the deadbolt and stepped back to give myself room to move.

"It's open. Come in."

The door swung open easily, as though it was tissue paper, which was my first hint. The minute I saw the woman I started abruptly. I recognized her. We'd played softball together in high school.

Mary Connolly had always been a bit butch. Short and stocky with golden-brown eyes and naturally black hair that she kept just a little bit shorter than any of the other girls in school. It never occurred to me at the time that she might be a wolf, but as soon as she walked through the door, I just knew.

There'd been rumors in school that she was gay and more rumors that we were an item. As far as I knew she wasn't. *We* certainly weren't. Back then I'd been keeping busy with the pre-broken-nose Michael. But I remembered she was tough as nails. It didn't look like time had softened her. I couldn't criticize. I haven't exactly softened up either.

"Hi, Mary. Long time no see."

She smiled, but there was a hard edge to it. "Nice to know I'm memorable after all these years. May I come in? We need to talk."

Mary was always one for getting right to the point, which I'd always liked about her. I tucked the knives back in the sheathes, which made one corner of her mouth turn up. I couldn't tell if it was because she was impressed that I'd been ready to fight, or that she thought it was cute but futile, which was a distinct possibility.

I still remembered watching her beat the crap out of one of the boys from a rival school, after he'd nearly raped one of the girls on our team. He wound up in the hospital for a month, and she got suspended for a week. I probably should have too, since I didn't stop her. Heck, I think I remember applauding. While my nickname was *the Terminator,* hers was *the Enforcer.* She could have beat the crap out of me back then. I didn't honestly know who would prevail now.

"I don't have any time to talk right now, Mary. I have to go—"

"Find Bryan," she completed with a serious nod. "I know. That's why I'm here."

I didn't sit down completely, but I rested my tail on the arm of one chair and swung my hand to offer her the couch. Mary didn't sit either. She stepped forward and mimicked my move. She sat on the other chair's arm, directly across from me. Check. My move.

"This doesn't have anything to do with the wolves."

One eyebrow raised, but then she gracefully shrugged. "So, you know I'm a lycanthrope. No matter. I was going to tell you anyway. But I'm not *just* a wolf, Kate. I'm the Acca of Denver."

It was my turn to show surprise, but not because she was Acca. That didn't shock me at all. Like me, she wouldn't be able to stand to be anything less than the top dog . . . er, wolf. "I thought we already had a meeting scheduled."

She nodded and crossed her arms over her chest. "We did. We do. But Bryan's kidnapping upped the stakes. I'm here to offer the assistance of my pack to find him."

I pursed my lips and dropped my gaze to the floor for a moment while trying to figure out why she would make such an offer. I jingled my keys in my hand while I thought. Nope. It was beyond me. "Don't get me wrong, Mary. I appreciate the offer. But why would you care what happens to my brother? This has nothing to do with the wolves."

She chuckled darkly and shook her head. "Well, first—I actually liked Bryan. So, that's one reason. And second, this has *everything* to do with the wolves. We need Bryan found, and you need our help to find him. What's the problem?"

I realized I was tapping one key on my leg as I stared at her blank expression, and stopped. "Just call me suspicious, I guess. I spent the majority of my life wolf-free, and in the last two days I've gotten one for a tenant, been threatened by another at a burger joint, and now the head of the pack stops by my home. You tell me—what's the problem with this picture?"

Her expression darkened. "Who threatened you?"

I shook my head. "No deal. What does Bryan's kidnapping have to do with Dusty?" I figured she'd know the name. They had to be connected.

Her bright smile was cut short, like turning off a switch. "You always were quick on your feet. Yes, you're right. This is about Dusty. I can't let you have Dusty, so I have to help you find Bryan. I'd rather not get involved at all, but life sucks some days."

I shook my head, tiny movements to try to get the little balls to fall into the right holes. "You know, I'm feeling a lot like I missed part of this whole conversation. Let's start from scratch. *Why* can't you let me have Dusty? *Why* do you have to help me find Bryan? *Why* are the wolves fighting with the Thrall at all?"

She slid off the chair arm to land with a soft plop on the overstuffed cushion. "I figured that you were on the same level of knowledge. My mistake." She made a sweeping gesture to ask me to join her. "Sit down. We have time. Monica won't harm a hair on his head for a little while yet."

I glanced at my watch. It was still early, but Mike would probably be calling any time. I grudgingly sat down on the front edge of the chair, but kept my body ready to bolt if I needed to. She noticed.

She steepled her fingers in front of her chin and gave me her full attention. "Okay, then, I'll make it brief. Monica wants you to be the Thrall queen."

"No duh, Mary. I know."

She made a little annoyed noise. "I'm just setting the stage here, so quit interrupting with what you know and don't know. We don't have time."

I shut up, because she was right.

"But Monica knows that you'd rather die—which I don't blame you for, by the way. Just so you know."

I nodded, but didn't comment, so she went on.

"The back-up choice is Dusty, but that's not why we're protecting her."

That raised my eyebrows.

"We started to protect her because of Matt Quinn. She had evidence that he's been skimming money from the city coffers, and doing bad things with Monica—some big plot that she won't even tell *me* about. Suffice it to say that Matt wants the evidence back, and her no longer able to testify. Dead is good, being the Thrall queen would be better, because she would have to honor agreements made by Monica."

"So, Matt *is* working with Monica in this. I knew he was bad news!"

Mary nodded. "The baddest. Anyway, Dusty told her friend Voneen about the documents she'd taken, and she helped Dusty run away. Dusty knew one of our wolves, Rob, from school. Just casually, but they text messaged and stuff. When Monica offered Voneen the queenship, she *knew* that Voneen would die. She had no psychic talent to speak of. But Monica intended to follow Voneen back to Dusty, who *does* have talent. I don't know what Matt is giving Monica to help him eliminate Dusty, but it doesn't matter. We have to ensure that Matt and Monica don't get their hands on her. When I agreed to protect her, I endangered the pack. Matt has sworn revenge against the wolves. In his position as councilman, he can make our lives a living hell. Tom getting kicked out of his place was just the beginning."

My eyes shifted to my watch again. "But I still don't know what Bryan has to do with this. If I can ensure that Dusty is safe with you, the pack can keep her. I never intended to give her back to Quinn. I'm not working for him."

"No, you're working for that slimeball, Dylan Shea. Not much better, Reilly. He's under Monica's thumb, so if he knows where she is, she'll know."

I wasn't going to discuss Dylan's recent allegiance shift, because it was immaterial. "So, again—what has Bryan got to do with this?"

Mary took a deep breath and I heard a grating sound as her teeth ground together. "Like I said, reality sucks. I'll be straight with you, Kate. I know you. Your brothers mean *everything* to you. If it's a choice between Bryan or Joe, and anyone else—you'll pick them. I can't afford that."

I felt my face fall into a look of disgust and anger. "*Fuck you*, Mary! That is just flat *insulting!* I would do no such thing! Dusty's not a trading card to be swapped for someone else's life. I'd die before I let *any* of them get killed."

Mary wasn't surprised by my anger. She just stared at me

calmly, and her next words put an icy chill down my spine that I couldn't seem to shake. "Monica *won't* kill them, Kate. She'll make them long for death; pray for release, but never get it. And she'll make sure that you get a front row seat, even if it's in your head. Bryan's an innocent. He wouldn't even understand. He'd only scream, and scream, and never know why. It's why you're so panicked right now. You know it. What will you risk to save him, Kate? *Who* will you risk? I won't lose Dusty, and I can't afford to have you sacrifice yourself."

She struck home with that one. Because part of me knew that I might well give myself to Monica before I'd let her hurt Bryan.

"And why is that any of your business? I said I won't let Dusty get hurt."

Her smile was sad but her eyes were fierce and determined. "I can't let you be the next Thrall queen, Kate. You're too damned tough and too smart. There's always been balance between the wolves and the Thrall. But Monica has upset that balance, and if you were queen, you'd take advantage of it. Kate Reilly and Queen Kate of the Thrall wouldn't be the same, and you know it. You know that the hive would take full advantage of every skill you possess to their advantage, and eliminate your honor, your morals, your belief in truth and faith and God. Everything that makes you *you*. You would be the Terminator for real, and your Hosts would be extensions of your wrath. We would *die*. By your hand. And you would enjoy each death. You would revel in the blood of your enemies."

She'd said it so calmly, but I couldn't seem to breathe past the reality of the words. Heaven help me, she was right. My mouth opened to speak, but I couldn't seem to be able to put words together.

She took a slow, deep breath. "So. We have to get Bryan back for you, and protect him until Monica is gone. I arranged for Chuck King's detective job, so that you'd have an apartment available for Tom to watch this building and your tenant, and already have my people following Joe and staking out the church. I don't worry about you, so long as the others are safe. I believe you can either kill Monica, or wait her out, so long as no one you love is in danger."

Mary stood up, but I couldn't seem to get my muscles to cooperate to do the same. But I could finally speak. "That's a lot of effort on your part just so *my* life stays sane. Should I be flattered?"

She shrugged and turned to leave. "Be flattered or don't. I'm just trying to protect my pack as best I can." Her hand was on the knob when she stopped. "Oh, and speaking of which—stay away from Tom, please."

I did stand then and walked toward her. "You don't get to pick who your pack does and doesn't date, Mary. That's stepping too far over the line."

The light from the table lamp caught her hair and gave it blue highlights as she turned. "Actually, every Acca gets to pick. Normally I don't, both because I don't care, and because I believe it's wrong. But this is an exception. Tom is one of the strongest males I've ever encountered. He retains his full human mind in animal form. His body proportion makes him blend in with humans. Those are incredibly rare and exciting things in our kind." She stopped and looked at me significantly. "It's very likely that he would pass those traits onto his children—"

I suddenly understood. "And I'm sterile because of the Thrall bite."

She nodded. "I have to protect my pack. You're a dominant female, and he will be attracted to you. He's handsome, and charming and—"

My chuckle was both sad and angry. Not at Tom, but at myself. "And not interested in me. Nor me in him."

Her jaw actually dropped a bit. "Really? That surprises me."

I crossed my arms over my chest, but they wrapped around like I was hugging myself instead. Maybe I was. "He made it very clear that we were on opposite sides of this issue, and offered to move out so we didn't have to live in the same building. The more I think about it, the better of an idea I think it is."

Mary waggled her head. "Well, I guess that's good—and

bad. I need to send out my best tracker to help you find Bryan. One who also has the ability to make sure that you're not captured." She stepped back and opened the door.

Tom was standing there, looking annoyed and embarrassed. Mary waved a hand at him, "Meet your tracker. He's the best I've got." She looked at Tom and I could feel a surge of energy flow from Mary that made him wince a little. "I thought you were lying when you asked not to do this, Tom. I guess I was wrong. But you *will* make every effort to get her brother to safety, and you *will* be civil to Kate."

He glared down at her for a moment, and didn't even look at me. His voice was filled with too many things to sort. "Of course, Acca. I will do as you command."

She stepped past him out the door, and her head barely reached his Adam's apple. "Don't take any unnecessary risks, Kate. If we have to fight the Thrall, we will, but I don't want my wolves to be cannon fodder, either."

Tom stepped in the door, and closed it. He walked to the window and stared down, while I gathered my purse and tried to figure out how not to make this a disaster. Apparently, he saw Mary walk away, because he turned around.

I stared into his stony face and gave him one of my own. "Look, you don't need to do this. I can find Bryan just fine, and I really don't need someone tagging along who is going to make my life miserable."

He continued to stare at me hostilely without speaking or blinking for a moment.

"Look," I said in annoyance. "If you've got something to say to me, just say it. I'm really not in the mood for the silent treatment today."

The first words out his mouth were a sarcastic snarl. "I never figured you for the passive-aggressive type, Kate. If you wanted me out of the building, you could have just said so. I thought head games were beneath you."

I raised my hands, palm up, and reared back a bit. "What in the hell are you talking about? Passive-aggressive? What does that mean?" He started to answer, and I amended. "No, I know what it *means,* but what do *you* mean by it?"

He settled into an aggressive stance and frowned. "Oh,

gee, I don't know. Maybe playing heavy metal music above my head so loud all night that it actually vibrated a picture off the wall and broke the frame. Wolves have sensitive ears, Kate. I decided it was intentional when I banged on the ceiling and you turned it *up*."

I shook my head and the words came out more sarcastic than I'd planned. Guilt does that to me. "Gosh, Tom, I guess the next time the queen Thrall and her entire hive are simultaneously mentally attacking me, I'll try to be more respectful with the *one thing* that actually helps me manage not to put a gun to my head and blow my brains out." I glared at him until I felt hot tears sear my eyes. I turned away as understanding finally filled his face.

I stalked into the kitchen and pulled off a paper towel from the roll to wipe my eyes. Today was sucking even worse than yesterday. When the tears threatened a second time, I slapped myself sharply across the face, and they faded. The sting in my cheek cleared my head. I needed to get moving. Daylight was burning.

When I turned around, Tom was standing there. "Kate, I . . . I don't know what to say. Why didn't you say something? I had no way of knowing you were being attacked. I would have helped."

I shook my head and pushed past him out toward the door. "I didn't need your help, Tom—then or today. I don't need your help or your pity, or anything else." I slid one of the knives from the wrist sheath and checked the edge while he watched. It wasn't perfect, but it would do. "I'm going to find Bryan. Come along or don't. But stay out of my way."

15

I didn't want to leave the laundry in the garage, or go back upstairs, so I stuffed it behind the seat. It didn't fit very well. The seat wouldn't lie flat, but hey—the day was already sucking. What was being uncomfortable to boot?

Yeah, Tom rode along. The business part of me actually hoped he'd stay behind, but a tiny little new piece wanted him to stay, despite being snippy with each other. I wanted his help and his comfort. It unnerved me a bit.

"So," I said to end five blocks of unbearable silence at a whopping twenty miles an hour. "If we're going to use your nose, do we need to go down to the church first?"

"Wherever he was taken from. Are you sure it was from the church?"

"It was the last place I saw him, anyway. It's too late in the season to escape the snow."

Tom looked at me with the oddest expression. "Huh? What does snow have to do with it?"

I shrugged and automatically shifted into third gear through sheer force of habit. Yeah, I regretted it. "What does snow have to do with *what?*"

"That's what you said—it's too late in the season to escape the snow."

I laughed and shook my head. "No I didn't. I said the church was the last place I saw him, and she probably took him out the alley exit."

"Uh, Kate? I think you might be losing it tod—" He looked out the window and suddenly reached across the car with both hands and grabbed the wheel "*WAIT!* Turn here!"

"Tom, what the hell?" I slammed both feet down on the brake and clutch simultaneously as he turned the wheel to the right. Edna's tires screeched as the old truck tried to take a corner at almost thirty-five. We made the turn without hitting the parked cars on the side, but my heart was pumping a mile a minute. I pulled over to the side next to the fire hydrant and tried to catch my breath. "Damn it, Tom! Are you trying to kill us?"

He was smiling. "Look up, Kate."

I scrunched in the seat a bit to look where he was pointing. A billboard rose over the road, advertising vacations in San Diego. "Uh, what am I looking at?"

"The tagline, Kate. 'Escape the snow in sunny San Diego.' It's summer. You're psychic. You *must* have seen this in your head and commented because it was out of place."

I thought about it for a moment. I couldn't dismiss the idea, because it was *exactly* how I'd found Bryan in a ditch in Boulder.

I opened my senses as we pulled back onto the street. The next intersection had a red light. I couldn't sense anything in my head. It was still a white sheet of humming. But then the light changed to green. I started into the intersection when a blue sedan ran the red in front of me. If it had gone through in normal traffic, I might not have even noticed, but the screeches and honking made me look. Bryan was in that car!

"Shit! It's Bryan!"

"What? Where?" asked Tom.

Maybe Bryan had seen my red truck so many times that he actually looked my way. Or maybe it was a fluke. In any event, Carol was watching the road. She swerved to avoid one car who was already halfway across the intersection. Unfortunately, I was in the wrong lane to follow her. I'd have to go another block and try to intercept her.

"There, in the blue sedan." I said, and my heart did happy thumps when Tom smiled proudly. Well, that and the fact that Bryan was alive!

I slammed Edna into first and floored the gas pedal. One nice thing about the old trucks. They actually put real engines in them. The big old valves opened up wide and the engine roared to throaty life. I leapt ahead of the car in the middle lane. The next light was going yellow and I floored it again. My head snapped back from the force as I changed lanes again. I prayed that God would keep all of the cops safely in their doughnut shops until the split second when I caught the sedan and needed them.

The next street was a one-way the wrong direction. I blazed forward again and caught the next left. I got lucky. The sedan had turned right and cut across me again. The tires protested as I frantically turned the corner.

Then luck failed. Carol caught sight of me in the rearview. She whipped into the center lane, cutting off a motorcycle who slammed on his brakes and fishtailed wildly. I managed to pull in behind the motorcycle just long enough to go around a cross-town bus that was stopped in traffic at the corner.

I urged Edna even faster and caught the sedan again. Carol took me by surprise by making a sudden left into a park. She snapped through a chain holding a sign reading, "Restricted to Official Vehicles Only."

"She's either panicked or insane!" Tom shouted.

"Yeah? Well, so am I!" I followed her and prayed that nobody was out walking their pets. The paths in the park are wide enough to admit a truck with a plow to keep the sidewalk clear, but the corners are sharp and meandering. I shouldn't have glanced down at my speedometer. We were traveling almost forty through a busy public park. The sedan rounded the curve and confronted two cyclists. They scattered off the sidewalk and crashed into a bush.

We couldn't keep up this pace. Someone was going to get killed. I looked closely and noticed that she and Bryan were wearing seat belts, so I took a chance. It was risky, but this had to end. The next curve went around a large, obviously ancient spruce. I sped up and clipped her bumper. She missed the curve and shot off the concrete. I prayed again for Bryan's safety and for Carol's.

I wanted her alive so *I* could kill her.

She slammed on the brakes but the impact was inevitable. The huge tree shook as the front of the car buried itself into the mass of branches. The boughs slowed the car enough so that when the bumper hit the massive trunk, it did little more than vibrate the tree.

I stopped Edna and we both jumped out of the cab. Carol panicked and started to sprint across the park. Tom took off after her.

I was more concerned about Bryan. I fought to break branches away from the passenger door so I could make sure he was okay. When I finally moved the last branch from the window, I saw him sitting staring in wonder at the windshield. The mass of green was too much for him to comprehend.

I struggled to open the door. He turned and smiled at me and reached up to touch the needles surrounding us both. I reached across him and unbuckled the belt and helped him slide out of the car.

Tom showed up a minute later, with sweat painting his brow. He bent over with hands on his knees while he tried to catch his breath. "Damn, she was fast. She got in a truck at the end of the block and they got away. She must have been planning to ditch this car anyway."

I didn't bother to call the police about the sedan. I didn't have time. Carol and her unknown friend knew I was here, which meant Monica would know, too. I was betting the Thrall queen would have a better response time than DPD. In any case, I wasn't waiting around to find out. If I wound up getting charged with leaving the scene, so be it.

We got Bryan back to the church without incident. Mike apparently hadn't slept. The pale face and dark circles under his eyes made him look like he was wearing makeup. His relief at seeing Bryan almost made him weep.

I didn't get a chance to introduce Tom, because he was angrily walking up to the vacant-eyed teenager I'd seen earlier. Mike and I were both taken aback when he addressed her. "Tiffany, I thought you were watching out for him! What the *hel* . . . I mean, what the *heck* happened?"

Life and intelligence flowed into the girl's eyes in a rush that was like watching a flower bloom in time-lapse. A flush reddened her face to her hair roots as she stared at Tom's angry face. "I'm sorry, Tom. I made the mistake of assuming that the people who worked here were above suspicion. It won't happen again. I won't leave his side."

Mike walked over to the pair as though in a trance, and put gentle hands on Tiffany's face, cupping her jaw. His amazed smile looked like those carved on the statues above him. "You're not a zombie? But how—?"

Tom sighed and ran fingers through his dark hair while the girl smiled back at Mike. "I'm very sorry, Father Michael. But our Acca felt Bryan might be a target, so we put someone here undercover. If you have no objection, we'd like to keep Tiffany here. We're the only ones who know she's not what she appears. She's a very good actress, and can quickly reach any of us. But after this incident, I think we'll also post two of our younger male wolves as guards, just until Monica is no longer a threat."

Mike the priest vanished for a moment, and Mike the hockey player took his place. He looked at Tom with a ferocity that surprised us both. Clenched fists tightened ropes of thick muscle that would have made his old coach proud. He must still be visiting a weight room. "If your people have to fight, I'll expect them to *eliminate* any threat to my charges or my parishioners. Is that clear?"

I jerked back a bit, because this was the first time that Mike had ever openly showed hostility toward the Thrall. Tom smiled. "Perfectly. Thank you, Father."

Mike turned and walked back to me. He placed a strong hand on my shoulder. "Promise me you'll be careful?" His blue eyes were pain filled but serious.

"Do my best." It was an honest answer. I would do my best. Neither one of us could know if it would be good enough.

When Tom and I walked out of the church, he followed me around to my side of the truck. Before I could react, he pulled me to him in a tight embrace and whispered in my ear. "I'm so sorry for everything I said before, Kate. But I've got to let Mary know we've got Bryan back and get the guards situated. Go ahead without me. I'll be home in a few hours." He pressed his lips against my temple briefly. "Please be careful." He released me, winked and then disappeared in a blur of movement.

While I was still terrified about Bryan, and terrified about Monica, feeling Tom's arms around me made a little part of me happy. That same nagging bit liked hearing him whisper words like *sorry, please* and *careful,* and that he'd be home in a few hours.

Not Mary's threats, not smart little wolf cubs, and not even the Thrall could erase my smile as I got in the truck. Eek!

16

My plan was to go home, grab some lunch and head back to the church to stay with Bryan. I hated that I couldn't trust anyone else to do it.

But reality is what happens while you're making plans. The attack began before I reached the building, and in broad daylight. You know how tinnitus sounds? There seems to be a pop, and then a buzzing or ringing in your ear. You can't hear things around you—only the buzzing. It usually goes away in a few minutes and doctors claim it's nothing serious.

This didn't go away, and it was very, very serious. At first, I was able to hold it off, but somehow Monica had convinced the other queens to join her to bring me to her. Or, maybe they were never on my side at all. It could all have been a trick.

I heard Connie listening to country-western in her apartment, so I went upstairs and dug through the chest of drawers to get my CD Walkman. I figured some hard rock would help, and wouldn't annoy church visitors who prefer inspirational music.

But before I could put in new batteries, Monica's voice appeared in mind.

It's time, Kathleen. I've been patient up to this point. But my patience is at an end.

I pulled out the four AA cells and dug in the junk drawer in my kitchen for replacements. I smiled darkly as I popped them in. *Well, guess what, Monica? My patience is gone, too. You added that final straw when you took Bryan. Agreement or not, queens or not—you're going down!*

She laughed. The bitch had the nerve to laugh. *Oh, dear, sweet Katie. You have no idea just how patient I've been. I may die, my Hosts and Herd may all die, but* you're *the one who is 'going down'.*

Her laughter took on that "bwahahah" quality of every villain in every movie in history, and then fire filled my mind, turning it to silly putty. It was so abrupt that the batteries fell to the floor from my limp fingers. I found myself on my knees on the floor and didn't remember falling. I would like to say that it felt like an ice pick to my mind, because that's what everyone thinks of when they imagine a mental attack.

But this was closer to sandpaper—red hot sandpaper that left slow, smoking trails of dead cells in its wake. I couldn't think, I couldn't see. All I could do was scream over and over until my throat was hoarse.

You see, Kate? I've been practicing, and have discovered many amazing things about the human brain. I do love the sound of people screaming. That first slice was only a taste, sweet Kathleen. Perhaps your legs next, hmmm?

And she was as good as her word. I couldn't shield, I couldn't do anything to ignore the instant, dreadful pain that started in my toes and raced upward all the way to my hips. I had to open my eyes between screams to confirm that nobody was slowly flaying my flesh with a dull knife. I tried to stand, but my muscles wouldn't respond.

That should be long enough, don't you think? We wouldn't want to damage your muscles so you can't crawl *to me, would we? So, are you going to accept your fate, or do I continue?* Her voice was pure evil, and filled with a hatred so vibrant it was nearly joyous.

The pain ceased so suddenly that my whole body spasmed.

She was letting me make a choice, and I did. I slammed up every shield I could find within myself. My fingers were clumsy as I fought to get the batteries in the player before she returned. Because I knew she would return. She wanted me dead.

I hurried to the couch. There were pillows and things to hold onto. I turned up the player to the highest setting, and winced as the bass vibrated the player in my hand and through my head. I had to beat this. I knew I could, but before I could figure out how, Monica's voice replaced the music for the first time ever. The player was still spinning, but the music wasn't reaching my ears.

You know, it's funny. I've actually gotten a taste for AC/DC since you've played it so often through the years.

Something about the way she said that—but I didn't get a chance to even voice the question before she answered it.

Oh, yes. I've been with you the whole time. I've watched you live your infinitely dreary life. I know your penchant for pasties, and rum raisin ice cream. I know your favorite shampoo and everyone *who is important to you.* I saw her fangs flash in my mind and the scar on my leg began to ache. Her next words chilled my blood. *Have you checked in on your friend, Peg, lately? No? How about that sweet old man in Tel Aviv? Didn't he have some grandchildren? Wouldn't they make darling Hosts? But you can save them; save them all. Just let go and feel the hive. We're here for you. We've always been here for you. You're one of us.*

I was suddenly standing in the basement over Larry again, and Monica had hold of my leg. But this time I felt her draw me against her. She nuzzled my neck and then sharp fangs pierced my skin. Her mind reached for mine, touching me— turning me. I started to slip away, started to fall into the welcoming arms of the hive.

"NO! No—no—no!"

I woke screaming in a cold sweat, my heart racing. The CD had finished. There was silence in my ears, but not in my head. Had it been a dream? The pain had felt so real, but Thrall shouldn't be able to cause pain.

The buzzing and whispering grew louder with each passing second, as more and more Thrall woke from their sleep to join in the attack. I glanced at my watch. It was nearly dark. I'd been out all blinking afternoon! Who had they captured? Who was the next chip to use against me?

I raced to the phone, but never got the receiver off the base.

Hahaha! Not a dream, Kate—not a dream at all! Pain slammed into my body so hard that I stumbled and fell against the table. I barely managed to move enough not to crack open my forehead.

Get out of my head, you bitch! I put up walls of heavy stone in my mind, strong enough to withstand the worst possible winds. But Monica waved it aside as though it were a sheer curtain.

Poor, poor Katie. You just don't understand yet, do you? I command you. I own you. I am your QUEEN!

My skull began to ache, then burn. The flesh should be melting, running off the bone. I screamed as fast as I could draw breath but nothing relieved the torture. Then my worst nightmare came true. I felt my left arm raise, and I wasn't doing it. The fingers curled into claws and reached for my face. I grabbed it with my right hand and held it away like a snapping dog on a chain. Fear caused the screaming this time, because my right was the injured arm, so my left was stronger. But my screams weren't nearly as loud as Monica's laughter in my head.

I heard pounding on the door, but was too busy preventing my own fingernails from giving me a *Little Shop of Horrors* facial.

The front door burst inward and Tom raced in the room. He took one look and seemed to know exactly what was going on. He grabbed me and pulled me against his chest, even as I tried to stop him. I didn't know what the evil possessed hand would do to him, and I'd never forgive myself.

"Tom! No! You don't unders—"

"No, Kate. I *do* understand." He pressed my head down to his chest, and slid his other hand up the back of my shirt. A fast wind swirled around my body, giving me shivers that blended with the pinpricks of pain as his hand pulled at the bandages on my back. The wind raced through my mind, cooling the fire and the pain. My left arm dropped to my side as though the string had been cut.

I could suddenly breathe, and that startled me. "What . . . how . . . ?"

He didn't respond right away. He released my head a bit so I could see his face. He looked shaken and concerned. "Enemy predators means we have a balance of power, Kate. The Thrall can't touch our minds. We can extend that power to those we—well, those who matter to us."

I saw a touch of awe on my face reflected in his dark pupils. "You can block them? Can you keep Monica out of my head until she dies?"

He nodded, but then chagrin slid over his features. "Well, as long as we're touching, anyway. You're lucky that it also works as a super pain killer. I can't heal your damage, but you won't feel it. Skin to skin works best, but I can probably manage it if we're both in the same room. I don't know. I've never tried to extend my power that much. But the Acca has calculated that Monica only has another day or so to live, so I can probably stay nearby that long. I hope it's only a day, because my vacation is over tomorrow."

Oh. Um. Again my split personality reared its ugly heads. He needed to stay nearby, touching me, for a whole day. Yay! But he needed to stay nearby, *touching me, for a whole day.*

The thought of touching reminded me abruptly of Bryan, and Peg and Gerry and a flow of adrenaline replaced the embarrassment. I started to pull away. He let me pull back a bit, but not completely away. "How's Bryan? Is everything okay at the church? Has anyone heard from Joe?"

He nodded and let out a slow breath. "Everything is fine at the church. Rob, Mark, and Tiffany are there now. Joe checked in as soon as he arrived back from California. He tried to call here, but you didn't answer, so he sent me over to check on you. I'm glad he did."

I let a burst of air through my lips. "Yeah. I'm glad, too. I didn't even hear the phone ring." But how could I have, with the CD player and Monica's loud, haunting laughter scorching my brain?

Phone . . . *phone!* I pulled away from Tom sharply and headed for the phone. I had to call Peg, and what time was it in Tel Aviv? But I didn't make it more than two steps before the queen bitch of all time was in my head again, trying to take control of my body. Tom felt it. He stepped forward and grabbed my hand before it attacked me again. It was gradual this time, but I felt Monica fade into the background— hissing and spitting the whole way.

I closed my eyes and felt the fear slowly fade. "Thanks." I whispered the word, not wanting to look at him.

He pulled me toward him and wrapped me in an embrace. I opened my eyes, startled, and was drawn into the depths of his molten chocolate gaze. "You need to let me help, Kate. You can't do this alone. Not today. Monica is panicked. She's throwing everything she has at you."

A brittle laugh escaped my lips. "Yeah. No shit. But she threatened my friends in my head. They don't live around here, and don't have wolves to protect them. I have to call them—make sure they're okay."

He nodded and followed me to the table, holding my hand. We walked that same way to the couch. He had a nice grip, firm and strong without being overpowering or sweaty.

I dialed Peg's cell phone by heart and was surprised when she picked up. When she's in the air, she has to turn it off.

"Peg! Thank God! Are you okay?"

"Kate? Is that you?" She let out a small annoyed sound. "So it's already made the news over there, huh? I guess I shouldn't be surprised."

"Made the news?" I asked with a note of confusion in my voice. "I haven't watched the news. What's up?"

"You're not calling about the attempted hijacking? Then why were you calling?"

"Hijacking! Jeez Louise! Are you okay?" I glanced over at Tom to see him smirking at my catch phrase. I realized he'd never heard it from me.

"Yeah, yeah. I'm fine. The air marshal took the guy down in about ten seconds. He didn't seem to be going for the cockpit, though. He pulled a ceramic knife and put it at my throat. I don't know what he thought he was trying to do. But the other passengers jumped the guy and then the air marshal handcuffed him. Boy, some guys can be so stupid! But, I guess that's another thing they'll add to the list of hand searches. Those things don't show up on the detector. But why were you calling, if you didn't know?"

I hesitated for a heartbeat, wondering whether to tell her. Was it just a stupid wanna-be terrorist, or had Monica attempted to threaten her? I just didn't know. When I didn't answer for a moment, her voice lowered an octave and dragged out in warning. "*Kaate?* Ahem! Talk to me, girl. What should I know?"

I sighed and looked at Tom for advice. He just shrugged his shoulders and squeezed my hand.

I closed my eyes and took a deep breath, letting it out slow into the receiver so she would know I was still on the line. When I started to talk, it came out in a steady stream of words on a single breath. God, it felt so good to tell someone who understood. "It's Monica, Peg. She's almost at the end of her life and wants . . . well, she wants *me* to be the next queen. Of course, I told her where to go and how to get there. But she's started to threaten people I know to get me to cooperate. She tried to kidnap Bryan yesterday, and almost succeeded. She specifically mentioned your name and one of the guys I know in Tel Aviv. Are you *certain* it was just some whacked out guy? Could he have been a Thrall Host?"

The next long pause was hers. "A Host? You think a Host was trying to grab me? Okay, like, *eeww!* So, let me get this straight. The whacked out vampire lady who bit you wants you to be her successor and is grabbing family and friends of yours? God, Kate! You need to, like, *move* or something! Go live on some deserted beach in the Philippines." I could hear her shake her head as the hair brushed the phone. "No, never mind. You'd find trouble there, too."

I didn't really disagree, so I didn't comment. But Tom smiled the tiniest bit.

She sighed and it spoke volumes. It was the same sigh I wish I could use, but I was the one being sighed *about.* "No, I don't know it wasn't a Thrall Host. I suppose I should notify the Gendarmerie. I'm in Paris, by the way, until they clear us to take off again. I don't know what they can do about it, but they're looking at it from a terrorist angle, instead of the concept that the guy might actually have been after *me*." Her breath flowed out again in another burst, this time the sound of martyred patience. "Well, you are an *interesting* person to be friends with, Kate. Are *you* okay? How are Joe and Bryan? Anything at all *good* going on in your life? Cute guys, shopping, shoes—*anything?* Or just big baddies around every corner?"

I looked over at Tom, whose face was completely neutral. "As the song goes, 'I get by with a little help from my friends.' Joe and Bryan are okay, and, um, I'm . . . *okay.*" I didn't want to get into gossipy stuff with the stuff of the gossip sitting on the couch with me.

"Well, okay then. I'll let you know if I find out anything. Maybe there's a Not Prey on the police here who can question the guy. What's the bitch—I mean, what's the *queen's* name again?"

I had to smile and chuckle. "Monica. Queen Monica. Thanks, Peg. And *please* watch your back for a few days until this is over."

"Oh, hey! That is *so* not an issue anymore. I will be sticking to my pilots like glue until further notice. Thanks for the warning, Kate. Really." Her voice softened into warm, soft fluff. "I wouldn't be much of a hostage if you didn't care enough to be worried. I'm flattered. So take care of yourself, so *I* don't have to worry."

We hung up before I started to cry. Tom didn't say a word. He just reached in his pocket and pulled out a real cloth handkerchief. I hadn't seen one of those in ages. There was even a monogrammed 'B' on the corner.

I didn't need it yet, but it was still early in the day.

I couldn't reach anyone in Tel Aviv, which could be no big deal or could be bad. I left a vague message, asking someone to call me back. I was just there, so they might out of curiosity. I did reach Joe at the church. He sounded relieved, but his voice held that dark edge of fear when you know that the boat is about to sink, or the tornado is on the horizon. There was nothing to say to each other, other than offer love, hope and prayer.

By the time I stood to put the phone back, it was oh-dark-thirty. I glanced at Tom, who was still holding my hand like a crush in junior high.

The battles were fought, and there were only hours and hours of unknown until dawn. Somehow I knew tomorrow was it. Damn that psychic sense. I would end up alive and human, dead and human or something not quite either one. Everything was fuzzy. I'd just have to wait and see.

So there I stood in my own living room, holding the hand of an amazingly gorgeous man. He was looking at me very seriously, and had just recently made my body feel all sorts of fun things. To top it off, he was going to have to touch me all night or the bad things would get me. Even worse, I actually felt safe for the first time in a very long while.

What in the hell had I gotten myself into?

17

"So," I said nervously, and realized my hand had started to sweat a bit. "What do we do now? Cards? Backgammon? I have comedy videos."

"I'm personally up for *bed*." He probably noticed when I flinched enough to have swatted a fly. He chuckled a bit and smiled. I noticed that his eyes were looking tired. "Sleep, Kate. I mean we both need to get some sleep. But we should probably be in the same location, whether the bed or the couch, or sleeping bags on the floor. I didn't do so hot at extending my power when you walked to the phone. I can try again if you want—"

I waved my free hand. I shouldn't be such a nervous nelly. He was a nice guy. He'd been honorable and sweet, and I was just being paranoid for no reason. "No. It's fine. We'll use the bed. But I would like to get changed in private if that's okay."

He thought about it for a moment. "That's dangerous, but maybe we can work it out. How about if you change in the bathroom upstairs and I just strip down to my jeans right on the other side of the door? I should be able to stay awake most of the night, but in case I fall asleep, there's a wider mass of skin to draw energy from to cover you. Would that be okay?"

Oh, and what a mass of skin it was. I coughed to cover up my drooling. "Okay, yeah. That should work."

And it did. I could hear the hive in the background, and Monica pounded on the door of my mind. But my own shielding, combined with Tom's, was enough.

When I had dressed, washed my face, combed out my braid, brushed my teeth and popped the last pill like a somewhat-below-average good girl, I caught my reflection in the mirror. I actually looked pretty good, although I couldn't believe I grabbed the nightshirt I did out of the closet. I don't know what possessed me. It's perfectly decent, mind you. Cream colored satin that goes to my knees, with cap sleeves and a short v-neck. Nothing sexy at all, except no bra. I can't stand to wear a bra to bed. It itches and twists. I was wearing undies, though. Never mind that I normally wear oversized junky T-shirt with pithy sayings, and had never actually put on this gown since Peg gave it to me for Christmas two years ago.

Yeah, yeah. I know. But none of the T-shirts looked, well, *nice* enough.

The look I got when I stepped out of the bath made me realize that perhaps the gown wasn't quite as decent as I'd thought. I glanced down. No, nothing revealed or even hinted at much. But Tom's eyes took on a bottomless weight that made my stomach lurch and my knees weak.

He didn't say anything. He just held out his hand. I took it, feeling very much like a bride on my wedding night, and I couldn't figure out why. Maybe it was because I don't do casual sex, and the look on his face was anything *but* casual.

He gave me first shot at which side. I picked my normal one, on the right. I stretched out while he walked around the bed, throwing a wave of raw power in his wake. I was starting to be able to actually feel the rush of white noise in my head. It had been so very long since my head had been quiet. Maybe I actually *could* sleep tonight and not dream.

My stomach jerked again as Tom crawled onto the other side of the king-sized bed. There was a rolling, sensuous quality to his movements—the animal inside him. There was nothing heated about the movements, only the fact that he was him. It was the sheer naturalness of him that made him so incredibly sexy.

He took my hand again and picked it up. He pressed it to his lips with his eyes closed. "Get some sleep, Kate. I'll stay awake as long as I can. I'm a light sleeper from working at the station, so if anything happens, I'll wake up."

I took his word for it, and rolled onto my side, facing him, while he picked up a book from the night stand. Since I hadn't been reading lately, he must have taken it from the shelves near the bathroom while I was dressing.

So he could read comfortably, I switched hand holding to putting my hand on his arm and closed my eyes.

I only remember one dream, and it was a happy one. I was a child again, playing in the grass behind our house with Fred Basset. Yeah, yeah. I know. But Fred was the best dog a girl could have. He was cute in that floppy, sad-eyed sort of way, and loved to play ball. We had just played a romping game of ball and then I rolled down the hill of dandelions, while Fred chased me. He pounced on me and I hugged him, just reveling in the joy of life. I felt the warmth of his body and his slow, even breathing that raised my arm up—

Too high. My arm was raising too high for floppy little Fred. My eyes opened just a hair, while still in that dreamy contented state. I found myself nearly on top of Tom's warm, naked torso. My head was resting on his chest, and one leg was wrapped around his thigh. His hand was on my head, stroking my hair absently while he read the last few pages of the novel. He'd rested the edge of the book on my shoulder and was turning pages with a finger.

I flicked my eyes to the night stand. It was already two o'clock in the morning. I didn't move a muscle. I just tried to figure out how to extricate myself without it being obvious and insulting.

He finished the last page and closed the book. He reached over with one arm and placed it carefully on the night stand and then looked down at my head. I could just see him out of the corner of one eye, because my hair was cascading over his chest and covering my face.

"What is it about you, Kate Reilly, that I find so utterly irresistible?" His words were soft, not even quite a whisper, and they made my heart skip a beat. He kept stroking my hair, which felt amazingly nice. He carefully lifted my arm away from his chest so he could lay down, which was my cue to awaken.

"Tom?" I asked sleepily, and he froze. "What time is it?"

"Almost two o'clock. Everything's fine. Go back to sleep."

I rolled off of him and looked into his face with half-closed eyes that really were still a bit asleep. He seemed disappointed about me moving.

I yawned, and took the bull by the horns. "I'm sorry I got all wrapped around you. I'll roll over so I don't bother you."

He leaned over me before I could move. His eyes were warm, but heat was growing deep inside. "Why in the world would you be sorry? I can't think of anything better than to have your warm—"

He placed one hand on my waist. "Soft—"

His face moved closer to me while my heart and stomach both fluttered at different speeds.

"Luscious—" His other hand reached up to stroke slowly down the side of my face while a delicious shiver rolled down my spine.

"Body wrapped around me. In fact, I think I'd like to do it again." Tom brought his lips against mine lightly. A violent shudder passed through me and he felt it. He gave up any pretense and leaned into me. He kissed me deep and long, opening my mouth with his, while his hand explored the length of my satin-clad body and he slid down until he was lying beside me. He ended the kiss slowly, with a final tug on my lower lip with his teeth. His smile was full of promise and made my heart flutter.

"But let's make sure you don't get hurt any worse. You might not feel the pain, but you're still injured." He rolled me over until I was on top of him. Gravity dropped my knees to the bed and I was straddling him. It felt good.

I couldn't deny it anymore. I wanted this. I wanted him. I reached over to turn out the lamp.

His hand stopped me. "What are you doing?"

I started to reach again. "Turning out the light. I'm pretty sure we're going to . . . well, you know. Right?"

"Oh, we're going to. But the light stays on."

I suddenly felt panicked, but couldn't figure out why. I found myself reaching for the lamp switch again, only to have him pull back my arm.

He smiled at me, a teasing grin. "You've never done this before, have you?"

I didn't know what he meant. "I'm not a virgin, Tom."

He shook his head. "That's not what I meant. You've never made love with the lights on before, have you?" He used his free hand to slide down the satin to cup my breast and squeeze it, making it so I couldn't speak. My nipples were just suddenly hard and visible through the fabric. "You've never watched a man make your body react. Never watched the reflection of your own climax in his eyes. Hmm?"

My mouth was suddenly dry. He was right. Sex was, well, it was for the dark. It wasn't a daylight activity. Or, at least, it hadn't been for Mike or for Dylan, and they were my only experiences. They were both like me—close the doors, shut out the lights, and grope.

"I . . . um, isn't your pack a matriarchal society? Aren't *I* supposed to be in charge?" The best defense is a good offense.

His look was still teasing, but there was an underlying seriousness I didn't understand. He nodded and the transformation to serious was complete, even though his hand remained firmly on my breast. "Yes. You are supposed to be in charge, Kate. You're supposed to be the leader. Unfortunately, you haven't got a *clue* what that means."

I felt cool air on my tongue, which told me my jaw had dropped. "I know what it means, Tom."

He shook his head and thrust his hips upward, making me gasp. "No you don't, Kate. You wear your Not Prey status like a shield, or some sort of invisibility cloak. You leap into battle without consulting anyone, or even thinking about the consequences. That's not leading. That's just plain pig-headedness and foolhardy to boot."

His hand released my wrist and slid in between my legs. I nearly lost my balance as his finger rubbed me through the cotton. I didn't like what he was saying, but oh man—how he was saying it!

"You need to know the talents of the people around you, and utilize them to your advantage." He thrust upward with his hips again, while both hands were moving simultaneously on very sensitive spots.

I couldn't seem to catch my breath as I replied. "I do utilize people's talents. But usually I'm better at them than they are."

He raised his brows and removed both of his hands. He steepled his fingers just under his lip. "Yeah? So prove it. Teach me how to use my talents to please you. Do yourself up proud while I watch and learn."

I blushed to the roots of my hair. Surely he didn't expect me to—"That's not what I meant, Tom."

His eyes were serious, but his hands moved to my thighs. "But don't you see, Kate? That's what being in charge *is*. You don't know what other people are capable of, because you don't know what *you're* capable of. You keep throwing yourself into the void, hoping against hope that you'll pull out a miracle at the last second." He slid his hands up the gown and repeatedly flicked both nipples through the satin until they were hard as pebbles and I was groaning weakly.

"But you're not going to change your entire mindset tonight. So, I'm in charge until you learn how." Then he sat up and put his open mouth on one breast while that hand dropped to my panties again. He licked and sucked through the fabric until I could barely think, while his hand teased the skin on the edges of the elastic between my legs.

"Tom, I . . . *Oh, God!*" I shouted as he suddenly inserted one finger inside me and moved his face up to kiss me deeply. All I could think to do was hold onto his forearms so I didn't fall over while his hips rocked me up and down on his finger and his thumb toyed with my nub.

The next thing I knew he had leaned back and removed his

hands from me. With blazing heat in his gaze, he lifted the nightshirt up, exposing my breasts. "While I really like the slick-wrapping, I want your skin against mine—*now*. Arms up."

I obeyed and he pulled the gown off of me. Before I could bring my arms back down, Tom had wrapped his arms around my back and was alternately nipping and sucking both of my breasts, licking along the permanent tan lines from long-forgotten, bikini-clad summers on the beach. His hips pressed against me urgently.

I ran my fingers through his hair and made noises I didn't know I could make. He leaned back just enough to ask, "Do you really like these panties?"

I shook my head, not trusting myself to speak. I had a sneaking suspicion what he meant, and the thought excited me more deeply than I'd expected. His mouth found mine and his tongue explored my teeth and gums as I felt his hands snake down my body to the tiny little spaghetti strap bikini bottoms I wore. Part of me knew, or hoped, this might happen. The slim piece of fabric was no match for his strength and I heard each of the straps rip in turn. He leaned back far enough to slowly, ever so slowly, pull the cloth from under me. I was completely naked over him and wanted him that way too.

I scooted up his body just a bit so he could pull his pants and briefs down and kick them off. I explored his chest and his nipples while he did, and it made him smile darkly.

It wasn't until I felt his erection pressing at my back did I remember. "You should know, Tom. I'm sterile. I can never have children."

He raised his brows. "And yet you're on birth control. Interesting."

"How—?" But then I remembered that he had been in my bathroom to get bandages, and I hadn't bothered to put away the prescriptions from the pharmacy. "It's a hormone imbalance. I apparently inherited it from my mother. Birth control is just a handy side effect. But useless in my case."

"So, in either event, we're safe." His smile was teasing, challenging as his fingers began to stroke my nipple again.

"Not from Mary," I gasped. "She warned me to stay away from you."

The chuckle was as dark as his smile. "Not doing too well, are you?" He lifted my hips without any effort and hovered my entire body over his groin. I could feel the throbbing erection push against me, making my head spin. I needed him inside me. I was wet and hungry and wanted him—Heaven help me, how I wanted him. I tried to pull myself down, but he wouldn't let me.

"Don't worry. I'll handle Mary. You just worry about handling . . . *me*." He dropped me and the full length of him impaled me like a spear. I cried out from sheer pleasure as he filled me completely. He was thick and long and every moaning thrust turned my insides into jelly. I felt a tightening that was both thrilling and frightening in its intensity. It had been so very long since I'd done this.

I leaned forward, changing the angle, and rested my hands on the bed above Tom's shoulders. The scent of him was amazing. His cologne, the musk of his sweat and something in his hair. It combined to create an odor that affected my brain like a drug. I leaned down more and breathed in along his neck and exhaled harshly into his ear. He let out a deep groan and tightened his grip, moving his hands down my waist. He grabbed my hips and drove himself inside me. Just when I thought I was ready to climax, he pushed me backward, and backward, and backward, until I was nearly lying prone on the bed. He held my waist tightly while he stroked relentlessly in and out of me. It was almost too much. I was so very close and couldn't even think.

Bright white light filled my vision and I screamed, needing release. He pulled me forward until I was upright again, without ever missing a single beat. My eyes were closed, enjoying the sensation in the quiet darkness behind the lids.

"Look at me, Kate. I want to see that this isn't just for tonight. I want to see something deeper in your eyes than just lust." He slowed his movements, just when I needed him to speed up. I opened my eyes with panic. Once his gaze had caught me, I couldn't look away. And I could see my own reflection in the dark pupils. I could see every movement we made—from his hands on my breasts to his hips thrusting up and into me.

Faster and faster he moved, while I watched like a voyeur. He dropped one hand and started to toy with me while he slapped against me harder. I was so wet that there was a sucking sound with each stroke.

It was almost too much I was so very close. I threw back my head to let myself go, but he pulled me back. "No, Kate. I want to see. You're gorgeous and so sexy I can hardly stand it. I want to take you further than you've ever gone with anyone else, because I seem to have fallen in love with you."

I watched my own wild-eyed gaze in his pupils and realized that I very might well be in love with him, too.

His movements were finally too much and I nearly shrieked as I dug my nails into his arms.

"Tom!" The orgasm took me by surprise, pulling a second scream from my throat and dropping me bonelessly to his chest. The violent spasms of the climax made me lightheaded enough that the room spun. Each breath felt like I was starving for air.

He got more excited. His voice dropped nearly an octave to a deep rumble. "Yeah, that's it. That's what I wanted, Kate. I wanted to see it in your eyes, hear you scream my name before I—" I felt his whole body rise up and it felt like he nearly doubled in size inside me as he climaxed with a grunt and a tightening of his hands on my hip and neck. The extra size moving inside me caused a second, mini-climax in me, and I cried out again.

We shook and writhed on each other's sweat-soaked bodies while light sparkled in my vision and he continued to push himself inside me until he was spent.

We lay like that for long minutes until our hearts slowed and we stopped panting.

He was the first to speak. He chuckled and it bounced me on his chest. "Oh, I could do this every day. To hell with Mary."

18

The bare beginnings of daylight arrived and we were still in each other's arms. I was liking the concept of love with Tom an awful lot, which made me nervous. This level of comfort was right where the boot had dropped with Dylan. Of course, that was a subject I didn't even want to think about, especially while lying cuddled in the arms of another man.

I got up without waking him. I needed a shower and I wanted to think. It occurred to me while hot water was beating on my head and stinging my back that I *could* think. The hive was quiet. Had Monica already died? Was the danger over? I wasn't sure whether to risk opening my senses.

But then what I'm starting to affectionately refer to as my "spidey-sense" started to tingle. The witch wasn't dead. She hadn't been crushed by a falling house. No, she was in her castle, planning evil things. I knew it. But I also knew that today was the day. I could chase after fate, or try to run from it, but it would find me.

My first instinct was to chase after it, but Tom's words last night had stuck in my head. I had people willing to help. They had resources and abilities and I hadn't been giving anyone any credit for brains or brawn or anything else. I would be insulted as hell if anyone didn't feel they could rely on *me,* and here I was doing just that. So, I would let the wolves watch Bryan and Joe, no matter how much it made my skin crawl not to be involved. Of course, I knew that Joe could fight, and Mike could as well. Mike might even be a better fighter than me, when push came to shove.

But I would personally check to make sure that Dusty was okay, because that was still nagging at the back of my mind. Verifying the situation and not trusting aren't the same thing at all. Are they?

Oh, and I was going to avoid large fields of red poppies until the day was over.

A few minutes later, I was reasonably dry and wrapped in a towel in front of the mirror, trying to figure out what to do with my hair. Shampooing had brought back memories of the last time I'd damaged my shoulder. *Up* is not a direction a sprained rotator cuff likes to travel. You'd be surprised how fast you change your mind about doing it. Yes, I can make suds with one hand and clean myself reasonably well. Toweling dry is a bit more of a trick, and wrapping *hair* in a towel is an amazingly similar motion to shifting into third. I don't recommend it.

Tom entered the bath while I was scrubbing my face and reached arms around me to snuggle. He rested his head on my shoulder and stared at me in the mirror. There's a certain look that a guy gets after sex. It's part contented cat and part dog protecting his bowl. But when the look also includes that deep down warmth that has nothing to do with lust, and everything to do with helping fold the laundry—well, that makes me feel all cotton candy and roller coasters inside.

He wiggled his eyebrows after a second and flexed his fingers in my waist. I flinched involuntarily and he took that as an invitation to tickle me into a fit of giggles. He turned me around while I was still out of breath and kissed me. It was a long, slow taste that was happy, but not hungry, and the feeling of his arms around me was amazing.

"I see you managed to take a shower without me. How's the head holding up? I can never tell when they're around."

"Monica's ignoring me for the moment. She's planning diabolical things in her evil lair." My words were light, but we both understood the underlying seriousness. He backed up when I reached over to plug in the hair dryer and leaned against the wall with his arms crossed over his muscled chest. With his tousled hair, sleepy eyes and tight blue jeans, he was the stuff of calendars right where he stood.

"You going to be able to do that? That shoulder's pretty beat up. If you survive this, you'll probably need to get that looked at."

Ah, nothing like the guy you're dating, that you might well *love*, being so full of hope.

I gave him a little sarcastic look. "Thanks for the vote of confidence, *dearest*."

He shrugged one shoulder. "You don't strike me as the 'rainbows and sunshine' sort to want to hear lies, *darling*. If it'll make you feel any better, there's a good chance that I won't survive either. We'll be a modern day Romeo and Juliet."

True. Too true for this early. "I'll need some coffee before I think about that too much."

He winked. "Already started. You're almost out of sugar, by the way."

I bent over to take off the towel, and winced as I started to ease the knots out of my hair. "I don't use sugar. I take mine black."

"Yeah, but I take *mine* with sugar and cream. So pick up some sugar next shopping trip."

The implication was clear, and I grinned privately. The smile was off my face before I stood up, but he knew anyway because he was grinning too. I picked up the hair dryer and gasped from the immediate slicing pain behind one eye. I almost dropped it before switching it to my left hand. But I couldn't brush with the right either.

Tom stepped away from the wall with a shake of his head and took the howling appliance from my hand. "Here. Let me." And he did. Damned if he didn't brush my hair, dry it and even braid it. That part surprised me, and I said so. He smiled sadly. "My sister used to wear braids, but she kept chewing on the ends and snapping the rubber bands. So, I'd rebraid it before Mom saw and got mad."

His voice went soft and he finished braiding without speaking. It was probably the wrong topic to start on, so I didn't ask if he missed them. How could he *not?*

I just knew that I didn't want to ever have to face someone asking me that sort of question, so I had to eliminate Monica. I wouldn't risk Bryan and Joe joining my parents, and Tom's family, in a memory album.

The phone rang and Tom offered to get it while I was cinching the strap on my second wrist sheath. Again, I was dressed all in black for that somber, 'I-won't-take-any-shit-from-you' message. The sun wasn't even fully up but I was already sweltering in my jeans, T-shirt, neck guard with accompanying dickie, and my Rockies jacket. Oh, and the knives. Mustn't forget the knives.

I heard creaking of wood as he padded back up the stairs. "That was Mary," he said before I could see him. "She wants to move up the meeting. Can we go there now? Something's got her spooked, and I don't like it. I think she wanted to cancel, but I convinced her to honor her agreement to you."

While I didn't like to put him in the middle of me and Mary, I had to admit I was pleased he picked me.

Tom was quick in the shower, but he insisted on taking one. He even went to his apartment to get fresh clothes. Driving to the meeting I stayed about six miles over the posted limit, and kept a close eye out for cop cars. I was armed, and injured, and left the scene of an accident yesterday. Even speeding, it was another twenty minutes before we reached the address. Tom hadn't touched me, or even smiled at me the whole way, making me believe he really was worried.

The Shamrock Motel is on the corner of Colfax and Corbin. It's a low rent, high-turnover establishment built in a U shape with the parking lot embraced between the two "legs." The irony wasn't lost on me.

What little paint that still clung to the main building was white. The doors and shutters were a painful fluorescent green. Matching green window boxes hung crookedly beneath the darkened windows. Each was decorated with cut-outs in the shape of shamrocks. The boxes displayed the desiccated remains of what were once brightly colored artificial flowers. Over the years, they've faded to sepia tones. There are two floors but only ten rooms. It wouldn't have been hard to find 150 even if they hadn't had Jake waiting outside the door.

He was leaning against the wall of the building. He wore faded black jeans and a white T-shirt that bore a stylized werewolf glaring at me with red eyes. Not exactly low-key.

I pulled the truck into a parking space near where he stood. By the time we'd climbed down from the cab, Jake was there to greet us. He seemed nervous, looking up and around him often. I started to ask, but Tom shook his head, so I kept silent.

Tom wore mirrored sunglasses that hid his eyes. Trying to read his expression was pointless. He was keeping it deliberately neutral.

"You're late." Jake's voice was unemotional. He didn't smile when he spoke but he stood straighter as we approached.

"We got here as quick as we could." My voice was just as flat. I tried not to let any fear or worry come through.

Jake didn't answer me. He just tapped lightly three times on the door. It swung open to reveal a tiny, shabby room with three occupants. Tom started to hold the door open for me but a glance at my face changed his mind. Instead, he turned his back on me and walked through the doorway ahead of me, letting me use his body as a shield. It was a very deliberate gesture of trust. Good to know he trusted me.

The room was exactly what I'd expected. A dive. The carpet was a matted multi-color green shag that was old enough to have almost come back into fashion. A tattered jungle print spread covered the sway-backed double bed. The scratched headboard had been fastened to the water-stained wall with shiny silver bolts that were far and away the newest things in the room. The drapes matched the bedspread, but hung unevenly on a rod that was only tentatively attached. There was no television. The people who came here were expected to entertain each other.

Jake shut the door behind me, remaining outside to guard. With the door closed and five of us inside, the motel room was very crowded. I lowered myself onto the edge of the bed, being careful not to fall into the center crater. There wasn't anywhere else to sit. A skinny, teenaged, blond male dressed in leather and chains had taken a seat on the windowsill and a girl in high goth was perched on the dresser. Tom had left the bathroom door open and was sitting on the closed toilet seat. The glint of sunlight off the glasses unnerved me. Why did he keep them on inside?

I only spared a quick glance at the teenagers. Never one to waste time, Mary nodded her head briefly in response. "Kate, there's somebody I want you to meet." She motioned to the slender teenager on the scarred dresser. "That is Dusty Walker."

I looked the girl up and down, trying to picture her in white lace and naturally blonde hair. She didn't even match the photos I'd shown to Martha. She was wearing dread locks dyed a purplish black that matched her chipped fingernail polish. The torn lace-over blouse with bell sleeves was worn over a purple tank top and camo trousers in multicolor green with pink splotches. Perfect, I suppose, for hiding in peony bushes. I bit my tongue on the sarcastic comment, concentrating on counting her piercings. She had seven silver hoop earrings in her left ear and three in her right. They went well with the ring in her nose and the tongue stud clicking against her teeth.

"Hi." I gave Dusty my friendliest smile. She didn't return it. Instead, she fidgeted in her seat until the kid from the windowsill came over and put his arm around her.

"Dusty has agreed to be our pack surrogate in exchange for protection." Mary said calmly.

"I'd figured that out."

Dusty spoke up, her voice high and strained. "I took evidence when I left home. Told him if he didn't leave me alone I'd go public with it."

"So Mary told me. For the record, that was stupid." The words popped out of my mouth before I could stop them. I'd met her stepdad and agreed with Mary that if the Thrall didn't take her, there was always good old fashioned murder.

Dusty flinched and the blond with his arm around her waist growled. It was a low, menacing sound that raised the hairs on the back of my neck. I found myself reaching instinctively for my left wrist sheath.

"Enough! *Rob*—" Mary made the name a warning. He backed down, but he wasn't happy about it.

"I won't go back!" Dusty rested one hand on Rob's thigh for moral support, but her voice was steady and her chin jutted forward stubbornly.

"Did I ask you to?" I answered.

Her body jerked back toward the mirror, her eyes widening with shock. "But—"

"Look, I'm not here because of Matt Quinn."

"You're not?" Rob and Dusty said it at the same time, and both seemed stunned and disbelieving.

Mary gave a disgusted snort. "No, you're here because of that damned Irishman."

I dropped my chin in annoyance. "He *has* a name, Mary."

She shook her head. "Fine. You're an idiot about Dylan."

"Not anymore." I was surprised how much I meant it. Mary's eyebrows disappeared beneath her dark bangs, as if she was equally surprised. She glanced at me and then Tom, but only got her own shiny reflection in return. Ah. That was the reason for the sunglasses!

Tom snorted. I looked at him and was rewarded with a sour smile that wasn't at all happy. But if it wasn't faked, and I couldn't really tell for sure, then it was jealousy. I couldn't deny he had the right to feel that way at this point.

"What does Uncle Dylan have to do with anything?" Dusty interrupted. She was completely oblivious to anything in the room that didn't involve her directly. "And why would he come to you?"

"He wants you safe. He left me to decide what that means."

I could see Dusty's back go up. Her eyes were iced daggers from under the purple mop. "And who the hell are you to decide?"

Mary scowled, but I held my hand out in a placating gesture.

"I'm nobody as far as you're concerned. But your uncle knows me, and trusts me. And whether you like it or not, I agreed to do my best to keep you safe. And just so you know what we're talking about—"

When I stood, I was less than a foot away from her and our eyes were nearly level. I'd thought about this a lot on the way over, since Tom hadn't been in a chatty mood.

"Safe is going to bed and actually being able to sleep because you know you're not being hunted. It's waking in the morning without fear for your life. Safe is knowing that you don't need to rely on someone else's protection, because putting that much trust in anybody is just a bad idea." I briefly glanced at Tom with those last words. He nodded, understanding that it wasn't just said for Dusty's benefit.

She was listening intently and it seemed that she was weighing the definition against her present situation. "Safety doesn't guarantee happiness, but it's damned difficult living your life always looking over your shoulder."

She was nodding thoughtfully by the time I concluded, and the blond wolf by her side was no longer shielding her from me.

When she spoke, her voice was flat and hard. "My best friend, Voneen, was going to be the new Thrall queen. She was really excited, you know? I didn't know much about them, but Voneen said that Monica was really pretty and very nice. And the sex . . . well, the sex is supposed to be *really incredible*. They can work with your mind so that it's just an explosion of sensation. Voneen liked that, a lot. And she would be in charge. *She'd* be the one with the money and the power. She made it sound *wonderful*."

She wrapped thin arms around her body. Rob snuggled in closer to her. I just stood and listened. It was all she wanted from me. "Voneen came home late that night. She said they'd wanted her to stay, but she snuck out. She looked fine at first.

There was a weird swelling in her arm but it went away after a bit." Dusty took a deep breath and closed her eyes. "About midnight, Voneen decided to take a hot bath. She was feeling strange. A few minutes after she closed the door I started to hear really weird noises. I knocked and called to her but she didn't answer. So I tried to open the door. It was locked. The apartment we were in had really shitty doors, though, so I put my shoulder against it and popped it open."

Dusty raised her head until her eyes met mine. Angry tears glittered and slithered down her cheek. "Voneen was on the floor in convulsions. I tried to keep her still and splashed some bath water on her face. She didn't even know I was there. Her eyes were rolled back in her head and all you could see was white, like she was blind. She was actually frothing at the mouth. I'd seen dogs do that but never a person!"

Dusty was trembling in earnest now and Rob was holding her shaking form. "We didn't have a phone. I screamed until I was blue but none of the neighbors came. I held her and rocked her and hoped she'd be okay. Eventually, she stopped convulsing. I was so glad that I laughed and tried to wake her up."

"But she wouldn't wake up, would she?"

Dusty shook her head and bit at her lower lip. Rob was rubbing her lower back and nuzzling her neck. "She was dead. I ran screaming downstairs. Finally an old black lady came and helped me. She told me to leave because the police would take me. So I left. I ran into Rob and Jake at the 7-11, and they called Tom to pick me up. I couldn't go to the police. They would've called my stepdad."

Dusty concluded "Mary told me that when the Host isn't mentally strong enough to handle the hive mind—well, that's what happens. I can't go home, Matt will kill me. And I won't let what happened to Voneen happen to me. I'll kill *myself* first."

I nodded at her in agreement. "I know. If you just had to worry about the Thrall, I'd suggest you disappear for a few weeks. Monica will be dead soon and she'd have to find another Host." I didn't bother to mention my involvement. It would destroy what little trust I might have built with her. I had no doubt she'd sell me to the vamps to escape Voneen's fate, and she'd expect me to do the same.

"You could go to the country, somewhere where the food supply is too limited to support a nest. Once Monica died, you'd be out of the woods." I took a deep breath and continued. "But your stepfather is another problem. Based on what you just said, he's not going to feel safe with you alive and in possession of your own body."

I turned to Mary. "Which brings us to the wolves." I addressed my next question to her. "Can you handle the Thrall and her father? Can you protect her? *Will* you protect her?"

She gave me a smile that was all pointed teeth. I didn't know the wolves could do that, but maybe that was why she was boss. Good enough.

"All right then. If Dusty signs on as surrogate, what will her position within the pack be?"

Mary settled back into the ugly hospital green chair. "You know that female wolves are sterile."

"I've heard that but didn't know if it was accurate until we spoke the other day."

She nodded once. Her so-black hair framed her round face. Her hazel eyes were intense; they willed me to listen and believe. We'd see.

"I am sterile. So are the three females in our dyad; not pack. The pack is the hunting group; the dyad consists of the mating pair and a small group that protects them and helps raise the young. I am Acca, the leader. Collectively, the groups form the Canis. Dusty would be part of the dyad, but not the pack. We would insulate her from the hunt. I decide whether and when the dyad needs to expand in size. Right now, we need to grow to survive."

I interrupted with an upraised finger. "Where does the term Acca originate?" I'd never heard it.

"So far as anyone has been able to learn, a pre-Roman peasant, Acca Laurentia, was the first werewolf to co-exist with the humans. It was she who organized the first Canis, and each of our leaders is named in her honor. Among the humans she's best known as a supposed mistress of Hercules and then later the wife of a shepherd to King Numitor. She rescued a pair of infants from the river, eating herbs so that she could suckle them. The infants were Romulus and Remus."

She sat in calm silence, waiting for my next question.

"What would Dusty's role be in the dyad? Would she get to continue her education, have a career, or would she just be some sort of . . . well, *brood mare?*"

Mary actually smiled; a flash of warmth and compassion directed at the girl. "The surrogate is probably the most important member of the Dyad, and she has a great deal of authority. Bearing our young and raising them will be a large part of her life, but she will have plenty of help. If she wishes, she will have time to pursue other interests."

There was a thought that had been nagging at the back of my mind since I'd realized the plan. I crossed my arms over my chest and leaned against the door so I could see everyone. "By whom? Will she be forced to accept any and all comers? Will all of your males try to get her pregnant?" More specifically, would Tom?

I couldn't help but glance at him. He took off his sunglasses for a moment, and met my eyes. Mary frowned.

"Naturally you'd be interested in that." I started to protest, but she waved it off. "No, you're right to be concerned. We offered Dusty her choice of any available male, all of whom had qualities worth breeding. Tom is one of the males that Dusty may choose from. As I said earlier, until she chooses, Tom is off-limits to you."

Tom showed no outward sign of emotion when my eyes flicked to him, but he twitched his finger when I opened my mouth. I closed it again, but Mary took even that as a challenge. Her jaw was set firmly, and her eyes flashed angrily. "Our society has rules for a reason, Kate. The future of our entire race is at stake with the addition of each surrogate and the choosing of her mate. My people count on me to think of their future. While I try to be lenient, duty sometimes tramples over free will. The surrogate has the full authority of the Canis behind her. If you both continue to defy me, the punishments will continue—if not from me, then from other females in the dyad without my knowledge. Tom will heal before he has to return to his job tomorrow, but please don't make him disobey our rules again."

What did she mean, *Tom will heal?* Again I looked to him for answers, but got none. What hadn't I noticed this morning, even with the lights on? Is that why they were on? Was I supposed to have noticed an injury and failed the exam?

Jeez Louise! What in the seven levels of hell had I gotten myself involved in? I opened my mouth to say . . . something. I'm not sure what, but she interrupted.

"It's only fair to tell you—there's a very good chance that Jake has found a second surrogate for us. If that's true and if both girls are young and healthy, the odds are very good that Tom will be free to be with whoever he chooses soon."

I stood there blinking like an idiot. I looked from Mary to Tom to Dusty. I glanced from Tom again to the skinny kid with chains. Dusty caught the look and interpreted it correctly. She flashed me a dimpled grin, giving a quick shrug. "Yeah, I'm probably going to mate with Rob. Tom's cute, but he's too old. Not my type." She reached over and petted Rob's leg. He nuzzled into her contentedly.

"Ooookay then." I nodded to Mary, swallowing down the fury inside me. Tom is a big boy. If he can't defend himself, it wasn't my job. But we would have to talk about what role Mary would have in our lives if we continued to see each other. I took a deep breath and tried to think of the big picture. Dusty's life was at stake. *My* life was at stake. "If you can't keep her safe, nobody can." I knew what I needed to know about Dusty. She might be a little young to be tying herself permanently to the wolves but it was certainly better and safer than anything I could come up with. Truth be told, she might even be happy. She and Rob certainly seemed to be getting on well enough.

With the Dusty situation in hand, I was left with only the Thrall, Dylan, and Tom to worry about. Of course, if I lost to the vampires, there would be no more mess with Dylan or Tom.

I turned toward the door, intending to leave things at that, but I saw a blur of movement out of the corner of my eye. I spun around to find that Rob had slid off his perch on the dresser and was crouched as though to spring. I was in a bad spot with no room to move, but I was pleased to see that Tom had instinctively started to rise.

"I don't trust her. There's something she's not telling us."

Mary rose in a blur of speed to stand next to him in the small space. "You will *not* insult an honored guest of this pack. It is for me to decide whether Kate can be trusted or not." Her words were a throaty growl that sent shivers down my spine. He was taller, bigger than she was, but it meant nothing. The air around her nearly crackled with power and the one eye I could see blazed with anger. "You agreed to accept my authority in all things when you joined our pack, Rob. Or would you perhaps prefer to return to the detention facility? It can be arranged."

Detention facility? I was definitely missing something in this conversation. But Rob dropped to the ground, cramming his skinny body into the small space between the foot of the bed and the dresser to grovel. First at her feet, then mine. It was uncomfortable as hell. I fought down the urge to squirm and said a silent prayer for help.

"Please forgive me, Acca. I meant no disrespect. Forgive me, honored guest." Rob was laying sprawled with his belly on the ratty carpet, legs under the rickety bed. I tried to act calm. It wasn't easy. He was licking my boots. I was obviously expected to do something. Trick was, I had no idea what. I looked over at Tom. He made a motion with his hand like he was petting a dog. I squatted down and, God help me, patted his spiked blond head. He whimpered, leaning into the caress.

I patted him again, and rose in one smooth movement. "No insult taken." I said it out loud to Mary.

"Thank you. As Not Prey, you're my equal. I wouldn't want to insult you."

"Ah." When in doubt, make neutral noises. Her eyes started sparkling, and little crinkles of amusement appeared at their corners but she didn't say anything to ruin the effect.

"Tell Dylan the girl's all right, but no more. We'll make sure it's the truth."

"Works for me." I glanced into the bathroom. Tom's expression was inscrutable. I wanted to say something . . . but not here, not in front of an audience.

"We'll *talk* later." The look that accompanied the words said that talking might be second, or third, on the list, but it was carefully neutral enough that Mary couldn't know anything for certain.

"Right." There was nothing more to say, so I turned to walk away. Dusty's voice stopped me with my hand on the knob.

"You're actually okay with my being a surrogate?" Her voice was timid when she asked and she looked nervously at Mary, as if afraid she'd be punished for asking.

"You're underage—but it's not like I could stop you. Besides," I was being completely frank, "I trust everyone in this room one hell of a lot more than I do Matt Quinn, and I wouldn't give my worst enemy to the Thrall."

Her blue eyes went wide and her mouth formed a silent "O" of surprise. Rob had risen to his knees so I had to reach around him to extend my hand to Mary. "Good luck keeping the kid safe. I wouldn't trust the stepfather as far as I can throw him. He was waving an awful lot of money around. My guess is I'm not the only one looking for her."

"Thanks for the warning." She took my hand and shook it. I nodded farewell and walked out of the room and back into the bright afternoon sunshine.

19

Tom sprinted to catch up with me in the short distance to where I'd parked Edna. He touched my shoulder and I felt a shudder pass through me. Mary stood at the entrance to the motel room, but didn't make any motion to approach or stop Tom from talking with me.

His voice was low, nearly a whisper, making me wonder just how good wolves' hearing was "Kate, I'm sorry about that. Normally, Mary's a terrific Acca, but she's under a lot of pressure right now from others in the dyad. Dusty is a very controversial choice for surrogate because of her background. She's drawing too much attention to the wolves."

He slipped his hands around my waist and pulled me against him. "I need to stay here. I'll get a ride back home. I didn't want you to know about the ribs, but I don't care if I have to take a beating every day for the rest of my life, Kate. They can't change how I feel about you. I—oh, to hell with it!" He pulled me tight against him and gave me a kiss that left me breathless and speechless. It was a fierce joining of lips and limbs that made me feel both comforted and possessed, and turned my stomach to butter. It was as if he was trying to fill me up with his power like he had filled me with his body only hours ago.

It took me a few seconds to recover enough to whisper, "We're going to make it through this. I swear it to you. No Romeo and Juliet. And when it's all over we are *definitely* going to talk." He smiled and drew back from me. My knees were jelly as he sprinted back up the stairs to disappear back inside the room, past a very annoyed Acca. I could still feel the phantom tingling from where his lips had pressed.

But then everything changed. I was removing the truck keys from my pocket when all of the hairs on the back of my neck stood on end in unison. Someone was watching me. I was guessing that Mary had posted more guards than Jake for our meeting, but considering everything I'd learned today I didn't want to take any chances. As I slid the key into the door lock I used the window reflection to check behind me. Upstairs, a curtain twitched.

Time slowed; became surreal. So many things happened at once that I could only catch flashes of action—glimpses of still photographs. The door to room 150 opened again. Mary stood framed in the doorway. Dusty was a full head taller, and a half-step behind. A flash of light glinted from the drawn curtain. It reflected off my truck door.

"*MARY! Look out!*" She glanced at me and then to where I pointed in a fluid movement as quick as a hummingbird in mid-flight. She shoved Dusty backward with one hand and transformed in a blast of pure power just as a gunshot crack sounded. Half a dozen wolves bounded from various directions, all converging on the shooter's room. One of the wolves came from Room 150, sailing over the head of the Acca. The first werewolf to arrive leapt onto the hood of the car beside me then jumped onto the second floor balcony. The wolf's chest exploded in a rain of blood and bone as a second shot rang out. The furred body fell backward with a lifeless thud that dented the roof of the parked car. My psychic sense told me that the wolf wasn't Tom—thank God." His lifeblood flowed in thick rivulets over the white paint and down the cracked windshield.

A high-pitched scream from the shooter's room chased me as I ran to where Dusty lay. Blood pooled beneath her and her eyes were open and startled. The scream behind me ended in an abrupt gurgle as I dropped to my knees beside her, heedless of the blood soaking into my jeans.

She whimpered, her eyes wide with panic and shock.

Her shoulder was shattered. I could see shards of white bone protruding through the ruptured skin. Blood flowed steadily, but wasn't spurting, thank God. If Mary hadn't shoved her out of the way . . . I didn't want to think about that. I had too much to do. I rose and sprinted into the bathroom to grab what I hoped were relatively clean towels. By the time I was back at her side, Mary was there. She was calm and cool as the other wolves slavered and howled around the shooter, many of them wet with fresh blood. She knelt naked beside me. Without a word, I handed her towels and she began applying direct pressure to the wound despite Dusty's screaming protests. I ran down to the truck, to my cell phone. It was time to call 911. Someone probably already had but in this neighborhood it was better to be sure.

The wolves were back. They stood guard in a semi-circle around their companions in the doorway, their thick neck ruffs bristling, bloodied fangs bared. Was one of them Tom? I didn't think I wanted to know.

Events returned to normal time. I reached into the truck cab and grabbed my cell phone. Just that small movement hurt enough to make me wince, which made me wonder just how bad the damage to my shoulder was becoming. I stifled the thought, and made my way carefully over to the gathered werewolves. I stopped bare inches from the guarded perimeter.

"The police and an ambulance are on their way." I announced. "You probably better get dressed—and they'd better change back."

I pulled my laundry bag from behind the seat. Tossing it onto the ground caused another shooting pain to radiate from my shoulder into my neck. My breath caught in an involuntary gasp. All of the wolves immediately raised their noses to the air. I'd assumed they'd heard me, but could they smell pain? I made my way very tentatively between the snarling animals to the fallen girl. They moved smoothly; parted and allowed me to pass and then closed ranks once more. I nudged Mary aside, taking her place applying pressure to the wound. It hurt my shoulder. A lot. But I did it anyway. Mary stared at me for a long moment over the wounded girl. Her gaze tried to extract information but I wasn't giving any. I just kept my eyes and attention on the wounded girl. Dusty's blood was still flowing, but more slowly. I hoped the ambulance would get here soon.

Mary disappeared into the room with the bag, reappearing just as the police and the first ambulance arrived.

The black sports bra was loose on her small chest, while the matching shorts were stretched uncomfortably tight over her ample hips. The rest of the wolves had vanished. I wasn't sure where. I hoped they'd reappear. There were bodies on the ground and Tom was a paramedic. I wasn't. But most of all, involved parties at a shooting don't just get to walk away—on two legs or four.

I was a bit concerned that Tom didn't reappear to check on Dusty—or *me*, but all of the wolves had become scarce. I couldn't blame them. The police aren't supposed to be prejudiced against the wolves, but they are. I was betting the body upstairs had been ripped apart; another thing I wanted to avoid thinking about. The cops might shoot first and ask questions later.

I was cooling my heels in Edna's front seat when the nice policeman came to get me. He escorted me through the crowd of emergency workers and police to stand before a black man in a navy suit. Detective John Brooks was more imposing than you would expect from someone who stood a mere 5'7". But his suit looked liked it had been specially fitted to accommodate the kind of torso that can only be obtained through hours of hard work on weights. The dark brown eyes that stared out from that ebony face had seen it all. The power of an awesome intelligence and equally formidable will was in that gaze. I had heard through the grapevine that he, too, was Not Prey. One look at him made me believe it. I could tell from his glance that he recognized me as well. Not a surprise. After all, not many women in Denver stand 6'1" and wear sweaters and jackets in the middle of summer.

"John Brooks." He extended a broad-fingered hand to me, I shook my head no, holding up my bloodstained palms. He nodded acknowledgment, but his eyes went very dark.

"Kate Reilly."

"You're Not Prey." He observed, running his hand over a smoothly shaved pate. It wasn't a nervous gesture, just a human one.

"So are you."

"Why are you dressed for vampires on a warm summer day?"

I gave him a tight-lipped smile. "Long story."

He returned the smile, but it was the kind where the person knows they have the upper hand, and that made me nervous. "I look forward to hearing it, since you can't lie to me."

My eyes went wide. I realized in a flash that he was right. Custom dictated that Brooks and I were equals. If I lied to him I was displaying prey behavior. Everything would be null and void. Then I realized that it didn't really bother me. I'm not much of a liar, and I had nothing to hide. I smiled again and replied truthfully. "I wouldn't anyway."

He gave a genuine smile that lit up his face, and I realized with a start that he was actually quite handsome. I suppose it shouldn't have surprised me, but it did. He was a man whose impression of strength so dominated his nature that the "softer" qualities were noticed later, if ever.

"That's what they all say." His brown eyes sparkled when he said it and small laugh lines appeared at the corner of his eyes.

"Ah, but do they mean it?"

"Almost never," he admitted. "Come with me." He led me into one of the first floor hotel rooms, letting us in with a key one of the uniforms had acquired from the manager.

The room was an almost mirror image of 150, but done in shades of dark blue with a water theme instead of jungle. The window air conditioning unit was noisily blasting frigid air in a direct line toward the bathroom door. It occurred to me that he'd chosen the room with my outfit in mind. I gave him a nod of appreciation.

He returned my nod and lowered himself into the battered chair, gesturing for me to sit on the bed.

"Mind if I wash my hands?" The blood was dried and it was going to be a bitch to get off. The bloody jeans were hopeless, but I didn't have any options. I'd given the werewolves my only spare clothes. The police had come while I was tending to Dusty, so he knew the blood was hers, but that didn't mean he wouldn't test it to make sure. Still, it was worth a try.

He surprised me by saying, "Sure. While you do, you can start telling me that long story of yours."

"Rumor has it Monica is dying." I used her proper name. I was fairly sure he'd recognize it. He did.

The water pipes were noisy so he waited for me to finish washing before he continued his questioning. I grabbed a flimsy white towel from the rack and walked back to the main room drying my hands. The small movement hurt my shoulder more than it should, damn it. Not good.

"She hasn't got an heir?"

I nodded. "She's got two in mind. Me and the girl with the gunshot wound."

I perched on the edge of the dresser so that I wouldn't get blood on the bed. It creaked in complaint. I could feel the veneer peeling up beneath my palms. It made me wonder if I should sit on the bed after all.

"She wants *you* for a Queen Host?"

"So I'm told."

"Shit!" He flexed and tensed his hands into fists again and again. It was a nervous gesture that went well with the tic that had appeared in his right cheek. "What's that got to do with this mess?" He leaned back causing the chair to creak in protest.

"Maybe something—maybe nothing. I do know that the girl's stepfather has plenty of money and good reason to want her dead."

He nodded in acknowledgment.

"You're armed?"

I nodded and showed him the sheaths, "Knives. I have a concealed carry permit."

"Let's see it."

I pulled the black leather wallet I carry from my back pocket and handed it to him. He examined the permit carefully, slid it back in its sleeve and returned the wallet.

"Good." His jaw set, but he shifted uneasily in his seat. I didn't blame him. Thinking of the Thrall is enough to make anyone uneasy. The more you know of them, the worse it is. Detective Brooks and I shared more knowledge than was ever going to be comfortable.

"So." He reached into the inside pocket of his suit coat to withdraw a small black notebook and slim silver pen. "What happened here today?"

I gave him a quick rundown. We then spent considerably longer going over details. Repeatedly. Detective Brooks was thorough, and if he actually did trust me to tell him the truth it didn't show. I didn't blame him. I didn't even mind. It felt good to be somewhere cool and relatively safe.

"You think the girl's stepfather was responsible?"

"That would be my guess. The guy in the window had a rifle with a scope—and she's the one who got shot. The Thrall aren't big into guns. If it were up to me I'd give her police protection. No visitors, check all doctor IDs, the works."

"It's not up to you and it's not that easy."

My brow furrowed.

He looked at me hard and long. Then he nodded once as if he'd made an internal decision. He put down the pen and pad. Then he stood, opened the door and asked the uniform outside to leave for a few minutes. That raised my eyebrows.

"There are things you should probably know if you're going to go against Monica," he said as he sat down again. He fidgeted; was clearly nervous. "The nest is a lot bigger than it was with Larry. Monica wants power, and a lot of it. Her Hosts aren't just psychically talented, they're well placed, influential. She's got at least one person in the mayor's office, city council, business leaders. She even infected someone at the U.S. Mint. The Herd extends into the hospitals, the fire department and even the police. If Monica is determined, I can't guarantee the girl's safety, even with guards."

My eyes widened. Brooks' warning finally answered something that had been bugging me. Dylan had said they'd caused the wreck but I couldn't figure out why. Now I knew. Monica's people at the hospitals could have netted me that morning. If I were drugged or injured, I would be in no condition to put up a fight while she infected me. Wow. Monica showing up at St. E's meant that she had been covering *all* of the hospitals.

My eyes widened. I didn't have any appropriate phrases to cover the magnitude of the plot. "Damn!"

"No shit." He was talking to me like an equal. I knew it was unusual and I appreciated it, so I returned the favor.

"If you don't protect Dusty, the wolves will. Depending on how determined the stepdad and Monica are, that could get very messy."

"Do you know which of the wolves took down the shooter?"

"Haven't got a clue." I admitted with a shake of my head. "I was downstairs the whole time—and I don't know who looks like what in animal form."

He nodded sagely and jotted down some more notes.

"But you'd say it was self-defense?"

"Absolutely. He shot at the girl first. Then he killed one of the wolves. He wasn't going to be giving himself up."

"Even if they gave him the chance. Which they didn't."

"I wouldn't know. I was downstairs the whole time."

His gaze on me was the cold hard stare of a lifer cop. "Then why do you keep saying *he* when you refer to the shooter?"

I blinked. I'd just assumed the shooter was male. How incredibly sexist.

My expression must have been priceless because Brooks laughed out loud. "Lucky guess?" His voice sparkled with amusement. All I could do was nod.

Brooks rose from the chair and stretched. I started to get up with him, but he gestured for me to stay put. "I'm going to go talk to some of the other witnesses now, but there's something that the Acca wanted me to tell you. One of her wolves is missing—that firefighter, Tom Bishop." I felt my heart still. Where could he be? Was he the one who took down the shooter? Was he going after the stepdad?

Brooks never noticed my shock and fear. "You stay here. I may have some more questions. There'll be a uniform outside if you need anything—and to make sure you stay put. I've heard a lot about you. 'Kay?"

"Uhm, yeah—right."

20

It was a long wait. Hours passed, and I do mean lots of hours. The police took away my cell phone and the one in the room wasn't hooked up, so I couldn't call Joe or Mike. What must they be thinking after not hearing from me all day? News vans surrounded the place, so they would probably know that something was up, but be worried out of their minds.

The light seeping through the cracks in the poorly hung drapes dimmed as the sun finished cresting at noon. I didn't bother turning on the room lamp. I wished I'd tucked a deck of cards in my pocket the way I usually do. At least then I could play solitaire. I know about a dozen different varieties. The cards help me pass the time waiting in airports. I hadn't planned to be doing much waiting today, so they were still sitting on top of my dresser.

At first I paced, but there wasn't much room to do that. I could hear the sound of heavy footfalls up and down the stairs and across the balcony as a multitude of cops, crime photographers, newsmen and the like trooped around the crime scene. Sirens kept sounding as more and more people arrived.

The lights flickered on the drapes like a bad neon sign.

It gave me plenty of time to assess things in my life. Where could Tom have gone that he wouldn't have notified Mary? I thought about the kiss and what he said—*"They can't change how I feel about you."* But how did I feel about him?

I hadn't gone to the room to see the mangled corpse. I presumed that was all that remained of the shooter. And while I'm not into the whole vegan scene, I had never really asked just what Tom served himself for dinner when he wasn't eating apples or cheese omelets. Maybe I didn't want to know. For all I knew he might have been the one to take down the assassin.

If I managed to survive the wrath of Monica and Matt Quinn and even Mary, I'd probably have to screw up my courage and ask Tom about his life as a wolf. I wasn't kidding when I told him I don't do casual. But to be in a serious relationship, you can't afford to take things for granted. That much I learned from Dylan.

And what *about* Dylan? I'd loved him with all my heart but he'd betrayed me long before he became a Host. I'd thought I was over him. But my heart hadn't listened my head when he kissed me. I'd responded to him and missed his touch and loving words. *"I won't let you get away a second time."* A part of me was thrilled at the ferocity in his voice, but most of me was terrified. I wasn't sure I would survive being with him.

From zero suitors for years to two in a day—both of which could get me killed. Just my luck.

Finally, a uniformed officer knocked and eased the door open. "Brooks says you can go now. Your story checks out."

I rose from the bed and retrieved my jacket from where I'd set it on the chair. My jeans were stiff and uncomfortable with dried blood. It made me wonder about Dusty. I opened my mouth to ask but the officer beat me to it.

"I'm supposed to tell you that the girl's under police protection. The stepfather is raising holy hell about it. If it doesn't check out, Brooks is going to be damned pissed." He added an aside, "You *don't* want to piss him off."

"You're right about that." I agreed as I passed through the door he held open for me.

It took a minute for my eyes to adjust after the dim lighting of the room. The sun was well on toward setting, but glaring television lights had taken its place as handsome newscasters in TV makeup "reported from the scene." People were milling everywhere. There was a crowd being held back by uniformed officers.

My truck was blocked in by a Channel 4 News van. I stopped, wondering how I could get it moved without alerting anyone to the fact that I was a witness to the "terrifying events of this morning." It was then that I felt the first brush of her mind against mine.

I froze in place, shivering despite the 85 degree heat. My eyes strained to scan the crowd beyond the glare of the lights. Monica was here. I could feel it. But more than that, I felt *all* of them now. I shuddered under the awareness and attention of the dozens of Thrall Hosts interspersed in the crowd. How many more were Herd? A flash of blonde hair appeared, calm and poised. Carol's true nature was revealed, although I wasn't very surprised. She had outrun Tom. A second face appeared from the crowd. It made my heart fall. Celeste's vacant eyes stared at me without any hint of recognition. Further in the background, Officer Phillips, out of uniform, wearing a crisp red polo shirt and jeans, his eyes staring blankly at me.

I struggled to swallow, my throat suddenly dry. I could hear the thunder of my heart in my own ears and felt Monica's fierce joy at my terror. I had thought I was ready. There was no ready. But her joy brought forth a rush of my own anger in response. I would not go quietly. I'd die before I let her make me a Host.

Do you really think we'll give you that choice?

Her voice was amused and musical in my mind. The minute she "spoke" my eyes found her in the crowd. She stepped forward so that our gazes locked unobstructed.

Fuck you. I screamed into her mind and then tried to shut down the link. But again, I couldn't seem to manage it. At least it was daylight, so her powers weren't complete. This close in full dark, she'd have me for lunch. That she was here at all said how little time she had remaining.

The illusion she'd projected vanished as we mentally struggled. For the first time I got to see her as she really was. She looked like hell. The years of being Host and Queen had ravaged her body. Her hair fell in lank hunks around a sunken sallow face. The skin stretched like withered parchment across a death's head. A red satin dress hung loosely on her skeletal frame. I wondered how the others saw her.

Her mind, however, hadn't diminished a bit—nor had her malice. I felt it beating against my consciousness in hot waves of pure hatred. She was the Queen and her power was joined and strengthened by that of her offspring. The psychic force pounding at my brain was double that of when I fought Larry. Maybe even more. She tried to overwhelm me with the sheer power of her will, and I felt sweat break out on my forehead as I fought against her. I had no music, I had nothing to occupy my mind, so I began to hum heavy metal and imagine I could hear the thrumming beat in my ears.

I felt rather than saw movement to either side of me. Mary in my gym clothes to my left, and Detective Brooks, a solid rock to my right. It helped. I had no idea how, but just having them near me pushed back some of that awesome power, giving me the breathing space I needed.

You have allies. How . . . cute.

"*I am* not *prey!*" I said it with both mind and voice.

Nor are they. But the rest . . .

She must be broadcasting our conversation to the others. I felt Brooks flinch at the realization of what she was implying. There were literally dozens of innocent humans milling around. It would be a blood bath.

The Channel 4 reporter had good instincts. She tapped the cameraman on the shoulder and turned in the direction of our confrontation. Monica hissed at the glare of the lights.

Ignore us. This is none of your concern.

The reporter's pretty face went blank. With slow reluctance she turned away, her attention drawn again in the direction of the motel.

Now, where were we?

You're bluffing! I smiled tightly. *Kill this many people and the humans will wipe out nests all over the world.*

I felt the surge of power that hit her, bringing her up short like an attack dog at the end of its chain.

I heard a bevy of voices in my head. They whispered and called to me, barely reaching over the thrum of power that was Monica. *She must breed, Mary Kathleen, and now. This is affecting her mind. We cannot control her should it continue.*

Fine, I will challenge her to a duel, one on one.

Monica shook her head, I watched as she freed herself from the constraints of the other queens.

Unacceptable. Should you challenge me, I will instruct my children to begin the slaughter. The first one will be the wolf you took to your bed. I have him hidden. He is safe—for now.

I felt my heart still, and heard Mary growl beside me. "Hurt one of my wolves, vampire, and it will be *war.*"

Monica hissed then. Her lips pulled back to reveal her fangs. I had a flash of awareness. She had left it almost too long. She hadn't expected my trip out of town. Will alone kept her Host body going as system after system shut down. She must breed *now.* She would do anything to avoid a challenge she could not win. In a one-on-one match-up against me she would lose. There was simply not enough strength left in her failing body. Tom would die if I didn't agree. All of the people here would die. Monica had nothing left to lose.

"What do you want?" Brooks words made it seem like he had heard Monica's mental comments.

I think you know what I want. And she'll give it to me. Unless, of course, you want me to begin the slaughter. There are more of my children than the small group here. Many others are spread over the city awaiting my command.

"The police are armed." Brook's voice lowered to a growling bass. "We can kill you here and now. Your people will die."

Without an heir they'll die anyway. And how many humans are you willing to kill, Katie? How many, when you know we only want you?

I grated at her using a familiar name for me. But she was

right. There is no one more dangerous than someone with nothing to lose.

"I'll do it." Brooks squared his shoulders. He was pale, and a nervous tic had appeared beneath his left eye but he stood firm. He knew as well as I did that Monica was desperate enough to try anything.

She shook her head slowly. The greasy hair barely moved. *A noble gesture, but futile. A queen needs an abundance of psychic talent. You are very nearly a null. It's why you can't speak to me with your mind. No, it must be Kathleen. By choice or by force. It really doesn't matter which.*

"I am Not Prey." I spoke the words aloud for Brooks's benefit. "You can negotiate with me. You can challenge me. But you can *not* force me."

I will give you their lives. You will give me yours.

I schooled my features to neutrality and began bargaining in earnest. *Not acceptable. I will not consent to anything that gives me a less than fifty percent chance of survival.*

If we do not agree?

I will challenge you to a duel. One on one. Your fellow queens will not let you refuse. You can't fight both them and me. You will lose and your children will die.

Not without taking as many humans with us as we can.

As a single force the Thrall took a menacing step forward. There were more than I had originally counted—twenty, maybe thirty, which meant that she had blinded me. It also meant that she could make good on her threat without a strain. One of the uniforms spooked and started to reach for his weapon. In a blur of speed the nearest vampire grabbed his arm, snapping it with the ease of a dry twig. He screamed and dropped to the ground. His partner moved to his side and was immediately kicked in the face hard enough to knock him out.

Cops everywhere reached for their weapons.

"NOBODY MOVE." Brooks authoritative bellow got the desired result. People froze in mid-motion but the entire situation was balanced on a hairsbreadth of disaster as police officers' hands hovered over the butts of their guns.

I stared at Monica, my back straight, trying with every

ounce of my will to prove to her that I was not willing to play the martyr.

ENOUGH! Monica's voice was a sibilant hiss in my mind. *State your terms.*

The dickering began in earnest.

21

*I*t must have looked odd. Two women standing in a spreading well of tense silence, not speaking a word. The only sound was the whirr of cameras recording the event and the whimpering of the cop with the broken arm. He had not been allowed to move, nor was anyone allowed to assist. I don't know how long it went on. It seemed like forever.

Never negotiate with a psychic. Every time an idea would occur to me as to how I could increase my odds of survival, she sensed it and would try to negotiate countermeasures. Back and forth we went. Finally, it was decided. I stood shaking and terrified knowing that in less than five minutes I would be letting that *thing* lay its eggs in a vein of my left arm.

"Brooks, you took notes. Could you please read back the agreement?" My voice was steady, almost calm. It didn't show the slightest sign of panic. I was proud of that.

The news cameras turned to record what he said, but I don't think he noticed. His eyes were glued to the notebook in his hand. His dark skin had paled, and his hand trembled. But while his voice was taut he read the terms loud and clear.

"Monica and all of the Thrall Hosts and Herd she commands will allow every other non-Herd, non-Host presently here to leave unmolested. No Thrall will interfere with them in any way for the next forty-eight hours. They will not *ever* extract any vengeance or punishment from any of them for any actions they may take in the next forty-eight hours with regard to helping you in your attempt to not become queen. She will not take control of any of your limbs to use against you or cause you mental pain for any reason."

"In exchange—you, Mary Kathleen Reilly, will allow Monica to lay eggs in the vein of your left forearm for thirty seconds. You will not make any attempt to manually remove the eggs from your arm for at least two hours from the end of the thirty seconds during which Monica lays the eggs in your arm. You will not go to any medical professional for assistance in dealing with the eggs. You will not attempt suicide during the next seventy-two hours. And you will allow one of the nestlings to accompany you to make sure that your allies do not go against the negotiated terms." His voice ground to a halt.

"Monica, do you agree to those terms on behalf of yourself and your people?" I asked.

I do, but of course I can only speak for those I control. You will need to negotiate with the other Thrall queens separately. And you, Kathleen? She continued to speak into all of our minds. I think it was to prove that she still could.

I took a deep breath. I could do this. I could do this. God help me, I was going to do this. "I do."

Monica stepped forward. A space cleared between us like magic. As I stepped forward she gave a triumphant, anticipatory smile that bared blackened gums. *I can taste your fear.*

Fuck you. Just do it. With the cameras rolling I didn't say it out loud. My mother had raised me to be a lady—and ladies don't use that kind of language in public. Instead, I stripped off my Rockies jacket and handed it to Mary. Next the knife and sheath. Finally I shoved up the left sleeve of my sweater, baring a length of pale white forearm.

It was time. I took a deep breath and stepped silently forward. As I stopped in front of her and extended my left arm I asked, "Who's going to time this?"

"Give me a watch." Rob's voice answered. I pulled my watch from my pocket and handed it to him, then stepped back to where Monica stood waiting.

We were face to face at last. I grimaced with disgust. The failing of her Host's body was nauseating. Her body and breath stank of disease and rot. I tasted bile in the back of my throat as my stomach threatened to repeat but I fought it down. I couldn't stop the automatic flinch as I took a closer look at her and got a whiff of the decaying stench emanating from her. Multiple skin lesions had been artfully covered with the palest foundation available but there was no hiding the fact that the end was near. My nose was trying to convince my stomach to heave. She noticed when I shrank back from her and it made her more angry. I knew that she would not only lay her eggs—she would make it *hurt*.

Monica took my arm in both of her hands, raising it to her lips. I watched as her lips pulled back to reveal ivory fangs, the only teeth left in the blackened gums. My stomach clenched again and I fought back nausea. I could do this. I *had* to do this. I turned my head and spotted Rob. He was wearing only a pair of jean cut-offs the exact color of his eyes and my black sports watch. I gave a slight nod. His voice rang out in response.

"Now."

The pain was sharp and immediate. She filled my mind and blood with flowing lava. It wasn't outside the terms. It just really is that painful. I fought the urge to strike out; forced myself to stand rigidly still. I kept my eyes locked on Rob staring at the watch that adorned his wrist.

After what seemed an eternity he ended it. "Time."

Monica pulled back so quickly that a single tiny egg fell from her mouth onto the ground with a soft wet splat. I felt a shudder of sorrow pass through the collected Thrall at its loss. Still, Monica was satisfied. Twelve eggs were nestled in my vein. She was certain that one, at least, would survive.

I blinked. My ears popped and hearing returned in a blast of screaming sirens that faded into the distance. Monica and all but one of the Thrall were gone. I hadn't noticed them depart. Everyone else, human and wolf, stood immobile; mesmerized. The control she still had was impressive as hell and more than terrifying.

You'll be able to do it yourself soon. Her words were a warm hiss, a terrifying hint that she expected to prevail.

Not if I can help it!

I looked for my watch but it was gone. "How long were we out?" I muttered. Rob shook his head—looking around in alarm at the sea of blank faces.

"Shit!" He glanced at his watch. "Fifty minutes!"

"Stupid, stupid, stupid!" The bloodsucking bitch had used a loophole. I hadn't negotiated for her not to use mind control to pass the time! Damn it! I should have known that she would try to cheat.

Her voice in my mind was annoyed and flat. *I am within the terms of our bargain to have enthralled you for the full time, Kate. Do not condemn me for merely protecting my children from the wrath of your allies!*

I didn't answer her. Technically it was not a lie. She would have been within the terms. If she was strong enough. But she wasn't. I knew it as well as I knew my own name. I didn't know how I knew, but it didn't matter. The certainty was enough. I felt her hiss of rage inside my head, then blessed silence.

People started coming out of it, shaking themselves like dogs shedding water. Brooks was among the first to come to himself. He looked as displeased at having been put under as I felt. He kept muttering "Fifty minutes. They could've slaughtered us all."

It wasn't comforting. Neither was the fact that my arm was already starting to swell. The wound had closed—the coagulant in Monica's saliva had seen to that. But the eggs had grown. I could see twelve individual spheres pressing against the surface of my arm. They pulsed and grew with each beat of my heart as they fed on the blood coursing through my arm. My breath was coming fast and shallow as I watched them move like maggots under my skin. I struggled not to rip open the arm with my own fingernails.

"Now what?" It was Mary who spoke. All of the wolves seemed fine but most of the humans were still staring va-

cantly into space. Pickpocket heaven, if anyone walking by
could even see us.

"I need to get out of here but my truck's blocked in."

"Where are we going?" Mary asked. I raised my eyebrow
in inquiry. *We?*

Her hands moved to her hips and she looked at me sternly.
"Don't look at me like that, Mary Kathleen Reilly! You saved
Dusty when you yelled out that warning and you saved the
rest of us by letting that *thing* infest you. We're allies. I'm
sticking to you like glue."

She grimaced and failed to suppress a shudder. "Besides, I
told you. You are the last person on the planet I want as a
queen vampire."

"No shit. I'll drive." Brooks answered and led us in the direction of a plain dark blue Ford sedan. Mary, Rob, and I
were followed by a thin dark-haired man wearing a rumpled
suit.

"Where are we going?" He asked.

"Ask the lady." Brooks opened the rear door of the car.
Mary climbed in first. Rob got in the front seat between
Brooks and the partner he introduced as "Detective Adams."

"That was one hell of a thing you did." Adams shook his
head as he slammed the car door shut. He reached over the
back of the front seat to shake my right hand. "A hell of a
thing." His voice sounded almost awestruck, which made me
uncomfortable as hell.

"Thanks." I wasn't sure what else to say. "We need to stop
by a liquor store—fast."

"Right." Brooks turned the key in the ignition but before he
could put the car in gear there was a tap on the window. The
vampire. We'd forgotten the vampire.

"Shit." Brooks swore with feeling. "Adams, out of the car."

"But—"

"Out."

Adams reluctantly climbed out and the vamp took his
place in the front passenger seat. I felt ill. My arm throbbed.
I wished the damned air conditioning would start working.
My mind kept fading in and out as more blood was consumed
by the eggs. Not a good sign.

"I need to stop the blood flow to the arm." I hadn't realized I'd said it out loud.

"A tourniquet would work." Rob suggested.

Brooks turned his head briefly enough to offer, "Use her bootlace."

The Host was in the car now. Rob had scooted as close to Brooks as the vehicle would allow without interfering with the other man's driving. He tried to get as far from the creature as he could get in the small confines of the front seat. The vampire didn't seem any happier to be there than we were to have him. He looked to be in his early twenties. Still healthy enough to be handsome in a Tom Cruise-ish sort of way. He was probably still able to lure victims in with sex. As his looks faded, he'd have to rely on other methods.

Mary bent down and began unlacing my left boot. As she pulled the leather strap free, my last knife sheath came loose. She tucked it somewhere out of sight.

I was out again. I don't know for how long. But there was a tourniquet on my arm that hurt like a bitch—and the car was parked in the lot of a liquor store on Colfax not far from the turn-off I usually take to Our Lady when I'm on this end of town.

"How long?" I didn't need to ask more. Nobody in the car could fail to notice my bouts of senselessness. Rob answered. "Three, maybe four minutes. Mind telling us why we're here?"

"Alcohol. Someone told me that the eggs and hatchlings can't stand alcohol." I watched the vamp's face when I said it. He flinched; his eyes hardened with Monica's annoyance. It made me believe that Dylan hadn't lied after all. Thank God. If we both lived through this, I'd thank him.

"And ice." Mary offered. "Without regular blood flow you may lose that arm if you don't ice it."

"Definitely ice." Brooks agreed. "Do you have any preference as to what type of alcohol?" I shook my head. He climbed out of the car, leaving the rest of us sitting in strained silence. I closed my eyes and faded out again.

"Kate—" I came back to myself to find Mary shaking me. We were parked in the lot of a small liquor store. A brown paper bag was sitting on the floor at my feet, and it appeared that they'd been trying to wake me for awhile. The Host looked pleased as pie. "Where now?"

"How long as it been since she bit me?"

Rob glanced again at my watch. "One hour forty three minutes."

Right. I wanted them out. I wanted them out *now*. But I had to wait. I had to abide by the letter of the law. A sudden thought occurred to me. "Brooks, read me the agreement again.

I forced myself to stay alert long enough to listen to the part about getting medical treatment. It was worth the wait. I found myself smiling, which brought a very attractive frown to the vamp. "Anybody got a cell phone?"

Brooks reached over Rob's body to open the glove box and pulled out a small silver model that he handed to Mary over the top of the seat.

I recited a number, but let her dial. It was all I could do to concentrate on staying awake. The venom in my veins from the bite was meant to lull me, giving the eggs time to hatch. Then the hatchling would have time to make its way through my veins to the base of my brain. I didn't intend to make it that easy. Already I could feel their awareness in my arm. Twelve individual identities in various stages of waking. All twelve were feeling the pangs of hunger at the blood supply being cut off.

One . . . one felt the first stirrings of a personality. I felt her anger; her fear. She was aware of the vampire in the front seat, aware of all of her nest mates. Monica's Host was dying. There was no help for it. But the rest of the nest and the Herds *would* live. She would make it so. I felt the force of her will like a blow to my skull. Only the sound of the nurse at the at the other end of the phone line kept me awake and aware.

"I need to speak to Dr. Reilly."

I heard the phone shuffle and Dr. MacDougal's voice came on the line. "Kate? Is that you? Thank *God*." His voice was tight. "They said that a werewolf was dead on the scene at the Shamrock—and a woman was admitted to Denver General with a gunshot to the chest. But they won't release identities. I thought . . ."

"Not me." I cut him off. "But I'm in trouble. I need to talk to Joe."

"Kate . . . he's . . . he's been taken. A group of Thrall Hosts killed two nurses and kidnapped him from the middle of a surgery."

My breathing stilled and my mind screamed with all of the fury of my being. *MONICA! You BITCH! Where is my brother?*

Her voice in my mind was a tinkle of dark amusement. *Just a small insurance policy, Kathleen. We only discussed safe passage for those in attendance at the motel.*

She was right, and I hated myself in that moment. Tom— and Joe. I'd risked them both. My head spun as my safe world collapsed around me.

"Kate? Are you there? What's happening?" I'd forgotten about Dr. MacDougal.

"Miles, this is very important. I'm not allowed to ask for medical assistance . . ."

"Kate, what . . . Oh God! Do you mea—"

"I'm going somewhere safe, Miles. I've gone where I feel *safe*."

There was silence on the line for a moment, and I breathed a sigh of relief when he responded softly. "I understand. Tell Father Michael I said hello."

I closed my eyes and handed the phone back to Mary. Miles MacDougal would swim through shark-infested waters to find a way to get a doctor to the church. Mary hit the end button and tossed it over the seat to Rob, who was grinning as he put it back into the glove box.

The vampire was seething. His handsome face had taken on an ugly, mottled flush. "You—"

"I did *not* go to him. I am not *going to* him. I have not broken the truce."

I watched his eyes go blank as he consulted with the rest of the nest. After a long moment he reluctantly admitted. "You have not broken the truce."

22

By the time we pulled into the parking lot of Our Lady of Perpetual Hope, my arm was red and cold from the ice. I had forced down almost half of one bottle of Jack Daniels that Brooks had picked up at the liquor store. It's illegal to have an open bottle in a car—but the cop wasn't complaining and I wasn't about to wait. The problem, however, was that the soon-to-be hatchling in my arm had started fighting back. She was using every ounce of her will to try to have the liquor not *stay* down, and convince me to remove the tourniquet for more than just the couple of seconds necessary to save the arm. So far I was winning. I hadn't thrown up and the tourniquet was in place. But each time the struggle was harder. Either she was growing stronger, I was getting weaker, or both.

"Oh my God." Mary's voice was awestruck and horrified. "Would you *look* at them all."

I opened eyes I hadn't realized I'd closed and saw what she meant. Standing in the bright afternoon sunlight were well over a hundred of people. Every Host and nearly every member of the Herd had encircled the church—trampling

Michael's carefully-tended flower beds. They were blocking the sidewalks so that no one could get into, or out of, the church.

"They can't interfere with us." Brooks glared at the Host to his right.

"No." Rob agreed with a low growl, his eyes narrowing dangerously. "But they can stop the doctors from getting here. That's why they're here, isn't it?" The vamp flinched under the intensity of the werewolf's gaze.

His voice was calm but pleased. "We are not breaking truce."

My internal curse was met with a chuckle from Monica and her egg.

My voice sounded tired, weak. "Mary, call Miles at St. Elizabeth's. Tell him not to come—and *why*. He's so damned stubborn he'll try to get here and get himself killed in the process."

Rob retrieved the phone again. He was still growling. So was Mary. The tension in the car was thick enough to cut. Mary's voice on the phone was calm as she gave MacDougal the news. His response wasn't. Everyone in the car could hear him swear.

"Mary."

She turned to face me, phone extended. "Tell him I said thanks. Ask him not to do anything stupid. Somebody has to take care of Bryan if Joe and I don't make it."

She interrupted his tirade and told him. The silence in the car was deafening. After a long moment, I heard him answer. "I understand."

Mary ended the call. There wasn't anything more to say. We were at one hour, fifty-seven minutes. I glanced down at the growing string of pearls under my skin. The skin was becoming purple as the structure of the vein broke down under the constant feeding. "Mary. If this goes badly—take off the arm. I know you can."

"Somebody will take care of it." She gave me a confident look.

"I'll do it." Rob met my gaze over the car seat with calm surety. "You have my word."

The vampire hissed. Rob whirled to face the Host and snarled. It was all he could do not to rip out his throat. Mary was likewise having a difficult time controlling her emotions.

"You shut the fuck *up!*" Rob pointed a finger into the vamp's chest. "The agreement says she can't kill herself. It doesn't say a *thing* about amputation."

"I really hope it doesn't come to that." Mary whispered as she squeezed my good hand.

Her and me both.

The Hosts and Herd pulled back to clear a path for us to the front door of the church. Monica stood at the front, slightly apart from the others. She was weak enough to be swaying on her feet but her eyes held the sheer power of the combined Thrall Nest. Her gaze was only for me. I returned the stare with one of my own and the things I said in my mind should never reach air. My watch started beeping on Rob's wrist as the two-hour mark elapsed. It was time to get those *damned* things out of my arm.

The doors were locked. I was amazed. In my entire life, Our Lady Parish had never locked its doors before 9:00 p.m. Mind you, I didn't blame Mike—considering the company. But I was still shocked. Rob pounded his fist on the painted wood and I raised my voice to call out. "Mike, it's Katie. I've got friends with me. Let us in!"

I heard the key turn in the lock of the big doors. A moment later, Mike held it open as our motley party quickly stepped inside the brightly lit foyer of the church. He started to block the Thrall Host from coming in. Rob had to explain that he was part of the deal. Neither the vamp nor Mike looked particularly happy about it. That told me Mike's opinion of the Thrall was changing pretty fast.

Mary, meanwhile, was staring at my brother Bryan. He was a breathing empty-eyed statue near the baptismal font. She knew what happened, but had never actually seen him this way. The last time Mary had seen him was as a bright, handsome football star at our graduation. I could see the moment she understood my request of Miles.

I heard the key turn to lock the door but my eyes were on the angels in the ceiling as I prayed for help and courage.

"Let's do it." My voice sounded stronger; more confident than I felt.

"But Joe—"

"Joe isn't coming, Michael." Mary said softly. "They took him. He's a hostage until this is over. So is Tom."

"*Damn them!* Damn them all to Hell!" Mike would probably need a stint in the confessional after this was over. I didn't answer. There was no more time and nothing to say. I lay down on the cool, smooth marble of the foyer, placing my left wrist against one of the ribs of the railing overlooking the font. "Brooks, do you have your cuffs? I want to make sure I hold my arm *really* still."

Brooks set down the paper bag with the bottles and retrieved his handcuffs from their holster on his belt. He cuffed my wrist to the nearest rib.

His eyes were fierce as they met mine. I was struggling to hold on, so I took some strength from his sheer determination. He took charge like the good cop he was.

"I need a sharp knife and a bowl. You," he pointed to Mary. "Hold down her legs. You—Rob? You pin her wrists to the floor. Vampire—get the hell out of the way." He pointed to the far end of the room. "Stand over by those far doors. If you even blink, you're out of here and Monica can send someone else." He looked around to see who hadn't been assigned.

"Father—watch the Host as soon as we start. Make sure he doesn't interfere."

The Tom Cruise double nodded once but watched the eggs with eager eyes. "We will not break the truce."

"Whatever." I could tell that Brooks just wanted to shoot him to get him out of the way, but it wasn't that easy.

"Here's a knife." Mary handed him the sheath that had fallen from my boot. "It's sharp."

Michael reappeared in the door of his office carrying the empty silver fruit bowl. At Brooks's command, he poured whiskey into the bowl until it was almost a third full. He then knelt beside me between Rob and Mary. I could hear him murmuring a prayer of blessing over the whiskey before standing so he was between the four of us and the vampire.

I tried to ignore it as Brooks came at me with the knife drawn. I stared up at the pleasantly painted sky and felt *them*. My mind was dominated by the individual beings throbbing with life in my left arm. They were so *alive,* though still unhatched. But the strongest by far was *her.* I knew that in just a minute or two more she'd escape her shell and swim through my bloodstream in search of the nesting spot.

The knife was keen and the ice had numbed my arm well. I barely felt the slice that opened my skin to expose a smooth string of eggs laying inside my largest vein. I didn't want to look, but I couldn't help myself. Brooks had to use delicate movements to open the vein without nicking the eggs. The yolk from one egg hatching would hit my body like a drug. More than one would flood my system and kill me with the speed of a snake. He needed to remove the eggs intact to keep from killing me. He opened a small section of vein without severing it. There wasn't much blood. The tourniquet was doing its job well, and the eggs themselves were absorbing most of the blood through their shells. Brooks used the tip of the knife to pry the egg through the hole he had created. It was the size of a seed pearl, rubbery and covered with thick blood. As I watched, the blood was absorbed through the shell and the egg rippled with interior movement. A wave of nausea hit me and a cold sweat broke out on my brow. I turned my head, fighting down the flow of bile. I heard a sizzle and a mental scream as it was dropped in the alcohol.

A small tug. Soft swearing as Brooks tried to remove the second egg, and found it stuck. "What I wouldn't give for tweezers right now." He muttered.

"Bryan." Michael called my brother over. "Kneel here." He knelt beside me where Mike had been. "Hold this steady." He handed my brother the bowl and stood.

The vampire was suddenly in front of Mike. I had forgotten to explain that he couldn't help. I was so wrapped up with watching Brooks and the eggs that I couldn't even think of what to say. The Host's lips pulled back to bare ivory fangs. He hissed in warning. "You may not aid! It is forbidden."

The weight on my wrists lifted. I felt a wave of heat—

heard the sounds of struggle. I turned my head in time to see a pony-sized gray wolf leap at the vampire before he could strike at Michael. I saw fangs sink into the thick fur, heard the wolf scream. Mary reached over and did double duty by holding both of my feet. I opened my mouth to call out to Rob, but the hard crack of the vampire's skull sounded against the marble floor. When Rob stepped back, the vampire wasn't moving. *She* and Monica were horrified and furious. In less than an instant something began to happen outside. The doors of the church shuddered under rhythmic blows from many bodies.

Mike didn't stay to watch the struggle. "I'll be right back." He sprinted through the archway and up the aisle. I knew he was going to cut through the basement and go to the rectory, but tried not to think about it. I didn't want Monica or the hatchling to know.

The arched front doors shuddered again. There was no way the flimsy locks would hold under the assault. As if from a distance I heard Rob swear. He must have changed back to human. He ran naked into Mike's office. I watched him grab the crucifix from Mike's office and jam the long pole through the brass door handles.

Another tug at my arm brought me back to Brooks. The second egg was loose from my arm, balanced on the tip of the knife blade. I felt a wave of panic as the nestling realized what was happening. It was aware enough to understand death. I screamed then, long and loud. But over the screams I heard the sizzle of the egg hitting the alcohol. A flash of searing pain cut across my brain. Then it was over. Brooks moved on to the next victim.

Michael was back. He'd brought tweezers with him and the black bag he takes with him when he goes to the hospital to administer last rights. As if from a distance I saw Brooks take the tweezers, heard Michael begin the rites created by the church to aid the gravely ill.

I closed my eyes, unable even to think clearly enough to pray. All I could do was concentrate on keeping my body still—on not fighting, but as the process dragged on, my will was weakening.

The tweezers speeded the process. Egg after egg was re-moved to char in the silver bowl. I felt each death. Each individual personality silenced. More than that, I felt the rage of the thousands of Thrall throughout the world at the murder of their young.

Time slipped by as Monica enthralled me; called to me. I was *nothing* compared to her children. I *must* stop them. I tried to steel my will, but it was useless. My back arched and I struggled to free myself from the iron grip of the wolves who had to use all of their strength to keep me pinned to the floor. Brooks pulled back, unable to perform delicate work because of the thrashing of my body.

Minute after minute sped by as I fought. The children grew stronger. Their minds became mine as I joined the Nest. Brooks knelt on my pony tail to hold my head down. I swore at him, spat at him. I pulled against the handcuff until my wrist bled and the wood cracked. Mary was forced to kneel on my left shoulder—while Rob did the same to my right. I screamed from the pressure on my swollen arm, but he didn't ease up. Completely pinned, unable to move, I watched in blind fury as another child was removed from me.

Monica fell to her knees as the eighth egg burned. She collapsed with the death of the ninth. I felt a white-hot explosion of pain as her Host died. I screamed in fear and pain. Nestlings and Herd around the church writhed and dropped to the ground in death throes and I couldn't help them.

NO! A voice roared it in my mind. It was her. The strongest egg. I felt the rubbery skin of the shell split as she tore against it with all of her strength. They would *live*. She would *make the Nest live!*

I came to myself for an instant. "Shit! One of them's hatched."

I turned my head to look at Brooks. It was the last move I made before the toxin from the egg yolk hit. I couldn't move; I was suddenly numb and completely paralyzed. But my mind . . . my mind slipped the bonds of my body. I was free. The Host's awareness was pushed aside. She was nothing. I could look out from inside any human. I knew their thoughts, could feel their simple emotions. I felt the other queens all over the world. They waited for my birth; they offered me their strength of will.

I struggled to attack the humans' minds. Brooks was first. His mind blazed with intense determination. The Thrall, my people, were *things* to be defeated. To him, Kate, the Host— the inferior shell—was what mattered. He *would* save her. Try as I might, I could not break through. There was not enough talent yet to reach him.

Bryan, the Host's nestmate, held the bowl of infernal alcohol. My mind lingered behind his empty eyes, wandering through darkened passages. I searched for the spark of life, for something I could control. I found it trapped, closed off by burnt out and scarred tissue. He could be useful if I restored his mind. I probed and called to the spark. As if a door opened, I felt his mind start to awaken, but it was taking too long.

I looked out of the Host's eyes and saw the wolf who hurt my child. I tried to slide inside his mind, but the way was barred. The magic of his beast burned with hot orange fury and a strength of will that matched that of my warring Host.

I heard the thump of a body on the roof and it distracted me.

Kate's will pushed against mine, our twinned consciousness flew outward and I felt her thrill of recognition. *Tom!*

I fought for control, but the Host was stubborn. Together we watched as he backed up, ran with all his strength to the edge of the building and leapt onto the roof of the church. He staggered on landing, nearly losing his footing and dropping the medical bag he was carrying. He saved himself by throwing his arms around the steeple. The Host's surge of joy and pride made me snarl with rage. He would die for his interference.

No! I won't LET YOU! The Host fought for dominance, screaming in rage and defiance.

Once the wolf named Tom had steadied himself on the steeple, he held on with one arm and used one booted foot to kick through the shutters that closed off the bell tower. I heard his bellow of rage as his leg punched through the rotted floor of the bell tower. We all looked up at the sound.

"Father Michael! Get the door!" Tom's voice was a scream of rage, panic, and burning loyalty.

Mike rushed to the locked interior door, keys in hand.

"Katie—"

With a cry of fury the hatchling was pushed aside and I was once again Kate. I felt moisture on my face and my mind was again in my body. *My* mind, not the hatchling's. Tom knelt naked beside me. His hand stroked my face. His neck was a torn mess that was still dripping blood. He was crying. "You have to fight. You *have* to. I—I love you so much."

The pounding on the front doors continued. They were holding up better than I would have expected. Thank the Lord for craftsmen with pride in their work.

I couldn't speak. I could only look out at him with sad, haunted eyes. God help me, I was trying. But *She* was born and I was fading fast. I could feel her will pounding at my mind, ready to pounce and take over again at the first sign of weakness.

Tom brushed Brooks aside as I slipped away again. "Get out of the way. I need to get the ones that haven't hatched yet."

Tom took over with quick but steady determination. With a loud hissing and mental scream, the last eggs hit the bowl. *She,* however, was already swimming through the vein of my arm. The lack of circulation weakened *her* body. But nothing could weaken *her* will.

The hatchling hit the barrier formed by the tourniquet. *She* struggled, her panic increasing as the last of her siblings died.

I heard Mary speak as though from a distance. "Can you get the one that hatched?" Her voice was strangely calm as she addressed Tom.

There was a tense silence that spoke volumes. "No."

I watched as Mary nodded. She gave Tom a pitying look before calling out Rob's name. I knew what he would do. I knew it had to be done. But the look on Tom's face was horrified as he realized what was about to happen. He squeezed my hand and repeatedly kissed my forehead while tears streamed.

When the hatchling realized what was about to happen she

panicked. *She* screamed her will at me; tried desperately to make me remove the shoelace around my arm. I had to let her reach my mind. I was the Host. It was my *duty* to protect her! The effect of the toxin had worn off. I could move. Human hands with inhuman strength held me down as I screamed and thrashed.

In the background I felt the wave of heat as Rob changed to wolf form. There was no more time. In a last ditch effort to save herself and the last tattered remains of the nest *She* ripped through flesh and muscle using the sharp head horn that had cut through the shell of her egg. There was a small explosion of tissue and blood as she broke through my arm to open air.

For a moment, I felt the mental control weaken. *She* had to concentrate on breathing and moving through air instead of blood. She skittered across my pinned body—a slimy pulsating eyeless maggot, the tendrils that would become the ganglia dragging behind her. I slammed my mouth shut, screaming again and again through gritted teeth as I caught a glimpse of her plan in my mind. The mouth or the nose. She would go in through the mouth . . .

Brooks and the others flinched and recoiled from the sight of her. I heard their screams of surprise and alarm as she moved across my chest. A flash of light and power enveloped me as the rest of the wolves changed form in a rush of adrenaline. *She* kept moving; struggling across the foreign landscape of cloth and flesh. *She* was on my chin when I felt a splash of wetness across my chest and face.

I tasted the harsh bite of whiskey as she slid onto my lips, and her scream of pain was ripped from *my* throat. The whiskey flooded my nostrils until I couldn't breathe. It seared down my throat and into my lungs. With the last of my awareness before the pain took me, I heard a familiar, long-ago voice.

"Ka . . . tie?"

23

I woke in a hospital bed. As if in a dream, I tried to move my head and arms. A sting and ache in my left arm was my first shock of sensation. I looked down to see the arm tied to a board which was fastened to the bed. A long row of stitches was black against my pale skin. Wires and tubes snaked from my arm to disappear behind me. The other arm was wrapped in gauze. My mind was foggy, but it was *my* mind. I was Mary Kathleen Elizabeth Reilly and while I could hear the buzz of Thrall voices in my mind I wasn't one of them. I'd escaped. I felt the rage of the other queens at my joy but it didn't diminish it a bit. I looked again at my left arm. Still there. I closed my eyes under a wave of pure relief.

"Thank you God." It wasn't much of a prayer, but it was heartfelt.

I opened my eyes again, taking a look around the room.

Joe was asleep in one of the two guest chairs and I felt tears well. He was *alive!* He wore his usual hospital garb— blue shapeless scrubs with the St. Elizabeth logo printed on the front and one shoe. His left leg was in a walking brace and his face was a mass of bruises. What had happened? The scrubs were rumpled and looked like they'd been slept in. Obviously they had.

Michael snored peacefully in the other chair, his neck at a ridiculous angle that was guaranteed to cause him problems when he woke up. Still, he looked fine. Crisp as ever. Made me wonder what fabric those clerical uniforms are made out of. Bryan sat cross-legged on the tile floor. His neck was bent at a painful angle as he stared wide-eyed up at a television hung near the ceiling. Cartoon images rollicked mutely across the screen.

Bright daylight streamed through the slats of the vertical blinds, sending stripes of shadow across the floral wallpaper. It was a private room. One bed. There were bunches of flowers on the dresser along with a four-foot-tall stuffed wolf with a big red bow on its neck.

My thought processes weren't working very well but I didn't feel any pain. Even fuzzy logic dictated that one of the tubes running into the veins of my right arm must be painkillers. I remembered going into the church. Remembered getting my arm sliced open. Remembered being part of the Nest. Other than that, everything was a blur.

But somehow we'd won, and I still had the arm.

"Joe? What happened?" My voice was slurred and about an octave deeper than normal, but I could talk.

Mike and Joe both jerked awake at the sound of my voice.

"You're awake." Joe growled in a sleep-filled voice. "'Bout damned time."

"What happened to you? Is Tom okay? Did Miles find you?"

He stood up and walked the few steps to the bed and clasped my good hand. He looked almost embarrassed. "Dylan saved us. Never thought he had it in him. He kicked butt on half a dozen Thrall and freed Tom. Then he got me out of there right before a couple of Hosts were going to make me lunch. Tom's in the next room over. Broken ribs, fractured tibia and a nasty gash on his bicep from crashing down through the belfry floor. Miles sewed him up. My bet is that he'll be released later today. He'll be healed a lot quicker than you will be."

A part of me didn't want to know, but "Did Dylan . . . did he make it out?"

Joe shut his eyes and shook his head. "I don't think so. He stayed behind so we could escape. But they were all over him when we left, and I haven't heard from him since."

"You didn't think he'd wind up a hero, did you?" I wanted to be angry, but I was ashamed to admit that I agreed with him.

He growled and glared at me. When he replied, his voice was low and gruff, like it was just after we learned my parents had died. "Didn't think he had it in him. He saved our lives."

"KAY . . . TIE wake?"

The words from the end of the bed startled me. They were strangely childlike, but the voice was the same deep baritone I remembered from a dream.

"Bryan?" My eyes began to fog as he reached over and petted my hand like it was a puppy.

A bright smile lit his face and it cut through the rest of the fog. "Kay . . . tie." He recognized me. My brother recognized me.

Joe was smiling. "Amazing, isn't it? It happened right after the queen broke into the open. We don't know how or why."

Michael placed a gentle hand on Bryan's shoulder and added, "I think it was from seeing you being hurt. When you screamed, he took the bowl of whiskey and tossed it in your face just as the hatchling was slipping into your mouth. It died instantly."

Bryan was smiling broadly. It was the smile of a four-year-old child. Open, trusting, and so damned beautiful that I found myself crying. He gave me a puzzled look, but then launched himself into my arms.

Despite the awkwardness of the tubes and the bandages, I held him. I held him as though I'd never, ever let him go.

24

"I'm not quite ready to talk about it, Peg."

I stood in front of the apartment windows, staring down at the street below. Monica's death took the entire nest of Hosts and a good number of the Herd. In all, close to 160 people died that night, most of them in the churchyard of Our Lady of Perpetual Hope. In fact, photographs of the scene made the national news. There was a big hoopla for a few days nationally, but it faded after an attempted terrorist attack on the Statue of Liberty. Could I have saved the people? I just don't know, and that bothers me—a lot. But I couldn't talk about it yet, even with Peg, who is the closest thing I have to a best friend.

"I know it has to be bothering you, Kate. A lot of people you knew died. Try to talk to someone about it. Please?" She sighed sadly when I didn't respond for long moments, and then tried to brighten the mood. "Did you get the package yet?"

I glanced at the coffee table, and the massive wicker monstrosity with crumpled yellow film that resembled an Easter basket on steroids.

I smiled the smallest bit. "I cannot *believe* you took the

time to do this. Or is there some company out there that's warped enough to sell these?"

She chuckled. "Nope. I'm guilty all on my own. But I know how you are about coffee. And I'm all over the world every week. So, I just dropped into a few gift shops at a few airports, picked up that pretty reed basket in Kenya and poof, instant gift basket. I knew that you couldn't refuse a coffee basket!"

I'd been delighted when it arrived. There was enough Colombian and Kenyan and even German brews to feed my, and Tom's, caffeine addiction for months. We were still laughing when I hung up, but the happiness didn't last for long. I couldn't pick up the basket or even make my own coffee right now. But I didn't want to tell Peg that either. Tom thought my lingering nervousness was a result of feeling helpless. They had to do arthroscopic surgery on the shoulder *and* the elbow *and* I had a nice long row of stitches the arm where Monica laid her eggs. I *did* feel helpless. But that's not it.

Every time I was outside of the apartment, I could feel my skin crawl. Someone was watching me. I'd dropped my shields, tried to find whoever it is. Nothing. It was maddening.

I was reading a magazine a little later, which is not as easy as it sounds with only one arm. There was a knock on the door, then two more with a hard rap at the end. That was the signal. One of the wolves was at the door. Just to be safe, I let my senses flow outward, but couldn't feel any hive presence. I braced one heel against the bottom of the couch and rolled my body forward to get to a standing position. God, I hated this sling! Whoever was on the other side of the door was patient. Joe and Tom would keep knocking until I got there.

I unlocked the door and stepped back so I had room to move. "Come on in."

The door opened a fraction and stopped. It took another shove before Dusty Walker poked in her head. "Are you decent?" Her body was mostly still outside the door.

I raised my brows. "What are you doing here, Dusty?"

She smiled and gave a little laugh, which made her purple

hair bounce. "Just dropped by to give you a little present to make you feel better." She stepped fully into the doorway. She was wearing a black tank top with a skull and crossbones emblazoned across the chest. The black jeans and boots showed off her toned muscles. I glanced down to see that she was holding a glass vase with red carnations and baby's breath in one hand and a grey plastic box with a handle and a wire door. A small, oddly familiar *meow* came from the back of the cage. I let out a little squeal and bolted forward.

"*Blank?*" I tried to take the cage from Dusty, but the weight of it was too much for my elbow. She pulled back the cage, stepped across the entry and down into the pit, and set it on the couch. The flowers were placed next to the coffee gift basket.

I sat down on the couch and opened the wire door as Dusty returned to the front door to close it. She had to put her butt against it and brace her feet to get it to latch.

I could only hope he would remember me. Six years is a long time for a cat. I put a tentative hand inside the cage and let Blank sniff it. I needn't have worried. He licked my fingers and crawled out of the cage, directly into my lap. Then he curled up and started to purr. His long white fur was still silky, but he was heavy and well muscled compared to the adolescent puffball he had been when Dylan took him away. I had always hoped he would grow into his huge head and feet. I held up his head to look at him closely. His nose was criss-crossed with black lines of scars, some old and some fresh, but his eyes were clear. A throaty rumbling vibrated my palm.

I looked up at Dusty and could feel wetness edging my eyelids. "How . . . *where*—?"

Dusty smiled and it turned her back into the young girl in the photo Matt originally gave me. "The cat was Uncle Dylan's. It never liked Aunt Amanda. The cops let her out of jail to go to the memorial service and Mom and I dropped by her house afterward. I saw the cat scratch her, and I was afraid she was going to hurt it. I convinced her to let me take it home. I always thought that Blank was a better name than Snowball anyway, so I thought I'd bring it here."

Jail? I must have looked startled, because she elaborated. "Oh! Didn't you know? Aunt Amanda apparently tried to get someone at a pool hall to tell her where Uncle Dylan was, and it got ugly. The bouncer called the cops and the guy pressed charges. She's been locked up since before the whole thing went down at the motel. She even rated her own guard at the service."

I hadn't known that, but it would explain why she hadn't been bothering me. I didn't mind at all. I scratched under Blank's chin and smiled. "He was just a kitten when Dylan found him at the pound. His eyes were such a pale blue that they were nearly clear. He looked like a blank canvas, something that just needed a splash of color to be finished. So, he became *Blank*."

She threw herself sideways into the chair and then dropped her feet onto the floor after an annoyed look from me. "And . . . I was hoping that if I brought him, I might be able to ask you a favor."

I readjusted myself on the couch so that I didn't keep sinking back into the cushions. It's harder to get up when I get all squished. I didn't want to sound as suspicious as I felt, so I kept my question short.

"What's the favor?"

She took a deep breath and then looked at me squarely. "It's so bogus! The press found out Matt was at the church scene, and the news said Rob was there, too. He lost his job, and he hasn't found another one yet. We can't go home and live with Mom, so we were wondering—"

I stood up so fast that my shoulder screamed. "Oh no! I am not in any condition to have house guests. Especially ones that are actively trying to have babies, Dusty. As you can see, there isn't a room in this apartment with a *door!*"

She shook her head quickly and held up her hands in a mollifying manner. I could smell roast beef and onions on her breath as she stood as well. "No, no! I was just hoping we could stay in the apartment that's not quite done on the first floor. Tom mentioned you had one that was almost ready. Just until Rob can get back on his feet. I have some money. I can buy the appliances, and Rob said he would be happy to paint to your specifications." Her face was hopeful and scared at the same time. "We don't have anywhere else, and after what happened to Matt—"

Shit! That's right. I'd forgotten. Matt Quinn didn't die in the Thrall fallout. He'd been shot execution style, his body dumped by the side of I-25 not far from the exit to his house. It was a very professional hit, but there are no leads or suspects. The poor kid must be a nervous wreck, and I didn't blame her.

"I was going to ask you at Uncle Dylan's memorial, but I didn't see you. Did you go?"

I sighed and closed my eyes. "I miss Dylan, Dusty. I really wish I could've paid my final respects. He was stronger than any of us gave him credit for. But I know Amanda too well. She'll blame me for his death—"

It was as if my words summoned her.

The front door flew open and I jerked my head to the sound. It slammed into the wall with a crash that shook the wall of the building. She stood there, shaking with fury, her face contorted with rage.

"You're right, Kate. I *will* blame you for his death. They all died because of *you* and your damned *need* to *win*. You even had the gall to send *flowers* to my husband's funeral! You couldn't possibly think that a clueless deputy could keep me from making sure that you *pay,* did you?"

She leapt forward toward me. Dusty stood up in a rush and tried to stop her. "Aunt Amanda! No! Don't do this!"

Amanda grabbed her hair and literally threw her out of the way. Dusty hit the back of the chair and tumbled to the ground. She rolled to the side and got back to her feet. "I won't let you hurt her, Aunt Amanda!"

I was backing away from Amanda. I was in no condition to fight her, but I didn't want Dusty to get hurt either. "Dusty, go! Get out. Find Tom."

She nodded once and moved. Amanda tried to grab Dusty to stop her, but missed. She didn't follow the girl, but turned back to me. Her smile was a vicious baring of teeth as she pulled something out of her pocket. But she hid it behind her arm, so I couldn't tell what it was.

"So you're going to try to kill me? Is that it, Amanda?" I needed to stall. This time I really did need help. She was in a lot better shape than me.

The resulting laugh had that same maniacal edge that Monica's had at the end. "Oh no, Kate. Not right away. I want to hurt you first." She stepped slowly closer and I backed around the room, always keeping a piece of furniture between us.

"And what do you think can possibly still hurt me? I nearly lost my arm, I lost people I cared about. If you don't kill me, what's left?"

She revealed the item in her hand. It was an old fashioned metal syringe with twin finger loops and a thick veterinary-style needle.

She darted around the coffee table and nearly grabbed me. I just barely got behind the couch in time. "I'm going to finish what Monica started, Kate. I'm going to crown you queen."

I felt little hairs prick up on the back of my neck and a shiver crawl slowly up my spine. My voice cracked when I spoke. "That's not possible. Only another queen can lay eggs."

She slid her fingers into the metal guides and held out her other arm, where I could see a string of puncture wounds in a trailing line below her elbow. "I thought so, too, but there's another way. It wasn't easy to figure out how, but I've got the technique down. Once you're a queen, you'll be alone. All alone, like Monica was. Will you go insane? Or will you turn all your friends? What will you do to survive, Kate? Monica told me that not everything goes away. You'll remember them. You'll know what you've done, but you won't be able to stop yourself."

My heart was beating like a triphammer. She was insane. What the hell had she done to herself?

I grabbed the nearest potted plant left-handed and flung it in Amanda's face. Pain shot through my arm, and I knew that I'd torn open several stitches. She flinched just enough that she missed by a fraction of an inch. Blank darted up the stairs and hissed his outrage from the landing edge.

I ducked and spun, aiming a side kick at her knee but she twisted at the last second, the blow landing on her calf. It made her grunt, but she didn't go down. She grabbed for me again and caught my bad arm. I screamed as she threw me to the ground and kicked my other arm, tearing more stitches.

She let out a roar of victory. I could feel her hatred beating against my mind like a club. She ripped off the sling like it was tissue paper while I kicked at her back.

I kept blocking her as she brought down the syringe, but her speed was breathtaking. I'd never seen anything like it. It was taking everything I had just to avoid the blows she was aiming at me. I couldn't free my arm. She was just too strong. Where in the hell was the cavalry?

You'll be avenged, Queen Monica. I promised you she would pay. She spat each word directly into my mind and didn't even realize it. She doesn't have any psychic talent, but in that instant I found my weapon.

My hatchling had magnified my natural abilities. Lately it's been a constant fight to not only shield out the Thrall, but also the thoughts of anyone. All I had to do was concentrate on a person and I knew where they were and what they were doing. But I'd never tried to do what Monica had done so easily. Could I influence a person's actions? I had no choice but to try. Amanda would insert the syringe eventually. I was too far outmatched. Already I could see blood seeping through the thick bandage on my forearm. So I concentrated. I put every ounce of my strength and will into a sending directed at Amanda.

Amanda stiffened, her eyes glazing slightly. She staggered backward a half-step, her legs tangling in the broken foliage.

I couldn't have stopped it if I'd wanted to, but I didn't try. I just watched for that long, frozen second it took her to overbalance.

The crash of the window glass breaking was deafening. I threw my arm in front of my eyes, protecting my face from the flying shards. Her scream ended with a sickeningly wet thud. I dragged myself upright and staggered over to the window. I expected to see her horribly dead on the pavement three floors below. What I saw was far worse. There was blood, lots of blood, but no body. And in the distance, nearly out of sight, I caught a glimpse of something ducking into an alley.

Tom burst into the room at that moment in wolf form with Rob at his heels.

"What happened? Are you all right?" Rob asked as he dashed across the room. There was a shimmer of light that illuminated the fur of the huge gray wolf just before it shifted shape and Tom stood naked in front of me.

"What in the hell?" Rob's glance went from the shattered foliage to where the syringe had fallen, and from there to the shattered window.

"It was Amanda." I was still out of breath, panting from the mental and physical exertion, so the words came out oddly. "She fell."

He stepped up to the window ledge, looking down with something approaching awe. "It's three stories down to flat concrete. I'm not even sure one of us could survive that fall."

"I know."

Tom stepped up, pulling me close. Heedless of my bloody arm he held me tight. I could hear the pounding of his heart, feel it beating hard against my chest. "You're all right." He whispered the words into my hair. "Thank God you're all right."

Rob didn't notice. He just kept staring down at the bloodied pavement. "I'm going down there to take a sniff. She should *not* have been able to walk away from that. It's not *possible*." He turned and unlocked the window. I heard the rattling of metal as he bolted down the ladders.

Tom and I were alone. For a long moment he just held me. I felt him take a shuddering breath before he pushed me to arm's distance.

"Why didn't you let one of us stay up here with you? We were almost too late. Damn it Katie!" His arms dropped away from me. He turned away so that I couldn't see his face. *"You could've been killed."* His words were soft, but there was an undercurrent of anger that I didn't know how to deal with. What could I say? This was new to me. It's been a long time since I've had anyone in my life who'd *want* to protect me. In truth, I wasn't sure I wanted to be protected—even if at the moment I probably needed it.

The silence was stretching on too long. I had to say something. "Tom . . . I—"

He interrupted me before I could say anything more. Probably a good thing, since it looked like anything I might say would be the wrong thing.

"I love you, Katie." He stared at me, his open heart in those big brown eyes, "I *know* we haven't been together long, but I love you, and I don't want to lose you because of your damned stupid pride. I know you're tough. You're as much of a predator as I am—I get that. But can't you unbend just a little? Can't you let me in?"

"I love you, too, Tom." My voice was hoarse, my throat tight with tension and fear as the sunlight glinted off the metal syringe on the floor. "I want to let you in. I'm just not sure I know how."

His laugh was almost a sob, and painful to hear. "Can you at least promise me you'll try?"

"I promise." I brought my hand up to touch his face. His gaze stole my breath as surely as the kiss he laid on my lips.

"I love you, Katie Reilly. God help me, I do."

"I love you, too."

We kissed again, sealing our bargain. I reveled in the gentle probing of his tongue and lips, knowing that he wanted me, and that he could accept me, even when I couldn't accept myself.

He led me into the bathroom to dress my arm and check the damage to my shoulder and elbow.

"I think you should go to the doctor tomorrow. You've torn at least two stitches, but it doesn't look too bad otherwise. But Joe will want to look at them. The swelling is definitely up, but I don't have the tools here to do much good."

He was right. I'd be calling the doctor, both for my injuries and to figure out what in the hell was in that syringe. Could she really have figured out some way to make a queen without another queen? The room felt chilled, or maybe it was my blood that was running cold. Even Tom's touch couldn't seem to warm me completely.

Monica may be dead and gone, but that didn't mean I was safe. Not by a long shot. I have Tom, and I have friends, but I also have a brand new enemy. And she won't rest until she sees me dead—or worse.

Coming from Tor Romance in August 2006,
a new tale of the Sazi . . .

CAPTIVE MOON

BY C.T. ADAMS
& CATHY L. CLAMP

0-765-35401-2 / $6.99 ($9.99 CAN)

The sweet stench of rotting flesh on the breeze assaulted Antoine's nose, even before the buzzing of flies reached his ears.

"We are nearly at the site, Herr Monier. We are fortunate that it was cold last night. The carcasses have apparently been here for several days. The smell isn't nearly as bad as it could be."

Antoine stepped over a log hidden under the melting slush, and stopped just short of a clearing. He could see uniformed officers and even a few members of . . . the *harbor patrol?*—taking photographs and measurements under the towering beech trees outside of Stuttgart, Germany. The sun was about to crest the top of the nearest peak, but the shadow of the full moon still lingered on the opposite horizon. The gentle, sultry pull reached for the animal under his skin. His senses were still intensified by the invisible magic that played over his body. Any other time, the forest scents would be too intense to remain near prey long. But the death smell that permeated the valley stilled his natural urges.

The uniformed officer behind, the weighty tang of his blood sausage and porridge breakfast still hovering on his breath, couldn't smell the log under the snow as Antoine had. He tripped and dropped hands-first against a tree.

Antoine stopped, his nose sorting out the history of what had happened here. He caught Simon's scent and knew he was dead. The two-year-old tiger had been one of Antoine's favorites. A stab of pain and sadness rushed through him. *I failed him. What sort of Rex can't protect one of his own cats?*

Kommissar Reiner turned and raised one bushy brow, which disappeared under the brim of his cap. "Herr Monier? Are you well? We do not have to continue if you do not wish." The man's English was heavily accented, but far better than his French.

Antoine squared his shoulders and tucked a few loose strands of long blond hair behind one ear. *If Simon could endure his fate, then I can stand witness.* "I'm fine, Kommissar. Please show me the animals."

He entered the clearing and could only stare in shock and rage at the carnage. Big cats of every description lay in bloody, decaying heaps around the edges of a makeshift slaughterhouse. Bits of flesh, black with slow-moving flies, were splattered haphazardly over the ground.

Officers wearing mask-and-glove photographed the area. Crows watched from the branches of trees overhead. Their raucous caws, combined with the constant buzzing, set Antoine's nerves on a knife edge. Thankfully, the scent of fear and pain from the animals' final moments had dissipated. He wasn't sure how he would have responded to that.

"We believe the poachers were trafficking in tiger organs for the Far East black market. But we are not sure about the other great cats. Perhaps they could not find enough tigers to meet the demand."

Perhaps. But there's more here than meets the eye. A Sazi was here, I can definitely smell an injured female weretiger. While Antoine's nose wasn't nearly as sensitive as his twin's, the female shapeshifter who had been in this clearing had left her mark. *Sandalwood and tiger musk, with a hint of patchouli.* A quick sniff. *No, she's not among the dead. She was taken from here, very much alive.*

He'd identified as much as he could with his nose. Now his eyes began to take in details. Fiona and the rest of the council would want to know everything he saw, heard and smelled. If necessary, one of the Sazi seers could touch his mind and describe it at the meeting.

"Were you able to apprehend any of the poachers, Kommissar? How did you come to find this place?"

One of the police officers, looking a bit green around the gills, approached Reiner as they carefully skirted the bloody makeshift tables. He removed red-stained latex gloves before saluting.

Antoine could tell the Kommissar was going to ignore Hermann in favor of him—their annoying, high-profile visitor, but one look at the officer's face dissuaded him. He made a small motion of his hand. "One moment, Herr Monier." Antoine nodded politely and wandered a short distance away.

Was ist los, Hermann? Reiner lowered his voice and turned his back on the visitor; he couldn't know that it didn't matter. Antoine's supernatural senses would have been able to hear a conversation back inside the squad car.

Ich habe gerade Nachricht erhalten von Dietrich and Shapland, Kommissar. Sie sind ein wenig nervös wegen des Tigers auf dem Revier. Sie haben Zweifel, ob der Kaefig haelt. Sollen sie das Tier betaeuben?

Antoine stiffened as he listened to the conversation, while struggling to appear not to understand: "I have just received a report from Dietrich and Shapland, Inspector. They are nervous about the tiger at the station. They are worried that the cage will not hold it. Should they tranquilize the animal?"

It was so much easier to eavesdrop when the police believed he didn't speak German. Playing the part of the haughty Frenchman had been a useful idea of Margo's. But the Inspector's words dropped with the weight of lead. *They had a tiger at the station? Could it be the female Sazi? If they tranquilize her and the moon sets . . . Merde!*

Das waere ratsam! Wir müssen den Antrag stellen, um das Tier zu entsorgen. Bitte bring meine Nachricht zu Dietrich. Er hat die Lizenz für die Tranquelizer!

Antoine deliberately wandered around the far edge of the scene, being careful to take in every word. "Yes, that would be wise. We'll have to file the proper paperwork to dispose of the animal. Please relay my instructions to Dietrich. He is qualified with the tranquilizers."

Putain! What to do now? This could easily become a diplomatic incident. He began to tap his fingers on the front of his designer slacks. Hardly the appropriate clothing for today, but best for the image. Who should he call? He wasn't qualified to handle this. But he knew of no were tigers to contact in Germany, or even other species of were-cats, for that matter. *No, I need proof that the cat is Sazi—*

The Kommissar's voice, louder now, startled him. "Herr Monier, I am sorry for the interruption. What was your question?"

It was hardly a plan—reckless and bold. The council would never approve. Antoine took a deep breath and spoke quickly so he wouldn't lose his nerve. "I was asking about the cats. These all appear to be male. There are no female cats here. Where have you put *those* bodies?"

The Kommissar frowned and his eyebrows knitted into a single formidable line across his forehead. "Female? But no— you distinctly said you lost a *male* cat. It is in my report."

Antoine rose to his full six feet three height and crossed his arms over his chest. He pushed the tiniest bit of his Sazi power toward the other man. The Kommissar visibly shuddered. It was a risk, and it could go badly. Humans seldom reacted well to powerful Sazi, and those in authority sometimes treated them as threat. He would hate to wind up behind bars himself. "Non! I most certainly did *not* say it was a male. My lost tiger is *female*—mother to a pair of kittens who will die without their mother. Why on earth else would I get up at such an ungodly hour to follow you through a forest to see . . . this?" He swept his arm out wide, and set his face in tight, angry lines.

Without a word, the inspector stepped over to one of the men and grabbed a clipboard. He stalked back to his former position and turned the clipboard so that Antoine could see it. The powerful scent of his anger filled the air. *Actually, it does smell a bit like burning coffee. How very strange I've never noticed before.* He fought not to sneeze.

"You see, Herr Monier? It distinctly says *male* in my repor—"

Antoine waved his hand airily in the general direction of the clipboard without bothering to look at it. He knew full well what it said, but that didn't matter. "Your report doesn't interest me, Kommissar Reiner. Whoever took the details was mistaken. I am missing a *female*. Do you have a female tiger for me to view or not?"

Reiner looked at his report again and frowned deeply. Antoine sent out tendrils of magic, to eavesdrop on Reiner's thoughts. *The report says male. But I am to "cooperate." "It's a diplomatic courtesy," they told me. He says a female was lost. There is a female, and she has been especially difficult to handle.* An oddly amusing thought crept into Kommissar Reiner's mind. *There would be less paperwork to fill out if the Frenchman took the cat. Wilhelma Zoo has not yet opened . . . perhaps the tiger and our guest deserve each other.*

"Very well, Herr Monier, if you would like to see a female tiger, we were able to rescue one. It is at our station house, awaiting transport to Wilhelma Zoo. If you can *identify* this cat as yours, you are free to take it."

Antoine frowned. *"Identify* it? What would you consider identification? I certainly don't brand or tattoo my cats."

Reiner shrugged. "You said it was nursing. That should be obvious, at the very least. But any particular feature you remember—a missing claw, or damaged ear. A distinguishing feature that *we* can verify before *you* see the cat."

The words were very clear and seemingly innocent. But Antoine understood the inspector perfectly. Now he would just have to decide how to make good on his puffery. How in the world would he be able to positively identify a cat he'd never seen? *Well, Fiona always said I was the creative one in the family . . .*

Antoine turned on his heel and started back to his van, shaking the snow from his designer linen slacks after each step. Over his shoulder he shouted, "As you wish, Kommissar. I will meet you there and we will collect *my* cat."

* * *

Tahira woke to heat burning her skin. She tried to lift her front leg, but the drug still coursing through her made it difficult. Again she pushed against the door of the wire cage. It was weakening; bending outward, but she struggled against unconsciousness with each attempt. At least she'd been able to remove the dart quickly and had only pretended to be unconscious until the men left. But she'd never tried to hold her form beyond dawn, and it was already long past. Sunlight was slowly crawling up the wall, throwing shadows of herself, and her prison, across the floor.

I can't pass out. I must hold my animal form or they'll kill me. Well, they or her family. It hardly mattered which. She drew in a painful breath, snarled lightly, and searched ever more desperately for the waning moon magic. Every muscle was in agony and she could feel her bones straining to break and reform to human. The heat was unbearable and she looked longingly at the bowl of water just a few feet away. *But I don't dare move. If I concentrate on anything but holding this form, I'll lose control. I've risked us all with my recklessness. Rabi wouldn't have wanted this, no matter what his fate.*

She scanned the room again for the hundredeth time since she'd been brought here. There must be *something* she could use to free herself. If only the cage wasn't wire mesh. With bars, she could turn human and slide between them to free herself. If she was at full strength, she could easily break open the door, but the drugs from the policemen, combined with whatever her *original* captors had given her made that impossible. She could barely open her mouth enough to pant to cool herself.

Why had she planned this so stealthily that *nobody* knew where she was? If she had just told Grandmother, or Uncle Umar, they would have supported her. It was only stubbornness that had caused Grandfather to refuse to send a rescue party for Rabi in the first place. Apparently Tahira had inherited that stubbornness.

She readjusted her paw and winced. The light tingling under her fur was turning into prickling—stinging pinpoints like thousands of tiny ants were crawling and biting every inch of her body. The heat was increasing too. The constant whir of the exhaust fan buzzed in her ear. An abrupt crunching, grating sound sounded like it was directly overhead. She jumped when two sharp metallic slams echoed through the room, and she suddenly recognized the noises. She must be in a basement and the parking lot was directly above her. Voices now, in that harsh language that she didn't recognize. She wouldn't be able to hold out much longer. What was she going to do?

Hallo, Tiger. Was ist Ihr Name?

Tahira looked up and around. Nobody was in the room. She glanced at the barred window, but the sunshine was blinding to her sensitive eyes. The language was the same as she was hearing outside the door, but she didn't understand where it was coming from. Was there a microphone in the room?

Parlez-vous le français, le Tigre de Madame?

Was that French? Tahira shook her massive head. If she was starting to talk to herself in delirium, shouldn't she at least be able to understand the language? She growled again, and a startled yipe followed when her jaw snapped. It was starting. She couldn't hold it off anymore. She was going to change right here in front of witnesses and her family would be hunted like rabbits and slaughtered.

Do you speak *English*, tiger? We're running out of time!"

For heaven's sake! The voice *was* in her head! There was a distinct American accent to his words and relief flowed through her. She tried to think of what to say. Well, not quite *say*. She thought the words in her mind. **Uhm, yes—I speak English. Where are you? Who are you?**

Merde! At last! My name is Antoine and I'm in the outer room. Listen to me carefully. You are Sazi, correct?

Her head raised in unconscious reaction and she roared

loud and long. **I am *not* Sazi! I am Tahira of Hayalet Kabile!**

The guards in the outer room with Antoine jumped with the tiger's roar. *Hayalet Kabile.* Where had he heard that phrase before? *Hayal . . . Oh for the love of*—How could he forget? It was just mentioned at the last council meeting. The Hayalet Kabile were known as the "Ghost Tribe." The weretigers that lived along the Turkish/Iranian borderlands had declined to attend the great meeting of shapeshifters all those centuries ago. They were mentioned at the Sazi council meeting because Ahmad had brought along a clipping from the Discovery Channel Web site that said there had been a sighting of a supposedly "extinct" species of tiger, the Caspian, just last fall. The annoying werecobra, representative for the snakes, had asked what *Antoine* intended to do about it, since the Caspians were well known to be shifters, and he was the representative for the cats.

But the Hayalet Sahip, the head of the tribe, had refused an invitation to talk. Now there was one in the next room. Based on the roar of pain, she wouldn't be able to hold her form much longer. She was about to break the primary rule of both the Sazi and the Hayalet cultures. What a diplomatic nightmare!

"Merde!" he whispered harshly.

"Did you say something, Herr Monier?" Kommissar Reiner said, his mouth curled slightly in disdain. "Are you ready to make your identification of *your* cat?"

Antoine drummed his fingers on the table sharply. If he could only talk to the tiger—make her understand what was at stake. . . . *Yes, perhaps.* He turned sharply and reached for the doorknob, startling the inspector. "One moment, Kommissar. I've forgotten . . . my . . . uh, I'll be right back!"

He raced outside and pressed outward quickly with his waning magic. The tiger was directly under him.

Tahira, please listen to me. We don't have much time.

No response. But he could smell her fear, just behind the bars of the window.

Tahira of the Hayalet Kabile. I am Antoine Monier of the Sazi. Will you please speak to me? You are in great danger.

Another roar, powerful and haughty. **You need not worry about me, Sazi. I will end my own life before the humans see me in my day form.**

This doesn't have to happen, Tahira. I can help you. I've convinced the police that you're one of my tigers. But I need your cooperation

A snort of derision, but hope was replacing the fear. **And who are you that you believe you can own a tiger?**

Antoine walked out toward the van. A pair of pigeons pecking at gravel exploded into the air just as he reached the door. He managed to stop himself from automatically leaping into the air after them. **It's a complicated story, Tahira. But I and my cats entertain in shows all over the world. One of my tigers, Simon, was killed in the woods where you were held. But I have another Bengal named Babette. She just had kittens. I've convinced them that you are Babette.**

Her voice sounded suspicious but intrigued. **But even a human can tell the difference between a nursing and non-nursing tiger. Uhm . . . can't they?**

Antoine opened the van door and reached inside to grab a clipboard. He flipped his long braid back before swinging the door closed. He smiled and paced quickly along the edge of the carefully cleared walkway, expanding on his daring plan. **I don't know many humans who are willing to get close enough to check. But I'm an alpha, and have excellent illusion abilities. It would help if have any other identifying marks—perhaps ones that the officers have already seen? I promise that once the police have released you and are no longer watching, I will get you back to your Kabile—your tribe.**

Her soft alto was sad. **I will be dead to them. I'm already an outsider. I disappeared without permis-**

sion, trying to save my brother. But I didn't find him, and now I have bargained with a Sazi. I will be exiled . . . or killed.

She planned to cooperate. Thank heavens. A crunch of gravel behind him said another vehicle was arriving. He turned to see the occupants. Several of the members of the team from the forest were returning and he was out of time. **So you will allow me to assist you? The moon magic is nearly gone, but my power can hold you in form—if you'll allow me to. But I need something to identify you.**

I . . . you can hold someone past the dawn? But only sahibs hold that much power! Still . . . if you believe you can—I am missing part of my left ear.

Curious. What could have damaged a Saz—a shapeshifter—*enough* . . . A touch on Antoine's shoulder made him jump. Annoying that he hadn't heard or smelled the inspector walk up behind him. Distractions could be costly at this stage. "Herr Monier? Are you quite ready? The zoo is now open and if the cat is not yours, we must make a call to them."

"Yes, of course, inspector. Sorry for the delay." As he followed the inspector through the door, he threw a burst of magic ahead of him. He felt it penetrate the steel door in front of him and cover the tiger in the cage. The illusion was subtle, but he had to cast it broadly. Even Tahira would be able to see it when the time came. But he felt her shifting stop.

"How might we identify your tiger, Herr Monier?"

"There are several ways." He thrust the clipboard toward the inspector with feigned annoyance. "These are the customs forms for my animals. I thought you would want to see that I do indeed have a female Bengal with kittens."

Kommissar Reiner shuffled through the papers that Antoine recognized as the bill of lading, and confirmed for himself that Antoine had several different species of cats, in both genders. And, yes, there was a female Bengal. "There are no identifying features mentioned on this form."

Antoine forced his voice into a slightly condescending tone. "No, there are not, Kommissar Reiner. As you can see, there is nowhere on the form to insert them. It might be something to consider mentioning to the appropriate department. But, Babette—my female—is missing a piece of her left ear. And, as I said, she recently gave birth and is nursing."

He stared blankly at a print of a famous painting on the wall as the Kommissar questioned his men. No, they didn't notice whether the cat was nursing. That would require far too intimate contact. Even the dart didn't put the cat completely under. Yes, there was part of the left ear missing. It was in the report. Antoine suppressed a smile as the inspector reviewed the form.

The Kommissar smelled disappointed to find the written note about the defective ear on the paper, but he dutifully cleared his throat and removed a large ring of keys from his pocket. "It appears we *are* in possession of your tiger, Herr Monier. But I would like to see for myself that the cat is nursing. Tigers often fight in the wild and in captivity, so a damaged ear is not terribly—"

"Uncommon?" asked Antoine, with a sly smile. *He really doesn't want to let me win. But I already have.* Thank God. He concentrated on Babette and the cubs, let the memory of watching her nurse fill him until it was fixed in his mind. He felt for Tahira in the next room and let his magic bleed outward, blur the image of her belly until it matched the one in his mind. He shivered as the magic tied them together. He could almost see her in his mind now.

Reiner raised his brows. "Indeed." He swung open the steel door on oiled hinges and held it open so that Antoine could enter first. The negative pressure fan that kept the parking lot exhaust from filling the room assaulted Antoine's ears and he wondered how Tahira had managed to stay sane.

He stepped inside and got his first look at the woman, the tiger, he was helping. Her wide golden eyes looked startled as she inspected her chest and stomach. A burst of surprised scent quickly disappeared into the fan's flow. Antoine's followed the stare and he swore under his breath. He'd said it himself! She was a *Caspian* tiger, and that particular subspecies has a mane similar to a lion's with *long belly fur*.

Before the Kommissar could get past him to see, Antoine

concentrated carefully and blended the memory with the reality, like melting photographs into a single image.

He could see her surprise as her body betrayed her eyes. It was only when she ran her own nose over her fur that the illusion was dispelled. She froze when he spoke into her mind again.

You will need to greet me as though we are friends, and—He felt embarrassed to say the next words, but it had to be done. **Well . . . I will also—and I do apologize—but I will have to touch your stomach to prove to the inspector that you are nursing.**

Tahira started at the statement and immediately looked up. She felt her heartbeat race when she finally saw her benefactor. He was incredibly handsome, slender and fit. His blond hair was slicked back from his face, and the confident green-gold eyes grabbed her attention. He was so very young looking! Could he really be a sahip at such an age?

Then she looked more carefully. No, perhaps not so young. His heart-shaped jaw did bear a small golden beard, just covering his chin, and small wrinkles at the corners of his eyes made him at least in his late twenties. The eyes sparkled when he continued. **I normally wouldn't ask—,** came his voice, **But I don't think the Kommissar will believe you are mine otherwise.**

What he suggested did make sense. But he would have to put his hands on her naked chest. The form didn't matter, and he very well knew it! She would have frowned in her human form because he didn't seem too upset by the idea, either. But as a tiger all she could do was glare and pull back her lips in displeasure.

But one glance at the officer with him, the Kommissar, put the matter to rest. The narrow face was cold and his dark eyes serious and suspicious. There would be no discussion about the issue. He would have to see the evidence for himself, just as her Father would. Nobody else's word would do. But then a thought occurred to her. She hated that the words came out sounding a bit desperate.

If I am supposed to be a performing cat in your show, shouldn't I be able to obey commands? Couldn't you instruct me to roll over, or something like that?

She was a little annoyed when he chuckled. No doubt she smelled distinctly of embarrassment and fear. But his reply was polite and professional.

Is there room in there? I am quite certain that the Kommissar will not let you out of the cage, but I don't want to make you uncomfortable.

Tahira looked around and realized the Sazi was correct. There was barely room to stand and no room to make a full turn. If she tried to roll onto her back, she would be stuck there. **No, I suppose there isn't. But do only what you must—I warn you!**

He dipped his head slightly into a bow and remained serious, but his scent said something else entirely. He was amused at her discomfort. **As you wish, my lady.** He walked toward the cage with Reiner at his heels. She could hear his heart pound as he got closer, and she struggled against an increasing pressure that made her bones ache. She felt an uncomfortable pop, and realized that her bones were trying to reform. Why did it seem more difficult for him to keep her in form the closer he got?

"So, Herr Monier. Is this your cat? Can you prove your claim?"

Tahira watched the man—Antoine—offer a patronizing smile to the officer. "Of course she is." He turned to her and with complete confidence on his face, said, "Babette, let's go home. Are you all right, girl?" He stepped forward and reached past the cage grate to stroke her face. His hand was soft and gentle and smelled strongly of fur, along with a wonderful cologne that reminded her of freshly mown grass. She tried to offer a look that might appear adoring to the uniformed inspector. He was watching the interaction carefully, but not stepping too close to the cage. She rubbed her face against Antoine's hand as a house cat would and made soft kitten sounds. Hopefully, the officer would have no concept of proper greeting methods.

"Come now, Babette. I'll take you home to your cubs. Can you show the nice officer your belly? That's my girl." He turned to the Kommissar. "It's perfectly all right, Kommissar Reiner. You can step closer. Babette wouldn't hurt a fly. You wanted to see evidence of nursing, and you can't do it from back there."

Tahira struggled to remain completely passive while Antoine removed his hand from the cage and eased it through a lower square. He very carefully placed his flat palm on her side and let it remain there motionless as the inspector nervously stepped forward. The inspector reeked of fear, though he tried to hide the fact. She tried to fix her mind on the tangy scent of terror, remembering the tall grass that slid past her body as she stalked the old, limping deer. But her last hunt dissolved abruptly as Antoine ran a slow hand along her side and flank.

"You see, Kommissar? Here and . . . here."

His touch made her skin tingle. She'd never felt the touch of so powerful a sahip, and presumed that the tingling was an after-effect of his magic. But when his fingers slid through the fur of her belly, she suddenly knew better. It was magic, all right, but of a whole different kind.

Don't think about how good it feels. There's too much at stake. Rabi is counting on me. Rabi is countin— But her body wouldn't cooperate with her brain. Her stomach, and parts lower, clenched as his fingers skimmed along her fur. She closed her eyes and a small growl of pleasure slipped out. But just when she had decided to let herself revel in his touch, he stopped. Her eyes flew open in time to see the two men stepping toward the door. She hadn't realized that his hair was long. A wheat-colored braid hung almost to his belt. *What kind of cat is he?*

Antoine turned to her and winked. If she was in human form, she would have blushed.

We'll be right back. I appreciate your cooperation. We should be out of here in a few minutes.

"There is some paperwork for you to sign, Herr Monier," said Reiner as they closed the door. His voice sounded much friendlier. No less professional, but the tone and tenor were relaxed.

A few minutes later, she heard their voices again—this time in the parking lot above. "And you are certain that this van will hold the tiger, Herr Monier?" The man called Reiner must be inspecting the Sazi's vehicle, because she heard the squeaking of car springs, and then rattling metal.

"Without question, Kommissar," Antoine replied confidently. "We use this van frequently to transport our cats, and it has been inspected and approved by your government on numerous occasions. I do have the paperwork, if you wish to see it."

Reiner responded without a hint of worry. "No, I see no need. It is obvious that the cat knows and trusts you. It was quite calm when you entered the room and handled it. It reacted *completely* differently with my men."

Antoine laughed. "I don't doubt you! She is quite stressed right now. She needs to return to her cubs and have a meal and some quiet."

But shock filled her as Antoine stepped back into the room holding a *collar and leash*. **I am not a pet to follow along after you, Sazi!**

For the first time, he narrowed his eyes and dropped his head into a defensive position. Here then was the true sahip showing through. He fully expected to be obeyed without question. His gold and green eyes burned bright with intensity and a burst of magic hit her hard enough to sting each and every hair on her body. The words that seared into her head were terse and angry. **No, you are not a pet. What you are is a dangerous wild animal, and these men are afraid of you! They have guns and there are more of them than I can reasonably defend you against. I would suggest that you keep your annoyance to yourself and allow me to get you safety. I can't hold your form indefinitely, you know.**

Both his tone, and the truth of his statement made heat rise to her face. But her parents, her grandparents—they all said that the Sazi would use any excuse to subdue the Kabile, to subjugate them and turn them into shadows of humans with no free will. Yet, Antoine seemed to be trying to help. Or was he merely afraid to be found out himself?

She couldn't tell, but in freedom there was power. So she lowered her eyes when the cage door was opened and allowed the collar to be placed around her neck. He pulled on the leash and she stepped out of the cage and followed him through the police station. But then she saw him—the man who had kicked her head through the cage so the other could inject the drug. A snarl rose from her chest without warning. It was met with a sharp tug on the collar and another burst of biting magic.

Tahira fought down her anger. There was no time. *I should be thankful that I'm getting out of this alive so I can find Rabi.*

The guards followed them out to the van with hands on weapons, and remained there until the rear doors were safely shut and locked. The van was filled with the scent of other cats, large and small, some shapeshifters and some wild cats. But it smelled of comfort and peace, rather than anger or fear. The cats who had passed through this van were content, which surprised her. She'd heard horror stories about the treatment of cats in circuses and shows, and even worse stories about the sadistic Sazi.

A wave of relief made Tahira sigh as the police station grew smaller in the rear window. She jumped and turned as something lightly struck the back of her head. A cream colored silken shirt lay at her feet.

"I'm about to change you back. I thought you might want to cover yourself."

She looked up at the sound of his voice and caught sight of his eyes in the rear view mirror. The annoyance in his eyes matched his scent.

"I'm sorry for snarling back there, but—"

Antoine turned angry eyes back to the road. The very American accent in her voice was a worry. "It doesn't matter *why*. You nearly ruined your own escape. If you were Sazi, I would be forced to . . . but no, that doesn't matter right now."

With a thought, he released the flow of magic, and forcibly ignored the scream of pain as she shifted back to human form. She must be *quite* young to still scream.

There was a shuffling of fabric against skin and when he glanced back again, a fully grown, stunning woman was finishing buttoning the silk shirt. It stretched tight over the generous swell of her chest. She tucked slim, permanently tanned legs under her so she could raise to her knees. Thankfully, the shirt tails were long enough to cover everything, but Antoine found that he had to force a very appreciative gaze back to his driving. He wished he could ignore her enticing scent as easily.

He cleared his throat, and fought the customary attraction to a beautiful woman. "I . . . ahem, I expected you to be . . . *younger,* Tahira."

She half-crawled to the grating so she could see him as they talked. She dropped to a sitting position next to the grate, feet tight against her thighs. When he glanced in the mirror again, he couldn't stop his eyes from opening wide at what he saw. Without planning to, he laughed out loud. She was looking down, and her hair spilled over her face and shoulders. Wide portions of her hair were colored the bright russet of her namesake animal.

"You have . . . *stripes.*"

Tahira looked up in shock and immediately pulled her hair back and tucked it in the neck of her shirt while blushing furiously. Her scent was hot embarrassment and anger and she wouldn't meet his eyes in the mirror. "I'll dye it immediately when we reach a town. I swear. Please don't look badly on the Kabile for my defect."

Defect? Why on earth—

He softened his voice, let the amusement drop from it completely. "I don't consider them a *defect,* Tahira. I've simply never seen them appear before in human form. They're really quite lovely—as are you, by the way. Who told you they were a flaw?"

After a few moments of silence, where her scent was a mingling of emotions that included being worried and flattered, she responded. "Oh. Um . . . I . . . *thank you.* But in our tribe, they're looked down on as being low-caste—nearly as bad as a *sifena,* a halfling that must change on every night of the moon. Anything that would be noticed by townsfolk on casual inspection is a danger. If I lived with my grandparents I would probably be put down for these stupid orange hairs. But since I turned late in life—I only had my first change at twenty—they're hoping it will pass. But it's been two years, so I'm not real hopeful. Normally, I dye my hair during the moon. Fortunately, that's really easy at home in California. It's harder here in Turkey while I'm spending time with my mom's family. I wear a headscarf a lot of the time to cover my hair, even though I'm not Muslim."

"What do you mean, Turke—" Antoine saw her face in the mirror and noticed a large bruise that covered one eye and stained her cheekbone an angry red. He turned his head to confirm what he saw and exclaimed, "*Merde!* What happened to your face?"

She rose up to look in the mirror, which brought a grimace and a gentle probing with one finger. "That *does* look bad, doesn't it? That's why I snarled at that guard. He kicked me in the face through the cage."

Antoine's hands clutched the steering wheel until his knuckles were white and the plastic creaked in protest. Fury boiled inside him. The thought of someone—"He *kicked* you? *Pauvre con!* Why didn't you tell me at the station? I could easily have *discovered* it when I examined you and had him disciplined."

Tahira shrugged and sat down, carefully smoothing the fabric to cover her thighs. "What good would that do? Even if you'd made an accusation, they'd just claim that the men who'd captured me had done it." She pushed against her ribs and felt an answering twinge of pain. "And they did plenty— you just can't see the bruises anymore. Besides, I'll heal."

A shadow of a smile passed over his face. Their cultures might be very different, but they were also much alike.

She sighed and looked out the window through the grating. "I'm just hoping to get back to the village by nightfall. I'm not very good at directing people there when it's dark.

Grammy must be beside herself. I've been gone since before dawn."

Antoine nodded. Ah, yes. Back to the subject at hand. "Where do you think you are, Tahira? Do you know what day this is?" He asked the words calmly, without any emotion attached, but wasn't surprised when regarded him suspiciously.

"It's Friday, which—" She wrinkled her brow, and her face in the mirror grew more worried by the second. ". . . is a holiday in Turkey, and the police station shouldn't be open." They weren't speaking Turkish, either.

"No, it wouldn't and they weren't." Antoine agreed. He decided she needed to figure this out for herself before he intervened.

She looked out the window as another building flashed by. "Van is the closest city of this size, but the architecture is wrong."

A car ahead braked to avoid a small animal and the rear end skidded on the icy road before moving forward again. Antoine took his foot off the gas pedal in response. They slowed several kilometers an hour to a more appropriate speed. Yes, they would both *survive* an accident, but why risk one?

He listened to Tahira mumbling under her breath. Her scent was a blending of panic and worry that made his jaw clench. "Damn! I should have paid more attention in class. Franco? Grecian?"

"Baroque, mostly," Antoine offered. "A bit of Bauhaus in a few buildings." He decided to take the bull by the proverbial horns. "We're in Stuttgart, Germany, Tahira. And it's Thursday."

Tahira slumped against the expanded metal grating with a dropped jaw. It took two tries before she could get words out of her mouth, and even then they were a coarse whisper. "But . . . I was captured on Friday, and it was the first night of the moon. It's nearly Thanksgiving back in the States. It can't . . . the moon can't last for a whole week, can it?"

Antoine sighed heavily and felt his shoulders slump. If she really had lost her brother, there would be no hope of finding a trail after this long. He hated to tell her, but better now than later. "It's nearly Christmas, Tahira. My troupe and I were just about to return to America for the holiday. Can you remember *anything* about your captivity? Anything at all?"

"A *month?* But I couldn't have been a prisoner for a full month! What about Rabi?" She wiped sudden tears away with an angry hand. He could tell she was trying hard, but her chin quivered and her fists clenched as she fought to control her emotions. And there was no hiding her scent.

Antoine's voice was soft and gentle. "I'm so very sorry, Tahira. I hope your brother is still alive. When we get back to the show, you're welcome to full use of my satellite phone or the internet to make some calls."

The next curve brought the old tunnel into sight in the far distance. They were only a dozen miles from their camp. While Antoine had planned to stay near the auditorium where the show had been performed, the hotels were all sold out from a second convention, and they would have had to split the troupe. That was bad for the morale of the cats. So, they had obtained a special permit to set up the living trailers and an animal exercise tent in a field on the outskirts of the city.

He tried to ignore Tahira's wracking sobs in the back of the van. The reality of her situation had sunk home and there was little that could be done for the moment. By the time they arrived—

A light caught his attention and he flicked his eyes to the driver's side mirror. There was a police car on their tail and the blue lights were flashing. Well, perhaps it wasn't for him. He slowed and moved toward the edge of the road to give it room to pass. But there wasn't much room to move. The plows had been busy and the towering pile of ice covered dirty snow could easily take off his side mirror. But the police car also slowed and moved to the side. *Merde!* What now?

"Take off the shirt, Tahira!"

He said it harshly enough to stem her tears and look up in shock. "What?"

Antoine applied his foot to the brake - just enough to show compliance, but still stall for time. "The police are behind us again. They will be expecting a tiger, and I happen to like the shirt you're wearing."

She turned and looked out the tinted rear window. "Oh!" She hurried to obey.

He pulled the car over and sent a powerful burst of magic into the back of the van. "I'm sorry, but this is going to hurt."

He had to watch to make sure that the timing was right. She grunted, but didn't scream as raw energy ripped across her body, literally *pulling* the tiger inside to the surface. Bones broke and fur flowed like a waterfall over sharp rocks. It was over in seconds, leaving her panting and shaking on the carpet before the van had even come to a complete halt. He kept feeding power into her, until she roared in protest. He was surprised when a shock of fear scent flowed from the back. But there was no time to ease her fears.

Antoine rolled down the window and forced a smile onto his face. It was difficult. The strain of keeping her in animal form seemed to be increasing. He could feel sweat paint his brow and start to roll down his temple.

"*Guten tag.* Is there a problem, officer?"

Tahira fought back a growl, and he noticed. It was the same man she'd growled at in the station—the one who had kicked her. The officer was aware of the tiger's complete attention on him. He unconsciously backed away from the window a half-step. "You forgot to sign a document, Herr Monier. All of the documents *must* be signed."

Antoine bit back his first response. He couldn't afford to give the officer any reason to detain him further. He couldn't understand why it was so difficult to hold Tahira's form. It hadn't been like this earlier, but the more power he gave, the more she required. It was quickly draining him. His eyes were growing unfocused as he stared at the paper and the spot where the gloved finger pointed. He nearly dropped the pen from limp fingers while signing, and the German noticed.

"Are you well, Herr Monier? You look very pale suddenly. Should I follow you to your camp?"

Antoine's mouth felt dry and hot, and he had to lick his tongue over chapped lips. He managed a small smile and nodded. "I'm merely tired. I was up late performing and had little sleep before I received the call from your Kommissar." He pointed at the tunnel mouth. "But our camp is just on the other side of the mountain. So there's no problem. I appreciate the offer, but I don't believe I need an escort."

The officer wasn't buying it. Tahira must have seen his indecision, because she suddenly threw herself against the side window and let out a vicious roar, making the entire van rock. The officer blanched and stepped back in alarm. It was enough of a distraction. His eyes moved quickly between the large tiger and Antoine's pale face. "Very well, then, Herr Monier. I will leave you and your cat to make your way back."

Another roar and a powerful leap against the rear grate as the officer returned to his car nearly made him drop the clipboard. Antoine rolled up the window. "That alone tells his guilt. I believe he would be pleased to return and never see us again."

A dark chuckle that ended with an animal snarl came from deep within his chest. Tahira regarded him with a sideways glance. "Don't worry. I have plans for that one." Antoine stepped on the gas and quickly increased the distance between the two cars. "And now I think it's time for you to turn human again."

He threw a wave of power and waited for the change to occur.

But it didn't. Instead, the heat began to increase, so quickly that his head began to pound. He started breathing painfully, and noticed that Tahira was as well.

"Why aren't I changing?" Her speaking voice in animal form was nearly an octave deeper than when human. There was a delicious dark snarl at the end of each word.

"I don't know. Something is wrong. But just a few more miles—"

By the time the tunnel loomed in front of them, Antoine was having a hard time keeping the car on the road. *Just a few more minutes. But why can't I stop my magic?* Sweat was pouring freely down his face, stinging his eyes with salt. He heard Tahira collapse to the carpet and begin to pant heavily from exhaustion.

He leaned forward on the steering wheel to keep himself upright. His magic, his very life force, was being sucked away, and he didn't know why. Already spots of grey and white were edging his vision.

The darkness ahead seemed to stretch out, the light at the end narrowing to a pinpoint that disappeared into an inky blackness the headlights couldn't pierce. *What in the name of*—?

Twin red slits appeared above him and a gasp choked his throat as the eyes blinked and became the red irises of a giant snake. They were driving right into its maw! Antoine turned the wheel frantically, and slammed on the brake. He heard a distant scream and tearing metal, as though he was underwater.

Bone-jarring pain now in his shoulder, his leg, the side of his head.

More images passed in front of his eyes. He fought to end the vision as he always did, but the shimmering reflections entered him, filled him, and he couldn't turn away: A veiled woman dressed in black and gold, moving in a slow, sultry dance that sped up to music he couldn't hear; men and women chained to rocks, screaming and shriveling into husks of paper-thin flesh that stretched thin over twisted animal bones; the press of lips against his that tasted of cherry jam and sandalwood. A hold appeared in a stone cliff covered with brush; water, and a need to breathe so strong it seared his lungs. Blinding pain in his chest seemed to flay the skin from his bones from the inside out; and through it all, the eyes—those fiery eyes that his heart knew would burn the world to ash if he didn't intervene.

And then they rushed forward; enveloped him in sparkling power, and everything disappeared into blackness.